THE TROUBLE WITH DEATH AND DEMON GODS

CARY REDMOND, BOOK 7

KAT SIMONS

Published 2022 by T&D Publishing
Cover design: © 2022 Evernight Designs
Interior book design © 2022 T&D Publishing
ISBN-13: 978-1-944600-50-1 (Trade Paperback Edition)
ISBN-13: 978-1-944600-51-8 (Large Print Edition)

This is a work of fiction. All of the characters, places, organizations, and events portrayed are either products of the author's imagination or are used fictitiously. Any resemblance to actual persons, living or dead, business establishments, events, or locales is entirely coincidental.

First printing T&D Publishing edition: May 2022
For information, contact T&D Publishing: https://www.tanddpublishing.com

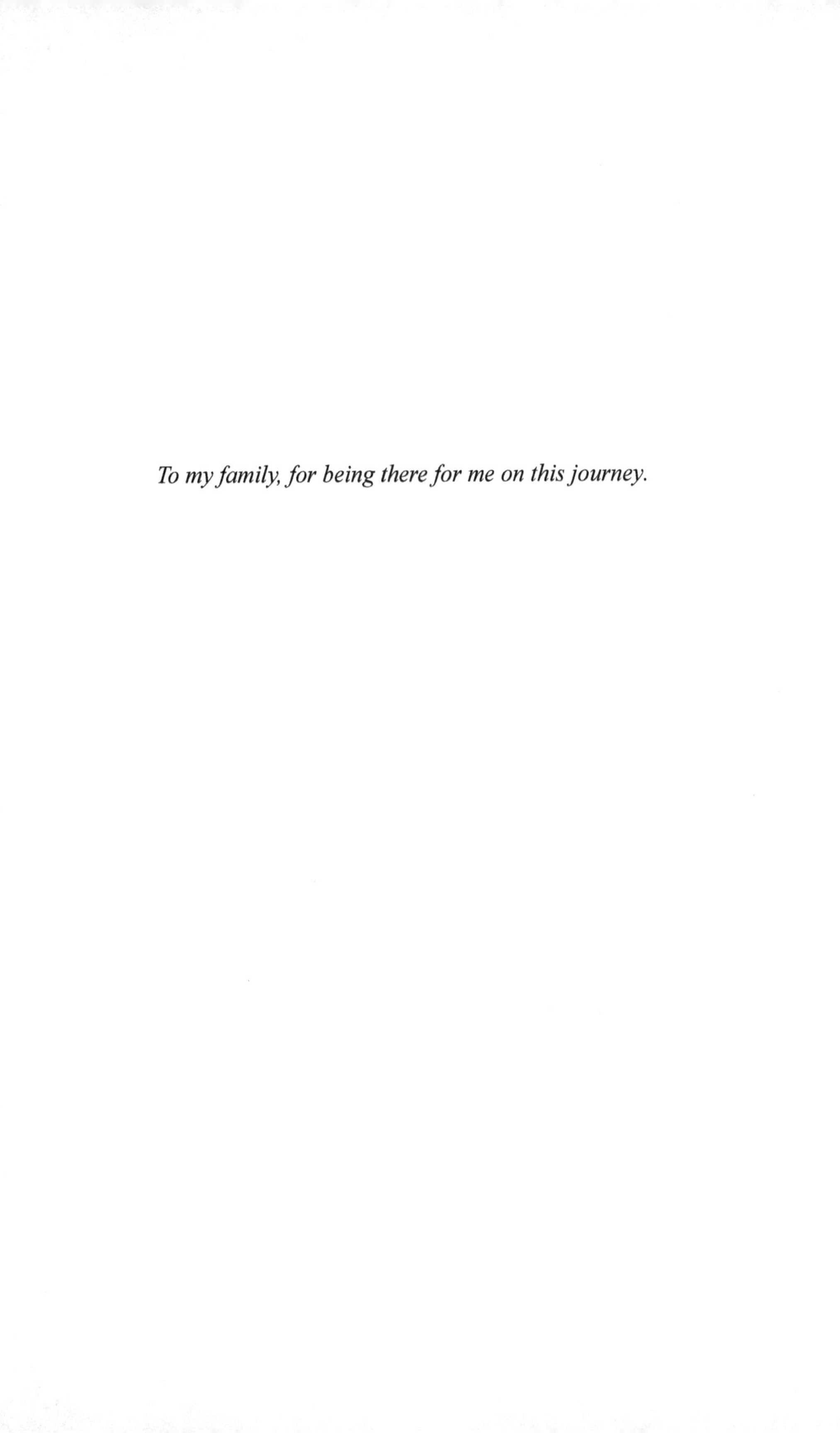

To my family, for being there for me on this journey.

1

ary pulled herself off the hard, navy blue mat, groaning only a little bit, and straightened her shoulders. The lovely scent of frankincense sticks burning by a small statue of the Buddha near the front desk of the dojo didn't completely hide Cary's sweat stink, but she'd take it. At least she wasn't bleeding.

"I'm not sure this is working," she said to her best-friend-current-torture-master and her bear shifter training partner.

"This is only the third time you've trained with Brandon," Lucy said in her sweet, high voice, putting her hands on her hips. "Give the process time."

Lucy Evans-Nakada, physically, was not what you might expect of a multi-blackbelt holding martial arts expert. She was a petit red-head, with brown eyes, pale skin, freckles across her nose, and a high-pitched, sweet voice that made her sound like a little girl. But she'd been training in martial arts since the age of two, including time spent in Japan studying under masters, and she could kick the ass of grown men—more than one at a time—without breaking a sweat.

She owned the dojo they were training in and had been teaching for years. And because she was one of Cary's best friends in the whole world, she tortured Cary here on a regular basis. To be fair, Cary was

1

trying to get better at the self-defense stuff. Her job as a magical Protector just kept getting more and more complicated, and knowing how to at least not freeze in the face of danger if her powers weren't working seemed like a really good idea.

Although, freezing in the face of danger was *precisely* the instinct that made her a good Protector. Get between bad guys and good guys and then just…stand there. That was her job description. The magic she channeled from her bosses rose up and shielded both her and the good guy. And all was right with the world.

At least in theory.

"You got up quicker than usual," Brandon said. "That's a marked improvement over the last two sessions."

She grunted in response.

Brandon Hawthorn, physically, *was* everything you might imagine a bear shifter to look like. Huge at six-foot-nine, at least, thickly-muscled, and when he didn't smile, pretty intimidating. He kept his dark hair cut very close to his head and was clean shaven, showing off a granite jawline any model might envy. His dark brown complexion was smooth, and his brown eyes hooded and hard to read. Until you looked directly at him and he smiled. Then suddenly you spotted the sweet, gentle man lurking behind the large, scary façade.

Being a bear shifter, however, meant he was faster and stronger than Cary. By a lot. And since he'd been training more diligently with Lucy for a lot longer than Cary, he was also a better martial artist. By a lot.

The first time they'd sparred—at Lucy's insistence—Cary had spent most of her session flat out on her back, staring up at the dojo's ceiling tiles. He was right about her getting up quicker now. But she had a feeling that was because he was pulling his punches.

"Are you two taking it easy on me?" she asked. "You're feeling sorry for me, aren't you?"

"Not…exactly," Lucy said, though she wouldn't meet Cary's gaze.

"Right." Cary huffed and straightened her training gi with a little more oomph than was absolutely necessary.

"It's mostly distraction," Brandon said, his deep voice gentle. "Not pity."

"You hate waiting," Lucy said.

Well, that was the damned truth. And she'd been waiting for two weeks. Which was starting to make her a little…difficult. Deacon would say that nicer, but he was her mate so he had to. But difficult was a good word for her snapping, brittle, irritable mood. Taking that mood out on her friends was unacceptable, though.

"I haven't been making your life miserable, have I?" she asked, now feeling worse than when they'd been tossing her onto her ass for the last hour. "Have I been grumping too much?"

"Not too much," Lucy assured. "Just enough. I'd be grumping, too. It's not like you're just waiting on a package or a repairman or something. Having to wait to stop the end of the world must be extremely frustrating."

More truth. Cary pressed a hand to her stomach to stop the jumping nerves—the real reason for her irritability, she was sure. Waiting for the world-ending confrontation between a demon god, the Angel of Death, and their demon offspring who, coincidentally, hated and wanted to kill Cary, was not exactly a fun experience.

Waiting for that confrontation without any signs of it actually happening was a whole lot worse.

If she was going to face—and maybe have to actually protect—one of her most deadly enemies, it'd be nice to just get it over with.

But no. That would be simple. And Cary's life never seemed to follow the simple path.

She let out another groan and sat on the mat, dropping abruptly enough both Lucy and Brandon took a step forward as if to catch her. She snorted. "I'm not fainting. I'm just tired. More emotionally, though, you know."

Lucy also dropped into a cross-legged seat on the mat. "Makes sense."

Brandon settled on his knees. "I get that."

She hadn't actual meant to unload the whole thing in front of Brandon, but it had just come spilling out during their last training session because she'd been too distracted to even attempt paying attention. He'd tossed her around the dojo like a ragdoll for all of ten minutes before Lucy called a halt and demanded an explanation for Cary's lack of effort. The whole thing just…spilled out.

Fortunately, according to Deacon, Brandon was a really good guy and could be trusted with the information. At least the parts of the story Cary had admitted to. Brandon was a professional fundraiser, and Deacon had worked with him in the past on fundraisers for Deacon's family business—they ran animal rescue shelters around the country, which was, of course, the reason she'd fallen in love with him because how was she supposed to resist that? It didn't hurt that he was a gorgeous, sexy leopard shifter who smelled like heaven and brought her donuts regularly. But the animal rescue job had really pushed his appeal over the top in Cary's mind.

The fact that her mate said she could trust Brandon had probably been the reason Cary had let go with all her pent-up anxiety.

"How's Sheldon doing?" Lucy asked quietly.

Ah, there was another thing that had her stretched too thin. The not quite twenty-year-old wizard who had at one point tried to kill Deacon, Cary had accidentally drained all his powers, his former master had tried to kill Cary for it—more than once—and now, maybe, possibly, Sheldon was no longer evil. But she wasn't sure about that, which only complicated things. Sheldon had most definitely been a bad guy. And he'd never really tried to atone for the evil—and murder—he'd committed before being drained of all his wizard magic. He hadn't even apologized. So he definitely wasn't a good guy.

Cary had been forced to protect him as part of her last job, which was the job that had gotten her into the waiting-on-the-world-ending-confrontation position she was in now. And because, for reasons Cary still couldn't grasp, he'd done something monumentally stupid and possibly suicidal, Sheldon had spent the last two weeks in a coma with his insides…well, not in good shape.

"He's hanging in there," she answered Lucy's question. "Thanks to Eriana's healing efforts."

Eriana was a Fae healer and a Protector mentor-in-training—

although Cary wasn't supposed to know that last part—and she had a very complicated past, and current, relationship with Cary's own former mentor Jaxer, also a Fae. Unfortunately, Cary hadn't been able to enjoy that drama because she'd had too much drama of her own.

"Has he woken up since…everything?" Lucy asked.

"No. Eriana isn't letting him. He's still got too much healing to do. But she says he's mending, so I suppose that's something."

"How's Deacon handling the whole Sheldon thing?"

"With a lot more…kindness than I would have expected."

The little shit had tried to kill Deacon. Cary had *met* Deacon because she'd had to save him from Sheldon and his nefarious plan to steal Deacon's body. There was no reason in the world, not even a little bit, for Deacon to have any concern at all for whether the former wizard healed or not. Yet he checked regularly with Eriana on Sheldon's progress, and had even been to see Sheldon in person once. She wasn't sure if he did all that for her sake—because Sheldon was so young, Cary's feelings about him were very very complicated—or if he did that for his own piece of mind. But the fact that Deacon hadn't ripped Sheldon's throat out yet was a miracle, and the fact that he seemed genuinely concerned that Sheldon *not* die was even more amazing.

"Your mate is a good man," Brandon said quietly. "Even when he doesn't think he is."

"You've known him a while?" She'd never talked to Brandon about Deacon, and only really once to Deacon about Brandon. She'd be interested to put the two men in the same room to see for herself how they got along.

But that was mostly because Brandon had eyes on one of her other best friends and Cary wanted to make sure that situation was a potential good thing and not a potential bad thing. Deacon getting a good super shifter sniff of Brandon would give him all the information Cary needed in regards to Brandon's feelings for Marianne. Brandon—being a shifter himself—would know that and likely only let Deacon get close enough to judge his motives if his motives were good.

And since thinking about Marianne—and her healing heart—and

Brandon was a lot less tormenting than considering the fact that one of her old demon enemies was, even now, on his way to Portland for this world-ending confrontation with his *parents*, Cary decided to get to know her sparring partner a little better.

Or she would have if they'd gotten the chance to actually have a conversation.

When Deacon stalked into the dojo, looking entirely too serious, thoughts of other conversations got ditched.

Cary came to her feet instantly. "What's wrong? What's happened?"

"Sheldon is awake," he said. "Eriana and Jaxer are with him. He's asking for you."

Shit. But also maybe good? Given the look on Deacon's face, she wasn't sure what to hope for. "I'll change. Give me two minutes." To Lucy and Brandon, "Thanks for the session. And for the not-pity distraction. I appreciate it."

"Call if you need us," Lucy said, giving her a brief hug.

Cary hurried back to the locker room to put on her street clothes, anxiety clawing at her gut.

2

Sheldon's apartment looked nothing like the first time Cary had seen it almost a year ago.

Then, it had been fully furnished, a big couch and TV in the living room, his bedroom a gaudy showcase of red carpet, leather, and animal prints—which given he'd been sacrificing shifters in an effort to take over their bodies, had been more than a little disturbing. The popping spells of lightning, hale, and fireballs throughout the living room had really added to the wizardy ambiance.

Now, none of that remained. It was a shell of a place with only a lumpy brown couch and empty wooden TV stand in the living room, a dust covered kitchen, and a stripped and utilitarian bed which Cary had had to donate sheets, blankets, and pillows for just so Sheldon could coma in comfort. Somehow, the bareness of it all was just as sad as the gaudy magic had been dangerous.

Thanks to a trait Cary hadn't even known she'd had at the time, Cary had—accidentally—drained all Sheldon's wizard magic. At least so much of it that he couldn't do magic anymore. Given his uses of it before she'd absorbed it all, this wasn't a bad thing. But the hollowness it had left in the former wizard was too obviously reflected in his now empty apartment.

When she'd been forced to come here again, to protect him from his own master, he hadn't actually been living in this apartment anymore. He'd chased away all the tenants on this floor using bought magic and had taken up residence in another apartment. But this empty space was what she thought of as Sheldon's apartment. The place she'd met Deacon. The place that had started her down the path that was her seventh year as a Protector. A test year. A year she was supposed to survive on her own without help from her bosses or mentor.

The year hadn't gone that way, exactly, but since no one had jumped out to say she'd broken the rules yet, and she only had two more months to go, she was going to assume all was well. And that because she'd saved the world a few times in the last year, if she managed to survive, she'd probably pass the test.

The survival part was the big question mark hanging over the last few months, though.

She walked into Sheldon's bedroom, Deacon at her back. His steps were so quiet on the hardwood floor that if she wasn't extremely aware of him at all times, she might have been able to forget he was right behind her. Thanks to the mate bond—or maybe just because Deacon was so very magnetic—she was always intimately aware of where he was, though. Initially, that had felt intrusive and weird.

Now, it was the most comforting thing in her life.

Sheldon was sitting up on the small bed, propped up on pillows— Cary's pillows—stacked behind him against the rickety wooden headboard. The first time Cary had been here, the bed had had a magical, rune-covered headboard. A headboard Deacon had been chained to. She blinked away the past memory to focus on the present.

Eriana hovered a few feet away from the bed, her expression carefully neutral. Jaxer stood behind her, leaning against the bedroom wall, his arms crossed over his chest. She caught his gaze, but she couldn't read his expression any more than she could read Eriana's. So much for hints about what she could expect.

She refocused on Sheldon. "How you feeling?" she asked him.

He was so pale he was almost translucent, which was saying something because he'd been pretty pale before. His dark hair was mated to his skull and shiny but not in a good way. His dark eyes were sunken, and his cheeks were hollow. He looked in pretty bad shape. But the mere fact that he was awake was a good sign.

Despite most of Sheldon's doctoring being done by a magical Fae healer, the room still had the smell of a hospital sickroom about it. Medicinal sharpness mixed with a sort of stale sweat and astringent disinfectants. A strong enough scent even Cary could pick it up. Which meant Deacon must have been hit in the face with it when he walked in.

Sheldon swallowed visibly, the bob of his Adam's apple sharp along his narrow throat. "I... I don't know how I'm feeling. Alive. Which I didn't expect."

Cary sighed. "Only because Eriana could heal you."

They both glanced at Eriana, whose only reaction was a raised brow.

In her human guise, the faery healer looked like a perfectly ordinary woman. Short pixie cut brown hair, brown-hazel eyes, pale skin and sharp features. A face that wasn't unattractive, but wasn't head-turning either. Just the sort of everyday ordinariness that most humans inhabited. She didn't stand out in a crowd, and you'd never guess there was so much more to her.

It was Fae glamour, of course. Unlike Jaxer, who was too vain to appear anything but gorgeous even with his blond-haired, blue-green-eyed "human" glamour in place, Eriana had chosen to present herself as unremarkable to the human world. Cary had seen her in her full Fae glory, though. And she was anything but unremarkable.

Sheldon, however, would only see the ordinary human woman. Cary wasn't even sure if he realized Eriana was Fae yet.

"Thanks," he said to Eriana. "I didn't realize you'd done the healing. It was bad."

Not a question, Cary noticed.

"You were in bad shape, yes," Eriana said. "Don't switch bodies with a demon again. It nearly cooked your insides."

Cary winced. For all she was an extraordinary healer, Eriana's bedside manner left a lot to be desired.

Sheldon winced too. "Being in his wasn't exactly a picnic either. I thought…"

He didn't finish, only turned his gaze back to his hands where they rested on top of the blanket covering his lap.

"You thought what?" Cary asked. "Because I seem to recall telling you *not* to try switching bodies with Oliver Holland. And then you went and did it anyway. I'd *love* to hear why you did such a stupid thing."

Sheldon scowled up at her. Given how pale and sunken he was, the scowl just looked sad and pathetic, not particularly threatening.

"I had a good reason."

"Sure, sure. I'm waiting to hear it."

"What did he say when he was in my body?"

"That he'd be leaving the Naga city soon and be back." Holland had said other things too. Things that didn't need to be said aloud yet.

"How long has it been?"

"Two weeks." Two fucking weeks!

"He's not here yet?"

"No. And before you ask, I have no idea what's happening with him. Whether he's out or not. His father hasn't shown up yet, so that's probably a good indication he hasn't left the Naga realm yet. No sign of the Angel of Death yet either."

The Angel was Holland's mother as it turned out. Which meant one of Cary's greatest and most dangerous enemies was also, unfortunately, unkillable. Not just technically immortal, the way most demons were. He was literally immune to death because of who his mother was. His father, a literal demon *god*, wanted to use his son's immunity to death to make himself immune to death as well—although she had no idea how Lud planned to do that—because if he didn't, he'd die at the hands of the Angel because it had been foreordained…or something.

It was a complicated family tangle, and she'd have preferred not to be anywhere near it when they worked it all out, but if the demon god succeeded, he'd destroy her realm just because it had provided sanctuary to his son for several centuries. And she didn't want her realm destroyed. So she was going to have to get into the middle of the family fight and make sure her greatest enemy wasn't reclaimed by his father.

She was really really really really *not* happy about this turn of events.

"Explain why you changed bodies with a demon, Sheldon?" she snapped, taking her pent-up stress and irritation out on the former wizard. Probably not her best moment. But she'd been so anxious, so on edge, she couldn't help it. "That stunt nearly killed you. Why risk that? For his immortality? Like your master wanted?"

"Not immortality," Sheldon said, scowling at the blanket on his lap. "Who does this belong to?"

"Me. Stop stalling."

"I'm not. You gave me a blanket?"

"You didn't leave any behind when you left for your lab, and destroyed your former master's lab, and then switched bodies with a demon. Stop. Stalling."

"I need some magic back," Sheldon ground out. "I need… something. I'm useless without it. I can't…do anything."

"The last time you had magic, what you did was murder people," she said.

Sheldon's hollowed cheeks splotched with red color, and Eriana stepped in. "Enough. He'll end up right back in a coma this way." To Sheldon, she said, "You wanted to tell Cary something. Tell her so she can leave and you can rest."

Sheldon pulled in a shaky breath, the gesture shivering across his shoulders visibly. He didn't look at her directly when he spoke, just kept his gaze on the blanket, plucking at the edges of it.

"While I was inside Holland's body, I… I couldn't understand most of his thoughts. They were…" He shuddered. "Too much. So much I didn't even comprehend. Some of what I could understand was bad, though. Really bad. The stuff of nightmares. Worse than what Zorianthus showed me. Worse than I've done." He shot Cary a defiant look.

She raised her brows and tucked her chin. Did he really want to argue that point with her right now? She viewed it as a monumental show of restraint that she kept her mouth shut in that moment.

"Mostly, I picked up images," Sheldon continued, "because Holland's thoughts are in a demon language that… I suspect if I'd been in my human body, it would have made my ears bleed to hear it."

Well that sounded horrific. She was absolutely certain she didn't want to hear Holland's native language in real life. His current voice already filled her nightmares.

"There are images of you in his thoughts," Sheldon said. "He's obsessed with you."

"I imagine with all the ways he wants to torture and kill me," Cary said. That wasn't a big secret.

"Stranger, though," Sheldon said. "Not kill you outright. Torture, yeah, but… He wants to keep you."

"Keep me? Like a pet?"

"Yes," Sheldon said. "A pet. A slave. A toy. He'd torture you while he kept you. But…he wants to keep you."

"That's super gross," Cary said, her stomach turning at the thought. For the first time, probably ever, she was actually pretty glad she could die. Cause she'd done that already, and while it hadn't been fun, doing it again sounded a *whole* lot more fun that being Holland's torture pet.

"And not happening," Deacon said, the growl in his voice deep enough to make her shiver.

She gave him a narrow-eyed glance. His eyes weren't glowing. Yet. But she got a feeling it wouldn't take much more for his leopard to rise to the surface.

"He knows you absorb magic now," Sheldon said. "He didn't while I was in his body. But if I saw his thoughts, he saw mine. He knows now."

"Yeah, he was kind enough to point that out," Cary said.

"That will make things worse for you. He'll want to use that ability, too."

"Still not happening." Mostly because any magic strong enough for Holland to find useful, if she absorbed and didn't release it, would kill her. Which was…weirdly good for her? That was going to fuck with her mind.

"He'll realize you might have absorbed some of his immortality," Sheldon said. He coughed and Eriana handed him a bottle of water. When he was done drinking, he said, "You need to remember that. Holland is smart. He'll think of that."

"I didn't, though," Cary said. Because she'd died. Eriana had to save her life. And even with Fae magic intervening, Cary had had to go into a healing sleep for ten days to recover from absorbing too much Faery magic. She not only *could* die she *had* died. "Trust me when I say I have not absorbed immortality."

Eriana gave Cary a look she couldn't interpret, but Cary would worry about that later. She didn't want Sheldon knowing any more about her than he already did. Including that she'd died in Faery not all that long ago.

"Is this what you wanted to tell me?" she asked Sheldon.

"Yes. You needed to know he's obsessed with you. When you're done protecting him from his father, he'll turn on you." Sheldon picked at the label on the bottle. "You knew that already."

"I suspected," she said. "Confirmation is good, though, because Holland is unpredictable. I would have expected him to try killing me outright. Knowing he has something else in mind is helpful. Thank you for telling me."

"Will you still protect him?"

"I have to. Can't have his father—who also hates me and wants to destroy me in painful ways—becoming indestructible. He'd destroy the entire world. And I absolutely have to stop that." She snorted. "Save the world. Seems to be part of my job description now."

And boy did she wish someone had warned her about *that* from the beginning.

"I didn't switch bodies with him for immortality," Sheldon said again, his chin tucked but his mouth set in a hard line. "I wanted…two things."

"You said already. You wanted magic."

"But not for why you think. That wasn't all, not the only reason."

She sighed. "Tell me or don't. But do it now. My patience has evaporated over the last two weeks and it was never very good to begin with."

Jaxer snorted. Cary gave him the evil eye. Or she would have if she knew how to give someone the evil eye. She idly fingered the charm on her necklace, a Fatima Hand given to her by a friend. She mostly wore it with fingers pointed up for good luck, though according to Jasmine, it could be worn with fingers down to protect from the evil eye. The charm had just a touch of good luck magic in it, magic that Cary was pretty sure came from Jasmine's aunt. She bet Jasmine's aunt knew how to give the evil eye.

"I wanted to be able to tell you what Holland was thinking," Sheldon said. "You didn't have any information. You needed it. And the Angel said I'd survive the body swap."

"The Angel could have lied. And there are better ways to get information than killing yourself."

"I didn't die."

"Only because Eriana saved you."

Eriana gave Cary another look Cary couldn't read so she ignored it.

"After all the times I swapped bodies with Zorianthus, I knew I'd have access to Holland's thoughts. At least some of them." Sheldon glanced at the floor. "I wanted to help because you… You helped me even though you don't like me."

She wasn't going to argue that point. She didn't like him. He'd tried to kill Deacon. He'd killed other shifters. And despite everything, he *still* hadn't done the atonement work for that. No apologies. Just excuses. No effort to do better. He couldn't fix what he'd done because the dead were still dead. But he could at least put in some sort of effort to make amends.

Unless, he thought this was that work?

"Is this your way of trying to…make up for what you did before?" she asked, her tone sharp even though she'd meant to keep it neutral.

"No," he said, still not meeting her gaze. "This was to help you."

"You said you did it to get some magic back, too. That isn't 'helping' me." She still didn't know what to think. About any of this. But especially about Sheldon.

"I didn't want the magic for the reasons you think."

She closed her eyes and shook her head. "Sure."

"I swear." His voice rose.

She opened her eyes to see him glaring at her. "You'll pardon me if I can't find it in me to believe you."

"I wanted to help *you*. I can't without magic of my own. I can't do witchcraft. It won't work. I need to be a wizard again. Otherwise, I'm just a useless lump who can't do anything. I'll be a brick, just standing there while you defend the whole goddamned realm. What good is that?"

"There are ways to help the world without magic. There are ways to help the world without body swapping with a demon. There are always other choices. And this one was a piss poor choice because it nearly killed you."

Sheldon flicked out a hand. "I knew you wouldn't understand."

"You're right. I don't. Being without magic isn't the end of the fucking world. Demon gods and the Angel of Death might be. But you not having magic is most certainly not."

"Maybe it is for me," he said quietly, sullenly.

She sucked in a breath and glanced at Eriana before staring hard at Sheldon again. "Are you trying to get yourself killed? Is that it?"

"No. I told you already, I'm not suicidal. I just want to be *me* again."

"You know my opinion of 'you' before. So I'm not going to encourage that."

"I don't have to do what I did before," he snapped. "I don't want to. I don't want to be the wizard Zorianthus tried to make me. But I *do* want to be a wizard again."

She pressed her lips together. There wasn't anything she could say in that moment that wouldn't just extend the argument. But she did have to know, "Did it work? Did you get any magic when you body swapped with a demon? Did you bring any of that back with you?"

He glanced at Eriana this time, but his mouth had gone flat and all the angry emotions drained from his expression.

Eriana answered for him. "No. The damage he sustained from having a demon in his body was too severe. His cells couldn't take the parts of the demon he brought back with him. To heal, those things needed to be removed."

"Did he even bring magic back?" she asked quietly. Was it even possible?

"No," Eriana said again, her tone clinically neutral. "Just damage and pain."

"And information," Sheldon said, though his expression was still flat. "I could at least get that done, at least that much."

Cary wasn't sure how to respond to the fact that he'd done all this to regain some of the magic he'd lost, because she was happier with him not having magic. He'd been dangerous with it. Still, a traitorous part of her recognized how miserable he was and there was empathy there she didn't particularly want to feel for him.

She was even less sure how to respond to the fact that he'd also done this to get information for her. The information he'd brought back was good, though. A confirmation of the fact that Holland wouldn't just be grateful for her help and go away. He'd turn on her. She could count on that now, not waffle about it. And that was worth at least another…

"Thank you. For the information. I don't want you ever doing anything like that again in the name of 'helping,' though. It could have cost you your life."

Sheldon shrugged. "No one would have cared."

"Sheldon…" She pressed her lips together and fought back the snap of anger. She shook her head. "Self pity is a bad look. You're alive. And people here made an effort to ensure that happened. Stop insulting them by feeling sorry for yourself." She cut her hand through the air. "This arguing isn't good for your recovery either," she said before Eriana could remind her. "I appreciate the information you brought back from Holland, and I appreciate you telling me. Now you can focus on getting well again." She glanced at Eriana. "How long until he's fully recovered?"

"He'll need another session, but he's almost healed. I wouldn't have brought him out of the coma otherwise."

Sheldon stared at Cary as Eriana spoke, but he didn't comment.

"Fine," Cary said. "I'll leave you to it, then." She turned to leave, Deacon following silently.

"Will I see you again?" Sheldon called. "Or are you done with me now?"

She snarled. "I have no fucking idea," she said.

The most honest answer she had.

3

Cary stomped into her house, tossed her keys into the bowl by the front door, and chucked the bag with her gi in it down the short hallway between her garage and living room, in the general direction of the laundry room. She was sure she'd regret not taking the gi out now and washing it, but she was too irritated and edgy and confused and upset for reasons she couldn't entirely explain. Laundry could wait.

"You want to talk," Deacon said, gently closing the door.

"Probably," she said. "I don't know what I'm feeling, though, or what I want to say, so you may just get a string of incoherent rage-gibberish from me in place of actual words."

"Fair enough. I have thoughts that will probably only come out as rage-gibberish, too."

She snorted, amused despite herself.

The dogs had jumped up from their beds under the big bay window in her living room, scrambling to greet her with enough enthusiasm to dim her bad mood.

"Hey guys," she said, dropping on her knees to hug her pack.

Fred, her terrier-collie cross who was the only mundane dog, stood braced against her arm, his short legs trembling with his excitement while she gave him an ear scratch with her free hand. He hopped away long enough to bounce off Deacon's thigh in greeting, then flopped onto the ground in front of her for a belly scratch. Pickles, her foo lion disguised as a basset hound, pressed her big head against Cary's hand as she got her own behind-the-ear scratch. Buck, her golden Lab who was really a demon dog, wagged his thick tail, thumping it against the floor as he got a hug and head scratch.

Coming home to her pack always helped release the frustrations of the day.

Once the welcome greetings finished, everyone—dogs, Deacon, and Cary—all made their way to the kitchen. The movement was habit. She let the dogs out into the backyard for a run and pee break, Deacon put on a pot of coffee for her and got himself a drink, usually milk. The rhythm of "being home" at the end of a day.

She smiled as they moved through the process, so familiar and settling, and more of her grumpiness faded.

Not all of it. But enough she thought she might be able to talk coherently. Maybe. Once she'd taken a few sips of coffee.

They settled in the living room, the dogs back in their beds under the big bay window that looked out onto the backyard, her and Deacon on the big overstuffed couch across from the fireplace, and Cary let that final step in the "coming home" process release the last of her jumping nerves. She settled against Deacon's side and for a long moment they just sat there, drinking their respective drinks and letting the quiet snuffles of sleeping dogs fill the silence.

"Better?" Deacon asked after a few minutes.

"Better," she said. "I don't know what to do about Sheldon. What to make of him."

"I know." He let out a long breath. "If it helps, I don't feel the urge to rip his throat out every time I see him now."

"Actually, that does help. But also emphasizes the complication of the situation." She sipped her coffee. He'd made her a pot of hazelnut, and the subtle, nutty aroma filled her senses as she took another deep breath. "I hate waiting too," she said.

"That I know."

She smiled and winced at the same time. "Holland is going to try and kill me at his earliest convenience. After torturing me and turning me into a pet."

"We suspected he would try."

"Having it confirmed is… I don't know. Reassuring doesn't seem like the right word."

"It's easier to plan and anticipate when you have all the information."

"Except I don't have it all. Because I still don't know when all this is going to happen." She waved a hand vaguely in the air. "Only that at some point in the near future, I have to protect someone who will then turn around and try to kill me. And we can't kill him back. He can't be killed. Except maybe by his father. But I can't let his father get him because then even more people die." She settled closer to Deacon's side. "I don't want to die," she murmured.

Despite having already done it once before, and in the end not remembering much of the experience—like childbirth, or so her sister told her, the memory of the pain had even faded so she didn't remember any of it that distinctly now—she still didn't want to go through it again with Holland. Knowing he didn't *just* want to kill her somehow made it all worse.

"I won't let him get you," Deacon said, pressing his lips against the top of her head. "I'll keep going for his throat. You'll have to protect me from his anger. He'll never get to you."

She smiled. The weird, but good thing, about Protector powers. They were tricky. Holland knew how to get around them. When she wasn't protecting someone, she could be killed as easily as anyone else. But when she was protecting someone, getting through her was pretty much impossible. To get around her powers, the person had to want to kill her and no one else. Their *intensions* mattered. Holland knew that. But he'd have to forgo his desire to kill anyone else within her realm of protection, and if Deacon kept trying to rip out his throat, Holland wouldn't be able to avoid being a threat to Deacon. Short of allowing his throat to be ripped out repeatedly and ignoring the shifter tearing him to pieces. Which Cary couldn't see Holland doing.

It might work. Not indefinitely. But it might work.

"Unfortunately, it doesn't solve the long term problem. Holland is…forever. And I'm not. You're not. He's got time. And patience that I don't have. And he'll just keep coming."

"We'll sick the demon hunters on him. Talk to Angie. There has to be something someone can do about him."

Angie was a witch, not a demon hunter, but she had ties to the demon hunting world that she never talked about. Just recently, Cary had learned—not from Angie but from Marianne who'd found out on accident—that Angie also had a secret boyfriend who was a demon hunter. A secret boyfriend she wasn't supposed to be seeing, or wasn't allowed to talk about. Or something like that. Cary wasn't sure. They hadn't talked about that little revelation yet. But only because Angie had been out of touch for the last two weeks.

Cary had called her after Sheldon had channeled Holland, to warn Angie that Holland was coming back. She knew Angie avoided demon things as much as she possibly could, and even though there was a convenient demon hunter in town, Cary wanted Angie to know in advance what was coming so she could be safe and away from it all. Angie had taken the news in a way Cary hadn't expected. She'd gotten very quiet, then said she had to go talk to some people and would be gone for a bit. She'd call when she got back.

Two weeks and no call. Angie was a powerful witch who was perfectly capable of taking care of herself, and had done so for longer than Cary had known her. Still, Cary worried. With everything happening, she worried a lot.

And of course, thanks to his super shifter sense of smell, Deacon zeroed in on the new direction of her worry without her having to say anything out loud.

"She hasn't texted?" he asked.

"Just that once a week ago." To let Cary know she was okay but still working on things. Whatever those things were. "I know she's fine. But…there's a lot going on. I warned her about Holland to keep her out of the demon stuff. I'm afraid she's gone and put herself right back into…whatever it is in her past she won't talk about. For me. And I really really hate that idea."

"She loves you. Just like you love her. You'd face your past for her?"

"Of course. But I don't have one to face." Before the Protector gig—which Angie knew all about—Cary had been a vet tech rethinking her career choice. She didn't have deeply buried secrets from a "time before." But if she did, "Of course I'd face anything for her."

"Would you expect her to do any less?"

"Stop making logical sense and good points," she grumped. "It's annoying."

He grinned and nuzzled her neck, which had the duel effect of relaxing her and distracting her from her grumpiness. Clever clever man.

"I just want them all safe," she murmured.

"All who? The girls."

"All everyone. Marianne, Lucy, and Angie. The leopards. Jaxer and Eriana. Wisat and Liruk. The world. You. Just…everyone. I'm a little tired. And I'm tired of the world continually being on the brink of destruction. It'd be delightful if all the mayhem would just settle down for like, I don't know, a month. Maybe two." She considered that. "Actually, I'd prefer a few years. A few quiet years where the world isn't trying to end. That'd be really nice."

He squeezed her shoulders. "Until then," he said, as if that would actually come to pass one day and it wasn't just a pipe dream, "we'll manage this current crisis. And you're better prepared to face Holland this time. We know what we're getting into at least. You've been training more with Lucy. And Rory."

Rory was a golden dragon—not a shifter, an actual honest-to-god ancient dragon. A good one. Who fought alongside an actual sword-wielding hero named Joan. And when Rory wasn't busy fighting legendary monsters with Joan, he showed up in Portland to help train Cary in the ways of dealing with the magic she absorbed.

"I am finally making some progress with that at least," she said. "That's something."

Rory was pretty sure all the magic absorption while *also* channeling Protector magic, which kept her from getting killed by all the magic she absorbed, had changed Cary on a fundamental level. But they still weren't sure how. Or what all this had done to her. She still felt perfectly normal. Like herself. But apparently, she wasn't the same self she'd been when she got tricked into becoming a Protector.

She *had*, however, managed to release magic on purpose three times in the last two weeks. Finally! This had been a big worry. That she absorbed magic, it built in her cells, and if she didn't release it, all that magic would kill her. Up to now, she'd always released big surges of magic without any control over the process. She'd hit a breaking point and then just...release everything in a big wave of mostly destruction.

Which wasn't the *best* way to deal with the magic absorption problem.

But! There was a light at the end of that tunnel. Rory had adjusted his teaching to take into account that her cells were changed. That she was changed. And even though they didn't know what all this had done to her, the change in the way he taught her to release magic had worked.

He'd had to let her absorb some dragon magic first, though, and that had been...weird. Dragon magic wasn't like other magic. Not that she could usually tell the difference between magicks. But Rory's kind wasn't something she had absorbed before, and knowing that had been a little disconcerting.

She'd managed though, taking in just a little bit—even a little bit of dragon magic was strong—and with Rory's coaching, sent it back into him. Well, most of it. He said she "dropped" some, whatever that meant. He didn't explain. But she wasn't holding his magic in her cells anymore and that was a relief.

After sort of mastering that—okay, she managed it once and he'd declared that good enough—he'd started teaching how to use the magic he gave her. And that was pretty cool.

The process Angie, and then Rory, had been trying to teach her before was just to release and let the magic go back into the ground.

But that never worked for her in any sort of planned way. What she could do, though, as it turned out, was *use* the magic. Throw it or cast it or whatever, the way an actual magic wielder might use their magic. Even do small spells. Almost like she *was* a magic wielder.

The ability was temporary because once she released the magic, it didn't rebuild in her the way it would in someone born with magic. She didn't innately possess it, so she didn't keep making it. But by using it in the same way someone with innate magic would use it, she could let it out of her body without mowing down everyone in the vicinity.

Which was good.

The tricky part was that she absorbed *all* kinds of magic. So she didn't just have to learn, say, how to cast spells like a witch, or form an energy bolt like a wizard. She needed to learn a combination of techniques to handle the hodgepodge of magic that all swirled together in her cells. How she had to use the magic was as unique as her ability to absorb it.

But she'd been practicing. And it was working. At least with dragon magic. Which was a huge relief.

"When does Rory come back?" Deacon asked.

"He didn't say. Depends on his and Joan's work. There's apparently still a goblin issue, and they need to be on hand for that."

"Fair enough. Not calling you in to help again, are they?"

"I will if they ask, but I think that last incident was special circumstances." She'd needed to protect some kids while Joan and Rory did their thing with the most recent goblin king's chaos. That was how she and Rory had met.

"You okay with that? Not knowing when he'll be back?"

She chuckled. Deacon knew her so well. "Of course not, but not knowing what might happen next in my life has become pretty standard practice. I'm used to it even if I don't like it. What I really really hate is knowing I have this big epic confrontation just…out there. And it's not happening."

"My mother wants to send some more leopards to Portland."

The seeming non sequitur had her turning to look at him. "Why?"

"So they'll be on hand. If you need backup."

"I do not want the leopards in danger because of me. Thank your mother for me, very politely, and then say no thanks."

"We've discussed this before. She's going to do what she thinks is right, no matter what. And right now, what she thinks is right is making sure there's backup for her son's mate." He set a finger very gently against her mouth when she opened it.

She scowled because the gesture was a distraction on more than just the keeping-her-quiet front. His touch always distracted her in sexy ways, and she lost too many arguments because of that.

"Before you argue," he said, his voice deep, "you should know, I agree with my mother on this. You will have backup. From us. We, all of the leopards who will move closer to Portland, all of them *want* to have your back. So stop arguing with us."

She let her shoulders relax but not her pout. "I don't want them hurt."

"And they don't want you hurt. So see, it's all fair and balanced."

"What did I say about making logical points?"

His serious expression softened into a grin that made her stomach do a funny dance.

"That grin isn't even a little bit fair, you know," she said. "What do you have to say about that?"

"I'm glad you think so?"

She snorted. Then leaned into him for a kiss. A kiss she definitely needed tonight.

If only it hadn't been interrupted by the tingling down her spine.

And the unexpected, but long overdue, appearance of her bosses.

4

"Where the hell have you two been?" Cary demanded, standing from the couch and setting her mug on the coffee table. "What the hell is going on?"

She hadn't seen her bosses since the whole Sheldon-Holland incident. They hadn't even dropped in randomly to give her another job while everyone waited on Holland to arrive. They hadn't brought her news from the Nagas. They had just vanished, suddenly, practically in the middle of a conversation. And not returned.

Which was really weird and extremely suspicious.

"Protector," Liruk greeted with a formal nod, her shoulders stiff and straight.

She looked more… Cary couldn't put her finger on it. Tense? Liruk was always the more demanding of her two bosses. She'd softened somewhat over the course of this year—which actually freaked Cary out a little—but for the most part, Liruk was the boss that made Cary feel like she wasn't working hard enough at her job and should really be doing better.

Wisat was always the more diplomatic boss, who took the softer route in his dealings with Cary. She'd finally gotten to see their good cop-bad cop routine from the outside not too long ago, and she'd been very impressed with it. When it wasn't directed at her.

At the moment, however, Wisat looked as stiff and closed off as Liruk, his usual gentle smile absent.

Even more suspicious.

She could never fully read either of her bosses, though, not unless they wanted her to. They were North American Fae, and spectacularly Fae looking. Liruk, with her long pearl white hair, golden brown skin, and golden horns poking out of her hair was everything white and gold. Only her eyes—a luminous shade of green—broke the color coordination. Wisat was almost her photonegative opposite. Where Liruk was white, Wisat was black—black hair, black robe—and where Liruk was gold, Wisat was red—red skin, red velvet-covered antlers formed into a halo over his head. The one thing they shared was the unreally green eyes. She still to this day had no idea if that was a trait common to their species of Fae, or if they were related and it was a familial trait.

Outside of them being Fae, and the fact that they'd created Protectors, she really didn't know that much about her bosses. Certainly not on a personal level. She'd worked with them for nearly seven years now. She had two more months of her seventh year test and then she'd have chalked up exactly seven years of working for them. And she didn't even know if they were related or just two individuals who worked together.

That was kind of sad, now that she thought about it.

"What's going on?" she asked again, her voice quieter to match their suspiciously reticent mood. "You both look… I don't know. Upset. Nervous. What's going on? Is it Holland?"

"This is… Not Holland," Wisat said. "And it is not what we would have…"

"The timing is poor," Liruk put in. She hissed something under her breath that sounded like, "Impossible." But Cary couldn't be sure.

"I'm really going to need a full explanation soon." She tried to rein in her impatience. She really did. But she had so very little patience left after the last two weeks, it was hard not to snap at them. "The hemming and hawing is going to make me snarl."

Wisat's mouth ticked up briefly at one side, a very faint show of amusement. But then his expression turned serious again.

Deacon had remained seated right after her bosses showed up, his way of trying not to be too threatening. He didn't always manage it. Sometimes he stood at her back like an angry predator ready to pounce. But her bosses and Deacon had a kind of…understanding between them. Deacon was on her side, no matter what, and they didn't even attempt to keep him from helping her. Technically, in her seventh year, she wasn't supposed to get help. But that rule applied to her mentor. To her bosses. *Not* to her boyfriend.

In all honesty, she'd had a lot more help this year than she'd been expecting, all from friends who weren't technically forbidden to help her. She wasn't sure she'd have made it this far without that help. And she wasn't sure what that said about her as a Protector—she always felt a little unable for her job—but she was still here. So far anyway.

That felt like a win.

"It is necessary for you to come with us," Liruk said, her chin lifting. "For a meeting."

"A meeting? With who? The Nagas or something like that?"

"No," Wisat said, his tone gentle but stiff. "With the… With the Elder."

"The elder? Which one?" There were a lot of elders in different communities. The tiger shifters had a whole council of them. There were elder gods—which she hoped never to meet—and elder human leaders, and elder leaders of smaller Fae communities, though that tended to be rarer. The "elder" could literally be anyone. And their vagueness brought Cary's snarl to the surface. She wasn't patient enough for this.

"The Elder of our people," Liruk said. "The Elder who oversees all Protectors."

Cary's eyes widened. Whoa. "Is this a good meeting or a bad meeting?"

Her stomach tightened and did a little flip that felt too much like nausea. Her shoulders tightened. This didn't feel like a good turn of events. She was still a few months away from finishing her seventh year. She doubted she was supposed to even know about this Elder person until then. Her bosses had made it clear there was a lot she didn't know and wasn't supposed to learn until the end of her seventh year trial—*if* she passed.

"You must come alone," Wisat said. "I'm sorry, Deacon. You cannot come with her for this."

Deacon growled, a quiet noise that nonetheless conveyed a lot of angry threat. "Is she in trouble?"

"It's necessary that she do this alone," Liruk said, avoiding answering Deacon's question.

"She'll be safe," Wisat said. "She won't come to…" He frowned a little and said, "She will be safe."

"Wait." Cary held up a hand. "You nearly said I won't come to harm. But then changed phrasing. Why? What harm could come to me, if I'll also simultaneously be safe? That doesn't make sense."

Deacon rose behind her, standing at her back now. "And I'm not leaving her to face the uncertainty alone."

Liruk let out a harsh breath, almost a show of exasperation, which was so unusual, Cary drew back. Liruk was frequently exasperated with Cary and made no bones about it, but the sound she'd just made was new. Like she wanted to cuss and wouldn't allow herself to.

That was interesting. But not in a good way.

"She must do this alone," Liruk said. "We will be there. She will be safe. But it's necessary. Part of the trial year. It cannot be avoided. Believe me, we've tried. There can be no delay. The Elder demands her presence and there's no avoiding it."

Cary could feel Deacon tensing behind her, and while she wasn't sure what he intended to do with all that coiled intensity, she knew none of it would help. She leaned into him, her back to his chest, because physical contact always calmed his leopard half and let the human half think more logically.

"It's not great timing," she said to Deacon, "but they say it's necessary, and they are my bosses. I'll go. Alone." She turned to face him. "And yes, I know that'll be hard for you. I get it. I understand. I wouldn't like this either if I were in your shoes. But it's my job."

He held her gaze, the faint glow of yellow in the depths showing his leopard, but not too near the surface. He wasn't going to lose control. He was unhappy, but she could practically feel the resignation in his sigh.

"I hate your job," he said, his voice gruff.

She smiled. "I know."

He'd told her that a lot since they met. Except her job was the reason she'd been able to rescue him from Sheldon. The reason they'd met. Because she did this job, she'd been able to save the world a few times. And while she got hurt occasionally, she'd managed to only die the once. And that was only because she'd purposefully stopped doing her job.

She might not always feel like she was a good Protector, and she worried constantly that she'd fail and people would die, but she'd managed to do a lot of good in the last seven years.

Deacon brushed hair that had escaped her ponytail back behind her ears, then let his palms frame her face. "I'd rather go with you. But I'll wait here until you get back."

"Thank you," she murmured, leaning in to his soft kiss. "Hopefully, I'll be back soon." She glanced over her shoulder at her bosses. "Right?"

"This will not take a very long time," Wisat assured.

Which wasn't exactly reassuring.

She let out a long breath and reluctantly pulled away from Deacon. "Okay, let's do this before I lose my nerve."

A tremble of adrenaline-fueled unease moved through her limbs as she stood between Liruk and Wisat, her gaze on Deacon. The dogs had moved to stand next to him, all of them staring at her in silence. Even Fred sat perfectly still.

She kept her gaze on her little family as Wisat held her elbow in a gentle touch.

And the room around her vanished.

5

─────────

he clearing they reappeared in was deep inside a forest Cary had never seen before. Trees as thick as buildings sored into the sky. Redwoods maybe? She wasn't sure. But they were still full with leaves and there was a faint scent of juniper or pine in the air. The ground under the trees was dark rich soil covered in thick leafy ferns. And here and there, Cary thought she saw fireflies dancing between the trunks.

The lighting was dim, but not dark. Late afternoon sunshine filtered through the trees and lit the ferns so they fairly glowed. The clearing was quiet, only a soft swishing of a breeze through the trees. No animal noises. For some reason, that didn't feel oppressive or odd. Just... She wasn't sure. The word sacred came to mind.

Damp, cool air made her shiver a little and she wrapped her arms around herself, wishing for her leather jacket—which she'd managed to forget since she hadn't known they'd be coming to a forest.

She wasn't sure what she'd been expecting. Nothing specific if she were honest. And for some reason, the forest seemed as good a place as any for her bosses to take her for this big meeting.

"Are we inside Faery?" she asked. Faery would be dangerous for her, with the whole absorbing magic thing and Faery being made out of magic. She'd died in Faery, even if only temporarily, and she wasn't particularly keen on being back inside the Fae realm, even if it was the North American region and not the English or Irish courts.

"Not directly," Wisat said, his voice quiet. The clearing seemed to call for quiet. "At a…crossing point. It's better that you're not inside Faery."

"I couldn't agree with that more," she said.

They stood in silence for several moments, Cary restless and worried. Then a soft sound, like the beat of a drum in the distance, a sound that rose to a level she could just hear, before fading away.

As the drum beat vanished, a new being appeared in front of her, materializing out of thin air the way Wisat and Liruk did in her home. Cary took several moments to study the newcomer because this was the first time she'd met any of Wisat and Liruk's people.

This Fae was a solid brown, from his brown hair which hung down to his knees, his brown skin, his brown robes. Not like a Brownie, though. He was too large for that. Human-sized. And his facial features more closely resembled Wisat's than any Brownie Cary had met. He had a loose rope belt hanging around his robes which was also a nearly black brown, but when she looked closely, there were hints of green running through the belt. Where Liruk had little goat horns, and Wisat had a halo of velvet-covered antler, the newcomer had the thick, curving horns of a bighorn sheep rising from the sides of his head and curling around so the points faced forward. Unlike the rest of him, the horns were a bright, vivid green. Brighter than the surrounding leaves. A color that matched his eyes.

Cary considered those green green eyes, so luminous they glowed like a green flame. Similar to Wisat and Liruk's. Almost the same. But there seemed to be more…age in the newcomer's eyes. She wasn't sure how. They were all of them immortal Fae. And they only showed "age" if they wanted to. There was nothing else about this particular Fae that said age. Nothing in his face, his posture. He held a long, wooden walking stick, but he didn't lean on it for support.

Yet she still got the distinct impression of age.

A trick? Or a real impression?

"Cary Redmond," Wisat said, his tone still quiet but very formal. "Kupal Umsta. Elder of the People. Creator of the Protectors."

Cary's eyes widened at this last. Did that mean he was Wisat and Liruk's boss? They'd never said they had one, but she'd gotten the impression there might be a boss or bosses out there somewhere because they occasionally slipped and said they didn't have a choice in something. Not often. But enough to have made her suspicious over the years.

And now, here he was. Wisat and Liruk's boss. Wow.

She waited for him to do something. Nod in greeting. Move. Give her a once-over glance. He remained perfectly still, staring at her without blinking.

Okay. Well, since this was her bosses' boss, she'd better at least make an attempt at being polite. She gave a little—awkward—head nod of greeting and forced herself not to bounce on her toes.

"Cary Redmond," Kupal Umsta intoned. "Protector of Portland."

His voice was powerful but not as deep as Cary had been expecting. A tenor not a base. But the sound had the kind of resonance that made her knees tremble.

Two others moved forward from the trees to flank Kupal Umsta then, not materializing next to him, but moving forward from the trees in a very obvious way. They didn't come fully into the clearing, though, staying back just enough to remain shadowy figures rather than solid beings she could study. One, though, seemed to have the vague form of a human with black wings. The other, a vaguely human body with a head like a dog.

Neither of the new entities spoke.

"Cary Redmond," Kupal Umsta said again, his tone not quite so echoey and formal now. But still filled with power. "You have been tested for the last ten months. You have been found wanting."

She winced at that. This wasn't starting good. She wanted to open her mouth to defend herself, but she wasn't sure how because she wasn't entirely sure yet what Kupal Umsta considered her failures.

Wisat moved a little closer to her, which felt protective and supportive, and Liruk moved a little closer to her on her other side, which surprisingly also felt supportive.

Silence hung in the air for a long moment. Long enough that Cary's nerves, already stretched, started to snap with the tension. She opened her mouth. Closed it again. Fisted and unfisted her hands at her sides. She wanted to say something, to defend herself maybe, or just…hear noise. But she bit her tongue—literally— to keep quiet and flexed her fists some more to keep from excessive fidgeting.

"The Old Ones have convened," Kupal Umsta said finally. "You will be stripped of your powers."

"What?" The exclamation came out sudden and loud in the otherwise quiet clearing. She was so shocked she couldn't actually think about what this meant for a full minute. She could only say again, "What?"

Wisat's gentle hand on her arm didn't help.

"Does this…" She stuttered and had to pull in a deep breath. She didn't seem to have enough oxygen for words. "Does this mean I failed? What does this mean? Does this mean… I don't… Am I not a Protector anymore?"

"You will be stripped of your powers," Kupal Umsta said again. "Your home will remain safe for the months remaining in your test year. You will receive payment for the remaining months of your test year."

"But then after that…?" She blinked hard a few times as spots danced in her vision. "I didn't want this job in the first place. I was tricked into taking it. And now you're just… Throwing me to the wolves? After all these years? I've *tried*. I know I'm not the best Protector, but I've *tried*. And…" She swallowed. Licked her dry lips. "What about Holland? Ho'Lud? The Angel of Death? The end of the world?"

"Another Protector will be assigned," Kupal Umsta said.

"But…"

She was breathing too fast. Her face was hot. She couldn't get enough air. She couldn't think. None of this made sense. She had two more months. She couldn't have failed already. She'd done everything she'd been asked to do. She saved the fucking world. At least twice already. Just this year. Sure, there'd been some mistakes. But some of them hadn't even been her fault. What the hell was happening?

Not a Protector anymore...

She felt tears building. And anger. And a weird sort of relief. And panic. And so much confusion she didn't know what to feel.

What... Just what?

"We have spoken," Kupal Umsta said, his tone returning to that resonance from earlier. Making her bones shake.

And before she could stutter out any more questions, Kupal Umsta vanished, gone in a blink. The two beings beside and behind him, the one with the black wings and the one with the dog's face, also faded away, but more slowly, their images lingering at the edge of the clearing for a long moment.

Then it was just a still-sputtering Cary, Wisat, and Liruk. Alone in the clearing.

6

Cary stared at her living room wall for a moment, vaguely aware of being brought wordlessly back to her home, vaguely aware of Deacon cupping her cheeks and saying something to her. But most of her brain was spinning in a circle around one sentence.

"I got fired."

"What?"

Deacon's sharp question finally brought her out of the fog. She looked up and met his golden eyes, a little yellow with his leopard but only at the edges. She wondered idly if that would get worse when she told him everything.

Or would he be relieved?

"I got fired," she repeated aloud. The words still didn't quite sound right. She glanced back at Wisat and Liruk who'd taken a few steps away to give her and Deacon space. The fact that they were still there was good. She had questions. She wasn't sure if they'd answer now that they weren't her bosses anymore. But she wanted to at least say these things aloud. "I'm not a Protector anymore."

Liruk raised her chin but didn't meet Cary's eyes directly, which was an interesting reaction, and Cary would think about it later when her brain worked properly again.

Quietly, Wisat said, "You have questions."

"Well, yeah. Like, only two months of severance after almost seven years? Two more months of..." She trailed off. She'd never told anyone about the glamour that protected her house. Not her best friends. Not Deacon. Only her bosses and Jaxer knew. She sort of thought she'd tell Deacon about it one day. But she didn't want to let it slip now when she was too stunned and emotionally mixed up to deal with the fall out.

The fact that she had enough sense in her head to do this much felt pretty impressive. She'd be a little proud of herself later for not just blurting out all the stuff in a moment of existential crisis.

"What then?" she finally asked Wisat. She still had enemies here. If they dropped the glamour after two months, there were a lot of people in Portland—and beyond—who'd happily hunt her down and kill her. And she'd have nothing to stop them since she wasn't even a Protector anymore.

Wisat and Liruk would know all this without her having to say it aloud. At least, they should.

"For the money," Wisat said with a shrug that looked difficult for him to make. "You will have two months to decide on a new career path. You've always claimed we tricked you into this. Now, you can find something you really want to do."

Why did that sound hollow and false? Like he was trying to say what she wanted to hear without actually believing it himself.

"The rest..." His gaze flicked to Deacon. "It will work out. The... memories of you as a Protector will fade. Even in the long-lived beings."

"Meaning what? The vampires won't come after me? Holland won't try to kill me?"

"What happens with Holland?" Deacon said.

She glanced up and realized he looked unreadable. He had that neutral look he got when he locked down his emotions, when he was exerting so much control over himself he was essentially an iceman. He hadn't had to do that, even around the other leopards, in a couple of months, since their mate bond had more fully settled into place. The fact that he had to shut down now was… Probably not good.

"There's a confrontation between Holland and his father due any day," Deacon continued in his iceman tone. "How is that being dealt with?"

"Another Protector," Liruk said, her gaze still steadfastly on the wall behind Cary. "More if necessary. Full Protectors who've passed their test year."

That one stung. Cary flinched.

"And Holland's memory of Cary will fade, too," Wisat said in his gentler, quieter tone.

"Wait." Cary straightened away from Deacon a little. "You're saying, everyone I've dealt with, even Holland, his demon god father, his Angel of Death mother, even those beings will forget I exist?"

Everything about getting fired felt horrible, not least of which was the confusion over *why* she'd been fired two months before the end of her test year. But this news, that even Holland would forget about her was…

Not bad. In fact, she might even like this news.

"They will all forget," Wisat said.

"It will take time," Liruk said, "but that is why there's a severance period. Once that is done, their memories will have faded. You can pass Holland in the street, and he will no longer know you. Though, I would advise against drawing his attention to you at that point."

Cary rolled her eyes. "Gee, you think?"

"You will be free to go on with your life. Whatever you choose to do." Wisat folded his hands in front of him and did meet her gaze. "You have done much good in your years as a Protector. This is not how I would have wished…this to go. But you did a good job."

"Then why was I just fired?" she asked.

Wisat sighed and dropped his gaze.

Liruk said, "You will be rid of us. That at least must make you happy."

But actually, it didn't. It didn't at all. They were a pain in her ass, and she frequently grumbled about them. She'd nicknamed them the

Nags, and she spent a lot of time railing against the way they dropped into her life and ordered her around.

But she wasn't happy at all about never seeing them again.

"Will your memories of me fade, too?" she asked. "Is that how this works? Will my memories of…everything fade?"

Would she lose Jaxer, too? She wouldn't lose Deacon. Her bond with him was something outside her life as a Protector. She was pretty sure she wouldn't lose her best friends, even though she'd only met Angie and Lucy because of being a Protector. But she wouldn't allow the memories of her friends to fade. What about the rest, though?

"Your memories will remain intact," Liruk said. "You are…safer with those memories."

She wasn't sure what that meant but she'd figure it out later. "So this is it, then? Not even a chance to finish the test year." She let out a breath. "I thought I had to die to get out of the test year without passing. Pass the year or die. Wasn't that what you said?"

"Well, technically," Wisat said, "you did die."

She flattened her mouth and gave him a look. "If you're trying to be funny, you really suck at it, you know."

"I know," he said with a little shrug.

She very nearly laughed at that. Except it was probably hysterical humor. Gallows humor? Anyway, the laugh didn't feel light and good. It felt dark and bitter. So she didn't let it out.

"What about…" She let her questions trail off. What about all of it really. Could Jaxer still be her friend? They were just getting to a place of reclaiming that friendship after a lot of emotional shit and now…

What about Sheldon? Who would protect him once he recovered? From himself even. Could she still go to the Bookstore? Studying paranormal stuff was no longer her job, but…

"What about the way I absorb magic?" she asked, a little breathless. "Without Protector shields, that will kill me the minute I come into contact with magic again."

Liruk's mouth flattened. "I would recommend continuing your study with the dragon."

"And, for a little while," Wisat said, "try to avoid magical attacks and magical realms."

"Not. Funny." She narrowed her eyes at Wisat.

"That time, I was not even attempting it," he said.

Shit.

Deacon wrapped his arms around her waist and pulled her back against his chest. He didn't usually hold her that way in front of her bosses. But as she let him take her weight, she realized she'd been on the verge of just dropping to the ground, exhausted and overwhelmed. She wasn't even sure what emotions she felt in that moment except that all of this just left her drained and hollow.

"Can I still talk to Jaxer? Eriana? Go to the Bookstore?" She murmured all that aloud without expecting answers. Her brain was just circling the same questions, over and over.

"The Bookstore is free and open to all who know about it," Liruk said. "You've done nothing to violate the rules of the store. I'm sure Renee will continue to welcome you there."

"As Jaxer is no longer your mentor, and you are no longer a Protector," Wisat said. "Any acquaintance you choose to maintain is entirely up to the two of you. But you should know he'll be reassigned to his next Protector soon. A friendship maybe be difficult to maintain at that point."

Cary swallowed, blinking hard against then prick of tears in her eyes, and nodded.

The change was so sudden. So abrupt. That had to be why should couldn't seem to process it. Why she just couldn't get her mind to accept this was all…over.

"Will I ever see you two again?" she asked without looking directly at them. Her gaze had settled on a spot on the floor, and she couldn't seem to drag it back up.

The silence that followed her question was heavy and the first tear dropped down her cheek. She wiped it away and dragged in a deep breath. "Well, good luck with Holland and all that. Try not to let the world end. I, uh, I suppose I have a new life to build and I'm gonna need time for that. So, yeah, don't let the world end."

She blinked hard and finally looked at them, forcing a smile that felt truly awful. "Thank you. For everything."

"Thank you, Prot—" Liruk blinked at her near slip. "Thank you, Cary."

"We wish you well," Wisat said, his tone quiet and sincere.

Without an actual goodbye, the two Fae vanished.

Leaving Cary with tears dripping down her face.

"Are you okay?" Deacon asked.

"No," she said. "I don't know why I'm crying."

"You're sad not to be a Protector anymore," he said.

"You can tell it's more than that. Super shifter sense of smell."

His arms tightened around her.

"It's not just losing a job I never asked for. There's relief. I'm not responsible for stopping the world from ending now. There's anger. I did this job as best I could for the last seven years and I still got fired. There's fear. What do I do now? And there's a lot of numbness. I can't believe this is actually happening."

She turned in his arms and rested her head against his chest, wrapping her arms around his waist. "It's the numbness that's making me cry, I think. The bewilderment. Tomorrow, the anger will hit. But now…"

He held her close, stroking a gentle hand over the back of her head as she let tears roll over her cheeks and soak into his shirt.

7

"I still can't reach Angie," Cary said to Marianne the next day. "She hasn't texted you? Called? Anything?"

Marianne sat on Cary's living room couch, looking cool and together in her work attire—an outfit that she had, of course, made herself—of wide-legged emerald colored pants and a white button up silk shirt with extra-long silk cuffs. Her makeup was, as usual for a work day, flawless. And she was back to wearing bright, rich lipsticks, this one a perfect-kiss-red which complemented both her dark brown skin and her perfectly shaped lips.

Her return to bright lipsticks and her shorter haircut had been a relief. After her breakup with her girlfriend, Marianne had gone through a phase of wearing long box braids and more muted lipstick shades. And while she'd still looked beautiful, those changes had been a very obvious sign of her grief. The fact that she felt comfortable enough to return to things she'd loved before—like bright lipstick—seemed like a good sign.

"I tried her cell yesterday, and again this morning," Marianne said, answering Cary's question. "Nothing. She's gone into a hole."

"This doesn't feel right." Cary sat in one of the two chairs flanking her coffee table. But she was restless and couldn't seem to sit for long.

She stood up almost as soon as she settled and started pacing the living room. Again.

Deacon had gone in to work that morning—at her insistence—because she needed room to think. But all she could think was, "I've been fired." And also, "I can't leave the house, or I might get killed." Neither of those two thoughts were helpful.

So she'd finally called her friends. She'd intended to invite Lucy and Marianne over for pizza and wine, an impromptu girls' night so she could tell them about getting fired and ask for advice on what to do next—after an appropriate period of time bemoaning the fact that she'd been sacked. And she'd texted Angie to see if she could video chat in on the girls' night—she wanted to discuss the situation with all three at once. But she never heard back from Angie. And now, her worry was spiking.

"I'm sure she's fine," Marianne said, though the faint frown creasing her normally smooth brow didn't match her words.

"It's been two weeks with only that single text last week. And I just got fired, so I can't run in and protect her—wherever she is—if she needs me to. And *she doesn't know that.*"

"You do remember she's a powerful witch who got along just fine before meeting you, right?" Marianne said.

"Yes, yes." Cary waved a hand in the air. "I know. But I love you guys, and now I can't help you if you need me and that is making me a little crazy."

"I noticed." Marianne patted the couch. "Sit. Drink your coffee. Tell me more about getting fired. What exactly did this elder say?"

Cary heaved a sigh. "I'm just going to have to repeat all this when Lucy gets here."

Marianne had been able to leave her assistant to manage her store for the afternoon, but Lucy had had one final class to teach before she was able to leave the dojo. Which meant she wasn't due for another hour.

"That's fine," Marianne said, "because maybe I see something different in the retelling. Or you do. Multiple tellings will be good for working out what happened." She glared. "Sit. You're making my head spin with all that pacing."

Cary rolled her eyes, but flopped down into the chair again. Her foot tapping, she reached for the cooling mug of coffee she'd left on the coffee table. "There's not a lot to tell, really. Wisat and Liruk took me to this clearing in the woods. A Fae with big horn sheep horns appeared, told me I would no longer be a Protector, and he vanished again."

"What happens with your pay?"

"Severance of the last two months of the test year. Then I have to find a way to make a living again." She groaned and ran a hand through her hair. "I haven't had a proper job in almost seven years. What the hell am I going to put on my resume? Who will hire me after that kind of gap? What am I going to do?"

"You could go back into veterinary work," Marianne suggested. She glanced toward the bay window and the dog beds, which were currently occupied by the dogs.

Fred and Buck were sleeping. Pickles had her head resting on her front paws, but her eyes were open and she was watching Cary and Marianne talk.

"I was going to leave that when the Protector gig happened. I don't think I want to go back."

"What else do you want to do with your life?"

"Ha! Like I know. I never got a chance to consider that. I was only just considering switching fields when I got tricked into this job. And now I don't have this job."

"Well, now you have time to consider it," Marianne said, in a practical tone that made Cary snarl. "Listen, if I can consider my future and my life post-Gina, you can consider your future and life post-Protector."

"That's not the same," Cary said. "Yours was worse. Losing a job is not the same as losing someone you love."

Marianne's expression softened. "The way you're reacting to this, I'm not so sure. You kind of seem like you'll miss the job."

"That's not it." Was it? "No. I just... I wasn't expecting this so I haven't mentally prepared for it."

Marianne adjusted her position to tuck one leg under her on the couch. She'd dropped her work shoes by the side of the couch when she'd come in. "If you had been prepared," she asked, "if they'd given you a choice to quit or to keep the job, what would you have done?"

Cary blinked and turned to stare at the coffee table. What would she do if she'd been given a choice? She'd never felt like becoming a Protector had been a choice. But she had *tried* to do the job all these years, to the best of her ability. Hell, she'd filled her attic with books and research materials so she could be better at her job. She'd trained and studied and…and sort of resigned herself to doing this job for the rest of her life. She wasn't sure if "resigned" was the right word. But it wasn't the wrong word either. She had just sort of assumed she was stuck with the task of being a Protector. And after a while, she hadn't felt "stuck" so much as just… Well, she'd felt like a Protector. It was what she did. She'd stopped questioning it.

She'd been pissed to learn about the seventh year and that she hadn't been given any warning a full test year was coming. She griped a lot about having to do the job, getting called away from other things *all the time* to go rescue people. She complained about not being able to have a normal life sometimes. And she didn't like hiding her real work from her parents, though she never wanted them to know the truth because they'd worry too much.

But in all that time, she'd never felt like she could quit. Even when she'd threatened to quit, when her bosses had told her the seventh year trial was a requirement, she hadn't felt like she really *could* quit. They'd told her they'd drop the glamour on her house if she tried. And she'd made too many enemies to risk that.

Now, though, her enemies' memories of her were going to fade. Soon she wouldn't need the glamour on her house to keep her safe because all the people who wanted to hurt her would forget about her. She'd be able to step away from the job and be safe.

That felt… She wasn't sure how to feel about it. And that was the worst part. She really didn't know *how* she felt.

"I have no idea," she finally answered Marianne's question. "If I'd been given the choice to quit, I don't know what I would have done." She made a face. "Probably would have depended on my mood and my last job."

Marianne snorted and sipped her tea.

"But to be honest, I never considered what I'd do beyond this job. I never thought about what I'd…be if I weren't a Protector."

Marianne frowned a little. "I understand that blind spot. I never thought about what I might do if Gina and I didn't grow old together. The idea of that not happening hadn't even crossed my mind in the last five, six years of our lives together. Right after we moved here from New York, before I'd gotten the store established, I worried. We'd only been together two years at that point. You think about what you might do that early, especially after moving across country for someone else's dream. But once we were settled here, and especially after she was able to open her nightclub, I thought… Well, I didn't. I just assumed we were in this for the long haul."

"I'm so sorry," Cary murmured.

Marianne waved a dismissive hand in the air. "No. I'm not saying all this for sympathy, or even to talk about my own situation. What I'm saying is that you were through that period of will-this/won't-this work. You were settled, committed. And that got ripped out from under you unexpectedly. Now you have to consider options you never had to think about before. I understand. And the best advice I can give is to take your time. No sudden changes. Don't worry about looking for a new career or job just yet. You have some time. Take it. Give yourself the room to mourn what was and come to terms with the fact that the future has changed. *Then* you can think about what you want to do."

Cary sighed and leaned back in her seat. "You're a very wise woman."

"Punch drunk, more like," Marianne said with a snort. Then she shrugged. "But I'm a survivor. So are you. You'll be fine. And we'll be here to help."

Cary felt tears prickling at the edge of her eyes. She blinked hard. "Thanks."

"Also, if you feel the need for a whole new look, come to me *first* before committing to something drastic, like a bob haircut or some such."

Cary chuckled. "I will." She settled further into the chair, no longer feeling quite so restless, and sipped her coffee. "To be honest, I don't feel the need for a makeover or anything. I don't know how I feel yet."

"That's fair. And another reason to give yourself time to work it out." Marianne glanced down at her tea mug before saying, "How did Deacon react?"

"He was…carefully neutral."

"He didn't want to show you how relieved he was."

Cary snorted. "Got it in one. I could tell, though. He was upset for my sake, because I was upset. But it was pretty obvious he heaved a deep deep sigh of relief at the news."

"I can't blame him. He loves you. And you keep getting into trouble because of this job."

"Probably an understatement." Cary considered the inside of her mug. "I'm pretty sure he forgot the upsides of my job, though."

"Like that you healed faster than a human?"

"And that I was aging slower." She often forgot that part herself. But the job as a Protector came with a few perks, and when your mate was a long-lived shapeshifter, aging more slowly than a typical human came in very handy. "I'll go back to aging at a normal human rate now. And I'll heal from injuries like a normal human. And he's going to be the leader of an entire group of shifters someday." She let out a shaky breath. "I was worried about that when I was channeling Protector magic. Now…"

Now, she'd be so far out of her depth it was ridiculous.

How did she even explain to the other shifters that she could no longer do the things she'd done before? None of them, apart from Deacon's mother, knew what she was— Or had been. She didn't go around telling people she was a Protector because it was safer that way. The leopard kids called her a superhero, even though she had honestly tried to dissuade them of that idea. How did she explain that she could no longer *do* any of those "superhero" things? That all that magic was now, just…gone.

"I'm more worried about the fact that you still absorb magic and now don't have the Protector magic to mitigate that," Marianne said. "The shifters will adapt. Your body isn't going to stop absorbing magic."

Cary ran a hand through her hair, loosening her ponytail. "Yeah, that crossed my mind and Deacon's. He might be relieved I won't be a Protector anymore, but the magic part... At least I've learned how to release what I absorb better. I just need to use it. So long as I avoid absorbing too much, I can just light some candles or something and get rid of it."

Well, okay, it wasn't quite that easy because which spells or whatever she used to dispel the magic had to be in line with the type of magic she absorbed. Still, it was at least possible now. They'd learned enough to know how to train her. Rory could help her whenever she absorbed something new. And...

"Frankly, I'm not likely to get thrown in front of magic now. It won't be my job. And before this job, outside of you, I didn't really encounter magical people. And I didn't know you were magic until after I had this job."

Marianne grinned. "I was magic before you knew about my magic."

"True." Cary tried to laugh, since Marianne had made the effort of a joke, but the chuckle sounded forced even to her.

"You'll still be around shapeshifters," Marianne pointed out. "And even though they're not magic per se, that might come into their world. You won't be able to fully avoid it."

"But little bits here and there should be manageable. I'll keep training with Rory. Learn different ways to use different kinds of magic. It should be okay." She shrugged. "At least we found out about the magic absorbing thing before I got sacked."

"And the wizard who was trying to kill you over that is dead."

"His memory of me would have faded. According to the Nags. All of them will forget me eventually." In the meantime, she was loath to leave her house.

"Eventually how long?" Marianne asked.

"By the time the severance period is up, according to Wisat and Liruk."

"What do you do between now and then? You have to survive two more months with no Protector magic but still a lot of enemies out there gunning for you?"

She shrugged. "I guess."

"And Holland? What about him?"

"They said another Protector, or Protectors, would be sent to handle that. Protectors who'd passed their seventh year." She snarled a little. "The thing is, I don't know what I did wrong. I mean, yes, Jaxer helped me a few times even though he wasn't supposed to, but most of the time it was something the Nags sent him to help me with, so I figured that was all allowed." She sighed. "But maybe it wasn't. And I got a lot of help from you all. And Deacon."

"That was always going to happen. We're your friends, not your work associates. Wisat, Liruk, and their boss can't tell any of us what to do."

Cary's smile felt more genuine this time. "Which is why I love you."

"Maybe it was because you died?" Marianne suggested. "Wasn't that the rub of the seventh year stuff. You either survive and come into your full powers, or you die and your family is compensated."

"Then they need to send me and my family more than just two months' salary as compensation." She flattened her mouth. "Wouldn't it just be that, the loophole of having died—for just a minute or two— that got me sacked. I mean, it's not like I stayed dead. And I died using my own stuff to save the world. I wasn't even channeling Protector magic in that moment."

"You were still protecting, though."

"Yeah, but not in a 'this is my job' kind of way. Plus, plus! I gave Faery the answer they needed to heal. That should count for something since my bosses and their boss all live in Faery."

"It should," Marianne agreed with a nod. She leaned forward and set her now empty tea mug on the table. "We can sit here guessing all day, though, and it won't change anything. You're not a Protector anymore. We have to come up with ways of keeping you safe for the next couple of months, until all those people who want to kill you forget about you."

Cary blinked a few times. "I hadn't considered... You'll help me stay safe?"

"Girl." Marianne scowled at her. "What did you think we'd do? Sit around drinking and commiserating and not actually *do* anything? Of course we'll do something. I can make you clothes with extra protective magic. Lucy can keep teaching you how to defend yourself against all comers. And Angie can make you wards and charms to fend off attacks. We've got you."

Cary sniffled. "I'm gonna cry now."

"Do," Marianne said, her tone softer. "It helps. Trust me."

She motioned Cary to the couch, and Cary went, letting Marianne wrap her up in a hug while tears streamed down her face.

"Don't be surprised if Deacon arranges a bodyguard for you, either," Marianne said softly. "It's what I'd do if I were him. He'll be very aware of the two month ticking clock."

"I really don't want a bodyguard. I don't want anyone getting hurt trying to keep me safe from people I pissed off."

"That's because you're used to being the bodyguard. But he'll need to do this for you, for his own peace of mind. I'd consider letting him. Just consider it. Either that or he'll just be attached to your hip for the next few months." Marianne shrugged. "That might not be so bad, though."

Cary chuckled. The cry and the hug and the joke actually did all help. "Thanks," she said. "For everything."

"Any time." Marianne kissed the top of her head. "Now. Go get you another cup of coffee. We're going to talk about your new wardrobe. And I have some really interesting ideas."

"Should I be scared?"

"Have I ever steered you wrong when it comes to fashion? Go get your coffee. This is going to be fun."

8

A long afternoon and a carb-filled lunch with Lucy and Marianne helped Cary's shaky mental state a lot. Especially after they established a clear plan for what Cary needed to do to stay safe over the next two months while people's—and more specifically vampires' and demons'—memories faded. Deacon returned just as Marianne and Lucy were leaving, the timing so perfect she narrowed her eyes at them all in the doorway.

"Yes, I texted him," Marianne said. "Do you really want to be alone right now?"

She flattened her mouth. She really didn't. She thought she'd wanted just that this morning, but the sound of her own thoughts pounding against her skull had been very unhelpful.

Marianne gave her a hug. "I'll start on a few things tonight. Tomorrow you come into the shop. We'll have you set up in no time."

Lucy's hug nearly pulled Cary off her feet. "Daily training from now on, not just every other day. I'll get the movements trained into your muscles and bones. You'll be kicking ass without any trouble, or any need for magic, soon."

"Thanks," she said to both of them. "Really. Thanks." Before they got off the front stoop, she said, "Call me if either of you hear from Angie. I'm still…worried."

They hadn't discussed Angie's absence for long, but they had talked about it. And Cary wasn't the only one worried about her, even though she was a super powerful witch and could take care of herself. But since there wasn't anything they could do until Angie got in touch with them, they'd moved on to the ways they could set Cary up for defending herself against old enemies without Protector magic. At least for the next couple of months.

Deacon pulled her into a hug, and a gentle kiss, as soon as she closed the door. She sank into the heat of him, the coming-home feeling of having his arms around her, the taste of him, the way his scent filled her, settled her. The depths and intensity of the mate bond still surprised her sometimes. This need to have him close and how much better she felt when he was with her. But she didn't feel any need to fight that feeling anymore. She was content to wallow in it, and savor the fact that, no matter what else was going on, she had Deacon to come home to. So to speak.

When he lifted his head, he held her gaze for a long moment. "You look less shocky. Less like you're going to break. That's good. The time with Marianne and Lucy must have helped."

"It did. A lot. And we have a plan. I feel better with a plan." She sucked at making them, but she was always reassured when there was one in place, even if it was a bad plan. This time, though, she didn't think the plan was bad—probably because Marianne came up with it and not her.

She got a refill on her coffee, even though she probably should have moved to decaf at this time of the evening, and got Deacon a milk, then they sat down and she told him everything she and her friends had discussed. The dogs made their need for a trip to the backyard known in the middle of the retelling, so she finished the details on the porch while they watched the dogs take advantage of the cool October evening air.

"I love the idea of Marianne making you clothes that will fend off magic," Deacon said.

They sat on the top step of her little wooden porch, his arm wrapped around her shoulders, pulling her close to his side. He was so warm, she almost didn't need the padded flannel she'd put on in deference to the cool air.

"Me too. She says she can do some stuff for physical attacks too, maybe work those into my jacket."

"Can she make you something with Kevlar in it?" he asked. "Since you're no longer Kevlar incarnate."

She chuckled at that. It was the way she liked to describe her job— Or at least, the way she'd described the job she used to have.

"Wow. I'm really going to have to get used to not thinking of myself as a Protector anymore. It's…habit. You know."

"It's okay if it takes time."

Fred raced up to them with a soggy tennis ball and dropped it on the step at their feet. Cary picked the ball up and threw it to the far wooden wall of her little yard. Fred raced after it, his little legs flying over the cut grass.

"Has Jaxer been in touch?" Deacon asked quietly.

"No." And the absence was noticeable. But… "I'm sure he'll stop in when he can. He's . got a lot on his plate. And Liruk and Wisat probably have him working with the other Protector or Protectors they're calling in to deal with the Holland situation."

"That is probably the one thing in all this that's a relief to me," Deacon said. "That you won't be the one facing Holland now."

She knocked against him with her shoulder. "The one thing?"

He let out a huffed combination of groan and chuckle. "Not been very subtle, have I?"

"No. But I understand. Marianne figured you'd be relieved, too, without me having to say anything."

"I really hate your job… Hated your job," he admitted. "But I also hate that you're so upset and shocked and sad. I didn't want to give you the impression I was celebrating something that's hurt you."

"I understand your relief. I don't think you've considered the downside. But I understand your relief."

"What downside? Outside of the fact that for two months you're still in danger."

"I'm going back to aging and healing normally. I won't have that slow aging thing and the fast healing thing that made living amongst shifters a lot easier." She dropped her voice to a near whisper when she said, "I'm going to die a lot sooner than you, even though my chances of growing old have just gone up significantly."

"The fact that the chances of us growing old together have *increased* now that you're not a Protector is what I like. Even if I will get to old a lot slower than you. I'll take all the years with you I can get."

Still. She wasn't sure he'd feel that same way in fifty years when she was an obviously old woman and he looked…well, like his mother. Older but not old. But she supposed they could deal with that when they got there. And he was right. Her chances of getting there were a lot better now. Growing old, even if she was doing it at a normal rate, gave them more years together than her getting killed trying to save the world. Again.

"What about the fact that I will heal like a normal human from now on?"

"We can accommodate that, too. There are human partners to shapeshifters, you know. Even among the leopards, though it's rare. They manage to do just fine. Look at my brother and his new mate."

That was true enough. Deacon's youngest brother Dylan had found his mate in a human woman, too. The probability of both of them having human mates was pretty astronomical. Leopards almost always mated with other leopards. But since Dylan was an astronomer and his mate was a genius physicist interested in cosmology, somehow the "astronomical" odds seemed appropriate.

"Marianne thought you might want to get me a leopard bodyguard," she said, keeping her gaze on the dogs.

"Marianne knows me better than I realized," he said, almost to himself.

Cary grinned. "She's a very smart woman."

"Yeah she is." He let out a low sigh. "Will that bother you?"

"Marianne being smart, or you trying to shackle some poor leopard with the obligation of being my bodyguard?"

"The bodyguard part," he said.

She glanced at him from the corner of her eyes. He looked like he wanted to laugh. Which was good. That had been her intention with her cheeky question.

"Yes," she said, "it will bother me that someone else might be in danger because of me. That always bothers me. And I don't want one of your people putting themselves into that position."

"They're your people now, too, you know."

She tried not to flinch. She knew that on some level and yet couldn't wrap her thinking around the idea. She liked the leopards she'd met so far. Most of them anyway. And she loved . being Deacon's mate. But as a human, the idea that the leopard shifters were "her people" still hadn't sunk in. She wasn't sure if it ever would fully.

"I'd still like to arrange it," he said, looking at her and holding her gaze. "Not forever. Just for a few months. I'll get someone you already know and get along with. And they'll only be around when I can't be. Will that work?"

"I'll still hate it. But I understand that instinct. I'd want to do the same thing for you." She rolled her eyes. "If you're expecting me to be gracious about it, you'll be waiting for a while. But if I can't talk you out of it, I guess I'll learn to deal with it."

"Thank you." He dropped a soft kiss onto her lips.

She tried to pretend she wasn't pleased with his obvious relief.

"Will you…" He hesitated, and that put her on edge. "Will you get mad if I take more time off work to spend it with you? To keep you safe."

"Mad? No. Annoyed and irritated… Yes. You don't have to do that. I'd really rather you didn't." His job was rescuing animals! It was an important job. She hated when he stopped working just for her.

"You know Caitlin can handle things here. She'll understand."

"No, she won't because she doesn't know what I do." She paused. Let out a breath. "Did. What I did. How will you explain you need to babysit me? For that matter, how will you explain to any of the leopards that I need a bodyguard? We're not telling them what my old job was," she said, raising a hand before he could suggest that. "I don't want anyone to know. I don't want them to know what Protectors are if they don't already. It's safer for all the Protectors. It'll be safer for whoever takes over in Portland."

Which was true. The less people who knew Protectors even existed, the safer all the Protectors were. But a less noble part of her psyche also just didn't want to explain to people how she'd gotten fired from a job she'd thought she was good at. She wasn't ready to talk about that yet. She still didn't even understand *why* she'd been fired. She'd break down in tears if she had to tell people outside of her closest friends about any of this. And she still hadn't fully worked out *why* she'd break down into tears either. So for now, the firing was something she'd discuss with only her nearest and dearest who already knew she was a Protector.

Had been a Protector.

Damn that was going to take some getting used to.

"We're coming up to our one year anniversary," Deacon said. "Halloween."

She grinned at that. She'd rescued him from Sheldon on Halloween night, and he'd realized with a few sniffs that she was his mate. Funny he considered that their anniversary. She hadn't even thought about it.

But her brows bunched with the non sequitur. "What does our anniversary have to do with anything?"

"I'll tell everyone I want a month off to spend with you to celebrate. No one will object or even think about it. The first year between mates is always…fraught."

She snort-laughed at that descriptor. She was pretty sure her and Deacon's first year had been more "fraught" than most mates.

"So most of them want to celebrate reaching the first anniversary," he finished.

"That explains you taking time off work in October. But not November."

"I can just say I want to extend the anniversary." He shrugged.

"You'll be stretching their credulity at that stage. And even if they bought that as an excuse for you not working much, how will you explain that I need a bodyguard?"

"I don't have to explain that," he said, not meeting her gaze. "The only reason you don't have one now is because you got mad when you realized the other leopards were already guarding you."

She scowled at the side of his face. After the incident with his ex-girlfriend and the cougar attacks last January, after she'd officially been introduced to his family and his people, she'd found herself spending a lot of time with the handful of leopard friends she'd made. It had taken her a while before she realized they weren't all spending that much time with her just because they liked her. They were around whenever Deacon wasn't—protecting her.

"That's because *I* was the Protector. I didn't need anyone protecting me."

He finally met her gaze, his chin lowered, his brows raised.

Her scowl deepened. "Okay, fine, sometimes I was vulnerable. But most of the time, I was just fine. And had survived just fine without you and the leopards guarding me."

"They want you safe. I want you safe. My people… I know you don't want to think about it yet, but they consider you their future leader because you're my mate. And they *like* you. All I'll have to say is that you're allowing me to give you a bodyguard finally, and I'll have a host of eager volunteers."

She winced. He was right. She didn't want to think about being anyone's leader. Especially not now. She was good with thinking of Deacon as their future king. He was born to it and he inhabited that duty well. Naturally. But she just wanted to be his mate. Not anything more than that. Especially not to leopard shifters when she wasn't one. And it wasn't because she didn't like the leopards. Most of them had been welcoming and wonderful. She just didn't feel able for the role of leader.

Though, to be fair, she'd never really felt able for the role of Protector, either.

"Does your dad have a bodyguard?" she asked, just to be irritating.

"He did. In the early years of their bond. Right after my mother took over the territory and brought the leopards together into a cohesive group. The way to get to her would have been to kill him. They both understood that. He always had someone guarding his back."

Well that took the air out of her argument. Damn.

"I said I'd agree to it," she muttered. "I didn't say I'd like it. I hate putting other people in danger for me."

"I know. But someday you need to accept that other people don't mind putting themselves in danger for you."

Accept? Not likely. But she didn't say that out loud. "So… What do we do for the next two months?"

She should probably tell him about the glamour on her house. Now that it was going to be taken away. She'd felt a little guilty not telling him all this time. But now he probably needed to know that after her two month's severance period, her house wouldn't be as safe as it was now.

She glanced at the dogs still nosing around the backyard. Well, with a demon dog and a foo lion and a really yappy mutt, the house might actually still be pretty safe. Especially if all the enemies she'd made over the years forgot she existed.

Pickles wandered close to the porch and flopped onto her stomach in the grass, resting her head on her front paws as she watched Buck and Fred. Would Pickles stay? She was a retired foo lion. She'd taken refuge in the Bookstore after losing her mate. Cary's house had probably served as a safe retirement place too because of the glamour. If Pickles felt she had to be on guard here, would that motivate her to find another home?

The thought made Cary want to cry. She loved her pack. She didn't want to lose any of them. Probably a conversation she'd need to have with Pickles soon. Not that Pickles answered in a conventional sense. But she was pretty good at getting across her meaning.

Cary let out a long sigh. So much to consider. So much would change. And she still hadn't really wrapped her mind around it.

"Pizza or Mexican food for dinner?" Deacon asked out of nowhere.

She half-frowned, half-smiled. Had her stomach rumbled?

Probably. She was hungry. Or maybe he was. "Mexican food tonight," she said. They'd had pizza last night. "And then I need to consider how I eat. I won't have the Protector healing anymore. Or any other benefits. I'll need to balance the foods I take in better so I don't collapse of malnutrition from living off coffee, donuts, and pizza."

Not that she could live off those even as a Protector. Well, coffee maybe. She needed her daily dose of coffee. But she'd used the excuse of stress to justify a lot of her food choices in the past. And she wasn't going to have that same excuse going forward.

"Pizza is good for you," Deacon said, squeezing her shoulder. "Carbs, protein, dairy, good fats in the oil, vegetables in the sauce."

She grinned. "You're just saying that to make me feel better about my pizza habit, but I approve, so I won't argue."

She patted his leg, intent on heading back inside. But a warning breeze from overhead stilled her movements. Buck and Pickles both walked up the porch steps and flanked Cary and Deacon.

Fred, oblivious to his surroundings, only started barking after the dragon had settled in the yard.

9

Rory was as impressive as a dragon should be. Gold scales, multi-faceted ruby red eyes, massive body that he was able to shrink enough to fit in Cary's small yard, a tail with spikes, a spiked ruff around the base of his skull, and enough sharp teeth in his mouth to almost make a person forget he breathed fire.

Almost.

Fortunately for Cary, Rory was one of the good guys.

"I didn't think we had a session tonight," she said as Rory lowered his massive head to almost eye level so she didn't have to crane her neck back to look up at him.

"We don't, Protector," Rory said.

She'd nearly adapted to the fact that while he sounded like he spoke aloud, in actuality, his voice was in her head. He could simultaneously "say" something to her and Deacon, though, so Deacon would be included in the conversation and feel like it was happening out loud too.

"But I have some free time while Joan recovers from our last adventure. She'll need to sleep for a bit."

"Was she hurt?" Cary started to rise.

"No," Rory assured. "She's just tired. And I'm not anymore. Are you free to work on your spells?"

Cary let out a little sigh. "Yeah, I'm free. But… I should tell you. I'm not a Protector anymore." And why the hell did she keep tearing up when she said that?

Rory's momentary silence spoke volumes. "What happened?" he asked.

"I was fired." She explained most of it, a quick overview, trying not to feel the hurt again. "So, while I do still need to learn to manage any magic I absorb, it's less likely I'll take in much from now on."

She tried to say this in a light tone, a kind of bright-side-to-everything tone. Instead, she just sounded sad, even to herself.

She wondered when that sadness would be overwhelmed by the anger. Because there was a lot of that there, too. But the anger was subsumed under her bewilderment. She didn't understand why she'd been fired and that still dominated her feelings. That and the sadness. She imagined the anger would overwhelm all the other confused emotions eventually.

"That is…" Rory paused for long enough Cary thought he might not say more. But he ended his sentence with, "Unexpected."

"Yeah. I wasn't expecting it either. In fact, I thought they'd let me at least get through the full seventh year test before…" Well, she wasn't sure.

She'd sort of assumed all along that *if*—and it was a very big if—she made it to the end of the year without getting killed—permanently —and without really screwing up—like letting the world end—she'd have passed her test. She mostly followed the rules, and when she'd broken rules, it had almost always been because Wisat and Liruk broke those rules in her favor. And yes, she'd grumped about the job. And the year-long test. But lots of people complained about their jobs, and the complaining wasn't what got them fired.

"What will you do now?" Rory asked.

"Get through the next two months and then… I have no idea. Figure it out, I guess. I haven't had a chance to really think about what I want to do with my life. I do still have to deal with the magic absorption thing, though. And now I don't have Protector shields to stop some of the magic getting through."

"Yes," Rory said. "I suggest not letting anyone but one of your teachers throw magic at you from now on."

She barked out a laugh at the obviousness of Rory's statement. The sound of Rory's soft chuckle in her head proved he'd attempted to make her laugh. And for some reason, the fact that a *dragon* had tried to make her laugh and lighten her sadness seemed so unreasonably sweet and ridiculous, she continued to laugh a bit longer.

"You could always become a hero," he said when she'd stopped chucking.

"Like Joan?" She shook her head. "That took years of training."

"And a dragon and a mythic sword," he added.

"Exactly. I might be starting into the hero game a little late."

"Not really. You've been one for almost seven years. You'd just need to shift the sort of training you do."

"Like sword fighting?" Lucy had tried to teach her a few techniques with wooden sticks. It hadn't gone well.

"For you, I would recommend learning how to use magic better. Figure out how to immediately cast what you absorb. Offensively. Use magic thrown at you to…fight the bad guys." Rory sounded amused by his turn of phrase on the last sentence.

Cary got caught on the idea of using magic offensively.

Her entire career in the preternatural world had involved defense. She was…had been a purely defensive weapon. She stood as a shield and that was typically all she did. Occasionally, more was required of her, and when that was necessary, her Protector magic gave her the skills she needed. But for the most part, all she had to do was just stand in the way of bad guys and she could keep the good guys safe.

The problem was, she'd never been able to *do* anything about the bad guys. She couldn't make them go away. She'd gotten really good at irritating them into giving up and leaving. And thanks to the magic absorption thing, she'd flatten bad guys a couple of times just by releasing all the build-up of magic. But not on purpose or with any sort of control over the process.

What would it be like to be able to actually…do something besides stand there?

"You're saying I could take whatever a bad guy threw at me and use it against them?"

"Theoretically," Rory said. "Yes. It's what you're training to do now—release the magic via spells and castings. You'd just…do that faster. In the moment."

She glanced at Deacon, frowning a little as the idea sunk in. "This wouldn't help me against shifters. Or pure preternatural strength like with a vampire. But…it would help with the magic wielding people who want to kill me."

"Like demons?" Deacon asked Rory this.

"Demon magic is still magic. Cary absorbs it." A little puff of smoke came from Rory's raised nostrils as he sighed. "Except I can't teach her how to use demon magic. And Angie won't be able to either. We would need someone more familiar with the way it's used to teach you."

"I'm not asking a demon to teach me how to use demon magic," Cary said. "That sounds like a deal I'd have to make, which would have repercussions. And also, I don't like demons. And really, going forward, I'd like to avoid them all together. Which makes the point of using demon magic moot."

"For two months, you still have to worry about Holland," Deacon said. "Knowing how to counter whatever he throws at you seems like a good idea."

"First of all, I think Holland will be too busy with his dad and mom to worry about me. If he somehow survives that mess… Well, hopefully, at that point he'll have forgotten who I am."

"And if he doesn't?" Deacon asked.

"Then I'm probably not going to have time to learn how to use demon magic in a way that will prevent him from killing me," she said bluntly. "I just need to avoid him. And avoiding demons in general seems like a good idea from now on. Actually summoning one to teach me magic doesn't sound like the better alternative."

"You could ask someone who is not a demon but is familiar with demons," Rory said. "A hunter might be able to help."

"I thought they just used will?"

"Couldn't hurt to ask. As you said, it's probably safer than summoning a demon."

Rory's ability to sometimes state the obvious was just astounding. "I guess I can ask Angie. If I ever hear from her again."

She muttered this last, but Deacon squeezed her shoulder tight, so he must have heard her. She was pretty sure Rory would have heard her too, since dragon hearing was as good, if not better than, shifter hearing. But Rory didn't ask questions. For which she was grateful, because she didn't have answers.

"I think I should probably just avoid bad guys with magic for... Well, from now on," she said after a moment. "But on the off chance I can't, shall we get to a lesson?"

Deacon kissed her cheek. "I'll go in and order some dinner. You two have fun."

Fred bound into the house after Deacon. Buck, after giving Rory a little nod, followed. Pickles sat on the porch next to Cary for a longer moment, staring at the dragon. The dragon stared back. Then Pickles stood up and ambled into the house after the others.

Cary narrowed her eyes at her basset hound-foo lion. She'd swear Pickles had been talking with Rory. She turned her narrowed gaze on Rory, asking a silent question.

He chose not to answer it.

"Do I have your permission to feed you a little dragon magic, Pro—"

Rory's voice cut off so suddenly, for a split second, Cary was *aware* she was hearing it in her head instead of out loud. That was...something.

"Cary," he finished. "May I feed you some magic so we can practice?"

She let his slip go. She couldn't seem to stop calling herself a Protector either.

10

*D*ragon magic felt different to other magic she absorbed. Well, not that she could tell the difference most of the time. Or had even noticed absorbing magic before. Thanks to the Protector shields, most of the magic thrown at her over the years had been deflected, only a little leaked through. Which was why she was still alive.

In the past, when she did absorb magic, the only thing she'd noticed was a tingling in her skin after the fact. Sometimes that tingling was mild, even pleasant. Sometimes it was a little more intense. When a lot of magic got thrown at her, she could start to feel like ants were crawling over her skin, and the only way to ease that irritation was to rub her skin to calm her nerves. Rarely, but occasionally, the tension built so much she felt like she was going to explode—an actual *real* possibility—if she took in any more.

In Faery, she had taken in too much. On purpose. With her shields down. She'd purposefully drawn in as much of the surrounding magic as possible to stop a disaster.

And that effort *had* killed her. Even if only for a moment.

With all the magic she'd taken in over the years, though, outside of the tingling, and the pain of having too much flow into her, she'd never felt anything different or unique about the different kinds of magic.

Except with Rory's dragon magic.

With dragon magic, at least Rory's kind, there was more than just a little tingling along her nerves. There was a warmth to it, like warm water soaking into her skin. It almost made her sleepy. Like she could sit in the middle of all that dragon magic and be content enough to take a long nap.

But falling asleep full of dragon magic seemed like a really bad idea.

Rory "fed" her the magic very gently. He pointed a single claw in her direction and breathed out something, and she felt the tingling start and then the warmth. Never so much she felt overwhelmed. But enough she noticed it there.

She wasn't sure what Rory did could be called a spell. Not like Angie. When she'd tried releasing magic with Angie, and Angie had had to feed her some magic, the feelings and sensations were completely different. In fact, with Angie's magic, it was almost easier. Well, not easier so much as less…strange. But she hadn't had a chance to do spells with Angie yet, so maybe using Angie's witch magic would feel stranger than just trying to release it.

To *use* dragon magic, she couldn't just recite a spell, though, like she'd have to learn to do with witch magic. No finger twists and whispered words. Dragon magic didn't work like any of the other magic she'd observed over the years. Which made trying to use it a lot trickier.

But also, in a weird way, a lot easier.

Because Rory's dragon magic was fire magic.

"Are you ready?" Rory asked.

She let out a long breath, settling her heartbeat, her worries and fears. "Think so," she murmured. Her attention turned inward as she focused on trying to feel the magic in her, to know it and understand it better. Understanding the shape and feel of it helped guide her in using it.

She stared at her hand, concentrating on the idea of fire, the shape of it, the heat. She let out another slow breath. Took hold of the small amount of magic in her cells, the dragon shaped magic, and turned it toward that image of fire, that image of heat and dancing flame.

A small flame rose on her fingertip, her first finger, the pointing finger as she thought of it. The little flame danced like it was on a candle wick, wavering this way and that in the evening breeze. She pulled in another slow breath, careful not to lose her concentration. Starting the fire without burning herself was only the beginning. Controlling the flame while the fire burned out all the magic was the trick. Avoiding catching her deck on fire, or her yard, the goal. Because that little dancing flame, while it looked tiny and innocuous, was dragon fire. And it spread faster and hotter than regular fire if not controlled.

Something Rory had drilled into her before they'd started these experiments.

There were other types of dragon fire. The type he and Joan used was a different type, according to him. But Cary wasn't able to handle more than this yet. Learn to crawl first, Rory had said. Then walk. This was crawling. For a dragon.

Or a human learning how to use dragon magic.

"Try to move your hand," Rory said quietly, his voice a whisper through her mind.

"If you're sure." The last time she'd tried to move while still holding the flame, several sparks had leapt from her control, and Rory had had to stamp out the minor fire while she froze in place so she wouldn't "spill" any more.

She started slow, and it reminded her of moving with a hot cup of coffee. Careful, even gestures. But not too careful. For some reason, as with coffee, when she tried to move too slowly and carefully, she just spilled more. She glided her hand to one side, watching the flame, holding it gently and compactly in her mind. There was a lot of visualization involved in her mind even as she watched the real-life flame wiggle on her fingertip.

When no little sparks jumped off, she was tempted to let out a relieved sigh. But she'd only managed to glide her hand about three inches to one side. She slowly moved her hand in the opposite direction. Pausing with a slight gasp when the flame wobbled a lot and a few little sparks seemed to dance away from the main source of heat. She held still while those little sparks reabsorbed into the fire. Waited another beat. Then continued her movement.

Slowly. Very very slowly. But not too slowly.

Once she'd made the movement to the opposite side, she did let out a breath. Another moment of waiting. The flame was lowering now. Not going out per se, but not as bright and hot and large as just a moment ago. Like the "wick" of her finger was too low in the wax and the flame didn't have enough room to really burn now. The dragon magic in her cells was almost used up. It didn't take long. Not with the amount she took in from Rory. But watching the little flame die of its own accord, as the magic literally burned off, was always fascinating.

She moved her hand back to where she'd started. Another panicked pause when a spark danced away from the main flame. But she managed *not* to start a fire this time. When the flame went out, she'd cheer about that.

"You will need to learn to put the flame out yourself," Rory said. "Without using it all up."

"Why? The point is to let the magic burn off, to get rid of it through using it. I want it all used up, not only half used. I don't want to keep any stored in my cells. Right?" She kept her gaze on the flickering fire as it grew smaller and smaller.

"That's only part of what you need to learn. Not just to let it burn out. But how to really, truly *use* it. How to control what you take in. Control isn't just how to burn it all out in one go. It's how you start *and* stop a spell."

Rory's taloned front foot waved in front of her, but she only saw it through her peripheral vision because if she didn't focus on the flame, she risked letting it get beyond her control.

"This is about what you said earlier. About me using magic... offensively. Instantly after taking it in."

"And maybe doing more with it. Yes. But you need to learn how to control the flow of magic through you. How to keep some and hold it in reserve for when you need it."

She watched the little fire on her fingertip shrink to the size of a flame on a matchstick as she considered Rory's comment. The idea still held a lot of appeal. If she could use magic—not just to burn it off but to actually do something with it—that could be helpful if she got into trouble around the shifters. Or if Marianne or Angie needed her help with something. She wouldn't be a helpless mundane human without even good fighting skills like Lucy.

But all this, being able to use magic like this, only worked when she absorbed it. And if she absorbed too much without releasing it, she died. She had to use that magic all up to keep her cells from exploding…

Except she *could* keep some magic stored without hurting herself. She'd done that over the years without any harm. Without even knowing that's what she was doing. She'd kept magic stored for long periods of time. All different kinds of magic too.

In fact, she'd done so much storing of mixed bags of magic, they were pretty sure her cells had changed at a fundamental level. That, while she might still be mostly human, she wasn't quite as ordinary a human as she'd been before all the exposure to magic. Rory thought— was pretty certain—she'd become something…different over time. Something more? She wasn't sure she'd call it more. She wasn't sure this was a good thing. But it was what it was. She absorbed magic. And she'd been able to hold it without dying for long periods of time. She couldn't have done that without it causing some changes in her.

They still didn't know what those changes were. There was no one to compare her to, no one who'd seen this before or studied it. Even Rory wasn't entirely sure what she'd…become, for lack of a better word. It was that mixture, that combination of many different types of magics that didn't normally occupy the same body, that was the real rub. The real reason they couldn't say for sure what changes had been made.

But changes had occurred. And even without the Protector magic flowing through her, she was different now.

The flame on her fingertip winked out, all the dragon magic used up. She flexed her hand absently as she considered what Rory had said.

Could she actually keep the magic? Not just burn out everything she took it, but keep some to use when she needed it? Should she do that? What would all that mix of magic become inside her? Once she held it, did it change? Did it go from being a wizard's magic, or a witch's, or a dragon's to something different? Or would she only be able to use it in its original form? Pull specific tendrils from the soup of all that magic to use it as it was originally intended? Was that even possible?

"We could experiment," Rory said, as if reading her thoughts.

He didn't do that without her permission. Which meant she'd been projecting those questions at him. Not just considering them herself, but asking him without meaning to.

But who else could give her answers?

"How could we do that experiment?"

"Your friend Angie and I could both give you magic," he said, settling down so his head rested on his forepaws.

When he did that, when he laid down in the grass with his huge head on his legs, his body relaxed, he reminded her of the dogs. A very large dog. But still, the impression made her smile.

"And then we see what I can do with the combination?" she asked, just to be clear.

"Better to experiment under controlled conditions than get hit with lots of magic of different kinds and not know what to do with it," he said, his tone matter-of-fact.

She scowled. He was right. Still… "I shouldn't be getting hit with lots of different kinds of magic anymore."

"It's still important to figure out what happens when you do, to experiment with how to use up the magic—or use it without using it all up—when we can control the conditions and ensure you're safe."

She did like the idea of knowing what to do, having a clue how her body would react, just in case. If "just in case" never happened, well that was fine. But if it did happen and she hadn't even tried to figure out what to do… She'd likely end up dead. All this training was in an effort to prevent that. No point half-assing it.

"Okay," she said. "When I hear from Angie, I'll suggest the experiment to her, see if she's willing to participate."

"She still hasn't been in touch?"

Cary shook her head. "Just one text a week ago. She isn't answering her phone or any of the texts we've sent since that last one."

"You're worried."

"Yeah."

Rory didn't give her the normal platitudes and reassurances. He just fell silent after making a little noise that sounded like sympathy in her head.

She waved away that worry as there was nothing she could do about it in the moment. "When—" she put emphasis on that word, "—I hear from Angie, I'll let her know about your experiment idea."

"For now, then, let's practice you holding my magic and not releasing it all at once."

"You told me that was bad for me, holding on to dragon magic for too long."

"This won't be for too long. Just long enough to get used to stopping and starting."

"I can barely move without 'spilling' flames. You sure we should try this already?"

"When better?" He straightened again, sitting up so his head rose above her. Then he asked, "Are you ready?"

She nodded and the warm flow of dragon magic seeped back into her. Her eyes drooped shut for a moment. Then she blinked back to her surroundings and said, "What do I do to stop the flame on command?"

"More visualizations," Rory said with a hint of humor in his voice.

She didn't groan, which she considered an act of supreme self-control.

They practice for another half hour. The first few times, Cary could only manage to make the flame flicker lower, but never really put it out and had to wait for the magic itself to burn off. But then, twice in a row, she cut the flame off with the suddenness of a snap. And got it going again.

"Good," Rory said. "Now, instead of on your fingertip, try your whole hand. I'll give you a little more this time."

"My whole hand?" Panic tightened her throat. "I really don't want to burn down my house."

"I'll stop any accidents. You can do this."

Cary pulled in a deep, steadying breath. "If you say so." She winced a little as more of Rory's magic seeped into her. Not because it hurt but because she wasn't sure she could do this part.

And she was right.

At least the first few times she tried. She got three fingers going at once, then panicked and put the whole thing out.

"At least I can put it out on my own," she said, hoping that would be enough.

Rory shook his head and made her practice more. Until she managed to encompass her entire hand in flame. Without panicking, without lighting herself on fire, without burning down her porch.

"When you get more accustomed to this," Rory said quietly, "I will teach you how to fold the fire into your palm and use it like a wizard bolt."

"Not today, though, right?" She stared at her hand, the way the fire danced over her skin. Then, before panic got the best of her again, she snapped her hand into a fist and cut off the fire. She breathed a sigh when the flames went out as she'd intended.

"Not today," Rory agreed. "You're getting tired. And your food has arrived."

She'd mentally allowed the delivery person from the Mexican food place to find her house when Deacon had gone in to call for food. She'd heard the doorbell a few minutes ago, too. Rory was right. After the magic lesson, she needed to eat. She'd been hungry before they started. She was starving now.

As she said her goodbyes to Rory, a part of her mind latched on to the reminder that in two months, she wouldn't have to give anyone permission to find her house anymore. They'd notice it, see it. People could just show up at her door randomly, without her expecting them. After almost seven years, that was going to take some getting used to.

She went inside and was met with the delicious smells of burritos and nachos, a bouncing greeting from her pack, and Deacon in the kitchen getting the food ready. For just that moment, she decided things would be okay. If this was her life now, she could get used to it. She could even love it. She still had a lot of questions. A lot of worries. And she'd have to figure out what sort of job she wanted to do. What she was even qualified for after all these years.

The idea of that sent her stress levels climbing. So for the moment, she let it all go and decided that, at least for tonight, she'd live in this moment and enjoy her company, her food, and knowing she wouldn't be interrupted by her bosses—her former bosses—with a job. She wouldn't have to rush out into the night to rescue someone. That was now someone else's job.

She could adapt to that. At least for tonight, she could let that worry go.

Anticipating an uninterrupted night of nachos and time alone with Deacon went a long way toward lifting her mood.

11

*C*ary hadn't anticipated the punch of panic and fear that would follow her the minute she left her home the next day to go to Marianne's shop. She probably should have. She'd been worried about leaving the day before. But an evening of Mexican food and Deacon had given her a sense of peace that had taken her through the morning.

The peace shattered when she stepped outside her door and realized just how vulnerable she was.

Not rushing back inside and hiding took an act of will.

"You okay?" Deacon asked, his hand on her lower back.

He'd insisted on taking the day off to go with her to Marianne's, and of course, she'd argued with him that it was unnecessary. But as her breath sped and her pulse pounded and she started to see spots at the edge of her vision, she decided he'd made an excellent decision and was extremely grateful for his strong, steady company. And even grateful for his super shifter smelling so she didn't have to explain that she was having a minor panic attack being outside.

"Just..." She swallowed. "No one has forgotten me yet. And I can't...I can't..." She forced air in and out of her lungs. She couldn't stay inside her house for the next two months. She knew she couldn't. She had to leave. But the panic had her edging back toward her door.

She pulled in a deep breath again, let it out very slowly through her mouth.

Okay, it was daytime, which meant even if there were vampires around, they'd be weak. And she had a truce with the vampires anyway. There shouldn't be any after her. Holland wasn't around because he had bigger things to worry about at the moment. There were currently no shifters who wanted her dead, and Deacon would be able to sniff any out if they came close anyway. The wizard who'd wanted her dead was himself dead so that wasn't a danger. And the other wizard who might have been an issue was currently laid up in bed still recovering from almost dying. Plus, he didn't have any magic left.

She was as safe as she was likely to get at the moment. So going to Marianne's and getting some upgraded protective clothing was safe. She could do this.

Another deep breath, another slow exhale. One more deep breath. "Okay," she said as the spots receded and her pulse slowed. "Okay." She swallowed. "Sorry. I… Wow. Didn't expect that."

"This will take time and adjusting," he murmured, kissing her gently on the top of her head. "And I will keep you safe."

"We spent the first part of our relationship with you 'keeping me safe' by ensuring I was always in front of you like a shield." When he'd let her protect him, that had kept them both safe. "What if we forget I can't do that anymore?"

"I won't," he said, very firmly. "I'm extremely aware of the fact that you can't be a shield anymore."

She wasn't sure whether to be relieved or appalled by that, so she just said, "Let's go."

"You're ready?"

"As I'll ever be." She knew she'd eventually get used to this. Eventually leaving the house wouldn't bring on a panic attack. But that was cold comfort as she scanned the street on the way to Deacon's SUV, parked in her driveway outside the closed garage door.

The drive to Marianne's shop downtown was uneventful. Finding street parking surprisingly easy. Deacon even managed to park within half a block of Marianne's door. All of which helped calm Cary's nerves further. Not having to walk far to get inside somewhere safe helped.

She wrapped her leather jacket a little tighter around her. It wasn't all that cold, the air had that damp crisp autumn feel to it that she usually loved. But the leather jacket felt like a familiar old friend, a bit of a security blanket when she was feeling vulnerable. Plus, with magic pockets, her keys, cellphone, and wallet never fell out, and that made this the best jacket ever created ever as far as she was concerned.

And it was just the tip of what Marianne could do.

As a magical weaver—the kind that actually could weave straw into gold, although she called that skill a parlor trick—Marianne could do amazing things with cloth and thread. Magical things that involved pockets that didn't make your pants bulge in weird ways, no matter what you put into those pockets, and bottomless purses and bags that could hold whole storehouses of stuff.

Her shop was a bright, tidy place with a lot of windows to let in whatever light there was on any given day, clean dark wooden floors, open space, and the lovely scent of material, starch, and cinnamon from Marianne's favorite scented candles. There were two people in the main reception area, waiting in chairs near the wall of windows that looked out onto the sidewalk. The large table in the main room, where Marianne showed client's sketches and helped them select fabrics, was covered in several bolts of jewel-toned shiny material and a scattering of sequins.

Cary was very curious about the clothing coming from those materials.

No sign of Marianne, but one of her three assistants, this one a recent hire named Lashana, manned the checkout desk as she rang up a third customer. Lashana, a short, curvy Black woman with purple hair and a flare for business-casual fashion, was a recent business school grad with student loans to pay, who couldn't find a job in finance that was more than an unpaid internship. She'd come in to Marianne's to have a hem fixed, Marianne had heard her story, and two days later hired her. According to Marianne, Lashana was such a wiz with both customer care and budget management, she'd be opening her own business soon enough.

When Lashana finished with the smiling client, she motioned Cary to the desk. "Marianne asked if you could wait for just a few minutes. She's finishing up with someone in back now."

"Sure. No problem."

Lashana leaned close and whispered, "She also said if you had Deacon with you, you should sit by the windows." Lashana grinned and flashed a sideways look at Deacon.

Cary chuckled and agreed.

All of Marianne's assistants were mundane humans, who wouldn't know shifters existed, nonetheless that whispering around them was rarely effective. So Deacon skillfully pretended he hadn't overheard Lashana's comment.

Until they sat down in the chairs on the opposite side of the front door from the other two clients. "I should start charging Marianne for this," he said, his lips quirked in a suppressed smile.

"She'd pay," Cary said. "Every time you're here, she gets a new client."

"She gets new clients because she's extraordinary at what she does," Deacon whispered.

"True enough. That's how she turns them into clients. But you get them through the door."

As if to prove her point, a young man pushed into the shop just then with a slightly stunned expression as he stared at Deacon. Cary had to hide her smirk. Lashana eased up to him, the consummate professional, asking if there was anything they could do for him. The young man blinked and looked around, taking in the place he'd walked into for the first time.

Cary had seen the scene play out a few times and it never ceased to amuse and impress her. Lashana guided the young man to the large table, pulled out some of Marianne's sketch books, discussed his clothing needs—turned out he did need a custom-made costume for a Halloween party at the end of the month. Lashana was happy to point out that Marianne made truly impressive, and unique, pieces at very reasonable prices. Would work with his budget. Would guarantee his satisfaction.

Cary watched the man go from a little stunned and bemused, to serious interest. His gaze did keep jumping to Deacon, but the lure of perfectly designed custom clothing by a true artist sucked him in.

"Chalk up another client for Marianne," Cary murmured.

"Lashana is very good at that too," Deacon murmured back.

"Yeah she is."

When Marianne walked out from the back room with yet another client, she took in the scene in the main room with a glance. Her gaze landed on the young man talking with Lashana, then skimmed over to Cary and Deacon sitting at the window, and she grinned.

After ringing out the client she'd been working with in the back, she stopped by Cary and Deacon. To Deacon, she said, "I really should just pay you to sit there."

"Ha! He just said the same thing." Cary grinned up at Marianne.

"I will, too." She winked at Deacon. "We'll talk later." To Cary, she said, "Can you wait a few more minutes? I'd like to finish up with the other two here, and I should have a talk with the new one Deacon lured in."

"You're very sure he's here because of me," Deacon said.

"Did he stumble in looking bemused?" Marianne asked Cary.

"He did."

"Mm hmm." Marianne nodded. "You just stay sitting right there, handsome. You're very good for my business."

Deacon chuckled as Marianne walked off to deal with her other customers.

When the general hubbub had calmed, and all her other customers were taken care of or could be left in the very capable hands of Lashana, Marianne brought Cary into the back. Deacon remained in the main room, partly to amuse Marianne, but also to watch the front door.

He didn't say anything to Cary out loud, and she didn't bring it up, but she knew he'd taken up the role of bodyguard for her. A part of her that was braver and more irritable wanted to argue with him, tell him he didn't have to do that. But the part of her still reeling from being fired wanted him guarding her back, watching the door to make sure no bad guys snuck up on her and caught her so vulnerable.

And since that was a little embarrassing, she chose to temporarily ignore the issue as she focused on her friend.

"I have some ideas to run past you," Marianne said. "But first, how are you holding up?"

"I'm shaky, and I had a panic attack when I left the house this morning. So, yeah, maybe not great."

Marianne pulled her into a hug. "Don't worry," she said. "We've got you. We'll keep you safe."

"Thanks." Tears prickled at her eyes. She sniffed and pulled away before she started blubbering. Deacon might worry if he heard her crying now. "What kind of amazing ideas have you had?"

Marianne studied her face a moment, then moved into all-business mode.

"Upgrades to your jacket for a start. I'm glad you wore it."

"I always wear it."

"Which is why we're going to add some more magic to it, give it a little stronger…frame I guess you could say. I'll add a little bit to the material so things like knives and bullets can't get through too easily."

"Why haven't I had that the whole time?"

"Because you haven't needed it. The only time you get stabbed or shot at is when you're protecting someone. You already had magic for that. No point in complicating matters."

The comment gave Cary a moment of pause, and she considered something that hadn't ever once crossed her mind. "Am I absorbing magic from this jacket? Will I absorb more if you add more?"

Up to this point, the jacket really only had magical pockets. And Marianne had recently added a spell around the cuffs, like a few shirts she'd made for Cary, that could staunch a bleeding wound. Those were emergency backup measures she'd never had to use. Usually, she got in the way of things that could cause bleeding before the bleeding started. Or, well, she used to. But there was still magic in the clothes Marianne made for her. Had she been absorbing that all these years without realizing it? Without even thinking about it, even after she'd learned about this weird ability of hers?

"Oh." Marianne set aside a bolt of material she'd picked up. "I hadn't considered that." She frowned. "When you're not in Faery or someplace made of magic, you only absorb magic when it's thrown at you, right?"

"As far as we can tell." She'd been able to pull magic in while in Faery, and she'd definitely absorbed ambient magic while there. But in her own realm, she didn't seem to have that worry.

"You have the jacket on now. Is your skin tingling?"

The sign that she was absorbing magic. "No."

"Does it every tingle while you have your jacket on and aren't getting in the way of other magic?"

"No." She widened her eyes. "That's a good sign, right?"

"I think so. Have you ever gotten tingly skin wearing anything I've made for you with magic in it?"

"Not that I remember. No."

"All right, then. I think we're safe enough. The clothes aren't 'throwing' magic at you, so you don't seem to be absorbing it. But we'll keep checking in every time I add something, just in case." Marianne made a face. "Would kind of defeat the purpose if my protective clothing made things worse."

Cary gave a little shiver. "Since we seem to be good, I'd like to keep trying whatever sort of protective stuff you have in mind." She slumped against a table. "I have to tell you, I'm pretty wigged out by… By knowing I have a bunch of scary people in this city who'd love to kill me, and I'm no longer able to stop them with Protector loopholes."

"I'm wigged out for you, too. Which is why we're here. Now, down to business…"

12

$\mathscr{A}$ half hour later, Marianne had taken possession of Cary's jacket—it took time to add the upgrades—and they'd sketched out a few shirts she could wear over her regular clothes that could help protect against magic. As Marianne explained it, they should diffuse anything thrown at Cary, breaking apart the spells so they were less effective.

"Should help with the magic absorption too," Marianne said, though she frowned and didn't look entirely certain.

She intended to add some mundane weapon "Kevlar-like" magic to the jacket, which would help deflect and offset attack with mundane weapons.

"But you're going to also have to train more with Lucy and make sure you use some of those skills if someone comes at you with a knife," she warned.

Cary tried not to wince. She'd managed to use the skills Lucy had been drilling into her exactly once in an actual Protector situation. Her instincts were to freeze in place, and the training didn't seem to be overriding that instinct. But now that she knew she didn't have shields to protect her and anyone around her when she froze, maybe her body would take the hint and switch to fight mode.

Anything was possible, she supposed.

Finally, Marianne showed her a sketch for some pants she thought might help. They weren't Cary's usual jeans but were made of a stronger leather and Marianne swore she could make them strong enough to fend off shifter claws and vampire teeth.

Cary frowned at the drawing sitting next to the material Marianne wanted to use. "I'm not usually a leather-pants wearing person," she said. "Those look…tight."

Marianne shook her head. "I'm going to be making them to fit you and your body. I will not put you into uncomfortable clothing, even clothing designed to be protective. They will pull on and zip up without you having to suck in your gut, because *that* would defeat the purpose too. I promise."

Cary nodded as she ran her finger over the butter-soft deep-brown leather, the color dark enough it was almost black, but not quite. Which was probably good. She'd feel like she was dressing to impress the vampires or something if she wore black leather.

"This is even animal-friendly fake leather," Marianne assured with a grin. "Specially made to be just like the real stuff, including having a lot of the inherent strength and durability of real leather. But without the requirement of skinning an animal that hasn't been used for food."

Marianne, like Cary, was an animal lover but not a vegetarian. They both believed in animals being treated with respect and humanely, but they also believed in the biology of human omnivorous eating habits.

"You think this will work?" Cary asked, still running her fingers over the soft faux-leather. "The training, the clothes…"

"It'll work," Marianne said. "And when Angie gets back, we'll get her to whip you up some potions you can toss at bad guys who might harass you."

"She's not going to have anything that will work against Holland."

Marianne pursed her lips. "You heard from Jaxer since all this happened?"

"No. Last time I saw him was at Sheldon's apartment just before I was fired. I haven't seen him since."

"I'd have thought he'd come by. Even if just to explain."

"Yeah, me too. But maybe he's not allowed. Maybe once I'm fired, he has to…cut off contact with me." Wisat and Liruk hadn't said he had to, but they'd implied he wouldn't be around much now. She'd been trying not to believe he'd disappear without at least saying goodbye.

Marianne dropped her chin and gave Cary a look. "We all know how he feels about you. If he didn't vanish before, when he was supposed to at the start of your test year, he's not going to do it now."

Cary made a face. Then said, "But you know things have changed between me and Jaxer, and between Jaxer and Deacon, since the whole thing in Faery. Jaxer isn't so… Well, he seems less, I don't know, hopeful? Interested? I'm not sure how to put it. And there seems to be a peace between him and Deacon now, a sort of understanding. Maybe. I'm not sure how to say all this. But Faery changed a lot. Maybe changed everything."

"You don't think Jaxer is still in love with you?"

"I have no idea. I kind of hope not. I actually kind of hope he's more interested in that complicated thing he's got with Eriana. But we haven't talked about it."

"Ask Deacon."

"Huh?"

"Ask Deacon. He can smell Jaxer's emotions, right?"

"Jaxer can make Deacon smell whatever he wants him to. I'm not sure that's something we can trust."

"Has he ever hidden how he feels about you from Deacon?"

"No." Cary scowled. "Which was part of the problem."

"Then he isn't likely to start hiding those feelings now," Marianne reasoned. "Ask Deacon. He'll have a clue."

Cary let out a long breath. "How did we get on to this topic?"

"I wanted to distract you. You looked upset."

"Talking about the Jaxer thing doesn't *not* upset me, though."

"But it's not the same as worrying about being killed by Oliver Holland."

"True. And I did temporarily forget about Holland."

"Until I brought him back up again." Marianne rolled her eyes. "Sorry."

"You tried. And it's not like this isn't all…part of the same thing I guess."

"I have to get some work done tonight, but you want to do something tomorrow night? Dinner? A little girls' night with Lucy if she's free? A mini-party instead of a girls' night if Deacon wants to hang out with us."

"Thanks," Cary said. "I might just need that. Can we play it by ear?"

"Of course."

She hugged Marianne again before they went out to the main room to settle the bill Cary insisted on paying.

"You're about to be out of work," Marianne reminded her. "I can wait to be paid until you get another job."

"I'm still getting paid for two more months, and you're doing special work for me. I will pay you now."

They had this argument a lot, even when Cary wasn't unemployed. She was not going to take advantage of her friend. Marianne had a business to run.

"Deacon brings me in enough work when you're both here to make up for anything I comp you, you know," Marianne said with a wink.

Cary laughed because she needed to. "I'm still paying you."

Marianne saw them out before returning to Lashana and another couple of clients who'd come in while she'd been in the back with Cary.

"She's really doing great business," Cary said as she and Deacon walked back to the car. "She's going to need to open a second shop soon."

"Lashana could run it," Deacon said. "She's very good with the customers."

Talking about something besides her own situation felt wonderful. Wallowing in her own fear and worry didn't change anything and just made her miserable. She'd rather think about Marianne opening a second boutique. So she did. All the way back to Deacon's SUV, they talked about what it would take for Marianne to have a second business, where she might open it, all the things that kept Cary from worrying.

And it worked at distracting her.

Right up until they heard the scream.

13

ary ran toward the scream without thinking, without pause. Without remembering.

The sidewalk was unfortunately not empty, too many people around in the middle of a business day. Everyone turned toward the scream, too. Which meant Cary had to push through and past bystanders just…standing there, murmuring.

Another scream and she pushed into a jog, rounding a corner to see a woman, holding a kid behind her while a man pulled at her arm.

And again, without even pausing, Cary rushed forward, pushing between the man and the woman and kid.

"No idea what's happening," she said, "but a little less shoving and pulling will be good."

Part of her brain registered that it was harder to get between the two people than it should be and that it took her a minute of physical effort to get the man's hand off the woman and put some space between the two people.

Deacon appeared next to her, also putting himself between the man and the woman and kid. That gave Cary enough space to take a breath and assess the situation.

"This is none of your business," the man said, his tone cold and sharp. "This is a family matter."

"Sure sure," Cary said.

She turned to face the woman. She was about Cary's height, with shoulder length, dark blond hair and brown eyes, her pale skin flushed, dressed in jeans and a thick flannel shirt. The boy she kept tucked behind her peeked around the woman's waist, his hair a few shades darker than hers, more brown than blond, but his wide dark eyes very similar to the woman's. Cary was terrible with kid ages, but she got the feeling he couldn't be much older than nine. His gaze darted between the man, the woman he was hiding behind, and Cary.

To the woman, Cary asked, "You related to either of these people?"

"He…" The woman swallowed, looking past Cary to the man. "He's my husband."

"Mm hmm." Cary kept her attention on the woman.

"Ex-husband," the woman clarified.

"Fair enough," Cary said, with enough feeling the woman smiled a little.

"And this is my son," the woman said, almost defiantly.

Cary waved to the boy. "Hi. Nice to meet you."

The boy didn't smile.

"You okay?" she asked him quietly, holding his gaze.

He nodded, but his grip on his mother's arm tightened.

"It's nothing," the woman said, pulling Cary's attention. The woman's gaze darted back to her ex-husband as she said, "He surprised me. That's why I screamed."

"I could see that. I'd scream too if someone grabbed me unexpectedly."

"I shouldn't have," the woman said. "It's… I was making too big a deal out of this."

"No, I'm sure you were startled. A scream is warranted," Cary said, trying to stay calm in the face of her own anger. The woman didn't need her to be angry too. She might even misunderstand it.

Cary felt some movement behind her and glanced over her shoulder.

Deacon held the man's hand wrenched up over his head. The man struggled against Deacon's grip, but with his super shifter strength, Deacon held the very human ex-husband easily and seemingly without effort.

"We have things to discuss," the man snarled, the early coldness vanishing as quickly as it had appeared.

"Mm hmm," Cary said again. She took him in in one glance—about six foot tall, thick shoulders, thin legs, clean shaven, dark hair and blue eyes, dressed in a dark gray business suit. His tie was loosened and he wasn't wearing a coat. There was a deep furrow between his brows as he scowled at her and the woman standing behind her.

"Let me go," the man snarled at Deacon.

"Don't raise your hand to my girlfriend," Deacon said, his voice very low. "Or anyone else for that matter."

Cary noticed Deacon didn't release his grip. He didn't move at all when the man shoved at him with his free hand. Deacon might as well have been a brick wall.

Cary focused on the woman. "You got a car around here somewhere? Maybe you and the ex should talk later. When there's less emotion. And maybe some lawyers or other…advocates around." Cary shrugged. "Or maybe you don't need to talk in person. Phones are good." Less chance anyone got hurt during a phone call. She didn't say that part out loud. She was incredible aware of the boy standing behind the woman. And none of this felt like a good situation for anyone involved.

The woman gave a little nod, her gaze dancing between her ex and Cary. "I'm parked around the corner." To the man, she said, "You need to discuss something, you can go through my lawyer. That was the arrangement." The woman pulled her shoulders straighter, her eyes not quite so wide, the flush in her skin fading.

She bundled her kid into her arms and started up the block. The kid looked back once, at Cary. He very pointedly didn't look at the man. Then he faced forward as his mother rushed him down the block.

The small crowd that had gathered to watch the scene dissipated and went back to whatever they'd been doing.

Cary faced the man and Deacon again. Deacon still hadn't released his arm.

"Let go of me," the man snarled at Deacon.

Deacon's gaze moved down the street. Cary followed his gaze. The woman was climbing into a car parked at the sidewalk. The boy was already in the back, his head just poking over the top of the seat. When the car started and pulled away from the curb, Deacon finally released the man.

Business Suit rubbed his wrist and glared at her and Deacon. "That was none of your business."

"Sure, sure," Cary said again.

The man snarled at them both and stalked away, in the opposite direction from the woman.

"Huh," Cary said, watching his back. "I was kind of expecting a parting shot, like 'you'll hear from my lawyers' or 'this isn't over' or something. I don't quite know what to do with the silent treatment."

"Come on," Deacon said, his voice still very deep.

He spoke quietly and his touch on her elbow as he guided her down the sidewalk was gentle, but she didn't miss the tension thrumming through his body or the way a muscle in his jaw jumped.

When they were ensconced in the SUV, she asked, "You okay?"

"No."

"Okay. Why?"

"You're not a Protector anymore." He gripped the steering wheel hard enough she heard the plastic groan.

"I know that. That's why we're here getting me some more protective clothes."

He turned toward her and she realized his eyes were glowing yellow, just a little, but enough to show her how close to the surface his animal side was. "You. Are. Not. A. Protector."

"Yes," she said with a snarl. "I know."

"Do you?" His voice was low, and his intensity turned it into a growl. "Because you ran in between that man and woman like you'd forgotten."

"I…" She stopped mid-rant. Faced the front window. "Oh shit."

"What if he'd had a knife? A gun? You aren't a Kevlar vest anymore."

Shit. She actually had forgotten. Well, not really forgotten so much as just didn't…stop to remember. She'd just acted.

She shook her head, hard. Part in denial and part as a way to wave off the incident. "Listen, anyone would have gotten involved there. The woman screamed. She was obviously afraid of her ex."

"No one else on the street got involved," he pointed out.

"All the more reason for us to get involved. She was in trouble. Her son could have been in trouble. And you are a shifter. Why did you grab his hand by the way?"

"He was going to hit you."

Shit. He actually would have succeeded in hitting her if Deacon hadn't been there. She didn't have a shield to deflect physical attacks anymore.

"Thank you for stopping him."

"Cary…" Deacon let out a long breath and carefully released his grip on the steering wheel.

She was pleased to see there weren't any dents or cracks. Good sign for his control.

"I know," he started. Paused. Let out another long breath. "I know you can't watch something like that and just let it go. It's one of the reasons I love you."

She smiled a little at that.

"But you are not a Protector anymore. You will not have a shield that comes up and keeps you safe from magical or mundane weapons. You have to *think* before charging in. You need to find another way to help that doesn't involved possible getting yourself killed."

She swallowed. She'd spent almost seven years learning how to not think. How to not hesitate. Just run in. Get there before the good guys got hurt. Then all would be well.

Except that wouldn't happen anymore.

"I can't just not stop someone harassing someone else," she murmured. "Especially with the kid there. It's… Hell, it's habit after all these years."

"You have to undo that habit, then," he said, very seriously. "You are not indestructible. I won't ask you not to help. That would be wrong on many levels." He held up a hand when she opened her mouth to thank him. "But you have to know that my primary concern is for you above strangers. And I do not want you killed."

It hung in the air unsaid, but she still heard the "again" at the end of that sentence.

"So what do I do?" she asked, and not rhetorically. "I can't stand by and watch. But if I run in, I risk getting hurt."

"Move in with more of a plan from now on. A way to defuse a situation without just physically putting your body in the way."

She groaned and dropped her head against the seat. "I suck at plans, though. You know that. My plans almost always involved…" She sighed. "Involved me having a shield that would go up at the right moment."

"I blame Jaxer for that, for the record."

She rolled her head to look at him. His eyes weren't as yellow anymore. Almost completely back to normal golden brown now. Which was good. "Why Jaxer? I'm the one who can't make good plans."

"He was supposed to train you better, to help you learn to be strategic." His eyes might be back to normal, but there was still a very distinct growl in his voice.

"He trained me well," Cary said, narrowing her eyes. "As best he could given what he had to work with."

"Stop. That insults you, and I won't have it."

"You'd rather blame Jaxer for my failing?"

"Yes."

Her lips twitched. And then she laughed. The laugh felt good.

He rolled his eyes, but he pulled her into a hug while she chuckled. And that felt good too.

When she stopped chuckling, she tightened her hug around him.

"I'll try to check my habits," she murmured. "I can't promise I won't try to stop things like what was happening earlier, but I can at least try to be more thoughtful about the running in part."

"That's all I ask." He kissed the top of her head. "And be sure you have on some of Marianne's protective clothes next time."

She smiled into his neck. "Deal."

14

ary spent the next two days either at Lucy's dojo or hiding in her house. The incident outside Marianne's shop, in hindsight, shook her. Because it had shaken Deacon. Because she'd jumped in so…automatically. Without thought. Deacon was right. She wasn't a Protector anymore. Jumping in between people in a dangerous situation wasn't an option now. It wasn't her job.

But she couldn't ignore stuff like that either. She just had to figure out a better way of diffusing tough situations. Couldn't just muscle through them now. Unfortunately, a non-muscling-through option involved being able to make a plan, to think strategically. She was not a great strategist.

"You can be taught strategy," Lucy said as she pulled Cary up off the mat. Again. "It just takes some time."

"You don't just jump into dangerous situations and start kicking people's butts just because you can," Cary said, bending over and putting her hands on her knees. A moment to catch her breath. "How do you handle stuff like that?"

"I don't seem to come across it as often as you do," Lucy said, her tone wry. "You're a trouble magnet."

Cary scowled. "Not on purpose. Is it my fault that asshole was

93

harassing his ex and her son on a public street?"

"Of course not. But that's what I mean. I don't just stumble on situations like that all the time. You do." Lucy motioned her into a defensive stance.

"But why me?" Cary said, not even flinching at the whine in her voice. "At least why me now? When it's not my job anymore?"

She settled into a wide-legged stance, most of her weight on her toes. They were just running through some practice exercises that were supposed to train Cary's muscle memory so she could react without thinking—and who knew thinking was such a handicap!—but so far, her muscles seemed to be unwilling to memorize these lessons.

Lucy lunged forward, then rolled to one side, a move that brought her up behind Cary. Cary followed the roll and turned her body so she was facing Lucy again as Lucy stepped in to grab her. Cary caught Lucy's arms, spun under them so both Lucy's arms were over one shoulder and ducked low, then lifted up and spun again, using momentum to toss Lucy over her head.

They'd practice this enough that Cary could now actually toss Lucy. The problem was always that Lucy just rolled with the throw and bobbed back up to her feet, facing Cary again, before Cary had time to regain her stance. The speed with which Lucy recovered from being thrown always amazed Cary—and distracted her from resetting her own position fast enough.

Which was how she ended up with her legs swept out from under her, lying flat on her back on the mat. Again.

"Still thinking too much," Lucy said.

"Mostly I'm thinking about how fast you recover after getting tossed on your ass, though. That's an improvement, right?"

Lucy snorted, but she didn't sound amused.

Cary rolled to her side and got back to her feet.

"Have you ever considered," Lucy said, "that the reason you keep coming across situations where someone needs protecting is because you are just naturally a protector. That the universe lines this stuff up for you?"

"No," Cary said. "And why would the universe continue to put me in that position when I am no longer equipped to deal with it?"

"Aren't you, though?" Lucy gestured to the currently empty dojo. "You've been training hard for months now. You've surpassed a number of my students who've been working longer at this than you have. You're about to have a whole wardrobe to help keep you safe. You're literally gearing up to be a protector without the magic."

"Are you saying I'm… Batman?" Cary wagged her eyebrows as she lowered her voice to take on the proper tone.

"Except you're not a billionaire."

"I don't have the super cool cars and stuff either." Although, she did have a secret attic where she kept all her books on the otherworldly and her computer with links to places on the web she couldn't go on her regular computer.

Oh. Would she lose that? Would Wisat and Liruk have her computer guru Chris come take the computer away now? She'd only had that access because it was a part of her job. She'd paid for all the books, they were hers, but the computer access to places she couldn't get to on her own…

And did it even matter if she lost that since she wasn't a Protector anymore?

"But my point is," Lucy continued, "you're lining up skills and equipment that will allow you to stay a Protector without having to work for anyone else."

"No." Cary shook her head. "No, that's not what I'm doing. I'm just making sure I can survive the next two months, until the people in this city that I've pissed off forget I exist."

"And then?"

"Well, that's the question, isn't it? I don't know what then. Except that I won't be a Protector anymore, or have my severance pay anymore, and I'll need a job."

"I hate to tell you this, sweetie," Lucy said, her hands on her hips. "But I think, even without getting paid, you're gonna keep trying to protect people."

"Nope," Cary said. "That thing outside Marianne's shop was a fluke. It's not my job anymore." She raised a hand when Lucy opened her mouth. "I won't be able to ignore people in trouble, but I doubt I'll keep attracting trouble now. The universe and all the bad guys in Portland will soon forget I exist, and I'll get on with my life like a normal, mundane human. I probably won't even come across people in trouble anymore. That'll be for the next Protector."

"Right," Lucy said, shaking her head. "I'll believe that when I see it. Until then, we're going to keep up your training because I don't trust you *not* to run into the middle of trouble."

Cary's turn to snort.

At the end of the session, as Cary tried to regain her regular breathing, while not snarling at Lucy's easy return to an ability to speak without gasping for air, she said, "Any news from Angie?"

"Haven't heard anything yet," Lucy said. "And I'm officially worried."

"Yeah, me too." She'd tried texting Angie three different times in the last couple of days. Nothing. "I'd say we should go help her, but I have no idea where she's gone."

"Would Jaxer know? He's known her longer than the rest of us. He might have a better idea about this mysterious demon hunter background of hers."

It was a good suggestion actually. Except, "I haven't talked to Jaxer either. Not since I was fired."

"He hasn't come around at all? That doesn't sound right."

Cary shrugged, trying for casual and not hurt. "He's probably busy with a new charge or whatever."

"Still, he was supposed to be your friend. The very least he could do was show up and explain why you were sacked."

Cary actually agreed with Lucy on that point, but she kept it to herself. "If he does show up, I'll ask if he knows where Angie is. In the meantime…" She lifted her hands in a helpless gesture. "I guess we just keep trying to reach her."

And hope that whatever Angie had gone to do—to help Cary!— that she was safe.

～

Cary left the dojo expecting to find Deacon waiting for her on the sidewalk. Instead, she found two different leopard shifters.

"Nicky! Jillian! What are you two doing here?" She hugged them in greeting.

She'd met the two women last January during her first—pretty disastrous—meeting with Deacon's family. They'd bonded over pretty dresses and the complications of having a mate, and been friends ever since.

She stepped back and narrowed her eyes. "Deacon asked you to babysit me, didn't he?"

Nicky grinned. "He said you agreed this time so we didn't have to be subtle." She'd recently let her blond bob grow a little longer, though it still swung in a lovely wave around her pretty, heart-shaped face. At the moment, her blue eyes showed none of the yellow of her animal.

Jillian made a face. Where Nicky had started letting her hair grow out, Jillian had buzzed hers farther, leaving only a small section of longer brown hair on the top to sweep at an angle across her brow. "We'd visit you even if he didn't ask us to—" She rolled her lips into her mouth.

Cary laughed. "You can call it what it is. Bodyguard. Yes, we discussed it. And no, I don't like it. But yes, I agreed to it." She shrugged. "Seemed like a good excuse for a visit, anyway."

Nicky clapped her hands and squeezed Cary's shoulders. "I understand you're getting a new wardrobe. I want in on that."

"I have a feeling you and Marianne will love each other," Cary said. She frowned a little. "But how long are you staying in Portland?" Nicky hated crowds. Being in the city drained her if she stayed too long. The mates lived on the coast of Oregon in a town small enough to suit Nicky. "And where are you staying while you're here?"

"We're staying at the Jones place," Jillian said. "Deacon gave us an apartment for the duration. No charge."

"Since we're bodyguarding his mate," Nicky said.

Cary snorted. But actually, she was glad to hear Deacon had done that. The Jones "place," which Deacon sometimes called his house, was actually a small apartment building in Nob Hill. Apparently, it used to be a house at some point in the past, so Deacon still referred to it that way. The apartment building was large enough that Deacon had the entire top floor as his suite—though they rarely stayed there—his sister Caitlin had the third floor mostly to herself, and outside of some offices on the first floor for the family business, the rest of the building was apartments any leopard shifter could take advantage of if they needed a place in Portland to live, either long term or short. Cary liked that the Joneses did that for their people.

"And we'll be staying for the next two weeks," Nicky said. "A real holiday!" She leaned in and lowered her voice. "And we'll come back as often as you need us."

"Even though…crowds?" Cary asked.

"Even though crowds," Nicky said. "I can manage for a friend."

Jillian nodded, wrapping an arm around Nicky when she leaned back from Cary.

"You two are beyond lovely," Cary said. She felt herself starting to tear up, so she sniffled and straightened her shoulders. "Let's get food. I'm hungry after my workout."

"Food." Jillian groaned and nodded emphatically.

They found an excellent Chinese food restaurant a few blocks from Lucy's dojo, settling in for plates of sweet and sour chicken, pork fried rice, beef and broccoli, egg rolls, chicken with cashew, a tofu dish Cary had never tried before, a few dishes with fish in them that Cary left for the two shifters, and egg drop soup because it was October and Nicky claimed soup was an autumn food requirement.

The restaurant was smallish, with a scattering of brown wood tables, red rugs, stereotypical Chinese restaurant knickknacks everywhere—they were smack in the middle of Chinatown and the tourists expected it—and smelled like a heaven of spice.

"We should have gotten the lemon chicken too," Nicky said.

"There are three of us and we got enough food to feed six people," Cary pointed out. Though, to be fair, the shifters could eat more than that without issue. She sometimes envied them their shifter metabolisms.

"I just love lemon chicken," Nicky said with a shrug.

Once the food was spread out on the table and everyone had filled a plate, Jillian leveled Cary with a serious look. "Deacon wouldn't tell us why you needed a bodyguard suddenly. I don't suppose you will."

She supposed she could come clean now, at least with Nicky and Jillian. She could trust them. But admitting to what she'd done for a living meant exposing other Protectors. She didn't want to do that.

"I wish I could," she said after a few minutes. "It's not my… information to share, though."

"Yet it requires *you* to have bodyguards?" Nicky asked, her eyebrows raised. She popped half an eggroll into her mouth as she waited for Cary's answer.

"I know, it doesn't make much sense. I'll be fine in a couple of months."

"What happens in a couple of months?" Jillian asked.

"The problem goes away." Cary shoved some rice into her mouth to avoid saying more.

Nicky and Jillian exchanged a look and then Nicky changed the topic to Cary's new wardrobe. A subject change Cary gratefully accepted, even though Nicky was disappointed to hear the new clothes didn't involve any fancy dresses.

"How can you go to all the trouble of getting new clothes specially made for you and not include *one* dress?"

"I don't wear dresses that often," she said with a shrug. And frankly, she hadn't considered a magic infused dress might be something that she'd require in the next couple of months. She suspected Marianne, however, would not object to making one.

After the meal, which Cary insisted on paying for—while she still had money coming in—they left the restaurant with Nicky shoving a handful of fortune cookies into her purse. Outside, the late afternoon was cold and crisp and cloudy. Cary pulled in a deep breath, realizing she felt more relaxed than she had in days. The unexpected meal out with friends she hadn't seen in a few months had been just the distraction she needed.

She blamed that distraction for not noticing the vampire until he stood right in front of her.

15

Nicky and Jillian moved in front of Cary so fast and so automatically, Cary blinked. Wow, they could be the Protectors with those moves. It took Cary a few seconds longer to register the situation. Not long. But the fact that she hadn't automatically pushed Nicky and Jillian behind her when confronted with the sight of the vampire was…strange.

And something she'd have to think about later.

"James," she greeted. Because it was always good to be polite to the Master vampire of your city.

For a Master, James's typical style could best be described as business modern, which was remarkably understated for a Master. He tended toward nice, well-tailored suits in dark colors, though not always black. And he did like the occasional pop of red. But he was capable of shrugging off vampire clichés, which he proved today by wearing a steel gray suit with a steel gray shirt and blue tie that looked good against his pale skin and short, blond-brown hair.

She'd only ever once seen him dress in anything more dramatic and historical, and that was the last time she'd been to the Portland hive. Then he'd gone with a sort of medieval king look, and the hive had been done up to look like a medieval banquet hall in a castle, right down to giant tapestries hanging on the walls. That had been interesting.

Old vampires tended to get very nostalgic about the period in which they were turned, and their aesthetic often harkened back to that period of time. If James had fallen into that trap, he'd given away that he was turned during the medieval period in Europe and was therefore susceptible to all the Christian symbols. For some reason, all the holy water and crosses lore only worked on vampires "born" during that period of history. No one had ever been able to explain to her why—or no one was willing to admit why.

According to Jaxer, James was English. She supposed it was entirely possible he had become a vampire in medieval Europe and did like the whole castle vibe. But given how smart James was, Cary didn't take anything for granted. He'd hardly make the "mistake" of letting the Protector in his territory know he had simple vulnerabilities.

At the moment, she and James were on a… Well, she wasn't sure if she'd call their relationship cordial. But they weren't, currently, enemies. Actually, if it weren't for the fact that he was a Master vampire she couldn't trust, and his entire hive sort of wanted her dead for her part in the death of the previous Master of Portland, she might even say she kind of liked James. Except she suspected James used her to get rid of the last Master of Portland so he could take over the hive without blood—cough, cough—on his own hands.

Too many blood puns available with vampires.

The last time she'd seen James had been the night she'd spoken to the Angel of Death. And the night the wizard who'd mentored Sheldon had been killed. After James had ripped his arm off for being disrespectful.

She had very complicated feelings about that night. And about James.

"To what do I owe the pleasure," she said, gesturing at the sky. It was cloudy and dim but still full daylight. The sun wouldn't set for hours yet. It was exceedingly rare for a Master to be out in the daytime since it left them vulnerable. Vampires didn't turn to dust in sun, but they did get weaker. Weak for a vampire was a relative term. Sun just left them with the same sort of strength as a human. For an immortal being with a great deal of power and strength after the sun went down, feeling virtually human in daylight was not a pleasant sensation. And most vampires avoided it. Masters almost never exposed themselves to this kind of vulnerability.

This was the second time James had done this to meet her.

"It's lovely to see you, Cary," James said, his smile carefully hiding his teeth.

He didn't always do that around her. In fact, the last time he'd come out in the daylight to see her, he'd flashed teeth-revealing smiles so easily it had been disconcerting. But she supposed they were on a public street at the moment and not in an empty apartment hallway.

James's gaze danced over the two shifters guarding her. "Will you introduce me to your friends?"

"Nicky, Jillian," Cary said, with a little nod to each, "this is James. Master of Portland."

There were humans around, walking along the sidewalks, driving past. This wasn't a busy street, but it wasn't empty. Still, there was no one in their immediate vicinity, not close enough to overhear the introductions, so she wanted to ensure the leopard shifters knew exactly who they were facing.

Nicky grinned, showing her teeth, and gave James a little finger wave. Jillian grunted a greeting.

James gave them both a regal nod. "Deacon's leopards," he murmured, his gaze moving to Cary.

An ordinary human couldn't meet a vampire's gaze. Hell, even a shifter had to be careful and avoid looking directly into a vampire's eyes. Even in full daylight, if the vampire was strong enough. Meeting a Master's gaze was always potentially deadly. Beyond strength, mesmerism was one of the vampire's greatest skills.

In times past, when Cary was protecting someone, she could meet a vampire's gaze with impunity, and often used that ability to throw them off. She'd almost always been able to meet James's gaze, because he'd always been a threat to someone around her. He knew she was a Protector—unfortunately, the stupid wizard who'd wanted to kill her had told all the vampires what she was—and for reasons only a vampire could parse out, James made a point of being a threat to those around her so her powers would work.

But she wasn't a Protector anymore. She wasn't in front of the shifters, keeping them safe. They were standing in front of her.

And she didn't dare meet James's gaze directly.

He was going to figure this out.

Fuck. The Master of Portland was about to realize she was no longer a Protector.

Vampires were as good at scent and hearing as shifters, which meant everyone there but Cary would hear her heart beating a little harder, and probably smell her panic. Lying to vampires and shifters was almost impossible if you weren't one, and Cary wasn't a great liar under even the best of circumstances.

But she was good at being impatient and grouchy. She was very very good at that. And being scared made her even better at being impatient and grouchy.

So she channeled her spike of fear into appearing, into *feeling* impatiently grouchy. "We were on our way to look at fashion magazine," she said. "What do you want?"

She kept her gaze moving around their surroundings as if impatient, as if making sure no one was around to overhear. The fact that they were on a public street, with other humans in the area, gave her a great excuse not to make it obvious she was avoiding James's gaze.

"The Angel wants a word," James said.

In her passing glances, she caught sight of his raised brows, but she ignored his speculative look. "I can't right now. Busy."

"Doing?"

"None of your business?"

"A job?"

"None. Of. Your. Business. Why the hell would the Angel want to talk to me anyway?"

"The whole…demon god thing," James said, echoing her speech pattern in a way that made her scowl.

If he were purposefully trying to make her grouchy for real, he'd just succeeded spectacularly. "That's been lingering for weeks. They have that much time on their hands, they can wait a bit longer." Another two months would be good.

Did she dare tell James she wasn't the Protector on that particular job anymore? The less the Master of Portland knew, the better. But she couldn't have him continually surprising her on city streets like this for the next two months. She'd never be able to put him off that long and he'd eventually figure out something was wrong. Hell, he probably knew something was wrong now given her jumpy gaze and the fact that she was standing *behind* the shifters instead of in front of them. But she couldn't talk about Protectors right then anyway because Jillian and Nicky didn't know they existed.

She let out a huff, and finally, as vaguely as possible, said, "Listen, the Angel is going to have to deal with…with another…with other people. I've been pulled from this job. It's someone else's problem."

She made a show of frowning, and grousing, and pretending she was super annoyed. Which was, technically, an easy act to pull off because she was super annoyed. She was also terrified under it all. She walked a very fine line here. But she was annoyed at being scared, and she was angry about being in this situation to begin with, and it was extremely easy to let that annoyance and anger rise to the surface.

In fact, she sort of hoped even her fear would look to be tied into her anger. Maybe, just maybe, James would misinterpret the source of her fear.

"I'm not happy about this, as you might guess," she said. "But…I have bosses. And I have to do what they say. It's just…the way of it."

She wasn't entirely sure how much James really knew about Protectors, but he was super old—likely older than he let on—and smart, and he knew what Protectors were. He'd also had time to learn more. She couldn't guarantee he *didn't* know some things. And erring on the side of some vague revelations was better than *hoping* he did or didn't know about the fact that Protectors worked for someone. In this case, being able to blame "bosses" for her inability to protect Oliver

Holland—which was technically true—also gave her cover to hide that she wasn't a Protector.

Though she continued to let her gaze skim over the area, she rolled her eyes to add to the appearance of irritation and let out a huff. From the corner of her eyes, she got the impression James's expression was speculative. But that could have been her own paranoia. Without being able to look at him directly, she couldn't say for sure. And even if she'd been able to look him in the eyes, she still couldn't read his expression unless he wanted her to.

"Does this have something to do with the shifters?" he asked, his voice quiet.

His tone impossible to decipher, damn it.

"It's complicated," she said, waving her hand and half snarling. "Anyway, send my apologies to the Angel. She'll have to deal with her son and his father on her own. Or…whatever. How are the triad?"

The question that had nothing directly to do with their current conversation made James pause, and Cary gave herself a little mental fist bump.

"They're fine and waiting to channel the Angel so that she can speak with you," James said, his tone more neutral than it had been a second ago.

Not that Cary had been able to read his tone, but there was a level of iciness in it now that hadn't been there before. Was he mad at the witch triad? Or was this something to do with Cary's attempt at a subject change?

"Send them my apologies, too," Cary said. She didn't actually like the three witches who'd worked for Oliver Holland and also channeled the Angel of Death. Although, if they hadn't tried to kill her once, she might have. Well, not the blond. She was never going to get along with the blond. "Are we done here?"

She was itching to be away from him. There was only so long she could keep her gaze scanning the streets and jumping around past his before he noticed. If he hadn't realized already she was doing this on purpose. And he'd certainly noticed she was behind the shifters instead of in front of them. He was suspicious, he'd have to be, and she didn't want to give him more data to mull over.

"I suppose we are," James said, very quietly. "Though I doubt the Angel will be pleased to have her situation fobbed off on another."

"Well, she can talk to my bosses about that," Cary said. "Maybe they'll change their minds."

"Mm."

Cary let her gaze pass by his again. She couldn't have read his expression if she'd had a year to study it without fear. She wasn't sure why she bothered.

"We'll speak again soon," he said.

"Sure sure." She waved a hand in the air again, pretending at an ease she didn't feel even a little bit.

And without another word, James turned and walked away, moving at human speeds, lifting his arm as if checking his watch. If an observer didn't know better, they'd never guess he was more than an ordinary man in a sleek gray business suit, strolling down the city street.

"That's gonna come back and bite you, isn't it?" Jillian said quietly.

"So long as *he* doesn't bite me, I think I'll survive," Cary said, equally quiet, her words for shifter ears only.

"Not sure it'll be that easy," Nicky said. When she turned to face Cary, there was a very faint yellow glow in her eyes.

And Cary realized it was the first time she'd seen Nicky's leopard rise to the surface that way.

"He'll be back. And whoever this Angel is, they're not going to leave you alone." Nicky spoke as if she was absolutely certain, not just making a guess. Maybe she picked some of that up in James's scent.

"Want to talk about it?" Jillian said. "We'll keep it to ourselves. We won't even tell Maria."

Keeping something from Deacon's mother, the queen of their people, was a big offer. And Cary acknowledged that for what it was. "I very much appreciate that offer," she said. "For the moment, I can't discuss it. But thank you."

"When you're ready," Jillian said. "We'll listen."

Cary studied the street where James had disappeared as worry churned in her gut. How the hell was she going to avoid the vampires for another two months if James kept tracking her down? He'd just proved that finding her when she was outside her own house was pathetically easy for him to do. How could she hold out for another two months when he insisted on meeting with her?

And how was she going to survive if the Angel of Death kept looking for her?

16

icky and Jillian followed Cary home, ensuring she got there safely. She, in turn, gave them permission to find her house and invited them in for a coffee while they all, without saying a word about it out loud, waited for Deacon to arrive.

The dogs took to Jillian immediately, and Pickles and Nicky struck up an, admittedly one-sided, conversation about pockets in fancy dresses. Both were very pro-pockets. Or so they all assumed that's what Pickles's occasional woofs meant. Fred was, for reasons Cary wouldn't figure out, pretty leery of Nicky at first. He'd been completely comfortable with Jillian and he considered Deacon a part of the pack, based on the way he treated Deacon. So it wasn't just the cat shifter thing. But eventually, he decided Nicky was acceptable in the house, and then he spent the rest of the time sitting up and begging her for a treat. Which Nicky, in a bid to be accepted, was happy to get him.

Deacon texted he was on his way about a half hour before he arrived home. And Cary still considered it funny they both thought of her place as "home" now when he literally had a massive suite in an apartment building his family *owned*. But she was glad they did. She liked her cozy house. She was grateful he was comfortable here. And she was also glad she owned the place outright, thanks to her previous job, since she was about to be out of that job and still hadn't decided what to do with her life.

She waited until Nicky and Jillian had said their goodbyes, and Fred, Buck and Pickles had welcomed Deacon home before she told him about the incident with James.

"Fuck," Deacon said. With feeling.

She was glad to see his eyes didn't get that yellow leopard-rising glow, but his jaw was tight and little lines formed on his forehead with his scowl.

"I was hoping to avoid him, too, but it happened," she said. "And at least it was in the middle of the day."

"But he'll know something is wrong now," Deacon said. He ran a hand through his hair and stared at the living room wall.

They hadn't even sat down yet. She gave him a little nudge toward the couch and they sat. She turned to face him, folding her legs up under her.

"I know this is bad," she said. "But with luck, my excuses put him off the…scent. So to speak."

"And if they didn't? Or if the Angel of Death still wants to talk to you? What if the witches track you down here?"

She settled back a little, holding his gaze. This last secret of hers, the one thing she'd never told him about her house, her job, was about to be a moot point. But if it meant he'd worry less over the next couple of months…

Hell, she'd intended to tell him eventually anyway.

"They won't find my house," she said. "At least not before they forget who I am."

"Why?"

His voice had gotten very neutral. Which immediately made her suspicious. And leery.

"So, you know how I have a secret attic with all my research? And I kept it secret from almost everyone so I didn't accidentally give it away to anyone?" She'd shown him the attic in the spring, because she'd wanted to stop hiding one thing from him.

He nodded, but didn't comment.

"Okay, so, part of the Protector job, a sort of perk of the job, is that the Nags put a kind of glamour on my house. A special kind. That means no one can find it without my permission. Not taxi drivers, not delivery people. My mailman couldn't find the place walking right past it if I didn't give him mental permission to *see* the house and the mailbox at the sidewalk. Shifters can't find the house by following scent. Vampires can't track it. No one who I exclude from this place can locate it. Even if they find the neighborhood and circle the block for hours."

For a long moment, he remained silent, his gaze on her face but his expression closed. Almost his iceman look, when he was so closed up she couldn't read him at all. He only did that when he had to control his emotions or risk hurting someone.

"This has been on your house the entire time I've known you?" he asked.

And that was his iceman tone. She let out a slow breath. "Yes. And no one knows about it. Not the girls. Not my family. No one but Jaxer and my... And Liruk and Wisat. Because it's safer that way. The less people know, the better the glamour works."

The problem with glamour magic was that if someone knew the spell was there, that it was a glamour, it got easier to see around it. Eventually. She wasn't sure if the same thing went for her bosses'... former bosses' glamour. But it was the reason Jaxer didn't like to be around kids. They saw through glamour. And once they did and alerted others to the reality underneath the disguise, the disguise crumbled.

"So while you're here, in this house, you're safe?" Deacon asked, his tone still very quiet, all the emotion washed from it.

"I am. At least for the next two months. It's part of the severance that the glamour stays in place until everyone's memories have faded." She shrugged. "It was the thing Wisat and Liruk used to get me to commit to the seventh year test."

"Meaning?"

"I asked what would happen if I refused to do the test, and they said they'd take away the glamour. My enemies would be able to find my home. No memories fading as an option."

A muscle in his jaw jumped. She raised her brows. The show of emotion was a little unexpected given he'd gone into his ultra-controlled defensive shell. Was it good or bad that tiny hint of anger got through his control?

"So while you're here, you're safe," he said again.

She gave a sort of nod-shrug that she hoped he understood. She was too leery of his mood to do more.

"This is why you had a panic attack leaving the house the other day, when we went to Marianne's. Because you knew you were safe inside the house in a way you weren't outside."

He hadn't asked a question. But she nodded in answer anyway.

"Would you have ever told me?"

"Eventually. I'd planned to. I wanted to pass my seventh year first. See where that left…everything."

"Everything?"

"My job. My supposed 'full' powers. Our relationship." She sighed. "To be honest, like the attic, it's a habit not to talk about the glamour. It's just this thing that exists but I don't say anything to anyone about it so it keeps existing."

"Not even Angie, Marianne, Lucy knew?"

"Nope."

"They've stayed here. House- and dog-sitting."

"And were happily surprised at how few visitors they got. I did have to learn how to give permission to their standard food delivery restaurants to find the place while I wasn't here. The first time Angie house-sat, she couldn't get any of the local delivery places to come out. She couldn't figure out why. I had to make up an excuse, and then ensure I gave the local restaurants permission to find the house every time after that."

"And Angie wasn't suspicious?"

"If she was, she didn't say anything about it. She might even know, since she's known about the existence of Protectors since before we met. If she does, she doesn't talk about it with me." She lifted her hands, palms up. "I'd have to ask her and might well do after the severance period is up."

Deacon fell quiet for a long moment, his expression still closed off.

She waited him out in silence, though not jumping in to make excuses or justify her actions took an act of will.

Finally, he said, "When did you give me permission to find your house?"

She felt her cheeks heating, but admitted, "I gave you permission on accident. Probably while we were still at the hospital that first night we met." When she'd rescued him from Sheldon and had gotten broken ribs for her trouble. Also all of Sheldon's magic, but they hadn't known that at the time.

Deacon had taken her to the hospital, stayed with her through the whole process, and put her in a taxi home. He'd shown up the next day at her door with the painkillers she'd forgotten all about. And she'd realized she'd wanted to see him again—despite thinking he might be a little delusional with this whole mate thing—or he wouldn't have been able to find her.

"You didn't mean to let me find your house?"

"I hadn't thought I'd see you again, so I didn't consciously consider it one way or another. If you'll remember, I didn't believe you about the whole mate thing. And also I was in a bit of pain what with the broken ribs and all." She was starting to sound defensive so she shut her mouth.

"And yet you still gave me permission to find you," he said.

"Apparently." She rolled her eyes because the way he said that left her feeling a little mortified and she wasn't even sure why.

"Have you ever…taken away that permission?"

"Of course not," she said, scowling. "Have you ever had trouble finding this place?"

"No. But you could, take away permission, if you wanted to?"

"Yes. At least for the next two months."

"With Jaxer?"

"Actually, yes. If I didn't want him to find my house, I could take away his permission and even though he was my mentor and knew the glamour existed, he wouldn't have been able to find the house. Only

Wisat and Liruk can get around the whole permission thing. Because it's their magic."

"Have you ever taken Jaxer's permission away?"

"No. Because he never pissed me off enough to actually do it. Though it was a close thing once or twice."

His jaw muscle jumped again.

"We're not doing this again, are we?" she said with exasperation. "I thought you and Jaxer had finally put all this jealousy crap behind you. You've been getting along so much better since Faery."

"We have," Deacon confirmed without cracking his neutral, icy expression.

"Then why are you angry he can find my house? He *was* my mentor. I kind of needed him to do my job."

Deacon nodded but didn't comment.

She sighed. "You're mad."

"I'm processing."

"You handled the attic better than this."

"You haven't asked me what emotions I'm processing."

"Anger?" she said with a snort.

"Relief," he said. "So much relief I'm lightheaded."

"Wait. What?" He definitely looked angry—or well, like he was carefully controlling his anger so he didn't actually show any emotion at all. That was not his relief face.

"It's a pretty profound relief which is mixed with a lot of…"

"Anger, annoyance, anger?"

"Terror. Because the thing that's been keeping you so safe over the years is about to go away."

"Ah." She wasn't sure how to respond herself now.

"It's a fear I've been living with for the last year—that someone would find you here and kill you—and I'm just realizing I didn't have to worry. All that time. I could have relaxed more."

She winced. "Sorry. I… Is that why we really stay here all the time?"

"No. I like your place better than mine."

She blinked. That was more blunt about the living situation than he'd been before.

"If I didn't," he said, "I'd have tried to convince you to move into my place, bring the dogs, ensure we had all the best security systems in place to keep you safe."

"Why *didn't* you do that, though, if you'd been so worried?"

"I don't know. I wondered that myself a few times. Now, I guess I know."

"Huh?"

"A part of me must have known we were safe here. You were safe here. Even without knowing. Even with my conscious mind worrying about it. My instincts must have known your house was a haven."

"So… That's a good thing, right?"

"And you let me find your home instinctively. Without consciously making the decision. Your instincts knew you could trust me, even if you didn't yet."

There was still no emotion in his tone so she wasn't sure if he thought that fact was good or bad. "I suppose so," she said slowly.

"For the record," he said, "I find that a huge relief, too."

"Huh?" she asked. Again.

"Because you're human and our mate bond isn't…the same for you. Not as…permanent."

"Yeah." Where was he going with this?

He shrugged. "It's a relief to know, on a subconscious level, you recognized the bond and accepted it from the start. You didn't want to, consciously, and you didn't trust it, but from the very beginning, a part of you recognized what was between us as quickly as I did. And I'm glad."

She narrowed her eyes. "You don't sound glad."

"I'm still processing all this."

"Is that good or bad?"

His mouth ticked up at the corner. A break in the iceman expression. "Good."

She let her shoulders relax, and she slumped against the arm of the couch. "Mad?"

"No."

"You sure?"

"Yes. This isn't mad. This is…"

"Processing," she said, and let out a little grin. She was okay with this if it was processing. "Though, the attic took a lot less processing time."

"The attic didn't affect your daily security. And it didn't have quite as many implications."

That was fair enough, she supposed. She'd also gone a lot longer hiding this particular secret than she had the attic.

"This shielding goes away in two months," he said.

"'Fraid so. It was part of the job. Like the paychecks."

Technically just direct deposits into her account. And she had no idea where Liruk and Wisat got money to pay the Protectors. Or bank accounts. Did they have bank accounts? They must or there wouldn't be direct deposits. But still. She'd needed the job at the time so she hadn't questioned *how* they could pay her. She just spent the money that showed up in her bank account every month.

"Without the glamour," she said, "do you think you'll want to… live somewhere else?" They'd never really discussed living here. Or at his place. They just stayed at her house all the time. And she did own it outright. She loved her house and had no intention of selling it. But everything was changing so she supposed they'd better have this conversation, too.

"You love it here. We'll stay here."

He still hadn't broken the iceman expression or tone, but the words were nice. And reassuring.

"We should probably make the fact that you moved in—months ago—a more formal thing eventually, huh?"

"We will. I've been waiting for you to finish your seventh year before…broaching the subject of our future."

She snorted. "Because we didn't know if I'd *have* a future?"

"Yes."

Wow. Not pulling any punches. Okay. "Well, looks like if I can get through the period of time it'll take for the supernatural bad guys in

Portland to forget me, I will have a future. I don't know what it'll look like. I have no idea what I'll do with myself."

"You have time for that."

"But I suppose this means I can plan for a future of some kind now, right?"

"It does."

"You're still really iceman right now. You okay?"

"Getting there."

"You're going to want to install alarms and stuff here, aren't you?"

"Maybe. But you have a foo lion and a demon dog in your pack, so we probably don't have to."

"They don't actually do foo lion things and demon dog things most of the time, you know. They're here to just be dogs."

"And dogs protect their homes," he said. "Pickles and Buck, and Fred for that matter, will protect you and this place."

"Fred? Seriously? Fred will sit up and beg if the intruder smells like bacon. He's not exactly the epitome of a guard dog."

A soft snort of almost amusement cracked the iceman exterior again. And this time the ice didn't flow back in to fill the crack. His mouth softened. The tension along his jaw loosened. His gaze gentled.

Suddenly, she was looking at Deacon as he normally was with her.

She smiled. "Finished processing, I see."

"It's a little scary the way you read my expression so well."

"I don't have super shifter smelling. I have to do something. Plus, you're really hot. I spend a lot of time studying your face."

The last of the tension in his shoulders eased. He pulled her across the couch into a hug, that turned into a kiss, that turned her brain to mush so she forgot what they'd been talking about.

He eased back from the kiss to put his forehead against hers. "Any more safety-related secrets I should know about?" he asked quietly.

"Nope. I noticed you didn't say 'secrets' in general."

"I want us to be open and able to tell each other everything. But I also know that 'everything' might take a life time. And I won't rush you."

"I really love you, you know that."

"I'm glad to hear it. Thank you for finally telling me about the glamour."

"Thank you for not getting pissy about the fact that I kept it to myself all this time."

He leaned back and raised his brows at her. "Pissy?"

"Yeah. You do do that sometimes."

"I don't get pissy," he said, scowling so fiercely she almost laughed.

"Grumpy? Angry? Pissed off?"

His grunted response only delighted her more and she pulled him in for another kiss. Relief left her a little giddy. And a lot randy.

Getting him naked seemed like an excellent way to end the conversation.

From the mere seconds it took them both to strip, she was pretty sure he felt the same way.

17

Leaving the house the next afternoon triggered less panic, but she still balked at the door, hesitating before taking that last step outside. This time, Deacon didn't ask if she was okay.

He asked, "Do you want to stay here? I can go get the stuff from Marianne. You'll feel better with your jacket."

He was right about that. Without her powers or her jacket, she felt pretty naked. In a bad way, not the fun way.

And she'd rather enjoy the fun way of being naked with Deacon than risk running into James again. But she couldn't hide in her house for the next two months. She was a little afraid if she did, she might not come out even after her severance period was up.

"Let's go. I'm good. James has bigger things to worry about. And it's daylight. His vampires won't come after me right now. Especially with you around." Shifters didn't get weaker in the daylight. The average vampire wouldn't want to deal with the humiliation of having a shifter kick their ass in full daylight.

She spent the drive talking herself out of her fear. She really didn't need to worry. Holland and the demons were someone else's problem now. The Angel probably knew Cary had been fired and was of no use to her by now. Being the literal Angel of Death, the Angel

118

no doubt knew all kinds of things like that. Cary carefully ignored the fact that the Angel had wanted to talk just yesterday, several days after Cary had been sacked. That was probably just a miscommunication.

And really if Death wanted to find her, there wasn't a whole lot she could do to stop that.

But she no longer had a wizard out to kill her. Sheldon wasn't a threat anymore either. At least not while he was still laid up from his injuries.

She should probably check on him. She didn't want to care or worry, but she did. When… If she saw Jaxer again, she'd ask about Sheldon. That "if" left a little hollow in her stomach she chose to ignore.

As they circled the block, looking for parking, she realized most of her enemies were otherwise occupied or dead. Even the English Faery queen—who may or may not count as an enemy—had a full plate keeping Faery from rotting by creating new Protectors in that part of the world. Cary should absolutely be safe from anyone who had wanted to kill her. There was no reason to worry.

Though the Holland thing still hung in the air. Even though she wasn't supposed to be a part of that anymore, she did want to know what was happening. She'd spent the weeks up to her firing waiting for that shoe to drop and then… Nothing. Cut out from the whole thing. And since the whole thing was a potentially world-ending situation, she kind of wanted to know if the world was actually going to end or not. She'd eat more pizza and ice cream if it was.

Not being able to help stop it, not being involved… She wasn't sure if she was upset about that, relieved, some weird combination of the two. It was nice not being responsible for saving the world, she supposed. But also leaving the fate of things to someone else felt weirdly irresponsible and left her edgy. She kept trying to convince herself it was someone else's problem and she needed to let it go. She was not entirely successful in this effort.

"Maybe Jaxer can let me know what happens?" she said aloud. "With Holland."

"If he's allowed to talk about it," Deacon said, his tone carefully neutral.

She wasn't sure what that tone—or lack of tone—was about but she didn't feel like getting into another "why are you grumpy about Jaxer?" conversation with him.

"I just feel…" She sighed. "I still feel like I'm waiting for the other shoe to drop, except now I'm not the one running in to stop the disaster after the shoe drops. I have to wait for someone else to do that. I'm not good at waiting."

He snorted. "An understatement."

She'd have rolled her eyes if he wasn't so right. "I sort of feel like I've abdicated responsibility for all this."

"Except you didn't. The responsibility was taken away from you."

"Harsh. True. But harsh." She sighed. "I still feel like I'm falling down on my job." She raised a hand before he could talk. "I know. I don't have a job anymore. It's habit. I just… I guess I'm still feeling adrift."

"It's only been a few days. Give yourself time."

She knew he was right. Of course he was. The words didn't seem to help, though.

She stared out the window. The sidewalks in this section of downtown were busy, a lot of pedestrians moving between stores, a lot of traffic. A weekday, she realized. She didn't always keep track of the days of the week. She'd been on-call as a Protector twenty-four-seven and that meant the concept of "weekend" had very little meaning. She usually only noticed the difference when she had plans for the weekend. And since her three best friends all ran their own businesses, even their girls' night was negotiable because weekends weren't necessarily days off for them either.

By the time Deacon found a parking spot, they had to walk a few blocks to reach Marianne's shop, but Cary was glad for the fresh air. And sunlight. There was a lot of it this morning and she was always grateful for autumn sunshine. There was something about the quality of the air in that light, the cooler temperature contrasting with sparkling sun. That fresh scent in the air, like everything was sharper and cleaner.

She pulled in a deep breath, letting the season clear some of the murk in her mind.

As they stopped at a crosswalk, Cary let her gaze move over all the weekday people walking around. And noticed one of the people across the street looked familiar. It took her a long moment to put the face in context. She was already halfway across the street when she realized why the woman looked so familiar, though without her son and a man screaming in her face, it was hard to pinpoint the memory. But it was definitely the same woman from last time she'd been in this neighborhood. The woman Cary had rushed in to help.

The woman's eyes widen when she spotted Cary. She waited on her side of the road for Cary to join her, raising her hand in greeting, smiling hesitantly. Cary waved back and opened her mouth to ask the woman how she was, realizing as she did, she'd never gotten her name.

In the next instant, she realized something else important.

The woman's ex was several paces behind her.

And as Cary neared, he pulled a gun from inside his coat.

Cary leapt between the woman and her ex, pulling the woman to the ground.

The exploding pain and burn that ripped through her shoulder happened in almost the exact moment that she heard the gun go off.

It took her a full twenty seconds to register that the burning went *into* her shoulder.

And that blood dripped down her back.

18

"Cary, Cary…" Deacon slid to the sidewalk next to her, panic in his voice.

Pain laced through her shoulder and chest, a burning siege of pain that left her not wanting to move or be touched. She could smell the mineraly scent of her own blood and that was probably not good. Not good for Deacon either.

"You know how I hate getting shot," she said to him as black spots danced at the edge of her vision. "Hurts a lot worse when the bullet goes in."

"Jesus," he muttered.

She got the impression of him stripping off his shirt and putting the material against the bleeding, burning hole in her shoulder. She hissed at the sting but he didn't let up on the pressure. There seemed to be a lot of noise and shouting, people on cellphones, but she wasn't able to focus on any of the chaos. Deacon barked a few orders at people. The woman was crying and apologizing, and Cary desperately wanted her to stop.

"Not your fault," she muttered to the woman but that pain in her shoulder hurt a lot and she wasn't sure she was talking out loud. She also thought she heard Marianne's voice in the mix, and a minute later

—or a second? Time had gone all weird—Marianne's face appeared in front of Cary.

More pressure on her shoulder. She looked down and realized she had blood on the front of her too. A part of her brain realized the bullet must have gone clean through and that sent a spike of adrenaline through her.

The woman! Innocent bystanders!

There was blood on the woman but no one was paying attention to her. And where was the man with the gun?

Cary struggled to pull away from all the people holding her down, but Deacon's hands were immovable.

Against her ear, he said, "Stay still. You're bleeding a lot. Ambulance is on the way. I can hear it. The man is unconscious and one of the humans is guarding the gun so he can't grab for it if he comes to. The woman wasn't hurt. The bullet that went through you and hit the sidewalk."

"Oh, that's good." She sagged in relief, and the surge of adrenaline left her trembling. Or maybe that was the gunshot wound.

Her vision was tunneling and the pain in her shoulder and chest hurt like hell. She could breathe, though. That must be good. Bullet missed her lungs. She hoped.

Marianne pressed something harder against the front of her shoulder. "This will help contain the bleeding," she said to Deacon, her voice low. The pressure on the back of her shoulder eased. Blood oozed hotly down her skin, then the pressure was back.

"One of your cool materials," she murmured to Marianne, trying to smile. Probably the same stuff she'd worked into some of Cary's shirts. Magic to help stop bleeding. Good stuff. Shame she didn't have one of those shirts on.

"Yes," Marianne said, her voice no-nonsense and stern. "Stay still and stop talking."

Cary hadn't thought she was talking much. And she wanted to argue with Marianne's tone. But everything hurt and she was shivering harder now. That might not be good.

She wasn't sure how much time passed because time was doing

weird wobbly things, but the next thing she knew, a couple of EMTs were pushing the crowds away and asking her questions, checking her injury, doing all the things ambulance people were good at. At least, she assumed that was what they were doing. The pain had moved her into a sort of detached place that felt more comfortable so she didn't feel like stirring herself enough to pay attention.

Something sharp against her arm. More pressure. And a stretcher. She kind of wanted to protest the stretcher, but she didn't have enough energy to stand so, yeah, stretcher was good.

"I haven't passed out," she murmured, mostly to herself. "Kind of surprised by that." What with blood loss and all. Probably thanks to Marianne's super material, keeping her from bleeding out.

Wow. The thought of bleeding out... Not something she'd considered possible in a long time. At least not from anything as mundane as a gunshot wound. Vampires, on the other hand, had caused her to consider significant blood loss as a possibility.

She was about to say some of this out loud when Deacon's face appeared over hers and she heard the ambulance doors closed.

"Stay quiet," he murmured. "Rest. You'll be better soon."

She nodded, then groaned. "I won't have this good medical insurance in a few months. Shit." She'd really had to take advantage of her good medical insurance while working as a Protector. She hated that she'd have to give it up.

"We'll talk about that later, too," Deacon said. His face was close to her, his scent a nice contrast to the stench of medicinal things and her own blood.

She focused more closely on him. There was a very faint glow in the depths of his golden eyes. A glow that most humans would be able to dismiss as a trick of the light. Thankfully. She'd hate for his worry over her to push him into revealing his nature on accident. His expression beyond that very faint glow as all iceman. Again. That was twice in less than twenty-four hours that he'd had to go iceman. That sucked. She hated that his worry had pushed him to needing that level of control. Again.

"I'll be fine," she murmured. "I'm breathing. That's good, right."

"Right," someone said from another part of the ambulance. Cary assumed it was one of the EMTs.

"See," she said. "Even the experts agree that breathing is good."

"I'll laugh at that after they stop the bleeding," Deacon said, his tone very controlled.

The sound of the siren, the feel of the ambulance moving, was comforting and also annoying. She hurt a little less now and wondered if they'd given her something for the pain or if she was just going numb. Deacon held her good hand and muttered things to the EMT without looking away from her face. She caught something about allergies, and smiled a little when he said none. It was nice having someone know her well enough he could answer medical questions for her. She'd always hated that part of having to go to the ER. All the questions. Though, to be fair, her injuries had always been so weird, her excuses so lame, her medical history so extensive, the questions were usually prompted by some doctor worried she was an abuse victim.

Didn't have to explain away this injury, though. Pretty obvious gunshot wound. Normal one where the bullet actually penetrated her skin.

Wow. She'd been shot. At some point, that was going to really freak her out.

At the hospital, the EMTs whisked her inside on the gurney, leaving Deacon to take care of the paperwork. Finally, someone gave her something that knocked her out.

And she went eagerly into the comforting pull of darkness and quiet.

19

*C*ary woke groggy and achy and disoriented. It took a few seconds to remember the gunshot, the ambulance ride. The hospital.

She glanced around. The room was pretty standard. Two beds separated by a curtain—no one was in the other bed so the curtain was pulled back—machines making noises, a TV hanging high on the wall —currently turned off—a metal poll next to her bed holding an IV with some clear liquid in it. She glanced down at her arm. The little inserted needle for the IV hurt. She was a little surprised she could feel it over the ache in her shoulder. That was either a good thing—excellent drugs —or a bad thing—she'd lost the arm. She flexed her hand on the side of her injured shoulder, looked at her fingers. Nope, still had the arm.

A single window flooded the room with light and gave Cary an industrial view of another part of the hospital across a parking lot. Deacon sprawled in a chair next to her bed, by the window, his legs stretched out and crossed at the ankles, his hands resting on his stomach, his eyes closed. She smiled a little at the sight of him resting, relieved he'd been able to. She'd worried she'd look around to see him pacing the room. Since he was asleep, she was probably out of the woods.

"I'm not sleeping," he murmured, opening his eyes to look at her.

"Your eyes were closed," she pointed out.

"I was thanking the universe that you were awake and alive."

"That's both sweet and horrifying."

"Yes," he said, straightening in his chair. "How do you feel?"

"Sore. Lot worse than ever before." She glanced down at the bandages covering her shoulder. Her left shoulder, she noticed. She hadn't paid attention to that detail before. Left. She was right-handed. That was some consolation she supposed. "Not gonna heal up fast like it used to," she said with a sigh.

"No. There was damage. But the bullet missed your lungs. And thanks to Marianne's cloth, you bled a lot less than you might have otherwise."

She looked closer at Deacon. There was a very very faint glow of his leopard in his eyes. Just a hint of yellow in the golden depths. But he hadn't gone full iceman emotionless to control it. Was that good or bad?

"You didn't die this time," he said, as if reading her thoughts.

"That made it easier to keep your…self controlled without shutting off your emotions?" She was genuinely curious. And it distracted from the ache in her shoulder. She'd kind of hoped that IV dripping into her arm had the good drugs in it. But maybe she'd burned through all the pain meds already. She'd ask a nurse.

"It helped," he said, too seriously. "And there are humans everywhere, coming in and out a lot. I had to keep a delicate balance. Couldn't afford to scare them, but they wouldn't believe I was your husband if I iced myself off too much."

"You told them I was your wife?"

Her stomach did a little funny flip and she wasn't sure why. They'd been together almost a year and they were mates. As far as leopard shifters were concerned, that was as permanent as it got. They were, for all intents and purposes, married. But… Well, she didn't think of them in those terms. And during previous trips to the hospital over the last year, he'd either said nothing about their relationship, or said he was her boyfriend.

For some reason, him telling the staff he was her husband felt… like something had changed.

"I didn't want arguments about me staying in your room, or emergency contacts," he said. He was still sprawled in the chair, not moving much as he spoke. "I figured this would be a longer stay than previous ones."

Damn. He was right. She couldn't just leave now that she was awake. Well, she could try. But she didn't have super fast Protector healing to fall back on. She had to worry about things like infections. And probably physiotherapy to help her shoulder recover. And there would be all kinds of restrictions so she didn't damage herself more.

Shit. Getting shot without Protector healing or shields sucked even worse than getting shot with them. She hated getting shot.

"Was the woman okay? What happened with her ex?"

"He was arrested. She was fine. Trevor was in earlier. He has some questions for you when you recover enough to talk."

"Bleh." She hated talking to the cops. She tried to avoid them. Before, they'd been a complication for her job. Now… She just didn't want that much attention. Or the questions.

"I'll make sure his partner isn't there when you talk to him."

"Thanks."

She got along well enough with Trevor. She really liked his wife, Sue Anne, and their kids. She and Deacon had been to their house a couple of times for dinner, and Cary had managed to maintain a semblance of normalcy so as not to spark Trevor's suspicions. But his partner…

Officer Calvin Bacon really didn't trust Cary and was super suspicious of everything she did. Having him sit in on the questions she'd have to answer about this would only make her stumble and seem guilty. She didn't have anything to be guilty of. She was the one who got shot! But she'd still feel like she was trying to hide something, and she was certain both Trevor and Bacon would see that.

"The doctors want to keep you here another couple of days," Deacon said. "To make sure there's no post-op complications."

She groaned. "I was afraid of that."

"I can probably help a little," said a voice from the doorway.

Cary turned to see a woman in scrubs come into the room. She had a messy bun of brown hair pilled on her head and a pretty face above a spectacular curvy body. Cary blinked. Wow. Super model playing nurse. She hadn't expected that. Then she looked the woman in the eyes. Green-blue eyes that looked…familiar.

Cary narrowed her own eyes. The woman smiled.

"Jaxer?" Cary asked.

"Hello, love. I wondered if you'd recognize me."

The voice was most definitely not Jaxer's. But there was a rhythm to it that was still familiar.

"You left a hint so I would," she said, gesturing to his eyes. Or her eyes in this case. "Why the disguise?"

"I like doing sexy nurse," he said. "People forget to question what I'm doing here and don't remember they've never seen me before. It's fun."

She rolled her eyes. "Your idea of fun is weird."

The gorgeous nurse grinned. And a moment later, the Jaxer Cary knew was standing there. Still dressed in scrubs, but he'd reverted to his normal, also ridiculously handsome, appearance. Though not the full Fae glory. None of the humans in the hospital would be able to take that level of stunning beauty. Her own brain balked at it.

"Is Eriana on her way?" Deacon asked.

There was no growl in his tone, no annoyance. He sounded tired. But not upset to have Jaxer there.

"She'll come in later," Jaxer said. "During the shift change so there're fewer humans around to contend with." He sat gently on the bed next to her. "How're you feeling?"

"Like I was shot. Eriana is coming?"

"She'll be able to speed up the healing on that wound. Keep you from having any permanent nerve or tendon damage."

"Oh." That was really nice of Eriana. And also, it would be really nice to not have permanent damage after her stupid move. "You've been here before this?"

"Right after you left surgery," Jaxer said. "Heard about the… incident through the grapevine."

"The same grapevine that fired me?" she asked.

He let out a long breath. "We have a lot to talk about."

"Probably." She glanced away when she felt an inexplicable burn of tears. "Guess I failed. I'm still not sure what I did wrong. They didn't bother to explain." She made a face and tried not to sniffle too obviously. "Sorry I failed."

"Stop," he said. "You didn't." He gripped her right hand, his fingers warm and tight.

She couldn't meet his gaze or she would cry, but she noticed Deacon didn't growl or hiss or object to Jaxer touching her.

"There are things…" Jaxer started. "More to what's happened than is obvious. And we'll need to talk. But not here."

Deacon gave Jaxer a nod. Jaxer stood. And a moment later, a newcomer walked into the room.

Cary didn't recognize the woman. She was tall and what Cary thought of as statuesque and handsome. A kind of striking appearance that made you look twice. Her black hair was pulled back in a tight, straight ponytail, here dark eyes were sharp and attentive. She wore a long white doctor's coat over her dark blue scrubs and had a stethoscope hanging out of one of the pockets.

"Dr. Sharma," Deacon greeted. To Cary, he said, "Dr. Sharma was your surgeon."

Ah.

"And how are you feeling this morning?" Dr. Sharma said, smiling. Her gaze danced over the others in the room, but she kept most of her attention on Cary.

Given Deacon and Jaxer's sheer magnetic good looks, she gave the doc credit for that restraint. "Sore," she said. "Any chance of more of the good drugs?"

The doctor chuckled. "I'll see what we can do. First, though." She came close to the bed and started testing Cary's sense of touch in her fingers and different parts of her arm. "The nurse will be in to change the bandages in a few minutes." She glanced back at Jaxer and gave a few murmured instructions about medicines and increasing some fluids in the IV.

Jaxer, in turn, entered the instructions into a computer on a rolling cart that Cary hadn't noticed before. Had that been there just a minute ago? Or was that Jaxer's glamour at work.

And how the hell did he know what the doctor was talking about?

When the exam was over, Dr. Sharma said, "Let us know if anything changes, or if you start to feel worse. At the moment, everything looks good. The surgery went well. And you should be back on your feet in a few days. You'll have to take it easy. No more jumping in front of moving bullets." She smiled at that. "But after a few weeks and some physio, you should be mostly back to normal."

"Thank you, doctor," Cary said. Once she was gone, Cary looked at Deacon. "Does everyone know how I got shot?"

"A bystander told the EMTs when they were stabilizing you for transport. You don't remember?"

"Little blurry now. Getting shot hurts."

His jaw tightened, but he said, "Word got around the hospital. The woman you saved was brought in for a check, and she told everyone what happened, too."

Cary winced. "That's embarrassing. I hope no one gets the wrong idea."

"What wrong idea would that be?" Jaxer asked.

"I don't know." She shrugged.

For reasons she couldn't entirely explain, she was extremely uncomfortable with the fact that people were talking about what she'd done. What she'd done had been stupid because she wasn't a Protector anymore. She was *really* grateful the woman was alive and hadn't been hurt. But she didn't feel like people should be talking about what she'd done.

"How'd you get that computer in here?" she asked Jaxer to distract from the uncomfortable conversation.

He waved his fingers and the computer disappeared.

"Now all that stuff the doctor order won't be in my record," she pointed out.

"It will. That was a real machine, not glamour. I just returned it to the nurses' station." When she raised her brows, he said, "Glamour's not my only magical skill, you know."

Actually, she did sometimes forget that.

"The iron in it didn't bother you?" she murmured. Like all Fae, Jaxer had an allergy to iron and almost everything in the modern world had some iron in it somewhere. His allergy was very mild, so he could be inside buildings and things without it bothering him. But he didn't get into cars often, and he rarely used elevators if he could avoid them. And she'd never seen him use a cellphone or computer.

"A little discomfort. Not too bad," he said. "I can manage touching a computer if it's not too long. Plastic keyboard keys help."

Huh. The fact that she was just learning this about him after all these years felt weird. Especially since she'd been fired and she wasn't entirely sure how much longer he'd be in her life.

"So what now?" she asked.

"Now, you heal," Jaxer said. "Eriana will be in soon. And when you get home… We have some things to discuss."

His brow pinched, an obvious sign of emotion he didn't usually show her. She wasn't sure what the emotion was because his whole face seemed set in worry lines but she couldn't tell if this was worry or frustration or annoyance or something else. Jaxer claimed she could read him well, and sometimes she could. Sometimes she knew if he was hiding things from her. But at the moment, she couldn't decipher the expression on his face.

And that made her nervous.

"Am I going to hate this discussion when we have it?" she asked.

"Probably." He shrugged.

Well at least he was being honest with her. "Sure you don't want to start the conversation now while I'm getting the good drugs?"

That cracked his expression and he smiled a little. "It does seem a waste not to take advantage of the opportunity," he said. "But, no, this is better discussed in private."

"Can you tell me what's happening with…Holland and all that? Is that breaking any rules?" Not that she hadn't obviously broken some rules already, or she wouldn't have been fired.

"It's not. And I will. It's actually a necessary part of our discussion."

That didn't bode well. She frowned at him. "What does that mean?"

"That there's a lot to talk about."

"I hate waiting."

He grinned. "I know." He finally glanced at Deacon, before turning back to her. "I'm glad you're awake and doing better, love," he said quietly. "I'll be back soon." He squeezed her fingers, and the next moment, the sexy nurse stood at the edge of her bed.

Cary shook her head. "Don't cause too much trouble like that."

The woman that was Jaxer chuckled—which wasn't a reassuring sound—waved, and sauntered out the door.

Leaving Cary with more questions than answers. Questions she'd have to wait to ask.

She hated waiting.

20

$\mathcal{E}$riana came into the room looking exactly like her normal human self. No elaborate glamours to make her blend in to the hospital staff. No scrubs or stethoscopes or white doctor coats. Her human guise was a significantly different look to her normal Fae look —bearable and ordinary compared to her Fae appearance—but she didn't bother with the costuming that Jaxer loved.

Cary greeted her with a wane smile and a little wave. She was sleepy again. She seemed to be sleepy all day long, but she couldn't get comfortable enough to actually drift off, which left her in a kind of numb consciousness that was irritating. She'd finally sent Deacon down to the cafeteria to eat—she wasn't sure when he had last but she suspected it had been some time before she was shot—and she'd been watching TV, a gameshow she'd never seen before, which did nothing to distract her. Or help her sleep. So the visit from Eriana was a nice reprieve.

"How does your shoulder feel?" Eriana asked. She wasn't sharp or abrupt. She wasn't particularly kind either. An impressively neutral tone.

At least Cary found it impressive. That exact balance between interest and unconcern. She wondered how Eriana did that. Maybe it was a healer thing.

"Hurts," she said. Even with the good drugs, the pain was there, a dull ache underneath the painkillers. "Thanks for coming. You didn't have to."

"Jaxer asked me to."

"Wouldn't have otherwise, huh?" Cary said with a grin.

She and Eriana sort of got along, and this wasn't the first time Eriana had used her healer skills to help Cary. Hell, she'd saved Cary's life in Faery. But after that, they'd never really developed what Cary would consider a friendship. A sort of working truce felt like a better description.

Cary couldn't really get a proper sense of Eriana and what the healer thought of things. So she did her best to be neutral friendly and tried not to badger the woman with questions. Especially questions about Jaxer. And her relationship with Jaxer—both now and all those years ago when they'd manage to do so much emotional damage to each other. Cary's curiosity about the two was almost overwhelming, so she considered her restraint a sign that she should apply for some sort of sainthood position.

Hey, maybe that could be her next job.

She frowned a little. Or maybe she needed to cut back on the good drugs.

"I would have still helped," Eriana said, surprising Cary. "You got hurt saving a life. That deserves proper care."

"Thanks." She adjusted on the bed as Eriana got close enough to examine the bandages covering Cary's wound. "You heard about the fact that I'm not... Anymore."

"I heard."

Though Cary was staring at her face, Eriana kept her attention on Cary's shoulder.

"You think I should have been fired?" Cary asked, curious.

"Not my place to say. I haven't known you long enough. Or the Protectors for that matter."

"You're being trained to be a mentor, though, right?"

Neither Eriana nor Jaxer would confirm that, even though it was the reason Eriana had remained in the human world. In this part of the human world. She'd asked Wisat and Liruk for a job, and since she was still in Portland, Cary had assumed they'd given her that job. Still, no one would say for sure and that was irritating. It didn't seem like it should be a big deal to tell her since she'd been in the room when Eriana had asked for the job. They'd actually been in *her* bedroom. It seemed only common curtesy to tell her what had happened.

Or maybe not anymore. Since she was no longer a part of the Protector world.

"The surgeon did a good job on this," Eriana said, ignoring Cary's question.

"You can tell even with the bandage on?"

"I can feel the work done." Eriana's hands weren't glowing like they did when she was actively healing. But obviously the glow wasn't the only sign she was doing healer things.

"Deacon told me Dr. Sharma is one of the best surgeons in town. Guess I got lucky she was working."

Eriana met Cary's gaze. "You think that was luck?"

"It wasn't?"

Eriana blinked slowly. A reaction that gave Cary nothing.

"I won't do too much while you're still in hospital," Eriana said, without answering Cary's question. Again. "It would concern the doctors if you healed overnight. When you get home, I'll finish the healing to ensure no permanent damage. You'll still want to do some of the physiotherapy the doctors here will recommend."

"Fair enough. Why did you come into the hospital, then?"

"Jaxer asked me to. And I can help a little from here. Enough you should be able to sleep better. Around all the intrusive interruptions." Her mouth flattened. "Human hospitals are strange places that don't seem well designed for recovery."

"Suppose it does look that way after Faery," Cary said with a shrug.

"Faery wasn't perfect," Eriana said quietly. She set her hands gently against the bandages covering the holes in Cary's shoulder. "I'll ensure no infection sets in," she said, her eyes drifting shut. A faint blue light covered her hands as she hovered them against Cary's wounds.

The sensation was hard to describe but the best words Cary had for it were soft heat. Too warm to be warmth, like a bath, but close to that. Just a bit hotter. And gentle, like the heat seeped in slowly enough not to agitate her already raw nerve endings. That heat soothed over the pain, and if Cary concentrated, she could almost feel her shoulder healing.

That was probably her imagination. She was pretty sure Eriana wasn't doing that much to the wound. Eriana was right that sudden leaps in healing would alert the doctors to something being…not quite right in this situation. But the sensation of the healing left Cary feeling like she'd been given the best painkillers in existence. Her skin tingled a little, which meant she was probably absorbing magic. She'd need to figure out how to discharge that. But she'd worry about that later. Her eyes drifted shut as sleepiness overwhelmed her.

When she opened her eyes, Eriana was gone. She glanced at the big round analogue clock on the wall. Huh. She'd slept. For a couple of hours. That had felt good.

Now that she was awake again, and alone, she had a moment to take stock. Her body didn't feel quite as horrible as it had before Eriana's visit. But she still felt like she had a hole in her shoulder.

Shit. She had a hole in her shoulder. What the hell had she been thinking?

Same as the first time. She hadn't been thinking. And she'd gotten shot this time. She could have been killed. If the bullet had hit even a little more to the right, it would have gone through a lung or her heart. She could have died before having a chance to realize she'd made a mistake.

This wasn't good.

When Deacon walked through the door, she said, "After almost seven years, it's a habit now. I'm not going to be able to stop, am I?"

He settled into the chair next to her bed, the one he'd been living in since she'd landed in hospital, and met her gaze. "You've been thinking."

"Sleep and less pain will do that to me. The problem is, I'm not going to stop jumping in front of people, am I?"

"Nope. And it is definitely a problem."

"Cause I don't have anything to keep me from getting killed anymore."

His mouth tightened and little lines formed between his brow. "I've been thinking the same thing. You're not going to be able to stop. Maybe with some practice. But not quick enough to keep you from getting hurt again. Maybe worse."

She turned her good hand up and reached for him. He gripped her fingers, carefully gentle. The contact didn't loosen the lines around his mouth or across his forehead, but he didn't have glowing eyes so that was something.

"What am I going to do?" she said. "Short of turning myself into a Batman superhero with all the gadgets."

He shrugged, his gaze on her hand. "I don't know."

She frowned a little, also staring at their twinned fingers. "I mean. I could do that." She'd scoffed at the idea when Lucy had suggested it. But now... Maybe it wasn't such a ridiculous idea after all.

He looked up. "Become Batman?"

She tried for a smile that actually felt genuine. "Not quite. Although I do have a secret bat cave. It's an attic but close enough. No, I was thinking about something Lucy said. Marianne can make me some pretty impressive clothing. Angie and Rory can teach me how to use the magic I absorb. I have the last seven years of learning under my belt. I'm getting better at the physical fighting stuff thanks to Lucy." She squeezed his hand. "I could... Maybe I *could* take all that and learn how to use it. And just..."

"Keep protecting people," he said.

"It could work. If I'm prepared for my own stupid knee-jerk reactions, I'm a lot less likely to get killed. It's not the same as having an impenetrable shield, I know, but with the right gear and a new focus for my training. Maybe. It could work."

"You want to turn yourself into an actual superhero."

"It's silly, isn't it? I'm not capable of it without the Nags' magic. You're right. You're right."

"No. That's not what I'm saying. I actually, terrifyingly, think you are capable of it."

"You do?"

"I've been thinking the same thing. That we need to set you up so you can do what you do safely. Or as safely as possible. The Protector stuff... That's your instinct. It's who you are on a level that's not easy to change. You're not going to stop without a lot of effort, and before you retrain your instincts, you will get killed."

She squeezed his hand again.

"So I've been thinking we need to find a way for you to keep jumping in to save people without your shields, and without you getting hurt."

"I can't believe you were thinking the same thing. I expected an argument."

"If I thought you could give up jumping into danger, I would be arguing for that. But that's not who you are. I love who you are. Now we need to make sure you survive yourself."

"Ha." But she actually felt a loosening in her chest that she hadn't felt since being fired, a relaxing of tension she hadn't recognized was constantly in the background. "You think we can?"

"I think we can," he said. "I think *you* can."

"It's a little scary to think about."

"Good. You'll take the new training seriously."

"I wouldn't do this half-assed," she said, with a slight scowl. "If I'm doing this, it's all in."

"Sleep on it. You're not jumping anywhere for another few days. Let the idea sink in. If you're still convinced this is what you want to do, I've got your back. We'll make it work."

She tugged his hand so he stood and leaned close enough for a kiss. "Thank you."

21

She slept on her idea for the next two days, and mulled, and considered. It was a ridiculous idea. An impossible one. She wasn't a superhero. She wasn't Batman. She was just an ordinary woman now.

Except...

She had extraordinary friends who could help her with spells and clothes and training. She had a dragon teaching her how to use any magic she absorbed. She had seven years of experience running into the kind of danger most people ran away from.

And she felt the need to try.

She was still mulling it over, though, when she returned home from the hospital. Still not convinced she could make it work. There was nothing she could do to recreate the impenetrable Protector shield she'd lost. No Angie-made spells, no Marianne-made magic clothes, no Lucy-tested training, no dragon-magic lessons could recreate that shield. Spells could be broken. Charms and talismans damaged. Magic clothes had to be literally tailored to specific circumstances and couldn't cover every possible scenario in one piece. It would take years to get as physically skilled at fighting as Lucy. And Cary wasn't always going to be

140

jumping into situations where she'd absorb magic she could turn around and use.

As evidenced by the healing hole in her shoulder.

There was also the very real possibility that without the shield she'd absorb too much magic and die before she could use it. She had no idea what the balance was with that. What her changed and altered cells could take after all these years of absorbing magic in a way that didn't kill her. Had she reached a point where she could take in more magic than she might have before and *not* die?

No one could tell her. No one knew. There were no books that covered that contingency.

As a Protector, she'd always worried about failing and the person she was protecting dying. That fear would triple if she tried this, because she didn't have the Protector magic to rely on. She'd be solely relying on herself and what she could do.

The thought was terrifying.

She walked through the front door of her house still swirling through the same line of thinking that had kept her occupied throughout her hospital stay. Breaking the train of thought only when her dogs rushed forward to greet her.

"Hey guys!" She sank to her knees for the usual hugs and pets, but she had to be careful of her arm so the whole thing was a bit awkward. Fortunately, Buck and Pickles seemed to realize her left shoulder was a no-touch place. Fred, on the other hand, had to be gently guided away from the injury twice before he stopped trying to throw himself against her bad shoulder.

"It'll be all better soon," she promised him, giving him an ear scratch. "After Eriana has a chance to really get in and fix things, I'll be able to hug and play freely again."

Deacon helped her to her feet—which was a lot harder to do with only one good arm. Marianne stood from her spot on the couch and greeted Cary with a gentle hug.

"You're not at work," Cary said.

"I wanted to be here when you got home," Marianne said. "Lashana is watching the store. She's got it handled."

"Thanks for house sitting and dog sitting," Cary said. "I hope they were good for you?"

"Very good. I love your pack." Marianne scratched Buck's head when he bumped against her hip.

It had occurred to Cary the last time Marianne had looked after the dogs for her that now that Marianne was no longer with Gina, who'd been allergic to pet dander, Marianne could have a dog of her own. She'd meant to discuss that with the girls, maybe even get Marianne a dog for her birthday, which was coming up soon. Given everything going on in Cary's life, and the fact that she hadn't heard from Angie since she'd had the idea, she should probably push it back to a Christmas present option. Still, she felt bad for forgetting, so she made a mental note to say something to Lucy and Angie soon. As soon as they heard from Angie again.

"How are you feeling?" Marianne asked.

"Sore and stiff and looking forward to magic healing. I have to say, I would be a whole lot more unhappy about getting shot if I didn't have a magic healer nearby to help." She one-arm hugged Marianne again. "Thanks for the cloth that slowed the bleeding. That stuff is brilliant."

"Try not to get shot again. That nearly gave me a heart attack."

"About that..." She let out a breath. "I may have something to discuss with you later, but I'm still thinking about it. I'll want to talk with Lucy and Angie, too."

Marianne narrowed her eyes. "Am I gonna like this conversation or hate it?"

"Not sure yet. That's why I'm still thinking."

"You let me know when you're ready to talk."

"Thanks." She settled heavily onto the couch. After several days in bed, standing up felt great, but she couldn't seem to do it for very long. "Speaking of Angie, have you heard from her?"

"Not yet. Not still. And I have to tell you, I'm really worried now."

"Me too. I know she can handle herself, but the silence is really bothering me."

"I'll try to track her down while you're getting your shoulder magically healed. If I can't, maybe we find a way to go looking for her."

"Yeah. Yeah, I think that's a good idea." Angie's silence and absence had stretched too long. Cary was glad she wasn't the only one really worried. "Keep me updated."

They talked about easier topics for a bit, until Cary's eyes started to droop, then as if they'd coordinated it, Marianne said her goodbyes and Deacon walked her to the door. She couldn't hear what they said at the door because she didn't have super shifter hearing and they kept their voices low.

So when Deacon settled on the couch next to her, she said, "Did you tell her about my idea?"

"Of course not," he said, sounding annoyed. "You said you aren't ready to talk about it yet."

She smiled, though her eyes were closed. She was gonna be asleep any minute now. Wow, normal healing took a long time. And left her exhausted. She'd forgotten. And no magical sleeps that miraculous cured all her ills anymore. She was going to miss that.

"What did you two say?" she asked, leaning against him because he'd sat on her good side and she could. "You're very warm," she murmured. "I love that."

He kissed the top of her head. "She asked about the surgery and your recovery. Infections. Any complications. She just needed some reassurance."

"I hate that she's worried about me." He was silent long enough, she stirred herself back to something like consciousness to look up at him. "Say it."

He raised his brows in question.

"I know you're not saying something. Just spit it out. You think I'll worry her more if I try this ridiculous superhero idea of mine, don't you?"

"I think you'll worry her more if you don't," he said on a sigh. "The same reason I think this might be the only way to keep you safe. You'll keep jumping. And keep getting hurt. Marianne knows you well enough to know that too."

She released a long breath and settled against him again, closing her eyes. "I'm too tired to think about it properly. But…"

"But?"

"I think I might have to try. I… I don't know how to be anyone else. This is who I am. At least now. I blame Jaxer."

"I blame him, too."

She grinned. None of this was Jaxer's fault, of course. And it was sort of rude to blame him. But he could take it. What was a little pettiness between friends.

As if saying his name summoned him, her doorbell rang. And kept ringing as someone held his annoying faery finger to it.

She chuckled. "I need to start teasing him about being Beetlejuice."

Her dad had loved that movie, so she'd seen it a lot when she was a kid. Which reminded her, she should probably call her mom and dad soon. Make sure they didn't hear about her getting shot from anyone but her. And if they hadn't heard, well, maybe she wouldn't tell them. Her parents thought she did research for a former professor who wrote popular science books. The less they knew about her actual—now-former—job, the better for everyone's nerves.

"Don't get up," Deacon said, rising himself to answer the door.

She kept her eyes closed because she was too tired to open them. There was more murmuring at the door. She heard Jaxer's voice. And Eriana's, though she only said a few words.

"Hi," Cary called to them all without opening her eyes. "I'm going to sleep. Good time for a healing. I'll be a better patient."

Jaxer's chuckle made her grin. She finally forced her eyes open to look at them. "I'm only joking a little. I'm about to fall asleep over here. Getting shot sucks. Can we do the healing stuff while I sleep?"

"We can," Eriana said as she came slowly into the house. She glanced at the dog pack, now arrayed under the bay window, soaking up some afternoon sunlight. Pickles lifted her head briefly and let out a low woof of greeting, but that was all the attention they paid Eriana.

Which was a little strange. Fred, at the least, should have gotten up to bounce off her leg in greeting.

Instead, all three went back to snoozing and ignoring the newcomers.

Huh. Buck didn't even stare at Jaxer. For a little while there, Buck and Jaxer had had a strange series of interactions, with Buck staring Jaxer down. But ever since Faery, Buck had stopped doing that. Had he stopped before Faery? She couldn't remember now. The staring had been strange enough. The fact that he'd randomly stopped staring was equally strange. She wished she could talk to Buck and find out what all that had been about.

She wished she could talk to all three now and find out why they were mostly ignoring Eriana.

She did know someone who could talk to animals. Jon Webber worked with Deacon's sister at the animal shelters now. Well, volunteered because he was too young to have a job. Though Cary knew for certain Caitlin slipped him money under the table for his "volunteer" work. Maybe she could ask Jon to come over and translate for her.

Eriana sat on the couch next to her, and Cary shook her head a little to refocus on the present.

"Just relax," Eriana said. "It's fine if you sleep. That will help. Not as much as a magical healing sleep, but sleep is always good."

"Yeah it is," Cary said with feeling. She loved a good sleep.

"Today, I'll work on repairing the inner damage caused by the bullet, the things the surgeon couldn't fix. I'll need another session, maybe tomorrow, to finish that work and seal the outer wound completely. Fair enough?"

"Perfect. So long as I can sleep, you can do whatever you need to do." She paused before closing her eyes to meet Eriana's. "And thanks. You've... You've done a lot for me. For us. Since Faery. And I appreciate that."

Eriana's expression was always hard for Cary to read. That moment was no different. But the little straightening of Eriana's shoulders, the way Eriana nodded, the way her gaze flickered away and back to Cary... There was something about the reaction Cary thought might be important.

Rather than reveal anything, though, Eriana just told Cary to close her eyes, and she started the healing. As Cary sank into her exhaustion, it occurred to her again that she was absorbing magic as Eriana worked. Healing magic. She'd better ask about that when she woke up, if there was a way she needed to dissipate it. Especially since this was the second time Eriana had done a healing on her, and she'd need to do this one more time. Maybe she could light some candles with the absorbed magic to get it back out of her system.

But that could wait. Eriana's healings didn't leave her tingling, like other magic thrown at her, anyway. They just left her feeling good.

And true to her tired word, she fell asleep.

22

$\mathcal{D}$eacon listened for Cary's breathing as she fell asleep, waited for her to be fully out before he faced Jaxer.

"You should have warned her she was about to be fired," he said, his tone low so he wouldn't disturb Eriana. There was a growl in his voice that hadn't been there in a while, at least in his dealings with Jaxer. Things had changed since Faery, in a way neither of them had discussed. But he hadn't had any overwhelming urges to strangle the faery since then, and he counted that as a win.

Until now, anyway. Because now, his mate was hurt, his mate was miserable, his mate was considering turning herself into a Protector without all the magic, and he was going to help her do it because it was the only way he could see to keep her safe.

And he hated every single part of that sentence. He wanted to take that anger out on someone. Jaxer had the bad luck of being that person.

Jaxer pulled in a deep breath and didn't meet Deacon's gaze. He didn't automatically defend himself either.

"Well," Deacon snarled, unable to control his frustration. "Why didn't you tell her? Why didn't you warn her?"

"Because she wasn't supposed to be 'fired'," Jaxer said.

"What?"

Another long breath. "This was supposed to be part of the test year."

"Getting fired?" Deacon's temper flashed hot. He snarled and leaned into Jaxer. "Explain that. Now."

"I need to explain it to Cary first."

"She's asleep. If you want the chance to talk to her when she wakes up, you need to explain to me now."

"This is her job. You can't interfere."

"Stop prevaricating and trying to piss me off more. It's not helping. Talk. Now. This is the second time you've told me something was happening with Cary that wasn't supposed to when it comes to this job."

The first time was when Jaxer admitted Cary wasn't supposed to be getting hurt through her Protector shields. And that he and her bosses didn't know why she got hurt. They'd eventually learned it was because she absorbed magic. But when Jaxer had first told Deacon that, Deacon had crushed a rock into dust. This moment wasn't any better. His leopard was right at the surface, his control thin, and he was certain he could pulverize a boulder in that moment. His anger at this situation was overwhelming, and he needed answers.

"My mate was shot. I'm about to rip heads off, Jaxer. Make sure it's not yours."

Jaxer's mouth flattened, but to his credit, he didn't attempt to turn this into more of a fight. He glanced around Deacon to the couch, where Eriana was still quietly working on Cary's shoulder.

"Let me tell her when she wakes up," he said when he faced Deacon again. "This is part of the test year. Or at least it was supposed to be. I have to explain it to her. But…" He raised a hand when Deacon opened his mouth. "I'll tell you what I can."

"You'll tell me everything."

"What I can," Jaxer emphasized. "Because there are some things I don't know."

"I hate everything you just said."

Jaxer snorted. "You're not the only one." He glanced once more at Eriana and Cary, then said, "The 'firing' is supposed to be part of the test. It doesn't happen with all Protectors during their seventh year. But at this point in the year, there's always some sort of…reversal to push the Protector. To push them into owning their role. Cary has always insisted she was tricked into this job. So it was decided—"

"By who?"

"By my bosses' boss," Jaxer said. "It was decided this particular test was best for her."

"Cutting her loose and letting her think she'd failed? That was best for her? Leaving her vulnerable while she kept jumping in to save people? That was best for her?"

"That's the thing. She wasn't supposed to get hurt. *If* she jumped in to help someone, *if* she kept doing her job even when she *knew* she didn't have the magic shields to help, that was supposed to be how she passed this test."

"Meaning?"

"Meaning, her Protector powers should have flowed back into her the minute she tried to save someone. When she jumped in the way of that bullet, her powers should have returned and stopped the bullet."

"That was the second time she jumped in to save someone," Deacon said. "The same woman as it turned out. But the shooting was the second time she put herself in danger to rescue someone."

"Second time?" Jaxer's frown turned fierce as he glared at the floor.

"Second. And yet, she was still shot. Still nearly killed. Again. No magic, Jaxer. No shields."

"And that's the part I can't explain," Jaxer said, his jaw tight. "I haven't been able to find Wisat and Liruk, either. They aren't giving me any answers."

"How about their boss?"

"I don't get to see him. The Mentors aren't allowed in his presence once we start officially working. I've only seen him once, just before taking on my first mentee. He doesn't deal with us otherwise. That's up to our immediate bosses. Wisat and Liruk in this case."

"Jaxer." Deacon's temper flashed so hot, the cliché of seeing red felt real. "They took away her ability to protect while Oliver Fucking

Holland is on his way here. While the fucking Angel of Death is still expecting to talk with her. James approached her in daylight to tell her the Angel wants to see to her. While a goddamn demon god is about to burst into the world again. A demon god who *hates* her. She. Is. In. Trouble." He had his jaw clenched so tight as he tried to hold in his temper, he was afraid he'd crack a tooth. "And you people have done this to her."

"I would never," Jaxer hissed, leaning in close to Deacon. "You know I wouldn't. You know how I feel about her. I don't want her hurt. I don't want her killed. And I'm as angry about this as you are. Rein in your leopard. You losing control won't help Cary."

Deacon blinked a few times. He glanced down and realized claws had burst out of his fingertips.

Fuck.

He retracted the claws, but the sight shook him. Badly enough he had to lean against a wall. He hadn't lost control like that since last January. Not even in Faery. And Faery was practically designed to challenge his control. Even after he was certain he'd lost Cary forever, the only thing he'd felt then was pain and hollowness. And a determination to follow her.

This was different. She'd risked herself in Faery. She'd purposefully taken that risk to save the world. She'd done that before, and he knew with absolutely certainty, she'd do it again. It was who she was, and he loved her as she was.

This was someone *else* putting her into danger. Someone *else* throwing her to the wolves. Leaving her vulnerable. Risking her life.

And he hated that with every ounce of his being.

Obviously so much, he couldn't control his nature as strictly as he normally did. Which made him dangerous to everyone around him, but most especially to his own people.

People he'd recently called in to Portland to help him keep his mate safe.

He closed his eyes and let out a long breath. "Sorry," he muttered to Jaxer, his eyes still closed.

"Trust me, I understand."

Deacon nodded. That was, unfortunately for all of them, true. Although, since Faery…

He wasn't sure how to describe it. He could still scent Jaxer's feelings for Cary. He still loved her. But it was almost like…like he'd stopped fighting to win her. Deacon hadn't been able to parse out the change completely since they'd gotten back, even though it had been a couple of months. He just knew Jaxer's intentions had changed toward her in some way. And that had made all the difference to how he and Jaxer got along.

Deacon acknowledged, reluctantly and only to himself, that the fact that Jaxer had been by his side when Cary died had been… Something. Comforting maybe. He hesitated to call it that. In that moment, Jaxer lost his father as well. And somewhere in all that grief had come an understanding between them.

He owed Jaxer better than an out-of-control temper for that moment alone he supposed. Especially since none of this was Jaxer's fault.

He wouldn't admit that to the faery. But he would keep his claws in.

"What now?" he asked. "What do we do? What do we tell her? How do we find out what went wrong?" He met Jaxer's gaze. "How do we fix this?"

"I don't know." He leaned against the wall next to Deacon and they both looked at Cary and Eriana on the couch, Cary sound asleep, a blue glow surrounding Eriana's hands as she worked on Cary's shoulder.

"Cary is going to turn herself into a Protector without the magic," Deacon said, his voice very low. "She's going to learn how to use the magic she absorbs. She'll get better protective clothes from Marianne. She'll train more with Lucy." He didn't look at Jaxer, but the spike of confusion and fear in his scent assured Deacon the man understood what this meant. "She'll keep trying to save people. She can't help it. It's who she is. And she knows that."

"She's not… She can't do that."

"She can. She will. And I'll help. Because it'll be the one way I can at least try to keep her from getting killed."

"She doesn't have… Deacon, without the Protector shields, there's no way she can fend off everything she'll encounter. She won't have a barrier to all that magic. The first time she's hit with a big enough shot of it…"

Jaxer didn't have to finish the sentence. Deacon knew what he was saying. Hell, they'd both seen the results of that already.

"She hasn't completely decided yet. She says she's still thinking about it. She understands the reality of what she's considering." He shrugged. "She'll still do it."

Jaxer's sigh was audible. "Fucking hell. She will, won't she."

Deacon nodded.

"We have to help her."

Deacon nodded again.

23

---

eacon and Jaxer watched the rest of the healing in silence from their place against the wall, the reality of what was happening hanging between them. The absence of answers a thick lump in Deacon's throat.

By the time Eriana finished, Cary was deeply asleep. Somewhat to Deacon's surprise, Eriana nudged Cary over so she was resting comfortably on the couch, then went down the hall toward the bedrooms without comment.

Deacon raised his brows at Jaxer. Jaxer shrugged.

Eriana came back out with a blanket and gently settled it over Cary.

The kindness surprised Deacon. Eriana had never warmed to Cary. They weren't at each other's throats. They just weren't particularly friendly. And Eriana's scent hadn't given him much of a reason for the faery's reaction to his mate. He'd have assumed jealousy, since Eriana was still—despite her best intentions—in love with Jaxer. At least that's what Deacon had been able to parse out of her scent. Given how Jaxer felt about Cary, he would have assumed jealousy would be the natural reason for Eriana's distance. But…that acrid punch of bitterness didn't seem to be there in the otherwise complex mix.

It was possible Eriana was changing her scent, hiding things she didn't want a shifter to know, using Fae magic. Jaxer was able to disguise his scent when he wanted to. When he bothered. But he was also excellent at glamour. Eriana was proficient with glamour magic because she was a Fae, but her skills weren't up to Jaxer's level. Her power was in her healing magic. Tough to say if she could hide something as volatile as jealousy from him.

"She'll probably sleep for a few hours," Eriana said quietly when she joined him and Jaxer. "I got a lot of the internal damage repaired. One more session will finish the job." She glanced over her shoulder, frowning.

"What?" Deacon asked, straightening from the wall. "What's wrong?"

"Nothing's wrong," Eriana said. "Outside of her getting shot. But something is…different."

"What are you talking about?"

"When I use magic on her, she absorbs it. Some of it anyway. Not just the magic I'm purposefully applying to the wounds and the healing. My healing magic is…renewable. I give some of it during a healing, with everyone, but she can't drain me the way she drained Sheldon because that's not how my magic works. With everyone else, what they take of my magic gets turned into natural functioning of their bodies. Mundane or Fae both, the magic is…transformed into the things their body would always do. They don't hold the base magic I use. She does."

Eriana faced them, still frowning. "That wound wasn't as bad as it should have been today. I saw her in the hospital. I saw the work the surgeon did. It was good, but it was very…human. There's a progression to human injuries. A natural flow and process. It's not an absolute, there are variations for individuals, but the process only goes so fast without magical help. And Cary was way ahead of where she should have been."

Deacon looked at Jaxer. "Did Wisat and Liruk leave her healing ability when they took the shields? We'd assumed her ability to heal faster than normal got taken away with the other Protector magic."

As well as her slower aging. The fact that she'd go back to aging like an ordinary human would eventually be something they'd have to deal with. She'd die a lot sooner than he would even if they both managed to grow old. But that seemed the least of their problems at the moment.

"All aspects of being a Protector were suspended," Jaxer said, his brow creased as he looked at Cary. "The healing, the shields... All of it. She was back to her ordinary human self for the test."

"Could the other things, like healing, have returned even though the shield didn't?"

Since all this was just supposed to be a test and she'd absolutely passed the test by trying to rescue people even knowing she didn't have the shield, maybe she was mostly back to Protector status just without the all important shields. Not that that made things much better. But her ability to heal fast after getting injured was at least something they could work with until they figured out how to get her shields back.

If they could get her shields back.

He only realized in that moment that he was expecting her to go back to being a full Protector once they figured out *why* the shield hadn't returned when it should have. As he'd watched Eriana heal her shoulder, and considered how best to help Cary take on the task of protecting others without the shield, he'd been thinking of that as a temporary fix, a short term solution to keep her alive until they figured out what went wrong with the test. A way to keep her doing her work —which she was going to do shield or not—until her bosses figured out how to get the magic to flow back into her again.

"It's all part of the same thing, the same magic," Jaxer said. "But maybe. Since nothing like this has happened before, at least not that I've heard, I have no idea."

"It doesn't feel like the Protector healing," Eriana said. "I felt that when I helped her recover after Faery. I wasn't working...alone, for lack of a better word, on that healing. I had help from the magic Wisat and Liruk gave her. But that's not what this is."

"It's your magic? What she's absorbed?" Deacon's heart started to beat a little faster, but he wasn't sure if it was from hope or terror. With Cary, those two emotions seemed to mix a lot.

"I can sense some of what she's absorbed from me in that healing, but it's still not just that. It's not *only* my magic. But it's not the Protector magic. It's…different. Something has changed."

"Is that good or bad?" Deacon asked, working to swallow the faint growl in his throat. Jaxer was right, letting his leopard take the lead wouldn't help Cary. But his control was strained.

Eriana shrugged. "I have no idea. She's healing. And healing faster than a human. That has to be good, right?"

"She must be using the magic she's absorbed to do that," Jaxer said, "so she's not going to be overwhelmed by it."

Which settled Deacon's rising fear. After Faery, he wanted to insulate Cary from all magic, just so nothing like that happened ever again. He wanted to refuse magic in their lives the way he refused to use his own magic. If she wasn't around it, she couldn't absorb it, she couldn't die from too much of it. But that wasn't going to happen. There was no way to keep her wrapped up in wool and safe from all magic. She was safer doing what she was doing, learning with the dragon how to use what she absorbed.

Still, he hated all of this and just wanted his mate safe.

"Does she need to absorb some magic from you first," Deacon asked Eriana, "before her body takes it and uses it to heal?"

"I barely did anything in the hospital," Eriana said. "I didn't use enough magic for her to be healing this way. I haven't done anything on that level with her since Faery. It's not just the fact that she's recently taken in my magic and was able to use it now. This isn't that simple."

Deacon closed his eyes. He didn't know what was happening to his mate and the frustration brought his leopard roaring to the surface, desperate to help her without knowing what to do. Which only made his leopard angry.

And dangerous.

"She's changing," Eriana said. She let out a sigh as she frowned a little. "I'm not sure how to explain this. She's never been precisely human. During the healings. I haven't worked on mundane humans in a very long time, but when I was training with Grainne, I did. In the human world. We had to be subtle of course." She waved a hand. "What I'm trying to say is that working on Cary has never felt exactly like working with someone…not magical. I assumed it was the Protector magic flowing through her at first. Then learning she absorbed some, I thought it was that."

"But?" Deacon cleared his throat, forcing down the growl she might misunderstand.

"Not really a 'but' so much as a 'now.' Now, I'm sure that what she's been absorbing is changing her." She glanced at Jaxer. "Did you know?"

"That she was changing?" He shrugged. "Rory introduced the idea, that it was possible all that magic was changing her at a cellular level. But none of us knew how or to what end."

"Or if it was something permanent, or something that would…wear off once she used the magic," Deacon added. "She got caught up in the Sheldon thing before we could really explore the idea. And after… Between waiting for the demon fight and getting fired, she's been distracted."

"Well, I can confirm that at a cellular level, she's not precisely a mundane human. Yet she's also not fully magical. Or at least she wasn't the last time I healed her." Eriana glanced back at Cary again. "But that seems to be changing."

"Wait," Jaxer said. "Are you telling us, she's becoming *more* magical? Less mundane?"

"Yes." Eriana looked at them both again. "I can't tell when the change started or if this is a change that's always been happening. I haven't known her long enough and haven't been her healer long enough to judge if this is happening faster than it did before, or if this is just the normal pace. She's still not… She still doesn't feel like a magical being would, or even like a shifter or vampire. There's still an underlying…mundaneness to her. It's not like anything I've worked with before to be honest. She's different."

"What does all this mean, though?" Deacon said, slowly, working to unclench his jaw. All he wanted was his mate to be safe. And the fact that the universe seemed to be conspiring against that did not help his control even a little bit.

"It means that I don't know what it means," Eriana said. "Any more than you do. Or anyone else for that matter. I've never known a human who absorbs magic. I know she's not ordinary, and hasn't been since I met her. I can tell you, based on this healing, that her body is using what it absorbs, even without her conscious effort. The magic isn't *just* building up in her cells. And it's not just changing them. She's using that magic—even if she's not doing it on purpose."

"Which is how she's healing faster than she should, but still not at the speeds she might as a Protector?"

"As far as I can tell," Eriana said. "If the Protector magic still flowed through her, that wound would have healed days ago. Probably after she slept for ten or twelve hours." She made a face. "Though if she was still channeling that magic should wouldn't have gotten so severely wounded by something as brutish as a gun."

Deacon was on the verge of pointing out Fae still used swords to fight, which were also a brutish way to kill someone. Hacking at limbs and stabbing through the gut wasn't any less "brutish" than a bullet ripping through delicate bone and muscles. But he didn't want to get the conversation off track.

He also realized, with some surprise, that the side issue about what was a more brutish weapon was more like something Cary would say.

Hmm.

"Could this have something to do with why the Protector magic didn't return when it should have?" Jaxer asked. "I know you're not —" He cut himself off. "Could the changes have affected the way the test was supposed to end?"

Deacon didn't miss the fact that Jaxer had nearly said something out loud he didn't intend to. Eriana had asked to train as a Mentor. Cary was certain that was happening and that Jaxer was the one teaching her. Deacon would bet money Jaxer's near slip was more evidence he was training Eriana. That was something Cary would loved to hear.

And the fact that she hadn't because she was sleeping because she'd been shot was something that made Deacon want to smash things.

His shook his head a little. He was unfocused and angry and not fully in control. Which he hated almost as much as Cary getting shot. What they were talking about was important. He had to concentrate on that and not his anger. Especially if he wanted to keep his leopard in line.

"It's possible," Eriana answered Jaxer's question. "But I can't be sure. Has anything like this happened with another Protector? Don't most of them usually have some kind of magic at their disposal? The ability to channel Protector magic isn't ordinarily affected by the Protector's innate magic. Why would Cary's?"

"Cary's 'magic' isn't innate," Deacon said. "And it's not just one kind."

Jaxer frowned at him, but his gaze was turned inward. Deacon waited him out, waiting for him to consider what was said. He flexed his fingers a few times to release some of his tension. It didn't help much.

"Cary didn't have any of this other magic when she first started channeling Protector magic," Jaxer said slowly. "She channeled Protector magic really easily too. Right from the beginning. There was no barrier, no...other magic that had to be taken into consideration. But... But that's not the case anymore." He started for the door. "I'm going to hunt down Wisat and Liruk. Wherever the hell they're hiding. I'll be back."

He walked out the door and disappeared into a sidewalk tree before Deacon could stop him and ask questions.

Deacon cursed and started to slam the door shut, stopping only at the last minute because he didn't want to wake Cary. He spun on Eriana, but she just looked at him with her neutral, resigned expression. Giving him nothing to rage at. And since he didn't want to rage at the person who'd just helped Cary heal, he closed his eyes and took a few moments to breathe and get his leopard leashed.

When he opened his eyes, Eriana nodded. "Your eyes aren't glowing anymore."

Said as if to reassure him. He shook his head. "Fuck."

"You love her. It's hard not to get mad." Again said so matter-of-factly.

"Can you tell me anything else about how she's healing faster? What's happening to her?"

"Only that something is happening. I don't know where it will end, where this all goes. I doubt anyone will. There's never been anyone like her, who does what she does, and survives it. She took in a whole lot of Faery magic and survived—"

"Because you brought her back," Deacon felt compelled to point out. "She wouldn't have if you hadn't been there."

"But she did. And before that, what…demon god magic. More demon magic. Wizards. Witches. Dragons. She's been building and combining a *lot* of powers that don't usually combine together." Eriana nodded back at Cary without looking away from Deacon. "Even that little necklace she wears all the time, with the blessed charm on it. That's a little bit of good luck magic she's been absorbing almost constantly."

Deacon snorted. "Good luck? She was just shot and nearly killed."

"She was shot in a place that didn't kill her. The bullet missed her lungs. Her heart. There's no permanent nerve damage."

"Thanks to you," Deacon pointed out again.

"And one of the best surgeons in Portland attending to her. Isn't that a nice coincidence that both an excellent surgeon and a Fae healer happened to be around after she got shot? Might even call it good luck."

Deacon blinked. He'd never considered that before.

"As far as I understand how this works from Jaxer, in this realm she only absorbs what's sent at her. But over the last nearly seven years, that's been a lot. It makes sense she wouldn't be the same as she was anymore. It's logical that she'd be changing."

"The problem is, we don't know how." He huffed out a breath, his gaze settling on his mate, on the steady, gentle rise and fall of her shoulders as she slept curled onto her uninjured side. "How can I keep her safe if I don't know what I'm fighting?" he asked quietly.

"Maybe this isn't something you have to fight," Eriana said, her voice also quieter. "Maybe all this is a good thing. She lives in a magical world now. She always will because of you. And she's proven she can't stop jumping in to save people, even if she wants to."

Deacon snorted.

"So her changing, and learning how to use those changes... That all sounds good to me." She paused. "I overheard you and Jaxer. About her plan to continue protecting even without the Protector magic. I think she can do it with the right training." She shrugged. "I don't know her as well as you, obviously. I haven't even known her very long. But... I think this was something she was born to do. And one way or the other, I think she'll succeed."

Deacon looked closer at Eriana. The healer's confidence in Cary and her plan caught him by surprise.

"She doesn't think you like her," he found himself saying.

"I didn't at first." Eriana's expression finally cracked a little to reveal a very faint smile. "She grows on you."

He might have laughed if he wasn't worried it would wake his mate.

"I'll leave you two to rest and be back tomorrow for the final healing." Her expression had returned to the neutral, impossible to read one she wore most of the time. She left with a little wave, and after a quick scan of the road, walked into the same sidewalk tree Jaxer had disappeared into.

Deacon returned to the living room, settling into one of the chairs bracketing the coffee table, so he could watch over his mate as she slept. Savoring the moment of peace, knowing she was okay. For now.

Even as he worried about the future.

Cary woke slowly, assessing the various aches and pains in her body. Not as many as before. In fact, she was feeling decently. Not as good as she usually did after a magical healing sleep, but better rested than the entire time she'd been in the hospital. She rolled her injured shoulder. A little stiff but not aching. That was good.

Slowly, she sat up. She was still on the couch, a blanket covering her. Deacon sat in the chair closest to her head. She smiled at his closed eyes.

"Do I have you to thank for the blanket?" she asked.

He opened his eyes and smiled back. "No. Eriana got it for you before I could."

That was a surprise. Eriana was an excellent healer with a less-than-excellent bedside manner most of the time. She always surprised Cary when she showed those little kindnesses.

"What time is it?" She looked around the living room. The clock on her TV cable box said it was after noon. She'd missed lunch. "Ha. No wonder I'm hungry. Arm injuries do not dampen my appetite."

"We'll order pizza as a welcome home present."

She grinned.

"How do you feel?"

"Better. Less achy, more stiff now. I'd say that's good news. Eriana really does do good work."

"She does." He glanced at his lap a moment before meeting her gaze again. "She... I'm not sure how to tell you this."

"Well starting that way just sent a rush of anxiety through my body, so maybe cut to the chase."

He let out a soft huff, not quite a laugh, and said, "She says you're healing faster than an ordinary human. Not as fast as you did as a Protector, but still faster than you should be healing without magical help."

"Really? Did she say how? Why?" Cary sat up a little straighter, pushing the blanket to one side of the couch.

Deacon joined her, sitting next to her uninjured side and taking her hand in his. Touching him had become such an important part of her life, she felt instantly settled with that small contact. A mate thing. Less worrying that it used to be.

"She doesn't know for sure, because of course none of us do. But she thinks it's something to do with all the magic you've absorbed over the years and the way you change it. And the way you're changing." He stared down at her hand. "She says, since the first time she healed you, she could tell you weren't just an ordinary human."

Cary let out a breath. "So Rory was right. All this...stuff *is* changing me." She'd known. Since Rory had brought it up, she'd had time to think and consider the idea. And she'd known, on some level, he was right. But hearing it confirmed by a healer, who could see those changes at the cellular level was...a lot. "I'm not sure what to do with this."

"Nothing different," Deacon said. "Keep training with Rory. Use what you absorb."

"But the changes could affect that, right? I mean... I don't know, it seems like it should."

"Maybe. But wouldn't Rory know that? He's the one who brought this all up in the first place."

"What did Eriana say about my healing faster? How fast?"

"She wasn't specific except that it was faster than a human and slower than a Protector."

"Hm. Not as good, but still might be helpful."

Deacon fell silent a moment before saying, "You're thinking of your plan."

"Yeah. I mean, I won't have a Protector shield anymore. I'll probably get hurt more." She sighed. She'd gotten hurt often enough as a Protector. Her medical records were a mess. Oh, shit… "I need to figure out some health insurance going forward," she said aloud, and made a face. "My medical records are going to complicate that."

"I'll set you up with our business insurance. I don't want you to worry about that."

"I don't work for your business. Can you do that?"

"Family can be included. You're my family."

Ah. That gave her a soft, melty feeling in her chest. She leaned in and kissed him. "Thank you. One less thing now, right?" She went back to contemplating her healing. "I think I'd better talk to Eriana about this healing business. See how fast it's happening."

"There's more," Deacon said. "Jaxer should be back soon with more information. I hope. But he didn't tell me I couldn't tell you this, so…"

Cary felt her gut tighten. "What?"

"Your powers were supposed to come back. The first time you dove in to save someone, knowing you didn't have the shield and doing it anyway? The shield was supposed to return. It was a test."

Cary blinked. She stared at his face for a long moment trying to make sense of the words that had just come out of his mouth because they were getting all jumbled up in her mind and she was positive she'd heard him wrong because he couldn't have just said…

"It was a test?"

He nodded.

"They fired me. They made me believe I'd failed. They threw me to the wolves. With Oliver Holland on his way here. The Angel of Death looking for me. Vampires hanging out in the background. A literal *demon god* about to descend on this world. And it was all...a test."

He nodded again.

She didn't miss the faint glow of his leopard in his eyes.

Which was good. Because knowing he was that angry, angry enough that his control was tenuous, made her feel a lot better about what she was about to say.

"Those son of a bitches!" She threw her blanket off her lap and rose to stalk the living room. She couldn't have remained sitting if she'd wanted to. The sudden lurch upward didn't do her shoulder any favors, but thanks to Eriana, she could stalk and rage without doing permanent damage. "Those absolute assholes. They were *testing* me? Within a test. They gave me *another test*? What the hell? What the fucking hell?"

She continued to stomp around and curse and rage because it helped release all the fear and anger and hurt.

The hurt nearly overwhelmed her. Like she'd been betrayed by people she thought she could trust. And she had, damn it. She had trusted Liruk and Wisat even when she fought with them. Even when she was mad, annoyed, or frustrated with them. Even in those times when she didn't like them very much. She'd still trusted them. Trusted they weren't *actively* trying to get her killed.

This smashed all that trust into tiny little sandy pieces of misery.

"A test. What the hell did they think I'd do after seven years? Stand by and just...watch people get hurt? Just go hide in my house for the next two months."

And damn but hadn't she been tempted to do just that at first. Which made all this worse. But that had been because she was afraid of the enemies she'd made, not because she wanted to stop helping people.

That thought just reminded her that her bosses had purposefully left her vulnerable to her enemies. One of them could have killed her before she even got a chance to protect someone and get her powers back.

She stopped in her pacing to face Deacon again. "I did jump in and save someone. Twice. Why the hell didn't I get my powers back?"

A muscle along Deacon's jaw jumped. A sign he was clenching his teeth. Hard.

"No one knows," he said.

The growl in his voice made the hairs on her neck rise. An instinctive reaction to the sound of a predator.

"No one knows," she repeated, slowly. Feeling her own internal predator rise—even though she didn't think she actually had one. But the anger. Oh, she had a lot of that. "No one knows!"

She couldn't take it all in. She was so overwhelmed by the anger and hurt she didn't know what to do with herself. She paced to one side of the room. Swung around and paced back. Buck looked up from his spot by the window to watch her. Pickles kept her head resting on her feet, but her eyes were open and she tracked Cary's circuit of the room. Fred, usually pretty oblivious, sat up and wagged his tail as she passed, then settled back on his bed, his chin resting on the edge of the enclosed pillow as he watched her, too.

She wanted to say something to reassure her little pack that everything was okay, except everything wasn't okay. The people she'd been working for for seven years had hung her out to dry. They'd taken away the shields that kept her and others safe *just* when one of her biggest enemies was on his way here and the possible destruction of the world loomed. And then they didn't know how to give her that shield back. They took it away without knowing how to reverse that process. She just... She couldn't wrap her mind around that.

Pausing mid-pace, she faced Deacon. His hands were clenched, one in his lap, the other on the back of the couch. His jaw was tight too. But he kept his seat and watched her pace. And to be honest, given they were both holding on to their control by a thread, she was impressed with his ability to sit there and *not* do something.

"Does this have to do with my...changing cells? The magic, the way I'm healing faster on my own. Is that why the shield didn't just pop back into place? Cause I'm different now?"

"You were channeling that shield as you changed. Why would that affect the shield?"

His tone was surprisingly lacking in growls given all the signs of his animal side living just beneath the surface of his civility. Again she was impressed.

"Because I've never had it taken away and returned. And that's the only thing that's changed since I first started channeling their magic. Maybe they just need to take my, I don't know, my knew self into account."

"If Jaxer can find Wisat and Liruk, we'll ask them," Deacon said. "Until then, I have a question you need to consider."

"What?" She started pacing again because the restlessness was making her itch. The anger was fading, a little, as she considered the problem at hand. How to get the shield to start flowing again? How to return to being a Protector before Holland got here?

"Do you still want to be a Protector?" Deacon asked.

She stopped, so suddenly she rocked back on her heels. "What?"

"You need to consider everything that's happened since you were supposedly fired. As well as the fact that they put you through all this in the first place. Do you still *want* to work for Wisat and Liruk? Do you still *want* to be a Protector?"

"I was about to turn myself into one using magic clothes and upping my training. If anything, I've proved I can't walk away even if I want to."

"But do you want to continue to do this *for them*?"

She blinked and dropped into one of the chairs bracketing her coffee table, facing the bay window. Outside, it was still bright and sunny. A crisp autumn day. For some reason, in that moment, all that sunshine felt weird. Given the conversation, shouldn't it be gloomy and gray? Maybe stormy. Yeah, this felt like a thunder and lightning storm kind of moment.

"Do I still want to work for Wisat and Liruk?"

No one had ever given her that choice before. Not from the very beginning. Never once had she said, Yes, I will do this job. Not once. She'd gone along with it, and not really put up a big fight. She liked keeping bad guys from hurting good guys. She liked that she and Buck hadn't been killed by the demon when she'd first become a Protector, and she'd loved saving lives. She hadn't much liked some of the situations she'd been forced into. She had major mixed feelings about having to protect bad guys sometimes—her mind jumped to Sheldon and then skittered away.

But she'd never really been given the option of saying, out loud, "Yes, I will," or "No, I will not," when it came to doing the job.

Did she still want to work for Wisat and Liruk? Did she want to work for anyone? Even if she was still going to gear up like a less billionary Batman and take to the streets to save people on her own.

Would she rather do that? Or would she rather go back to being beholden to bosses?

"I don't know," she said honestly. "I've never really even considered that question before."

"Now's the time," Deacon said, his voice quiet. "Before we bend the universe to return you to your previous job, you need to decide if you *want* that job. At least as it was." He pressed his lips together before saying, "We both know you'll keep protecting people, shield or not."

She huffed.

"Now you get to decide how you do that."

Huh. And wasn't that just…something. She got to choose. No longer someone who'd failed and was fired. Someone who'd made an active choice. And maybe quit.

Maybe.

Because Oliver Holland was still on the way. Along with his demon god father and Angel of Death mother. And none of that sounded like something she could face without Protector magic. Except…

There were other Protectors.

"Huh. You think Frank might help me?" she asked, without looking at Deacon. "When Holland gets here."

Because now she had no doubt he was still coming. That there weren't other Protectors lined up to take care of that problem. Her bosses, and their boss, had intended all along that she'd return to her former job. That she'd handle the Holland issue.

They'd left her vulnerable *knowing* there was no backup from other Protectors coming.

That sparked her rage all over again, but she swallowed it as she considered her own question. Would the one and only Protector she'd met—she wasn't supposed to meet the others until after she passed her seventh year—help her even though she was no longer a Protector and even though it might piss off his bosses?

Cary had helped him and his wife once. She didn't consider him to owe her anything for that help, but maybe he'd be willing to help her if she asked nicely? They still emailed, since she liked the updates on the baby god he was raising. And the baby pictures. Baby pictures were adorable.

But Frank had a lot on the line. A family. His own job as a Protector. Could she ask him for help knowing it might complicate his life?

She needed a shield, though. If she was going to face Holland, and —damn it—keep him safe from his father, and then survive Holland after she'd rescued him from his father, she needed more than magic clothing and a tentative-at-best handle on some of the various magics she'd absorbed over the years. She needed a shield she could work behind.

The way she'd always been a shield for Angie to work behind.

Which brought her back to worrying about Angie, but she'd have to do more of that later, because first she had to figure out how to move forward. And if she wanted to do that as a Protector—if they could even manage that—or if she wanted to reenter the world on her own.

"I think Frank would help if you asked," Deacon said. "To protect Holland?"

"To deal with Holland," she said. "He's still coming. That's why James came looking for me. That's why the Angel wants to see me. They don't know I've been fired—I mean tested out of my powers." She scowled. "And since Wisat and Liruk obviously didn't send anyone else in to take care of that problem, assuming I'd be back to my usual Protector self soon enough, that problem is still coming."

"I'm afraid you're right, Pro—Cary."

The sudden, strange voice dropping into her living room without the usual warning tingle along her spine made Cary screech, and snarl, and spin to face the newcomers in one ungainly move.

"What the fucking hell?" she shouted.

And launched out of her seat to face her former bosses.

Wisat and Liruk stood near Cary's fireplace in similar poses. Their hands clasped in front of them, their shoulders stiff. Where Wisat held his head up and met her gaze when she glared at him, Liruk's gaze was turned toward the floor. Wisat looked... Well, Cary couldn't read him, though she wanted to call his expression contrite. Liruk looked very obviously miserable.

Which was a shocking enough expression to temper Cary's second explosive, "What the fucking hell?" to a more moderate tone. She didn't take the roof off of her house with the explosion at any rate.

"May we explain?" Liruk said quietly.

"An explanation would be super," Cary snapped. "Better than I've gotten to date. And since I *got shot* because of this little test of yours. Really shot this time and not just a bruise. I could have died. So yeah, I think an explanation is over-fucking-due."

Liruk's mouth tightened at the edges, but she pulled in a breath and said, "This always happens during a test year."

"Failure? The Protector getting shot and almost killed? Powers being stripped away and not returned because...no one knows?"

Liruk's jaw tightened this time, and Cary could practically hear her teeth grinding. "There is always a point at which the Protector is pushed past anything they've done before. A…" She glanced at Wisat for a moment, then said, "A make or break moment."

"Yeah, well, you broke me. Happy?"

"That was not—" Liruk cut herself off as her voice started to rise and bowed her head again. "That was not our intent," she said more softly.

"And what was your intent?" Cary asked, not even trying to hide her snarl. She was so angry. So very angry. And she didn't know what to do with all her rage, so taking it out on her former bosses felt like a good option.

Deacon rose from the couch, much more slowly than Cary had, and came to stand at her back. When she glanced at him, she wasn't even a little surprised to see his eyes glowing yellow, his leopard right there. His movements were very slow and his jaw looked like granite. When she could *see* him trying to hold on to his control that way, she knew he wasn't in a good place. His anger raged right alongside her own.

But she didn't want him to rip Liruk or Wisat's heads off in real life —verbally was one thing, actual physical head removal was another; mainly it was a lot messier—so she leaned into him, giving him the physical contact he needed to help control his animal half.

"Our intent," Wisat said quietly, "was…"

"You have resisted your calling since you became a Protector," Liruk said, her tone hardening. "You have denied choosing this life and refused to believe you were made for it."

"I was never once given a chance to say, 'you know what, I don't want to do this. I'd rather go back to working in the veterinarian's office.' Not once was I given an option."

"You could have quit at any time," Liruk said.

"Right. And you made that so clear. You actually said to me, out loud, 'you can quit at any time.'"

"It was implied."

"No. It wasn't."

"You were destined for this," Liruk hissed. "How can you not see that? It's in your blood."

"Because I also found out that most Protectors *know* what's coming from a young age," she snapped. "They're given warning, a chance to learn *before* having to blindly run into dangerous situations. They *know what they're getting into*. I didn't. I was never given the option."

Liruk's mouth stretched into a flat line.

"You weren't supposed to learn about other Protectors and their experiences before the end of your test year," Wisat said, still keeping his voice quiet and calm.

The calm was starting to grate on Cary's nerves. "Yeah, well, that wasn't exactly my doing either, was it? You introduced us when you needed me to step in and save the day. Again."

Wisat let out an audible breath. "Still... Our point is that, even though we didn't find you when you were younger, you were still made for this job."

"Apparently your magic doesn't think so since it no longer wants to play with me."

And saying that out loud, in just that way, made a lump of pain rise to clog her throat. Rejection. That's what all this anger felt like underneath. Tricked. And betrayed. And...rejected. After everything she'd done for them, for the world. Rejected.

"That wasn't supposed to happen," Liruk said.

"So you've said. So everyone says. Yet here we are."

"It's...complicated," Wisat said.

"Of course it is. And now there's a demon god about to drop onto the world to kill his unkillable son before the Angel of Death kills the god, and you've stripped me of any ability to deal with that. Did you at *least* finally round up some Protectors to step in? A few days have passed since I got shot."

The two Fae exchanged a look that actually, literally set Cary's teeth on edge. She had to focus on relaxing her jaw before she broke a tooth.

"Have you done anything," she said slowly, "anything at all, to mitigate the world-destroying confrontation that's about to happen in our realm, or just...ignored it?"

"Kupal Umsta has not given us permission to send in the other Protectors," Liruk said.

"Does he know what's happening? What's about to happen?" Cary blinked and looked between her two former bosses. Were they serious? Was their boss really going to just leave the world at the mercies of an actual demon god and the Angel of Death and their very evil son?

Because she wasn't okay with that.

"The demon hunters are aware of the coming confrontation," Wisat said. "It is… The Elder feels it is more their place to deal with the demons."

"These aren't just any demons," Cary said. "They're going to need help. And impenetrable shields, like *Protectors*, standing between them and the bad guys would be super useful in this fight to save the realm."

She felt like she was losing her mind. Was she the only one who saw this situation as something to worry about? Was she the only one concerned?

Was there something she didn't know?

"We must concentrate on what has gone wrong with the return of your powers, Cary," Wisat said. "That's our focus."

"Yeah, well, what's gone wrong with powers you shouldn't have taken away to begin with is a little less important than the end of the world."

"The world is always in danger," Liruk snapped. "Why do you think we created Protectors?"

"Good question if you're not going to let them help," Cary snapped back.

Wisat raised a stilling hand as Liruk pulled herself up for more of an argument. The Fae's shoulders dropped, but she continued to scowl at the floor.

"Eriana says I'm changing," Cary said. "Changed. Different to a normal human now. Rory said that could be happening, and Eriana confirmed it after she helped with my shoulder. Is that why the magic didn't flow back? Is it some sort of… I don't know. Is it linked to that in some way? Like the pathway for me being able to channel magic has changed and you didn't take that into account?"

"You have been channeling the magic as these changes occurred,"

Wisat pointed out. "How would that have affected them now but not before?"

Same question Deacon had asked. "I don't know. I'm not an expert in your magic. Maybe it's because you cut the magic off from me and it doesn't know how to get back in? Maybe I changed again while I wasn't channeling it and that screwed things up. How the hell do I know?" She put her hands on her hips, still glaring at them.

"Did you absorb magic after your…test began?" Wisat asked.

"You mean after you pretended to fire me and then took away my powers? No. Not that I know of. Just what Eriana has used to heal me *after* I was shot."

"You have not worked with the dragon in that period of time?" Liruk asked.

Oh yeah. In her anger she'd nearly forgotten that. "Just once," she said, surlier than necessary. "And yes, he gave me some magic during our lesson, but I didn't keep any of it. He's careful about that. Beyond Rory's lesson, and Eriana's healing, no magic. Hell, I haven't even had my Marianne-made leather coat for a few days because she's upgrading it for me."

She paused to consider the time since losing her powers. She'd confronted mundane humans when she'd forgotten she wasn't a Protector anymore. She'd confronted James, but that had been during the daylight and she hadn't risked looking him in the eyes. And she wasn't sure you could call vampire mesmerism magic anyway. It kind of was, but not the traditional sort of magic like wizards and witches and dragons and cursed objects and things. The mesmerism was part of vampire nature, like strength, like a shifter's ability to shift. More a predator adaptation than what she normally thought of as magic. And she hadn't fallen victim to the mesmerism anyway, so whether it was magic or not, the point was moot. She'd spent time with shifters, but again, there was no magic there, just biology. Except for Deacon.

She frowned. Deacon had magic he refused to use. He was unique for a shifter that way. But in this realm, she had to have magic thrown at her to absorb it, and he never used his, so he obviously hadn't been tossing magic her way.

Unless he'd been doing it on accident through the mate bond.

That wasn't… That wasn't possible, though.

Was it?

"What's wrong?" Deacon asked, the first words he'd spoken since the Nags arrived. "Your scent just changed."

She faced him. "Is there…magic in a mate bond?"

"Or course not. Ordinary leopard shifters mate bond all the time. There's no magic in it. Just chemistry and pheromones."

"Yes, but you're not normal," she pointed out the obvious. "You have magic even if you refuse to use it. How much do we share because of the bond? There are physical consequences of being tied together, for both of us. Could I be…could I be absorbing something through the bond?"

He blinked and the yellow glow in his eyes faded a little as he stared down at her. "I have no idea. It's not something that's ever come up. Ever."

"Would your mother know?"

"Not any more than I do. Cary, there are so few people like you, so little known about how you work, the chances of someone like you having ended up with a shifter like me are astronomically small. I doubt there's ever been a situation like this before. Which means…"

"No one has any idea if I'm absorbing some of your magic through the mate bond," she said with a groan.

Damn it, she hated having such a rare skill—curse more like at this point—because no one knew a damned thing about it and how it worked and what happened to people like her in all these various situations because people like her invariably ended up dead well before they got to any of this various situations.

"How could we tell? Could we…run some sort of test or something? Maybe Eriana could help us figure it out? Or Rory?"

"Maybe." But he didn't sound particularly convinced.

"Well, shit." She faced Liruk and Wisat again. "How about you? Any ideas? Deacon, Eriana, and Marianne are the only people I've been around with magic. And Rory, or course. But Rory makes sure I drain off anything he's given me. Deacon doesn't use his magic.

Marianne isn't throwing hers at me. Eriana's all goes in to healing. And outside of them, I haven't had a chance to pull in any extra magic." Thankfully! "So could it be something to do with the mate bond?"

Liruk and Wisat exchanged a frown that Cary was certain she didn't like. She was also certain she wasn't going to like what they had to say.

"We don't know," Wisat said after a moment.

Confirming that Cary hated what they had to say.

"The mate bond could be interfering with the return of your ability to channel Protector magic," Liruk said. "That is another thing that has changed."

"But as you said, I was channeling the magic while that bond formed. How the hell could that mess things up now and not earlier?"

"Perhaps the bond is somehow…blocking our magic?" Wisat said sounding more uncertain than Cary had ever heard him.

"Because you do not want it and the bond between you and your mate is…protecting you from it," Liruk suggested.

"First, I haven't said whether I want the magic back or not yet. The bond hardly knows if I don't. Second, I was safer with Protector magic than without it. If this was some sort of unconscious effort by Deacon's magic or our mate bond, then it's counterproductive to keeping me safe."

"Bonded leopards experience an imperative to keep each other safe," Deacon said quietly. "Your job puts you in danger, but no more so than your nature."

She snorted. If that wasn't the unexpected truth.

"Channeling Protector magic is safer for Cary," Deacon continued. "My leopard wouldn't block it."

Since meeting, since learning how her magic worked, he'd gone out of his way to make sure she was protecting him when there was danger around so that her magic would work. To keep her safe, he had to let her protect him, and he'd done that often. In fact, it had become a sort of automatic reaction for them both. Which meant, if anything, the bond should *want* her to have Protector magic because it was how Deacon could keep her safe.

She rubbed her temples. "This is hurting my brain. I need answers. And there are no answers. And I'm really ticked off about that. I'm even more ticked off that you—" she pointed one finger at Wisat and Liruk, "—risked this just to *test* me."

"We test all Protectors this way during their seventh year," Liruk said.

"You take their magic, too?"

She hesitated, looking away before she said, "No. Some are tested…differently."

"But you just *had* to use this test for me."

"It was deemed appropriate."

"The timing sucked."

"Yes," she snapped and faced Cary again. "I'm well aware of that. I warned against it. But no one listened to me. And now here we are."

Cary blinked a few times at Liruk's outburst. There was a lot to parse out in those few sentences. But the thing that struck Cary the most was that *Liruk* had argued against testing her by taking away her magic. *Liruk*. The boss who'd always complained about the way Cary refused to accept she hadn't been tricked into the job. The boss who'd always pushed and criticized and made Cary believe she sucked at her job. That boss was the one who hadn't wanted to strip her of her powers.

"We don't have time to argue," Wisat said. "That won't answer the fundamental question."

"Which is?" Cary asked, still studying Liruk's mostly unreadable expression.

"Holland is coming," Wisat said.

"We've known that," Cary pointed out.

"The Nagas have finally released him," Wisat said. "He'll be here soon. And we have no idea how to return your Protector magic."

"You used to channel it better than any Protector we've dealt with," Liruk said quietly. "Easily. It flowed through you like it belonged to you." She lifted her chin. "Like you were made to be a Protector."

"Is that why you were always so hard on me?" Cary asked.

"You kept denying your nature. Denying that this was your destiny. And it angered me that you could not see your own potential."

Cary let her hands drop from her hips as she continued to study Liruk. "I'm not sure what to say to that."

"There is nothing to say. If we can't fix this problem..." She spread her hands, seeming as much at a loss as Cary felt.

And Oliver Holland was almost here.

Oh boy.

Cary's cellphone rang at the same moment someone set their finger to her doorbell and didn't let up.

"Can you let Jaxer in?" she asked Deacon as she answered her phone without looking at the call screen.

"Cary. Oh good. I was afraid you wouldn't be able to answer."

"Angie?" Cary felt a woosh of relief flood her system. "Are you okay? Where have you been? Why haven't you called? We've been so worried. Are you okay?"

"I'm fine. I'm sorry to have worried you. I've had…things to take care of."

"But you're okay?"

"Yes. Yes, I'm fine."

Cary dropped onto the couch suddenly, her knees wobbling from the relief.

"I'll tell you everything when we have time. But right now, Oliver Holland is waiting for you."

"Wait. What?" She sat up and looked at Deacon still standing by the door, now with Jaxer. Jaxer was scowling at Liruk and Wisat, but he faced her when she squeaked out her question to Angie.

"He's waiting for you. Lud will know he's back in this realm soon. You need to get to him before the god finds a way into this realm."

"How long do we have?"

"Not long. Apparently, the god has been working on getting back into this realm since you banished him. Or since Buck did. According to my contacts, he's close to breaking through. He's not going to come in by the usual ways either. He's been working on literally breaking through. No channeling through another host. No getting some poor human to summon him and then release him from the containment circle. He intends to just rip through the dimensional blocks between realms this time."

"He'll lose a lot of his power doing that, won't he?" Cary asked. She knew Deacon could hear all this, but had no idea if the others could. She'd have to explain later if they hadn't.

"He will. But apparently, it's worth that to him to get to Holland. According to my sources, they think the demon god is desperate. He knows the Angel of Death is waiting for him."

"Shit. Where is Holland now?"

"He'll meet you in the woods, a few miles from town." Angie gave her the highway and off ramp number she'd need to reach the particular location.

Cary met Deacon's fully yellow gaze. "Ang, I… I have a problem."

"What's happened?"

As succinctly as she could manage, she told Angie everything. How her powers were gone. How even though they should have come back, they hadn't. How no one knew why or how to fix the problem.

"Fucking hell," Angie said with feeling.

"Right," Cary said with equal feeling.

"I'll be to your house in the next hour. Don't go anywhere yet."

"Holland will wait?"

"He'll have to." Angie disconnected before Cary could say more.

"Well fuck," she said. Deacon nodded in agreement. "Did the rest of you hear all that or do I have to explain?"

"Please explain," Wisat said.

Which was a reveal Cary would remember for later. That he and Liruk couldn't overhear her phone conversations was good to know. Did that mean Jaxer couldn't either? She'd push him for that answer later. In the meantime, she relayed what Angie had said and that Angie was on her way now.

"We have to find a way to return you to Protector status," Liruk said.

"Yeah. I'm open to ideas."

"You will take the magic back?" Liruk asked. "That was still a question just a few minutes ago."

"Well, that was before the current crisis escalated timelines," she snapped. "I've run out of waffling time. I need Protector shields. And any other help I can get."

She turned back to her cellphone.

"Who are you calling?" Jaxer asked.

"I'm calling in the cavalry." She rang Marianne first.

By the time she was done, she had Marianne and Lucy on their way, Deacon had called Nicky, Jillian, and his sister Caitlin, who were on the way, and he was on the phone rounding up any other available leopard already in Portland.

"I could use some dragon help about now," Cary muttered, but she had no way to call Rory or Joan. Instead, she rang Frank.

When Wisat opened his mouth to object, Liruk gave him a look that quieted him. Another very interesting reveal. Liruk was siding with Cary breaking the rules. Except what rules now? They might not have actually fired her, but she was still no longer a Protector. For whatever reason. That meant Protector rules no longer applied to her.

She might have smirked if she wasn't so terrified.

Frank took in her quick explanation of the situation and said, "I'll be there in a few minutes. Do I have permission? Wait... Is that still necessary?"

"It is, and you do."

"I need to convince Elizabeth not to come with me first. She'll want to help you, too."

"Tell her she helps me by looking after your kids if that's useful."

Frank's grunt could have been called amusement. "See you soon. Wait!"

Cary paused before disconnecting.

"I'm going to bring a couple of friends with me, if that's okay? They're also Protectors."

"I'll take all the help I can get. You should know, though, there's a reason you all haven't been sent in to help by your bosses already. Protector involvement hasn't been approved."

"Yeah, well, protecting is what we do even without marching orders. And we protect our own."

She disconnected feeling all warm and squishy inside that Frank still considered her "one of their own" since she technically wasn't. She was also low-level excited to meet other Protectors.

"Frank's bringing more Protectors," she told Deacon.

"Good," he disconnected his own cellphone. "Lucas and Diana are coming. And I've left a message with Sherri."

"Their kids?"

"Will have someone watching them and keeping them safe."

"Okay." She glanced at the faces already in her living room. Wisat and Liruk hadn't left, though she'd kind of expected them to. "You two going to help or just paying witness to the chaos." She raised a hand when Liruk opened her mouth. "I'm not expecting you to be there, by the way. This isn't an accusation or a request for help. I just need to know your plan, so I know what I'm dealing with."

"We'll be there," Liruk said before Wisat could answer. "I will be."

She raised her brows at them both. Wisat gave a quiet nod of agreement.

"Thanks." She wasn't sure what they did beyond premonitions and sending the necessary magic through Protectors, but she'd take every bit of help.

And knowing, after everything, they had her back was...kind of amazing. A moment of revelation that put a new light on her relationship with her bosses—former bosses. Actually, even the former part of that was still up in the air. For now, it was good to know they stood with her.

Lucy was the first to arrive. "What do you need me to do?" she asked without preamble.

"Have my back and don't get dead," Cary said, giving her a hug. When she did, she noticed someone standing behind Lucy. "Brandon." She looked between the big bear shifter and Lucy.

"I told him you needed some help," Lucy said. "He was in the last class I had before coming here. He wanted to help, too."

"No harm in having a few extra bodies behind you when facing a demon and his dysfunctional family," Brandon said with a slow smile.

He glanced past her and his smile widened. "Hey, Deacon."

"Brandon. Thanks for coming."

Cary had just gotten Lucy and Brandon inside when Marianne arrived.

"I brought some things I think will help," she said her head down as she moved into the house. She glanced up, spotted Brandon, and stopped in her tracks. "Oh."

"Marianne," Brandon greeted, his already deep voice a little deeper.

"Brandon," Marianne greeted back.

If the situation weren't so dire, Cary would have been delighted by Marianne's reaction to seeing the bear shifter. The slow creep of her blush, darkening her cheeks, the way she straightened her shoulders, the way she started to smile before catching herself.

Cary exchanged a look with Lucy and worked not to grin herself. Then, because the situation was dire and they didn't have time for cute romantic interludes even though she would have loved to indulge in a cute romantic interlude, she said, "What did you bring?"

Marianne blinked her attention back to Cary. "Right. I have some things you need to wear." From inside an ordinary looking paper shopping bag, Marianne pulled out Cary's beloved leather jacket. "All fixed up and ready to go," she said. "I don't have the leather pants ready yet, but..." She reached in again and pulled out a pair of calf-high boots. "Eunice whipped these up for you."

"Just now?" Cary asked, taking the boots from Marianne. Eunice was Marianne's youngest sister, also a weaver, and the superior cobbler of the three sisters. "How did she get them to you? What do they do?" Eunice lived in North Carolina so the boots came via one of their bag or pocket tricks, Cary was sure.

"I have a place at the shop that lets us pass things back and forth," Marianne said vaguely. "The boots are protective, like everything else I've got for you. They'll also keep you grounded when you need to be and help you move a little faster when you need to. Nothing like a shifter. Don't get cocky. But they'll give you a little burst if you need it."

"Wow." Cary looked at the boots. "Thank Eunice for me when you get a chance."

"We keep Lud from destroying the world, I think that'll be thanks enough," Marianne said. She pulled out a pair of jeans from the paper bag which wasn't actually large enough to hold the boots, the leather jacket, and the jeans. But the size of a bag was never an issue for Marianne.

"These—" she held the jeans out for Cary to take, "—will help keep stabby things from getting through. I had these started for you before the current crisis."

"Very helpful," Cary said with feeling. Stabby things, like sacrificial knives, tended to be an issue when demons were involved, even when the demons themselves didn't necessarily need something as mundane as a knife or dagger.

"There's a little magic deflection built into the seams along the outer leg. You want to deflect or dissipate some of the magic thrown at you rather than absorb it, turn to one side or the other. It won't protect you from all the magic, but it'll keep you from absorbing all of it at once and without some control over the process."

"Wow," Cary said again, studying the innocuous looking seams. Except for a brief run of golden light down the blue thread, there was nothing about the seams that screamed, *these* have magic in them].

"Do I get a pair of those jeans?" Lucy asked, hopefully.

"No. You don't soak up magic." Marianne reached into the

shopping bag again and pulled out a black, zip up hoodie. "This is for you."

Lucy frowned as she took the hoodie. "What does it do besides keep me warm?"

Marianne snorted. "That, too. When that's zipped up, if you want to go invisible, just stand still. Perfectly still. No one will be able to see you."

"Like a ninja," Lucy said, wagging her eyebrows.

Since Lucy was, to Cary's way of thinking, already a sort of ninja, the joke didn't seem like a joke.

"Try it, you don't believe me," Marianne said, crossing her arms over her chest.

Lucy pulled on the hoodie. "I didn't say I didn't believe you," she protested as she zipped the hoodie up. "I know how talented you are."

"Hmm," Marianne said with a little sniff. "Then don't move or talk."

Lucy shrugged, then went still.

Cary blinked. "Woah."

Lucy turned her head toward Cary. "What?"

"Before you turned your head, you were…gone. Not standing there."

"Seriously?"

"Seriously."

"Can I see it work in a mirror?" she asked Marianne, her eyes wide.

"Help yourself." Marianne gestured toward the hallway that led back to the bedrooms and bathroom.

Lucy hurried away. Cary turned to Marianne. "That's cool. Can I get one of those?"

"Later. We need you visible right now. Holland thinks you're coming to protect him from his father. But he'll turn on you the minute Lud is dispatched. We need you visible during that fight with Lud to keep Holland distracted."

"Distracted from what?"

"From what the rest of us are going to do," Angie said from the doorway.

"Angie!" Cary pulled her friend into a big hug. "I'm so glad to see you."

"I'll explain what happened when all this is done, I promise," she said. "In the meantime, this is my...friend. Sebastian. He's a demon hunter."

Cary turned to the man still standing in the doorway. He was tall, and very handsome, dark skinned, his hair cut short and peppered with a few curls of gray, his brown eyes a perfectly ordinary shade of brown if you didn't look too closely and notice the red in their depths. A side effect of being a demon hunter—some of the demon realm leaked in after a while and a demon hunter's eyes went ever so slightly red.

"Nice to meet you," Cary said. To Angie she mouthed, "Finally?"

"Later," Angie said back. "It's complicated."

"So I gather."

Lucy came out of the bathroom, her eyes wide. "I can disappear!" She stopped when she spotted Angie. "Oh thank goodness you're safe."

She launched into a hug that knocked Angie back a step and made her chuckle. Since Angie was six foot tall and Lucy was barely five feet, the fact that Lucy could throw Angie's balance off was impressive.

"How can you disappear?" Angie asked.

"Marianne made me a hoodie that makes me invisible if I stand still. It's the best." Lucy pulled back to stare up at her. "We have a lot to talk about later." She looked around Angie at Sebastian and Angie made the introductions. "Lots and lots to talk about," Lucy said with a little grin.

"But first we have a disaster to stop," Cary said. "What's happened that we need to know?"

"Holland is waiting," Angie said. "He knows Lud is coming, and it can't be stopped now. The negotiation to get him released was... complicated. But it was managed without anyone getting killed so that was good."

"Definitely. The Nagas are fine?"

"As far as I know. I wasn't part of that negotiation."

"The demon hunters took care of it," Liruk said, startling Cary.

"You knew this was happening?" Cary asked.

"We arranged it," Wisat said. "They had negotiated his original sanctuary here. It was their responsibility to negotiate with the Nagas for his release."

"I…didn't know that part. I thought the Angel of Death was involved somewhere."

"She was," Angie said. "But again, I wasn't involved in that part."

"She didn't threaten the Nagas, did she?" Because Cary would not be happy about that.

"No," Wisat said. "She had no reason to. She doesn't…threaten as such. She's simply inevitable for most beings. Even supposedly immortal ones."

Liruk said, "Her appearance is often enough reminder of that fact and make all creatures…cooperative."

"That's terrifying on so many levels," Cary said, mostly to herself. "But you two knew all this was going on," she said to Wisat and Liruk, "and you never told me? Never thought stopping in to give me an update was a good idea?"

"We were too busy arguing on your behalf with our Elder," Liruk snapped. She flattened her mouth into a line before letting out a long breath. "He insisted on this test as the negotiations were underway."

"We did try to talk him out of it," Wisat said. "He wouldn't budge. He felt you would pass the test quickly, and so we shouldn't worry."

"Wait." Cary looked closer at her two former-but-possibly-still bosses. "He was convinced I'd pass quickly?"

"Yes," Wisat said simply.

It was like being hit between the eyes all over again. Only not with outrage or anger or hurt. Now, she didn't know what to feel beyond confusion.

She hadn't been a disappointment. And not only hadn't they fire her, they'd *assumed* she'd jump in to rescue someone so quickly that she'd have her powers back by the time the demon hunters and the Angel of Death negotiated the release of Holland.

Meanwhile, she thought she'd failed.

Yeah, she had no idea how to feel about that. Not even a little. She'd have to unpack it all later and examine the miasma of whatever was churning through her chest right now.

If they survived facing Lud again.

If she survived Holland.

27

 riana arrived not long after Cary had stuffed down a couple of peanut butter and jelly sandwiches, while everyone was coordinating the logistics of getting to the location where Holland was waiting.

And she brought Sheldon with her.

"No," Cary said, seeing the young man, standing but still looking the worse for wear from his last interaction with Holland. "No. You're not recovered yet. You have no powers left. And Holland has body hopped into you once. That happens again, he'll kill you. And you'll be an easy target for it now. No. You stay as far away from him as possible."

"I'm going," Sheldon said, his voice hoarse and deep from the damage having a literal demon inside his body had done to him. "You're not my boss."

"Ha! As if I would be."

"And you're not my mother."

"Which we're both glad about. Plus, I'm not old enough." She scowled.

"I'm seeing this through to the end. The old wizard's research is destroyed. I'm done with body swaps. But I've been inside Holland's body, heard the echoes of his thoughts and dreams…nightmares. You'll need me."

"To do what?" She softened her tone because she knew this was a sore spot for him, and even though she still didn't like him, she also didn't want to purposefully hurt him. "You don't have any magic anymore, Sheldon. How will you help? You'll be one more person we have to protect." And she wasn't a Protector at the moment. At least not the kind with a super convenient, impenetrable shield.

"I kept some of the spells the triad sold me," Sheldon said.

"And they'll be there, probably channeling the Angel of Death, which means they can break the spells they sold you. Also, remember, they sold you stuff that would let them secretly spy on you. What makes you think you can trust anything else they gave you?"

"I managed to…twist the ones I kept. I experimented on them. I can't make witch magic work. But I could use what they gave me and…improve on it."

She hung her head. "I don't want to know what you did, do I?" she muttered. But really, she needed to know, so she raised her head and said, "Tell me."

"Mostly they're illusion spells," Sheldon said.

"Illusions? Against demons?"

"Yes," he said, so confidently Cary blinked.

"Well. Okay then. If it's anything but illusions, though, warn me. I don't want any surprises. And I swear to the universe if you body swap with that demon again…" She had no idea what she'd do. Another swap with Holland would kill Sheldon. And for complicated reasons, she didn't want that to happen.

"I don't want to go through that again either," he said, with feeling. "Trust me."

She didn't trust him, though, and that was the problem. But she would rather have him where she could keep an eye on him than have him running around secretly trying to do…whatever he intended to do.

"Fine. But keep behind the Protectors, all right? No heroics."

"Protectors?" he asked, his brows raised.

She ignored the question to answer her front door when the bell chimed, announcing the arrival of the leopard shifters. Lucas, his mate Diana, Nicky and Jillian, even Sherri. And Deacon's sister Caitlin. All gathered to help Cary. She hated putting them in danger but it was beyond touching that they'd come to help when asked. Lucas and Sherri had been there the last time Lud descended on this realm. They'd lost some of their fellow leopards in that fight. They knew what to expect. And still they'd come to help.

The idea was overwhelming.

The only ones she hadn't heard from yet were the Protectors. Which was a little unnerving. She was really hoping for people with proper shields standing between her and the demon god because the demon god really hated her.

While Deacon made introductions, she went to talk to her dogs. Especially Buck.

Buck didn't seem to be going through the same things he'd gone through before Lud's last arrival. No fevers. No strange behavior. Either Buck had better control of his demon nature this time, or the effects just hadn't started yet and he'd go full demon dog again later.

Which she was sort of hoping to avoid.

"Okay, guys," she said to all three as she squatted down on the floor with them by their beds under the bay window. They'd remained there the entire time the house filled with people, watching but not jumping up to greet anyone. Not even Fred. "I've got to go do a thing. That mean demon god will be back." She looked at Buck. "Do not turn demon dog again if you can avoid it. I'm not sure it's good for you."

Pickles let out a low woof. Cary wasn't sure if that was a sign of agreement or not. Buck just pushed his head into her hand so she'd scratch harder.

She still wasn't feeling any extra heat from him. Hopefully that was a good sign. Last time Lud had descended on Portland, though, he'd spent a great deal of time coming in and out of this realm, taking sacrifices from the serial killer who'd summoned him, grooming the killer so that he could take over his body and enter this realm without losing any of his power. All that activity before she'd known Lud existed was probably why Buck had been so off. At least, that's what she'd assumed. This time around, since Lud wasn't bothered with the subtle, slower, power-saving reentry into this realm, the effects on Buck could be quite different. He could yet go demon dog.

"I just need you guys to stay safe," she murmured to the dogs. "And you'll be safe here."

Pickles gave Cary's knee a nudge, and Fred jumped up almost into her face to try and lick her. Buck stared at her, his tongue hanging out, looking very Labrador and very not demon dog. She took a deep breath. Everyone got hugs and scratches and some attention. And then she pushed to her feet.

"Remember," she told them, attempting to be stern, "you guys just stay here and safe. I'll be back soon."

She hoped.

ary wasn't sure why, but meeting Holland in an open field in the middle of these particular woods east of Portland, not too far from the Columbia River, seemed too perfectly choreographed. She hadn't realized when Angie had told her where Holland was waiting, but now that she was here, the memories were sharp and clear.

The large clearing, surrounded by fir trees with a few oaks scattered throughout, wasn't all that far from where Cary had faced Holland and his army less than a year ago. Of course this was where they'd meet again. The location had a weird sort of inevitability to it that gave her the creeps.

Because the last time she'd been in this area, facing Holland, someone had died because Cary had failed to rescue her.

The late afternoon sun painted a lovely, crisp autumn glow across the green field and surrounding forest. The air was fresh and a little damp, scented by the firs and loamy earth. There was just enough autumn warmth left in the day to make standing around outside pleasant, neither too hot nor too cold. Birds chirped in the trees but at a distance. Nothing too close. A beautiful setting.

If not for one of her greatest enemies standing smack in the middle of all that glorious beauty.

She studied the surrounding trees, but she couldn't see any signs of others. Just Holland. Standing alone in the middle of the clearing. Looking like this was an ordinary day. Although, his perfectly cut dark gray suit seemed a little out of place to the setting.

Oliver Holland looked much as he had the last time she'd seen him. He lived in the human guise of a distinguished, older white man with gray hair, a fit physique, and a snooty English accent. The lack of any red in his pale blue eyes always struck Cary as an impressive mask. The first time she'd met him, she'd had no idea he was a demon. Deacon had to tell her, and he'd only known because of the smell. Visually speaking, Holland made sure he appeared very human. And he'd pulled off that façade for a few centuries.

"Cary Redmond," he said as she slowly approached, his English accent rolling her name. "So nice to see you again."

"Uh huh." She stopped far enough away she could talk without shouting, but only just barely. Getting close to Holland seemed like a very bad idea, even though, technically, she was here to protect him. "You look good. No worse for wear."

He smiled. "There are worse things than being held captive by beings that are, fundamentally, decent. A different experience than being captive to a demon. Not nearly the same degree of torture my kind are capable of."

"Sure. Sure." Not that she ever wanted to find out.

Holland looked past her and his smile widened. "Leopard."

"Demon," Deacon greeted in an impressive deadpan.

Deacon had walked into the clearing with her, but the rest of her little army were currently scouting the woods. There had been so sign of Frank and the other Protectors before she'd left to meet Holland, so Wisat and Liruk had gone to find them. Since Protector involvement here wasn't "sanctioned," she hoped Frank and the others hadn't run into trouble.

"How many are with you?" Holland asked without bothering to look around.

"I don't know, what…?" She made a mental count. "Fourteen others here now. Few more on the way."

"You'll need all the help you can get."

"Yeah, your dad is an asshole."

"He is. He very much is."

"You're mom's a little scary."

"Well, we all fear Death. Even my father."

"He wants to sacrifice you, or something, so the Angel can't kill him, right? That's what all this is about. One fucking demon god who doesn't want to die and his ex who intends to kill him."

"That's what this is all about," Holland said. "My very existence is all down to this."

"That's got to be a bit of a mind fuck."

"If I were human, I imagine it would be." Holland spread his hands. "Demons have a slightly different perspective on these things."

She snorted. "Right. I imagine parents killing their kids is normal for demons?"

"For a certain level of demon…" He shrugged. His expression turned speculative. "I didn't think you'd follow through with protecting me. I thought you'd back out."

"I don't want your daddy burning down my world."

"He's only going to destroy this realm because you pissed him off."

She scowled. "No. It's because this world gave you sanctuary." She winced. "Probably just a bonus that destroying this realm would also destroy me."

Holland chuckled. "If anyone could upset my father, of course it had to be you, Ms. Redmond."

"Using the formal address? Okay. I'm assuming that means we're friends for now and you won't try to kill me until after daddy is dead."

"Things have to balance, Ms. Redmond. That's the problem. The crux of all this. Balance in the universe. Even demon gods must die eventually."

"Are you technically a demon god?" she asked. "Does that mean even you have to die eventually, even though your parentage means the Angel can't take you?"

"Everyone has to die eventually," he said. "Even the gods. All the gods."

"That didn't answer either of my questions." Which was pretty normal for a conversation with Holland. "When's daddy and mommy due to arrive? I assume we're in the middle of this clearing for a reason."

"You assume right," Holland said.

She waited but when he didn't say more, she sighed. "It's harder to do my job—" hey, she didn't stumble over the word this time! That was good because he'd have noticed and she didn't want him to know she wasn't technically a Protector anymore, "—if you keep things from me, you know?"

"All you have to do is stand there. Why do you need to know more?"

"I'm nosey."

Holland smiled, a slow, amused lifting of the lips she didn't trust for a moment. "I've missed you, Ms. Redmond. So very much."

"Right. I imagine I was on your mind a lot during your captivity."

"You were."

Deacon's low growl didn't bode well for what Holland was letting through in his scent. She didn't ask. She didn't really want to know how many ways Holland had imagined killing her. Sheldon had given her some hints and that was more than enough.

"Your leopard wants to kill me," Holland said, matter-of-factly.

"I imagine you'd like to do the same to him."

"He would be a powerful sacrifice."

"You could try," Deacon said.

And wow was there a lot of his leopard in his voice. Low and deep and rough and gravely. She glanced back at him. Yup, eyes glowing. He wasn't even attempting to control his rising animal side. Was that a show for Holland's sake, or was he really on the edge of losing control? He'd seemed more…on board with this whole protect-Holland thing on the way here. But Holland was a serious threat to her, and Deacon took those kinds of things personally.

She supposed she took threats to him personally, too. She had no more intention of letting Holland get at Deacon than Deacon had of letting Holland get to her. So…same page then. That was good.

Holland was smiling faintly when she faced him again. "We will have a lot to discuss once my father's been dispatched."

"Why didn't the Angel come for him the last time he was here? He really wreaked havoc, even sacrificed some power to tear into this realm in the end." Granted, he hadn't been outside a circle and *in* her realm for very long before Buck sent him packing. But he had been around. "I'd have thought if Death was after him, she'd have descended the minute he broke through. Especially since his attempts to break through caused issues for months ahead of his arrival. The reason you went looking for the Nagas' city." Buck going all demon dog. "There was warning of his coming well before you were in danger."

Cary thought back to her first meeting with the Angel and frowned. "Yeah, she said something about you being safe and content with the Nagas until the stupid wizard's search revealed where you were to your dad. She knew what was going on with that. She would have known what was going on ahead of his appearance. What's taking her so long to kill him?"

"She killed the wizard trying to kill you, didn't she?" Holland asked.

Ignoring *all* of her questions. She hated that. "Yup. Very handy. One less bad guy to worry about."

"You know I knew him?"

"He kept trying to get in on your immortality with a body swap, right? Pestered you for like…centuries. Why didn't she catch up to him sooner? Your mom, I mean. She is literal Death, and Zorianthus was avoiding her."

"That's what he called himself in this incarnation, was it?" Holland shook his head. "So dramatic."

"Unlike Holland… Naming yourself after your dad? Not even subtle."

"My nom de plume wasn't meant to be." He smiled faintly. "As for why Death hasn't caught up with my father yet… Killing any demon is harder than one might expect, even for the Angel of Death. And a demon god… Harder still."

"Yes, but everyone has to die. You just said that. Even demon gods. You're ignoring my questions." Including the one about Zorianthus being allowed to escape death for so long, but she cared less about that since the stupid wizard wasn't a threat any more.

"I'm getting there."

"By the time you do, we'll be exchanging words with your dad."

"My father isn't here yet." Holland let his gaze turn inward. "Soon. Unfortunately." He looked back at her. "I've spent years trying to avoid this confrontation. Centuries. It's why I've lived on this little planet and conducted myself relatively harmlessly for so long."

"Harmlessly? I watched you kill people. An innocent woman you claimed to love. One of your own henchmen. You claimed to have killed a Protector. And I got the impression there were some dead demon hunters in those years. Don't act like you're not the bad guy."

"Of course not. Ms. Redmond, I'm still a demon."

He said that like the whole idea was so obvious it was ridiculous that he should have to point it out.

"I'm not the one claiming your behavior was 'harmless,'" she snapped. "Get on with it. You were telling me what's taking your mom so long to kill your dad." And the fact that that sentence had come out of her mouth would always amaze her.

"She can't enter this realm incarnate. Not...easily. My father is trying to take advantage of that. The first time he attempted to enter and reclaim me, he was betting on the fact that he could succeed before she could. And he was right. It's much easier for a demon to enter this world than it is for an Angel to incarnate here."

"Which is why she body swaps with the witches? Why don't they just channel her like a medium? I dealt with that once, while you were gone. Had a medium channel a god, a real god, not a demon one, right in my presence. It was wild."

Holland blinked once, slowly, and Cary preened. She'd actually thrown him off a little. That didn't happen much with Holland.

"You've hit on an important point. Though I suspect accidentally," he said after a moment.

"The witches were always working with your mom, and that's why they dealt with you, right? That way you and your mom could communicate through them."

"It took me centuries to find a suitable triad for her. The power required... Even three witches might not have been enough if these particular ones weren't so strong. Their bond as a triad was particularly powerful. And since my father had finally found me in this realm, finding the triad was also a convenient discovery."

That was an interesting bit of information, but she was feeling the ticking of time and the need to understand some of this before Ho'Lud arrived. "Body swap instead of channeling... Why?"

"Angels can't possess a human body like demons can. She couldn't have incarnated in this realm that way."

"Sure, sure."

"And there aren't many mediums who could channel something like an angel. Even your god-channeling medium would have had a hard time containing an angel's spirit, their essence."

"I thought gods were higher in the rankings than angels." Actually, she didn't really know. Until she'd met the Angel, she'd assumed angels weren't real because she'd never met one. Jaxer had confirmed they were a real species, like demons and Fae. But maybe this inability to "incarnate," as Holland put it, explained *why* she'd never met one. They couldn't actually show up in this realm very easily.

"Angels and gods don't have the sort of relationship to each other that humans assume. Anymore than gods and demons do."

"Are demons and angels related?"

"Yes. But not in the way some religions on this planet assert."

"Got that part at least." She hadn't known where all this worked in with gods, so it was good to know she could keep them all in separate boxes. Things just got confusing otherwise. "Anyway, why are gods from other realms easier to channel through a medium than angels?"

"It takes a different sort of medium. And they're rare."

"But not impossible."

"None of this was supposed to happen in this plane of reality," Holland said. "In this realm. It was ordained to happen in my father's realm."

"Before or after he conceived you? And also, how did that even happen? Wait, no. I don't want to know. None of my business what your parents got up to centuries ago." Even the thought of how Ho'Lud and the Angel might make a demon child was just…more than her brain wanted to contemplate. The rest of this mind-blowing situation was more than enough. Her brain had nearly curled up and gone on vacation meeting the Angel of Death. Having to think about the act of reproduction in relation to that would probably push her over an edge she already didn't have a firm hold on.

Although, the fact that they had time for this conversation was…interesting.

"What are we waiting on?" she asked Holland.

"You've asked questions. I'm answering them. My father is still… in the process of getting here."

"Where are the witches? They're going to body swap with the Angel, right? That's how she's going to get here?" She'd been assuming that from the start. But after this conversation, she was starting to wonder if the Angel had found another way in.

"You keep getting us off track," Holland pointed out.

"I am not," she huffed. Though, actually, she probably was. Curiosity and asking questions were some of her superpowers, even though it usually got her into trouble.

"The Angel couldn't channel through a medium because she is Death. Not just a powerful being like a god, but actual Death."

"Mediums channel ghosts—when they don't specialize in gods. Ghosts are already dead. Isn't that close enough?" She'd avoided most things to do with mediums because of their relationship with the dead and ghosts. Somehow, she kept having to regret that avoidance. Which was irritating.

"She isn't a ghost. Death is…different."

"Yeah, I know," Cary said, mostly to herself.

Holland narrowed his eyes at her. "I've missed some things, being gone."

"And we're not going to talk about it." If Holland didn't already know she'd died once, all the better. It was bad enough he knew how to kill her when she was a Protector. She didn't even have that right now. "So the Angel can't just channel through a medium. She *has* to body swap?"

"Yes."

"What the hell does that do to the witches?" Again said mostly to herself.

She couldn't imagine inhabiting the physical form of the Angel of Death, in whatever realm it occupied. Especially since it involved sharing that form with two other humans. According to Sheldon, you knew the thoughts of the being you occupied, or what their thoughts were before the body swap. Or something like that. Anyway, Sheldon had heard Holland's thoughts when he'd swapped bodies with him. And they had been horrible. She couldn't imagine how terrifying the thoughts of Death must be.

"They've gained power in the exchange," Holland said with a pragmatic shrug. "They feel the exchange is worth the price."

"Okay, I guess." Not a price she'd pay. But then again, she'd never been driven to gain more power. She'd been content being a shield. It meant she couldn't always get rid of the bad guys, which was a pain in the ass, but she could always keep the good guys safe and she liked that part.

Huh. She really did like keeping good guys safe.

She blinked back to Holland. "So death comes to everyone in this realm, even vampires *can* die. So why can't the Angel kill your father here? Why didn't she try the last time he was here? I'm still waiting on that answer."

She couldn't tell if Holland had been stalling or really leading up to something, or a little of both. She liked the extra information he was giving her, but she wasn't a particularly patient person.

An assessment Deacon, and probably Jaxer, would call an understatement.

"She has to manifest, to incarnate, in physical form to kill a god," Holland said. "That's the rub. With mortal beings, the process of death happens without direct action on her part. With immortal beings... Those processes aren't automated, so to speak."

"Uh huh. Thus the 'immortal' part of immortal beings. So. The short answer is, she has to be *here* in her full form to kill your dad? And she can't just be *here* in her full form easily? Did I get that right?"

"Close enough," he said, folding his hands in front of him. He looked like he was about to give a speech to investors at a board meeting.

"So then how can she get here to kill your father if he comes into this realm? How does she get here *before* he reclaims you?"

Holland smiled, a slow widening of his mouth, narrowing of his eyes. "That's where you come in, Ms. Redmond."

29

$\mathcal{N}$othing about Holland's statement boded well for Cary, even a little bit.

The sun was lower in the sky now, touching the tops of the trees as the afternoon faded. Her friends were out in those trees somewhere. But the longer she stood around talking with Holland, the more she worried about them. What had they found out there? Had Holland brought a lot of people with him, an army like last time she'd faced him? Were the witches out there somewhere?

Anxiety crawled over her skin, the waiting making her want to fidget. Holland claiming she was a pivotal part of all this did not help her restlessness.

"How do *I* have anything to do with anything?" she asked. "Except being here to keep your dad from killing you to get your immunity to death."

"That's exactly the point," Holland said, spreading his hands slightly. "You keep my father from me. The Angel has time to incarnate in this realm."

His narrow-eyed smile gave Cary a shiver of apprehension, and she wasn't sure if it was just because Holland gave her the creeps or because her instincts knew something very bad lived beneath that smile.

"It was always just a matter of time, you see," he murmured. "A matter of time before my father's death was upon him. A matter of time before he found me in this realm. A matter of time before he tried to sacrifice me. A matter of time before the Angel can incarnate here. The one thing all of us have been working against. Time."

"I can't stop time, you know."

"But you can delay the inevitable. For as long as you remain upright, you can delay him."

Oh oh. She kept her expression as neutral as possible. But now that she couldn't channel Protector shields, *delaying* a demon god was a lot more complicated. And her Protector backup wasn't here. Frank could teleport. He could show up at any moment. But he didn't know exactly where she was, and if Wisat and Liruk couldn't find him to tell him…

She didn't have the usual stalling ability she'd had when all this got started. The very ability Holland was depending on.

Fucking hell.

"How does the Angel incarnate? What does that entail? Because, uh, I'm not sure how long I can stall your dad." She had to work hard not to let her anxiety out in her voice. She must have been giving something away, though, because Deacon rested a gentling hand against her lower back. The reassurance that he was there and had her back was great. But she was also incredibly aware of just how vulnerable they *all* were in that moment.

"For the Angel to incarnate," Holland said, very slowly, "there has to be…a trade."

That sounded even worse than him relying on Cary to delay Lud. "A trade?"

"Someone here, must…trade places with the Angel."

"You're talking about another body swap? Or are you talking about sacrifice?"

"More than a body swap. That only allows her to speak and see into this realm. It's not her here incarnate."

"Sacrifice? No. No one is being sacrificed. No." But if the Angel didn't arrive, Lud would get Holland. And the demon god would destroy her world.

Her heart pounded loudly and hard against her ribs. Spots swam at the edges of her vision. She felt the panic attack coming on, the sweep of nausea, the fear overwhelming her ability to think. She let out a slow breath, took in another one, trying to calm her pulse. Trying to concentrate on Deacon's hand at her back. The panic continued to lurk, just at the edges of her control.

"If it makes you feel better," Holland said, "the sacrifice isn't the usual sort, with all the blood letting and pain and torture. That's my father's modus operandi, not my mother's."

"Doesn't help." Because Death came either way. Torture or in sleep, Death arrived.

"Then perhaps knowing the sacrifice is a volunteer?"

"Nope. Not going to happen." And who the hell would volunteer for something like that?

"If it doesn't happen, Ms. Redmond, my father will claim me and destroy your world. Only the Angel of Death can stop him. And she must be here to do it."

"No." She didn't have an alternative for any of this. She just knew with every part of her body that she couldn't stand by and watch someone be sacrificed. She just couldn't. "I need other suggestions and alternatives. Because that one's not happening."

"There are no alternatives. If this had taken place in his realm, well…"

"Still need a sacrifice so she can incarnate there?" Cary asked.

"Not in the same way, no. There, she can manifest in a physical form without need of an exchange. Here, she's nothing but a ghost without the trade. Insubstantial and unable to kill a god."

Of course he had to mention ghosts. Of course he did. He had no way of knowing they were her ultimate terror. No way to know that she'd just about stepped away from reality at this point and the mention of the Angel as a ghost was pushing her over the thin edge of her sanity. Yet, still, he did it. Because demon. And enemy. And peerless asshole.

"How do I get all of you into Lud's realm, then?" she asked. This wasn't happening in her realm anymore. Not if this was the only option.

"How did you send him back to his realm before?"

"I had help."

From a demon dog who could open a portal into demon realms. But she'd asked him to stay home. And she didn't want to risk his life here either. Buck wasn't a normal demon dog. He didn't do demon dog things most of the time. She had no idea what going full demon dog again would do to him, if he'd be able to come back again. And she didn't want to take that risk.

"That help isn't an option this time," she said. "I need another one."

"I don't have one for you. I can't get you into his realm. I lost that ability when I came here. Cut it off actually. I was, as you might imagine, trying to avoid ever going back."

Deacon leaned in close to her ear. "You might not have an option. You might have to…ask him."

She knew he was talking about Buck, and being subtle about it so as not to give much away to Holland. Holland had met Buck, once, and knew what he was. But the less Holland knew about what Buck had done, the better.

"I don't know how that will affect him. If he'll be able to come back." She'd thought she'd lost him the first time he'd dragged Ho'Lud back to the demon realms. She would not risk that again. "And that was after Lud had been wounded," she reminded Deacon. By his own magic, which had been absorbed into and channeled back through some magical stones that Cary didn't currently have on her to help.

She could absorb the magic herself, now, of course, but that would kill her before she could use it.

Also, even wounded by his own magic, Lud had recovered and was returning to full strength when Buck had shown up. So her trying to fend him off with his own magic, even if she could take the power and not die, wasn't going to do much but stall him.

They still needed a way for Lud and the Angel of Death to be in the same place, at the same time, without it costing an innocent person—or dog—their lives.

"There has to be another way," Cary said aloud. "There has to be."

She looked at Holland, but he wasn't looking at her anymore. His gaze was turned inward. He blinked and refocused on her.

"I'm afraid we've run out of time for conversation, Ms. Redmond. My father is here."

30

At first, nothing changed. The breeze was soft and smelled of the nearby fir trees. The air was cooling with the sunset, but not cold. Even the distant sounds of birds farther away in the woods remained the same.

Cary's heartbeat hammered, but while she panicked, nothing else around her seemed any different at all.

And then the world ripped open, not fifty feet away.

The rip was a strangely awesome thing to behold. A literal tear in the air, cutting through the reality of her world to reveal a burning hellscape beyond. But the hellscape wasn't quite the red and glowing lava pit she'd expected of a demon realm. Oh there was heat, and a lot of red sky, and the very odious and obvious scent of sulfur coming through that crack in reality.

But there was also this golden glow around everything, including the tear in reality. The red skies had a gold glow. The light filtering through the tear was hazy with gold fog. Not white fog with sparkles. *Gold* fog. With sparkles. Literal gold edged the rip and sparkled in its own light. And gold fog flowed out through the hole and over the ground, sizzling in the grass. Gold that made things hiss and burn.

Made the grass crackle as it came into contact with this significantly cooler reality.

The sounds that came from that rip made her brain hurt. She couldn't describe them. They almost weren't audible. She could "hear" things, but it was more like her mind was registering that this thing was supposed to be sound except it was bypassing her ears altogether. Probably for the best since she was pretty sure the noise her brain was grappling with translating would make her ears bleed if they registered it. The best her brain could come up with was a combination of moan and hissing and screams. But there was a chattering under it all. A persistent chattering that was like nails on a chalkboard, making her nerves ache and burn.

The light was a strange and sore event for her eyes, too. That gold and red with sparkles, both too bright and like looking into a darkness she couldn't fathom. The combination of all these strange sensations on the parts of her body that were supposed to perceive those sensations was absolute chaos. She couldn't process it all and the result was a lot of chaotic "noise" in her brain that didn't translate to anything familiar. Even a little bit.

The first time Lud had come to her world, she'd been told this realm of his was impossible to reach for even most demons. It wasn't a place easily accessible. A human didn't just call a demon from this realm forth and expect them to answer. It was a plane of existence higher than that.

All this, in theory, made a kind of logical sense to Cary. She "got it" on a basic level. The reality of it all was something else altogether.

A demon god's realm was the very definition of insanity for a human.

Which she supposed made sense. Might even be the point.

Because her sanity definitely hung on my a very thin line as she watched the god himself stepped through that rip in reality.

He was blackness so deep it was like looking into the depths of space where no galaxies or stars disturbed the view. The deepest of light absorbing darknesses. His skin was the rock over a lava flow, chinking quietly as it cooled but through cracks in that black she could just see the silver red flow of lava. His eyes glowed red, with pupils like a cat's eyes in the center. But he was a shadow otherwise, almost impossible for her eyes to contemplate.

The chink chink of his rock skin moving made her skin crawl.

The rumble of his chuckle nearly broke the remaining thread of her sanity.

Ho'Lud. Here. In her realm.

And she was no longer a Protector.

Fuck.

From somewhere in the distance, Cary heard her name being called. She didn't want to look away from the demon god, but she thought the voice might have been Angie's. Her heart was hammering so hard she couldn't be certain. She had a hard time hearing anything over her own panic and that weird chittering sound coming out of Lud's rip in space.

She automatically stepped between the god and Holland and Deacon, which she realized as she made the move, was a ridiculous thing to do. She wasn't a Protector. The reminder screamed through her brain even as she kept trying to process the noises coming from the demon realm and the sounds she was hearing in other parts of the clearing.

She wasn't a Protector anymore. She couldn't stand against Lud with impunity and protect the people behind her. He was going to throw a fire ball at her and she was going to die. There was nothing between her and the demon to stop that.

And yet… For reason surpassing her own understanding, she didn't move from her place in front of Holland and Deacon. She was playacting like she was a real Protector still. She knew she was. And still, she didn't move.

Deacon's hand on her back clenched, digging into her jacket.

"Son," Lud said in his deep, rumbling voice.

Holland sighed loud enough it was almost comical. "You could have just let this go."

"It is time to fulfill your destiny."

"Yes, yes," Holland said. "And yet, here we are."

The god took one more step away from the rip in space and then froze. He reached out and touched something Cary couldn't see. But in her mind's eye, she saw a faint flicker of blue surrounding Lud. A circle of blue.

A containment circle.

She blinked a few times. She didn't normally see magic. Not like she was now. The sensation was almost as disorienting as trying to comprehend the demon realm at Lud's back. Except Angie had given her an infusion of her own magic on the way here. Enough for her to learn a single, quick spell while they drove here. Enough to hold onto some for the pending fight.

Not enough to drain Angie, and not enough to overwhelm Cary's cells. But enough to give Cary something she could call on if she needed to. Apparently, that little bit of magic from Angie gave Cary the ability to *see* a magical containment circle, too.

At least, she assumed that's why she could see the thing now. She'd ask Angie for sure later. If she survived of course. Which, knowing Lud was stuck inside a circle, seemed a lot more doable than it had just seconds ago.

"You contained him," she said to Holland, knowing he was the only one who could have.

"It won't hold," Holland said. "But it's an extra layer of delay. I hope you don't mind. I didn't want to rely completely on your powers, Ms. Redmond."

"No, no. It's all good. All the layers. Good. Right. Perfect. More layers the better." She might have been babbling. It was hard to tell. So she stopped talking just in case.

"I'm afraid I've frustrated your witch, though," Holland said, not sounding particularly bothered by the fact.

Cary finally looked away from the looming darkness of Lud and glanced behind Holland. Angie stood a few hundred yards away scowling at the thin air. When she touched a spot on the air, she hissed and pulled her hand back, shaking it. As if she'd touched something…hot.

"We're inside another circle?" Cary asked, her throat too dry so the words came out with a sort of strangled sound.

Because of *course* Holland had put them inside a circle while still containing his father inside yet another circle and all this kept her help from reaching them which Holland didn't know was necessary to all of them surviving this because he still thought she was a Protector.

Her head hurt. And not just from the sounds still spilling out of Lud's realm.

"Let Angie in," she barked at Holland. "Let the other's in. We need help with your father."

"Why?" Holland said, his gaze narrowing on her. "You brought a lot of people with you, backup I'm sure you assumed, but also potential sacrifices and blood to be spilled. Why?"

He spoke as if the god wasn't just a few yards away and they had all this time to talk again even though he was the one who'd said they were out of time.

Her brain wasn't working right. Something was wrong. She just couldn't quite put her finger on it.

"You want to kill me after he's gone," she said, still trying to force her brain to work.

"And I know how," he said. "Which, unfortunately, means my father does now too. We're in the same space. He can see through me. Did he ever tell you that? Despite my best efforts, he knows many of my thoughts."

"He knew me when we first met," she said, though only half attending to the conversation. She was trying to work out what felt so off about...everything. "He knew me from your head. Said some interesting things."

"About how I want you as my slave?"

"Own me and destroy me and all that. Usual stuff. Sheldon said the same thing. Figured your dad had some way into your head to know all that. Even if he didn't know which connected realm you were hiding in." Lud had followed Holland here and then couldn't find him beyond this realm in the Nagas' realm. But Lud had know about Cary through Holland.

What the hell was bothering her? Something about how casually Holland was acting with his father just a few feet away. About the way he kept looking at her instead of Lud.

The way the world stank of sulfur and that chittering sound made her ears hurt…

Sulfur stink.

Demon realms, and demons, almost always stank of sulfur. But…

The very very first time she'd encountered Lud, trapped with him inside a containment circle in a cemetery at midnight, with only one vulnerable woman who needed Cary's protection between her and the demon god, there'd been the smell of sulfur.

But…

But not this strong. In fact, she remembered very clearly thinking the stench was a lot less rotten eggy than she'd been expecting. Still there, still gag-inducing, and his minions had stank of it. So it wasn't like there'd been no sulfur. But…

Right now, the stench was a horrible coating of grossness on the back of her tongue. So strong she was sure Deacon's eyes, if she glanced at him, would be watering from it with his sensitive sense of smell. Overwhelmingly strong. Stronger than any sulfur stink she'd encountered before, even fending off a lot of big demons.

Why was the smell so strong now? Why so overpowering *now*?

What was wrong here?

"A circle inside a circle," she murmured.

Why? Why keep her backup away when they could only help against Lud? How could Holland contain his own father like this? So easily. Without the extra powers he'd needed just last year, the power he'd tried to gain through taking over the Nagas' city.

He'd said the containment circle was temporary, that Lud would get through soon. An extra layer of delay. That was fair enough.

Something still felt not quite right.

She hated dealing with demons.

"What's going on?" she asked. "Why does this feel wrong?"

"Cary?" Deacon murmured, stepping closer to her back.

"Not sure," she said back. "This isn't…right."

Holland smiled. "Ms. Redmond. Nothing about any of this is as it seems."

"Why?"

"Cary!" Angie shouted.

Cary wanted to face her, but she was afraid to take her gaze off Holland, keeping Lud in her peripheral vision. Except Lud wasn't doing anything. Just standing there. Not trying to break the circle. Not making threats, gloating. Nothing. Just…there.

She touched the little Fatima's Hand charm hanging on her necklace, a habit she'd developed in the months since she'd been gifted the charm. She stared at Holland, her fingers brushing over the soft gold, with its tiny bit of good luck magic. What was happening? What was wrong?

"That's not Lud," Cary said, quietly, not sure Holland would hear her.

"What?" Deacon asked.

"That's not his father. This is…" She raised her voice. "An illusion? Another demon? A trick of some kind. Why?"

"A test," Holland said.

"Of what?"

"You, of course," Holland said.

"You've tested me before. And got flattened. What's the point of this?"

"Because Protectors can't flatten armies of supernatural beings. I had months to consider that, Ms. Redmond. Months of wondering… how? Then learning, from the young wizard, that you absorbed magic. An interesting revelation."

She hated that he knew that about her, hated that he'd learned that during his body swap with Sheldon. But it didn't explain the fake Lud.

"How did you absorb my armies' magic and not die?" he murmured.

"No idea?"

"How could you use it? You're not a magic wielder. All you are is a Protector." He glanced at the supposed-Lud demon. "And now, maybe not even that."

Cary's throat tightened and her stomach dropped. "I'm not following you." She sucked at bluffing. She wasn't a good liar. And when she tried, she always gave herself away. But her confusion was genuine, so she hoped that came through.

He couldn't know. How could he know?

And if he did know...

Why was she here?

"The Angel needs to incarnate," Holland said. "And, as you guessed, my father is still on the way, but that isn't him. And the person who was supposed to delay the inevitable is... Not as she seems."

"Not sure what you mean," she said, which was true. No lies necessary. She couldn't be certain what Holland was alluding to.

"You've...changed," Holland said, "since we last met. In several ways. But I keep coming back to the fact that you, a human with nothing but Protector magic to channel, were able to absorb enough magic to destroy my army. To take me down. And not die. How?"

"Got me," she said. "I'm still not sure what I did that night." Which was another truth as far as it went. She had no idea how she'd taken all that magic and thrown it back at his army.

The technicality seemed important in that moment.

"Cary!" Angie called again.

Cary turned her head toward Angie without taking her gaze off Holland. "He says he's testing me," she shouted back at Angie. "Can you tell what he's done?"

Holland smiled at her. She didn't smile back.

"He knows," Angie shouted. "The triad said he knows."

Cary had assumed the witches were out there in the woods somewhere. The fact that they'd told Angie something useful seemed significant. But she said Holland knew. Knew what, exactly?

Holland's smile grew, but he shook his head and tisked. "Habits are hard to break, aren't they, Ms. Redmond? The way you moved between me and my supposed father. The way you still put us behind yourself, to protect us from him." He held her gaze. "Even though you're no longer a Protector."

31

Cary held very still as Holland's words settled around them. She was stuck inside a circle with him. Deacon at her back. Some demon—that at least wasn't Lud—standing a few feet away. And one of her greatest enemies in front of her. Telling her he knew she was no longer a Protector.

That she was no longer able to defend herself against him.

"How did you know?" she asked. "When did you know?"

"When you wouldn't come to the triad when James came looking for you," Holland said. "You hid behind the leopard shifters, and James could smell your fear."

Of course he could. And of course Holland had been communicating with James. Why not. The whole convoluted thing was just one enemy on top of another. All of them making sure the others knew she was in deep shit.

"What's the point of all this?" she said as Deacon's hand clenched in her jacket. She felt his muscles tensed, heard the very low growl seeping from him, but she couldn't look at him just then. She didn't dare look away from Holland.

"You were shot," Holland said. "How's your shoulder?"

"All better now. Little stiff. I'll get over it."

"How?"

"How what? How was I shot? See there's these things called bullets—"

"How are you all better now?"

"Faery healer. Very good at her job."

"Is that how you came back after your time with my mother?"

"Meaning?" She knew what he meant. She wasn't sure why she'd thought he might not know about her dying in Faery since he'd been in communication with his mother. She was stalling.

"You died in Faery. And yet. Here you are. How?"

"Good question." The fortunate luck of having a Faery healer there to bring her back. He'd guessed as much. She didn't have to play along by confirming.

"What did that do to you?" Holland asked, his voice low. "Dying. What did that do to you?"

"Got me. I don't really remember it." She'd remembered some of it right after waking up. Remembered the pain. Remembered the darkness. But most of her visceral memories of the moment had faded. And she couldn't recall *being* dead at all.

"I won't die," Holland said.

"Yeah."

"My father intends to kill me."

"How?"

"He'll take this body." He motioned down the length of his frame. "The one he's ensured exits. One that my mother can't destroy. He'll let me be destroyed in his old form. It's not a simple process. But as you might imagine, he's worked hard to perfect it. He'll swamp me, push me out, and steal my invulnerability to death."

"The way Zorianthus was doing with all his protégé to stay alive and beat death." The wizard had been training other wizards to body swamp with him, then he'd steal their bodies and magic to extend his own life. He'd done that for centuries before the Angel of Death had finally killed him. In front of Cary. In a really gross way. She imagined something similar awaited Lud at her hands.

"Just so," Holland said. "So you can see why I was less than amenable to the old wizard's plans. Too much like my own father's. Which I'd gone through a great deal of effort to avoid."

"So why are you testing me? Why all this? You need my help."

"Your help is less…helpful without your Protector magic, though, isn't it?" Holland said. He narrowed his eyes at her. "And yet, you're still useful to me."

"Why test me? Why all this subterfuge? What are you getting at?"

"You died and returned. You flattened my army. You were shot and recovered."

"Got a lot of help along the way with most of that," she pointed out. Even the flattening his army part. Because he'd been the one throwing all that magic at her that she'd been able to use against him. He hadn't meant to help her. But he had.

"Yes. Help. But there's more. What is it? What is different about you?"

"You've already said it. I'm not a Protector anymore. Got sacked."

His brows jumped up. "Sacked? Why?"

"Guess I sucked at the job," she said with a shrug. She knew better now. But frankly, the sting of her own failure still lurked under the surface. Enough that calling up those emotions was easy. And Holland would believe her.

"No," he said, almost to himself. "That's not what happened."

"'Fraid it is." She shrugged. "Why are we here?"

"My father is due. My mother is due. And you are no longer a Protector."

"Which means I don't need to be here."

"You still came."

"To stop your dad."

"With what?"

"My friends. My backup."

"They've been cut off from helping you." His gaze jumped behind her to Deacon. "Only the leopard left in here to do anything for you. And I have a demon waiting to crush you both before your help can get here." He gestured to the still encircled Lud-lookalike.

"I don't understand any of this, you know. What you're doing. Why you're doing it. You wanted my help. And then you wanted to kill me. Well, I came to help. Instead, you've ensured I can't. You want to die? Is that the point of all this?"

"The point of all this—" he swept his hands out, encompassing his surroundings, "—the point of my coming to this little planet, exiling myself here, was always my own survival. My father can't get here easily. My mother can't incarnate here. They can't use me in their feud."

"And that's out the window now. So why are you trying to keep me from stopping your father?"

"I'm not. I want to know how you will now. Now that you're no longer a shield."

"No idea," she admitted. "You've got me. It's why I brought backup."

"Mm." Holland tilted his head to one side to study her. "I have an option." He glanced at Deacon. "But you're not going to like it."

"I haven't liked anything to do with you from the start," she said. "Well, I did like that steak you bought me that one time. That was a good meal."

His lips twitched, but he didn't smile. Not even the calculating, slow smile he'd been giving her for most of this meeting. He just stared at her.

Finally, he said, "I ensured I couldn't go back to my father's realm when I came here. I ensured I cut off enough of my own power stepping into this realm that opening that rift back would be impossible. I thought he'd have a lot harder time tracing me here if I did that. And it did…delay him. Unfortunately, it was only a delay."

"You've said this already. Why the repeat?"

"I didn't eliminate my ability to move back into *a* demon realm," he said. "Just *his* demon realm."

She wasn't sure she liked the direction this was going. She glanced at the open rift. Narrowed her eyes. "Not an illusion."

"Not entirely."

"Where?"

"Somewhere my father can reach. But also somewhere my mother can reach."

"Will he go there?"

"He might follow. He'll come here first."

"I'm going to hate this idea of yours, aren't I?"

"Cary," Deacon said from behind her. "You can't go into a demon realm. They aren't places designed for human survival."

"Yeah, got that part," she said back. "Why didn't you go to this realm in the first place?" she asked Holland.

"I didn't have a Protector there."

"You don't have one here either." No point in prevaricating any more.

"Didn't you ask any to join you?"

He spoke as if he already knew she had. Damn it. "Of course I did. They aren't here yet."

"There's something else, though. Beyond the Protector business."

He continued to hold her gaze, and, she realized with a start, there was now red in the depths of his blue eyes. Red she'd never seen there before.

That couldn't be a good sign.

"I was in that young wizard's head long enough to know," Holland said quietly. "At least, to have an idea. All that magic absorbed. How have you survived?"

She shrugged, keeping her mouth shut so she didn't give anything away—anything more than he already knew. She was a little ticked off at feeling tricked when the only reason she was here was to stop the world from ending. With nothing but her group of friends and some well-designed magic clothes.

"You flattened my army with magic you took in," Holland murmured. Almost like he was talking to himself now. But too loud for that. "You really can do what the child wizard thinks, can't you? You really do absorb magic. And it doesn't kill you. That's why the old wizard hated you."

"Whatever you say." She tried for casual. Her voice squeaked a little on the you, making a mockery of her attempt.

"All that magic. You took it all in and didn't die," he continued, like she hadn't spoken. "Still here. Able to absorb magic. Not dead."

Holland knew all her secrets, now. Her ability to absorb magic—and that the ability should have killed her by now. Her lack of Protector magic. Everything. All her weaknesses.

All the ways her help was useless to him.

But more importantly to the world, all the ways her help was useless to her realm right now.

"Well," Holland said, lifting a brow as his contemplative expression rolled into something more pragmatic and firm. "That settles it, then."

"Settles what?" she asked warily.

"This." He lifted a hand and dropped it.

And the Lud-lookalike surged forward.

Cary moved to put herself between Deacon and the demon automatically, and again, only realized that was a mistake when Deacon screamed her name.

She felt his arms around her, and then suddenly she was across the clearing, at the edge of Holland's circle, next to Angie, with Deacon still holding her.

"I'm glad your reactions are more sensible than mine," she said to him as he set her back on her feet. "And shifter speed is a lovely thing."

"Not much use if we can't get out of this containment circle," he grunted, and shouldered the circle. He might as well have been leaning against a wall.

"What now?" Cary asked Angie as she watched the Lud-lookalike stalk toward them.

Its mouth twisted into a grin Cary new meant very bad things for them. Behind the demon, Holland stood where they'd left him, his expression contemplative. As if this was all some sort of interesting episode of a documentary.

"I can't get through this containment circle either," Angie said.

"Where are the others?"

"In the woods still. The triad was there along with James and some of his vampires."

"Because of course," Cary said with a sigh.

"They aren't doing anything. Just…stalling everyone. No one is fighting. Yet. And Sebastian is holding off another minion demon. The demon is contained, but only by Sebastian's will at this point."

"Where the hell did another demon come from?"

"Holland, I assume. It was with the triad and vampires. Every possible option for keeping the rest of us from getting to you. Holland wanted you alone."

"This is a test."

"Yup."

The Lud-lookalike pulled what looked like a long, flaming sword from his back. Cary whimpered.

"He knows I'm not a Protector anymore," Cary said, mostly to herself. "He already knew I absorb magic from Sheldon. Now, he knows I have no way to block it."

"That's what he's testing then," Angie said. "What you do now when magic is thrown at you. You're going to have to channel demon magic. You up for that."

"Not even a little bit."

"How the hell is she going to channel demon magic?" Deacon snarled, still trying to physically push his way through the barrier. "Without getting killed, I mean."

"Yeah, I'd rather not do that last thing. Again."

Deacon gave her a look and she shrugged. He hated the reminders that she'd died, and yet she kept bringing it up. If she survived, she'd have to talk to someone about that.

"It's not very different from channeling dragon magic and witch magic," Angie said.

"How would you know?"

Angie sighed. "I don't. I'm guessing. But it's the best I've got right now." She muttered something under her breath, made a quick, sharp gesture with her hands, and slammed them both against the invisible barrier between her and Cary.

A flash of blue light again in Cary's mind's eye. Bright enough she winced at the glare.

When she could see again, Angie was scowling at the barrier and cursing.

"Yeah, can't get through," she said. She glanced behind Cary and lowered her voice. "Okay, here's what you're going to do. When the demon throws magic from the tip of that sword, it's going to look like fire. Turn sideways so Marianne's clothes can help scatter some of it. And you're going to use your will to slow the fire down. The way Aidan showed you the last time you faced Lud."

"I can't do that," Cary squeaked. "I don't have demon hunter will!" She couldn't even will herself to resist cookie dough ice cream if she went down the ice cream isle in the grocery store.

"You can. You've done it before, and you're too stubborn for your own good. Use that stubbornness. That's what you need. Refuse to let the fire reach you."

"I can't."

Angie met her gaze, and there was a strange sort of energy in her eyes Cary had never noticed before, a brightening of the hazel green that almost felt like…power.

"You can," she said, her deep voice even deeper. "And when some of that fire gets through to you, I want you to flow it to center on your hand, the way you did with Rory's fire, then roll it into a ball, bundle it up in the center of your palm."

Cary had told her about her last lesson with Rory in the car here. And Angie had tried to teach her a basic witch spell to use. Cary had managed to recreate the spell, in the confines and safety of the car, where she could concentrate. She still felt woefully unable for any of this when faced with a huge demon stalking toward her.

"You can do this," Angie said. She glanced back at the approaching demon. "Now!"

Cary turned sideways automatically, and also automatically set herself between Deacon, Angie, and the rapidly approaching fire shooting out of the demon's sword.

One day, she'd stop doing that, she thought in the part of her mind that could watch all this without screaming hysterically. A very small, tiny part of her brain.

She pulled on the stubbornness that kept insisting she get between people and danger, thought about that feeling she'd had with Aiden so many months ago, willed the fire to slow down. Willed it with a sheer fierce stubbornness she'd been relying on for years.

She was more than a little surprised when it worked.

Or, sort of worked. The fire slowed a little, moving more like a leisurely cruising car rather than a speeding train.

But it still hit her with a blast of breath-stealing heat and strength like she'd just gotten mowed over by the cruising car. She stumbled a step even as the fire scatter around her, the spell Marianne had put into the jeans activating, sending the waves of heat leaping to either side of Cary.

Some still got through. But unlike ordinary fire, this didn't sear her skin or catch her clothes on fire. It rolled *into* her, soaked in with such intense heat she might as well have caught fire.

She thought she screamed but it was hard to tell against the roar of the fire in her head. Knowing she should be hurt, that this should be killing her, it took her several moments to recognize that it wasn't. That she was filling up with heat, and fire, that her cells were taking this in, but not igniting. She wasn't alight.

Demon fire wasn't like dragon magic. There was no warm, soothing bath feeling here. There was scorching heat, sun so hot on her skin, she'd have a burn, but…

Bearable.

She could breathe.

For some reason, being able to breathe surprised her.

She heard Deacon shouting at her, but she couldn't speak, couldn't say anything over the sound of the fire rushing into her.

Only some of it. Not all. Marianne was a genius.

She also thought she heard Angie's voice, telling her to use the fire, to control it. She might have heard Rory's voice, too. Or that might have been a hallucination. At this point, she couldn't tell.

She did force her eyes open, force her brain to concentrate on the fire filling her up, pouring into her. When she focused, when she brought all her attention to the magic getting through, getting into her, it felt more and more like sun's heat, a dry heat like a very hot day in the desert.

It almost felt…good.

She concentrated on that sense of good heat, the way a rush of heat might feel after being indoors with the air conditioner cranked up to arctic. The way that heat would feel so lovely and nice after being too cold.

Holding that sense of contentment with the heat, she looked down at her palm and thought about rolling the heat into a ball in the center of her hand, using the visualizations Rory had taught her. Seeing the fire grow into a little mini sun. It was kind of cute, sitting there in her hand, dancing in red heat that no longer felt quite so overwhelming. Hot still, but also good. The heat felt really good now. A campfire warming her on a cold night. A super hot shower after coming in from a walk in the snow. That dry desert heat she hadn't experienced since she was a teenager on a school field trip, but had loved.

The little red sun in her palm grew, and grew, until it was the size of a soccer ball. She bounced it in the air once, like a ball, and then looked at the Lud-lookalike demon. It still had its sword pointing at her, but the fire had stopped pouring out of the tip of the sword and the demon was frowning at the weapon like something was wrong. When the giant being gave the sword a shake, the way someone might a remote control that had stopped working, Cary almost laughed.

She bounced the ball of fire on her palm again. Wow, it didn't just scatter or jump off. She felt it attached to her palm almost, like there was a thin string linking it to her, keeping it where she wanted. More controlled than she'd felt with the little flame on her fingertip she'd formed with Rory's magic.

Did that mean she was more comfortable with demon magic?

That probably didn't reflect well on her.

She glanced back at the demon, looming large only a few yards away, just as it started toward them again. How did demons feel about having their magic thrown back at them?

No time like the present to find out.

Bouncing the soccer ball-sized sun on her palm one more time, she took a step back and, with all her might, threw the ball of fire at the demon.

She was no athlete and had been a disaster at softball in grade school. So she was a little surprised by the distance she got on the throw. The little sun flew through the air, slamming the demon right in the stomach. She'd been aiming for its chest, but the stomach was close enough.

At least she hadn't missed all together.

The demon roared and reared back from the hit, like the fire ball hurt. Like she'd managed to inflict damage.

Wow. She never got to do offensive things. At least, not on purpose. But she'd just thrown some magic at a demon and the demon had to stop and yell about it.

That was…good right?

Maybe not. Since the demon shook itself hard and raised its sword overhead and screamed loud enough to make her eardrums pulse in painful protest.

She forced herself to concentrate. There was still heat coursing through her body. She hadn't used all the magic yet. She tried to call on the rest, focused on forming another ball of flame on her hand, but the demon approached so fast, she started to panic and threw a ball of much smaller flame this time.

The hit knocked the demon back a step, made it howl again, but then it started toward them faster this time.

Shit.

"Step against the containment circle," Angie shouted. "Try to soak up some of the magic in it."

"Can I do that?" Cary screeched, even as she stumbled back against the barrier.

"Try," Deacon said, his voice low. "I'll stall."

"Wait, what? No!"

But it was too late.

He leapt forward, in his leopard form, and charged the demon.

33

---

*C*ary cursed and threw herself against the containment circle even as Deacon, in leopard form, dove beneath the demon's sword.

His effort to distract the monster worked. Lud-lookalike swiveled around to attack the racing leopard. Deacon moved so fast, he blurred into nothing more than a streak of black. Impossible for her to follow. Fortunately, he seemed impossible for the demon to follow too. The demon swung at that blur of motion, missed, roared, and swung its sword again, only to miss again.

Thank the universe for shifter speed.

She settled her back against the solid, invisible barrier of the containment circle, and the flare of blue light she'd seen in her mind's eye when Angie had tried to break through flashed again, this time in a blinding halo that encompassed her entire body. She squinted against the light, and tried to focus on taking some of that light inside her.

This time the feeling was like static, like little tiny shocks to her system. Not like any of the other individual magics she'd worked with. Still heat there. A demon had set the circle, after all. But not the burn. And not the warmth. Closer to something she felt with Angie's magic. Electrical but not directly into her skin. Like lightning that struck a few

229

feet away and the sizzle of that electricity coated her without actually touching her.

"What do I do with this once I soak it up?" she asked Angie.

She could feel the containment circle's magic flowing into her faster now. Which was…maybe not good. She didn't want to break the circle and release the Lud-lookalike onto the realm. Even if that did mean she could get out and the rest of her friends could get in. Although, there were also vampires and the triad out there somewhere. And another demon.

Angie was quiet for a long moment, long enough, Cary glanced back at her.

Her eyes were heavy lidded and half closed, though she still seemed to be looking at something right in front of her. After another silent moment, she said, "Move away. Now."

Cary jumped away from the circle. The blue flare she'd been haloed in, died instantly, making her blink against the sudden darkness.

When she could see again, she glanced down at her hands. Nothing outwardly looked different. But she could see a faint faint glow of blue at the very periphery of her vision. If she tried to turn and look at the light directly, though, it faded.

"Okay, what do I have to work with? And what has it done to me?"

"Marianne's clothes scattered some of it," Angie said. "You picked up enough, though. You should be able to build a magic shield."

"Like my old shield."

"Except it won't last as long. But it's designed to work against demons. Listen."

Angie outlined the spell and the hand gestures in quick sentences, getting Cary to repeat each separately twice. They both watched Deacon spin the demon around in circles, avoiding the swing of the demon's fire sword, but the process of having to focus on a spell, to get a spell right in order to help, was overwhelming Cary with impatience.

"Focus," Angie snapped.

Cary startled back to her.

"I know you're scared for him," Angie said, lowering her voice. "But you have to focus or the spell won't work. The magic will spill out of you uselessly into a half-assed mess. Or worse, something will backfire, and you'll both be hurt. Pay attention. Deacon has the demon for now."

There was a howl of pain and Cary's heartbeat jumped into her throat. But when she turned to look, terrified she'd taken too long to help Deacon, she realized the howl came from the demon. Deacon had somehow carved a gaping wound in the black rock across the demon's chest, revealing a rolling plane of lava beneath.

Deacon hadn't been able to do anything like that to the real Lud. Good confirmation this wasn't the god. Also good, Deacon could hurt the demon.

Bad that the demon looked even more pissed off now, though.

"Focus," Angie said again. "This kind of magic needs focus."

"Fine. Focus." Focus, she told herself too. She had to get this right.

From beyond the fight between Deacon and the demon, Holland stood with his head tilted to one side, watching the proceedings, a slight frown on his face. His serious expression didn't give away his thoughts. But he didn't look inclined to get involved either. That worried her. A lot.

Focus, damn it. She brought her attention back to Angie, to repeating the phrases Angie was drilling into her. She got the hand gestures wrong the first few times, and without being able to touch her, Angie had a hell of a time correcting the gestures. But Cary got them on the fourth attempt and worked her fingers again and again until she could feel the gestures without having to think about them too closely.

"Yes," Angie said. "Now. Words and gestures together. They'll build you a shield. A half shield. It'll only cover the front of you. You'll be able to block anyone from reaching Deacon if he's behind you, but you'll have to keep the shield between you and the demon. This isn't like your Protector shield. Things can sneak up behind you."

"Shit," she muttered. She missed her Protector shield. Offensive skills were nice. It was brilliant to not feel helpless. But she really preferred just being impenetrable. "Okay, once the shield is up, then what? It won't last indefinitely."

She leaned back into the circle a moment more, soaking in a little more magic to use for her shield.

"Push the demon toward the opening it walked through. Force it back into its realm."

"Holland won't just let me do that." Although, the way he was staying out of all this, maybe he would. This felt like a part of his test.

She hated tests.

But she hated demons running around her realm even more. Especially when they were chasing after her mate.

"You have to try it," Angie said. "Add some of your will to it."

"You keep thinking I have more willpower than I do."

"Aidan said you'd make a good demon hunter with some training. You have the will. You've just never trained it."

"Aidan lied," Cary said. Aidan was a legendary demon hunter. But she was *not* right about Cary's will. Cary was certain of that.

Angie snorted. "She wouldn't lie about this. You can do this, Cary. Let's go."

"I should have learned this stuff before the big epic showdown, huh?"

"We ran out of time. And didn't expect to lose your Protector shield."

"There is that." She pulled in a deep breath and waited for an opening.

Deacon threw himself over the top of the demon, forcing the creature to turn in an awkward arc as it swung at him with its hands now, reaching for the blur of black rather than trying to slice with its sword.

Was that good or bad? She had no idea, but she did get her opening.

She rushed forward, muttering the spell Angie had taught her, at the same time as she wove her fingers together in the very specific pattern. She stumbled on a rock in the grass, but maintained the finger positions so she didn't screw up the spell. She did pause in the middle of her recitation for an instant and had to hope she hadn't screwed things up because by then she was between the demon and Deacon.

With a final outward flip of her fingers, she raised her hands in front of her and said the final word of the spell. A blue light erupted in front of her, arching over her like an actual, ginormous shield, a half dome of light between her and the demon. When the demon dropped its sword onto the blue light, she winced and half closed her eyes.

But the shield held.

Her knees wobbled with her relief.

"Handy," Deacon said from behind her, back in his human form.

"Are you hurt?"

"No." A pause. Then. "It healed when I shifted."

She let out an annoyed grunt, but couldn't really get mad at him for getting hurt since she only *just* got back from the hospital for getting shot. She'd be a bit of a hypocrite if she did get mad at him. Still, she wasn't *happy* he'd gotten hurt stalling a demon so she could learn a shield spell.

The demon tried to force its sword down through her shield. She could feel the effort, feel the push of its strength in her shoulders, like she was holding a physical shield against the demon. But the blue light held.

"Now what?" Deacon asked.

"Push it toward the tear in reality. Before the magic wears out."

She felt strong still, like she had enough to hold this shield. But in the back of her mind, she was very aware that ever moment that passed as she used this magic, the magic was draining away from her.

She shoved forward. To her relief, the demon dropped back a step. This wasn't so different from using her Protector shield. Except she had to keep her hands up, physically positioning the shield like it was an actual physical thing and not just this movable barrier that circled her.

She shoved again, hoping her shoulder strength would hold out, and suddenly very grateful for all the training she'd been doing with Lucy. She might have ended up on her ass a lot, but she was in better shape now.

The demon pushed back, swinging its sword around again to slam it down on top of her shield. She winced, grunting as she stopped to brace.

Deacon took hold of her shoulders, adding his strength to the effort. When the demon lifted his sword, Cary shoved forward again, suddenly and as fast as she could move. Which, with Deacon's strength helping her push, was faster and harder than she'd anticipated.

The shove moved the demon back again. It stumbled and fell another few steps closer to the opening into its realm. The creature was huge, towering over her, so being able to make it stumble felt like an absurd accomplishment.

She pushed forward faster, hoping to keep it off balance, and made an attempt to focus her will. To *will* the creature back to its realm. She poured that stubborn need to have it gone into her movements, into the shield.

And the demon continued to give ground.

As they neared the rip in reality, where the golden demon realm opened onto her world, Cary shoved harder, glaring up at the Lud-lookalike as it roared and tried to shove back at her. Thanks to Deacon keeping her upright, she had the strength to hold. And boy, did she want this thing gone from her realm.

A part of her was very aware that Holland was *right there*. Waiting. Watching. Ready to strike. And she couldn't give him any attention because the stupid Lud-lookalike kept resisting going through the reality rip.

She growled and pushed at the demon again. "Go back, you bastard," she snarled. "You aren't welcome here. I have other things to worry about. Get back to your own damned realm." With a shout of anger and desperation, she pushed harder, forcing the demon back. Two more steps. One more step.

It slammed its sword into the ground and gripped it like a tree branch or something, resisting her shoves.

The fire sword sizzled the grass and the ground around it started to melt and harden like lava hitting water.

The whole thing, for reasons she couldn't put her finger on, really just pissed her off. Not only was it trying to stay here, where it didn't belong, it was damaging the earth!

She roared again and shoved harder, pushing the shield out in front of her like a blue battering ram. "Go! Back!"

She poured all her anger, all her irritation, all her fear into that last word, and slammed her shield against the demon's sword, against the demon's hands.

To her utter surprise, the creature roared as if in pain, released its sword, and flew backward into its own realm. Literally. Like a string attached to its back had been jerked hard, retracting the demon through the rip in reality.

The rip closed with a blink. Suddenly and without any swirling ceremony.

Just…demon through, rip closed.

The burning sword in the ground was the only evidence the demon had actually been there.

Cary blinked a few times. Then looked at the area behind what had been a jagged window into another realm.

Angie's demon hunter stood there.

Sebastian gave her a little salute and then moved swiftly back into the trees.

Cary blinked again. Uhm. Had he sent the demon packing? Or had he just helped her do it?

She'd ask later. Now, with the immediate demon threat gone, she felt the physical drain of holding the shield. She dropped her hands and the blue light winked out. Leaving her exhausted.

And with no protection from Holland.

Who stood on the other side of the sword.

Slowly clapping.

"Well done, Ms. Redmond," Holland said as he let his hands drop to his sides after one final clap. "I'm impressed."

"Uh huh." Cary sucked in a breath, and using Deacon's strength to stay upright more than she wanted to admit, she faced Holland.

The night air brushed coolly against her skin, drying her sweat from working all that demon magic. The surrounding woods were quiet. She couldn't hear any fighting. That probably boded well for the continued standoff between her friends and Holland's people. Nothing had broken the temporary truce, or whatever it was they had going out there. Which meant she had time for questions.

"Wanna explain all that?" she asked Holland, gesturing to the spot where the rip in reality had been just moments before.

"Crash course in what a human who can absorb magic can do," Holland said.

"Uh huh." She shook her head. "Not buying it. Try again."

"I had to know what you were capable of. My father isn't...the usual opponent."

"Yeah. I remember." She spread her hands. "Are we done with the tests now?"

"I don't know. Do you feel able to face my father? Have you learned enough in the last few moments?"

"What the ever-loving-fuck are you talking about?"

"You no longer have your Protector shields. You can, however, absorb magic. And use it. Do you know what usually happens with people like you, Ms. Redmond?"

"We die. Yeah. I've heard. Long history of very short lives."

"Except for you. You can do… Well, what most of the humans like you might have learned to do if they'd survived long enough."

Her head was starting to hurt, just a little at the temples. She wasn't sure if that was Holland's mind games and tests and tricks, or if it was the use of all that magic. "Listen, could you just let my friends in and we'll sort out your dad. We have to figure out how to get your mother here in a way that doesn't involve any sacrifices. I'm not good with sacrifices. Still."

"You aren't going to collapse from exhaustion yet?" Holland asked, sounding sincerely curious, if not particularly concerned.

"I can keep upright a bit longer." Which did sort of surprised her.

Whenever she channeled non-Protector magic, and released it—mostly on accident—it left her exhausted and often sent her to sleep. And frankly, she could feel that exhaustion at the edges of her awareness, creeping in, waiting for a vulnerable moment to overwhelm her. But for the moment, she had so much adrenaline coursing through her, she could push that exhaustion off. She'd sleep later. Once everyone—except Lud of course—survived all this.

"It's okay to rest now, Ms. Redmond," Holland said. "I might have exaggerated the time it will take for my father to get here."

She closed her eyes. Probably not the best of reactions around Holland. But Deacon would be watching him, and since Deacon still had a hand on her back, keeping her upright, he'd warn her if Holland did anything sudden.

"What?" she asked her demon nemesis.

"I had to see if you'd still be useful to me, Ms. Redmond. If, without your Protector powers, you could do…anything."

"Gee, thanks?" She opened her eyes. "So if your Lud-lookalike had killed me, then two birds, right? I can't help you, but I'm dead, so yay?"

"Oh, no. I would have stopped my Lud-lookalike, as you call him, short of killing you. I wouldn't give another demon the satisfaction of killing you. That's my prerogative."

She snorted.

"But until it's time to kill you," Holland said, "I needed to know what I could do with you."

Deacon growled. Cary snarled right along with him. In fact, her nerves fairly hummed with the anger coursing under her skin. The anger that felt so volatile and hot, she thought she might just throw herself at Holland and rip his throat out with her bare hands. She could even picture it. Clear as day. One hand wrapped around his throat. Her claws sliding out in a rush, piercing demon skin. Yanking back, tearing her claws through his throat…

She blinked. Uh. Wait.

What?

She turned a little to look up at Deacon. His eyes were solid, glowing yellow, his leopard right out in the open and only a hair's breath from coming out. He stared at Holland, his jaw tight, a little jump of the muscle in his cheek giving away the amount of anger he was holding in check. Barely.

She reached back and touched is chest, trying to draw his attention down to her. "I think you need to calm down a little," she whispered. "You're…leaking some of that anger into me. And I'm not sure I can physically manage the things I'm thinking of doing with…what I'm taking in from you."

He looked down at her, slowly, as if it was difficult to look away from Holland. But as he stared at her face, something moved through the solid granite of his expression. He blinked a few times and the glowing yellow in his eyes vanished suddenly. So suddenly she nearly gasped.

"Fuck," he muttered and took his hand off her back. "I…"

"Shh. It's okay. We'll talk about it later." The fact that, for the first time, he was using and releasing enough magic that she'd soaked some of it up was definitely something they'd need to deal with. But later. When they didn't have a demon studying them.

She faced Holland again, missing Deacon's touch but understanding he needed a moment to pull himself together. She made the effort to stay upright on her own. But it was an effort.

Holland looked between her and Deacon, his lips pursed, his eyes narrowed. An expression she didn't trust in the least. "So," she said to try and distract his attention from what had just happened. "What does all this testing bullshit mean? You think I'm useful to you now? Or not? Is daddy coming tonight? Or was this all just some sort of false alarm?"

"Not technically a false alarm," Holland said, his gaze still narrowed and moving between her and Deacon. "But we have more time than I indicated. Which we'll need."

"For what?"

"For your lessons, Ms. Redmond." His gaze settled on her again. And he smiled. Slowly.

Cary took an involuntary step backward.

Holland's grin turned into a knowing smirk. "Magic school," he said with a lot of irony, "is in session."

35

"You've got to be kidding me," Cary said, not for the first time. She had been staring at Holland for what felt like an hour but which was probably only a minute total. She was certain she'd heard him wrong.

What the hell did he mean by "magic school" and her "lessons"? And did she even really want to know the answers to those questions?

The clearing was very dark now, but a natural kind of dark. Ordinary even. With night bugs starting to chirp and the leaves shimmering with the faint, cold breeze.

A part of her became aware of people coming out of the woods. She hoped most of those people were her people. Her friends. But she also knew some of them would be vampires—who hated her—and Holland's witch triad—who also hated her—and whatever other allies Holland had brought with him. There as at least one demon there somewhere, as well, even though, according to Angie, Sebastian had contained it.

In the fight against Lud, they'd need all the help they could get. But combining forces with Holland's cohort felt wrong on so many levels.

Holland waved his hand in a sweeping gesture, almost like he was brushing something away from just in front of him. A moment later,

Angie was next to Cary, standing on the opposite side of her from Deacon.

"You okay?" she murmured, though she kept her attention on Holland.

"Tired," Cary said back, most of her attention still on Holland too —though from the corner of her eyes, she watched for her own allies, ensuring Marianne and Lucy were there and safe. When she saw them emerge from the woods, she let out a quiet, relieved breath.

"Gonna collapse?" Angie asked.

"Not yet."

"Good. I heard what he said."

"Did you understand it?" Because Cary was still trying to work out what Holland intended. "What the fuck?" she asked Holland directly. "Magic school?" That sounded like a joke. Something from a book or movie, and he was trying to be clever.

"You need to learn how to use all this magic you take in, Ms. Redmond," Holland said. "You haven't learned enough. You haven't practiced…hardly at all as far as I can see. You need some knowledge of what to do with the different kinds of magic. Without that, you'll die at my father's hand in moments, and I'll have to deal with him on my own. And I hate dealing with my father. I went to a great deal of trouble to try and avoid dealing with my father. I'd hate to have all that effort come to naught."

She wanted to ask what he meant. Again. But—unfortunately—she thought she might be getting the idea. She hated the idea. In every ounce of her being. But she was pretty sure she understood what he was getting at.

It was a terrible, terrible idea.

Which might just work.

And boy did she hate that even more.

"Spill the specifics," she said to Holland as Marianne and Lucy hurried up to stand with them.

"You take in magic. You can't stop it. You have to use it to get rid of it."

She wanted to close her eyes and sigh. She didn't. She'd only just figured out using the magic helped. The fact that he got that part so readily was a little humiliating. Her only consolation was that she was a lot younger than he was and hadn't had as much time to learn things. Seven years compared to a demon lifetime was…yeah, not long enough.

The fact that her dragon mentor had also not worked this out so fast and he'd been around for millennia did make her feel a little better, though.

And Holland had just watched her try to use the magic she took in. He had that advantage.

"You don't know the techniques," Holland finished. "And you have no idea what to do with demon power."

"Hey, I managed just fine, thank you very much," she snapped. She'd used up everything the Lud-lookalike had thrown at her and managed to wound him. Sort of. And yes, yes, not for very long. Still.

"That demon's power was nothing to my father's. Nothing to mine, to be blunt. A few blasts of fire aren't going to slow my father down. Even if you're using his own powers against him. Unless of course the first hit kills you. How are you preventing those blasts from killing you, by the way, without Protector shields?"

"I might have to talk to you and maybe even learn something from you, but I'm not telling you anything I don't have to."

Marianne patted her on the back, and Lucy nodded emphatically.

Holland's eyes narrowed as he took in the friends circling her.

Cary realized the rest had gathered too. She glanced back. No Protector's yet. And weirdly, no Jaxer. That was a little unnerving. Where had he gone?

But Erianna, Brandon, Angie's Sebastian, the leopards, even Sheldon were all standing at her back now. She couldn't protect any of them at the moment. And yet, they were all still there.

She faced Holland again. "Get back to the specifics. Are you going to give me some of your power to play with? Is that how this is going to work?"

Holland raised a brow. "I was thinking more along the lines of getting you used to using witch magic." He glanced at Angie. "And maybe have the demon hunter teach you a few…things." His gaze skimmed over Sebastian. "There's not much more you can learn about fighting in only a few hours. So the shifters will just be…" He shrugged.

"They're my muscle," Cary said.

Brandon and Deacon both grunted, in a tone that was so similar, she might have smiled under other circumstances.

"Muscle is useless against my father," Holland said.

"It'll be helpful if there are other demons."

She hoped. They'd lost two leopards in the last fight with Lud. She'd never really gotten over that. She tried not to blame herself, but she was the whole reason they'd been there, and so she did blame herself every time she thought about it. But she didn't have time to wallow in guilt now.

"You want me to fight a demon god," she said to Holland, meeting his remarkably non-red blue eyes. "I need more to work with. I need some of you."

There. The gauntlet had been thrown. If he was serious about this, he was going to have to hit her with a little of his own power. Give her something she could really work with against his dad.

Having Holland purposefully throw his demon powers at her when he wanted to kill her was probably not the best of ideas. And maybe she shouldn't have thrown this gauntlet. But he needed her help still. Or they wouldn't still be standing here talking. So he wasn't going to kill her. Yet.

She hoped.

He held her gaze for a long moment. "You're willing to risk it? I could kill you and be done with it."

"Yup. You could. And then just you and daddy and… What was it? Sacrifice? Usually sacrifice with demons. Probably a lot of pain for you I imagine. After the body swapping of course. Then you die at your mom's hand and nothing you can do about it except watch your dad walk away in your unkillable body. I suppose if that's what you want…"

Holland's eyes narrowed but just a little, just a hint of some readable emotion beyond his bland curiosity. She didn't look away. Even as the vampires came out of the woods to stand behind Holland. Their whispers and goading were, fortunately, just outside her hearing range. Poor Deacon and the other leopards would have to hear whatever the assholes were saying. But she got to happily ignore them.

"What do you say, Holland? A little exchange. To seal the deal, so to speak. I trust you not to kill me yet." Ha! Trust wasn't quite the right word here. "You trust me with some of your power?"

The witches moved through the vampires to stand next to Holland on one side. James came out of the midst of his hive to stand on Holland's other side.

She wanted to shake her head. Having all the people in the city that wanted her dead standing in a row, and them all figuring out how to work together… It was really bizarre.

To be fair, she didn't think James wanted her dead, even if the rest of his hive did. But now that he knew she wasn't a Protector, she couldn't count on that either. She was of no use to him anymore. So he might want her dead just because she knew too much about the hive.

"Actually, Ms. Redmond," Holland said, pulling her attention away from the circling crowd. "I think giving you a little of my power might just be the thing."

ary blinked a few times as she stared at Holland. The fact that an unkillable demon who hated her and wanted her dead, but also needed her just then, *wanted* to give her some of his powers seemed… Well, just wrong. And weird. And probably a trick.

She couldn't help feeling all this was a trick somehow. Holland wouldn't give her power just because. Even to train her so she could defend him against his father. There was a trick in here somewhere. Demons always had tricks.

"It's a trick," Angie said quietly near her ear.

Cary nearly burst out laughing. "Same exact thought."

"But," Angie said, "one that might work for you rather than against you."

"How?"

"You'll be a lot harder to kill with my magic coursing through those sponge-like cells of yours, Ms. Redmond," Holland said. Proving that whispering was pointless around him.

She should have known. "But only temporarily," she pointed out.

"Well, I wouldn't want to make that permanent after all." Holland smiled. "I wouldn't be in my best interest then, now, would it?"

She snorted. "The night is getting on. How long do we really have before your daddy arrives?"

Holland glanced at the witches.

The lead witch, a red-head named Justina smiled at Cary. "Well met, sister," she said. "I see you've more surprises for us."

"Sure sure. Not up to anything nefarious recently, I hope."

Justina smiled. "Depends on your definition."

Cary glanced at the two witches flanking Justina. The Black witch was dressed, as usual, in a level of sophisticated sexiness Cary really envied—this time in dark gray pants and a white sweater that glowed in the dark. Her head was still shaved, which showed off the sharp, angular gorgeousness of her flawless face. And her dark brown eyes were, as usual, impossible to read. She controlled her expression carefully, revealing only a very faint smile.

The oldest looking but weakest of the group still looked like a fresh-faced California surfer girl, with shoulder length blond hair, blue eyes, and a tan that looked a little unnatural in the Pacific Northwest autumn. She wore ripped jeans, slung low around her narrow hips, and a cropped sweatshirt that showed off her sculpted abs.

Justina, the leader of the group and the youngest looking witch, still dressed in the romantic hippy clothes she seemed to favor, this time a flowing, purple paisley print skirt under a thigh-length black poet-shirt. Her thick red hair flowed around her, a dark rich color against her light brown skin. Hazel eyes revealed absolutely nothing she didn't intend to show.

Cary only knew Justina's name. The other two had refused to provide any. Even James hadn't called them by name, outside of Justina, and Cary finally realized that was on purpose. The fact that she could know Justina's name but not the other two only emphasized to Cary how strong a witch Justina must be.

The last time she'd seen them all, they'd been unconscious on the floor of the vampire hive after swapping bodies with the Angel of Death. All three at once had had to swap bodies with the Angel just to make room.

"What says my mother about my father's approach?" Holland asked Justina.

The witch glanced at him, then closed her eyes and the other two witches followed suit. They moved in unison in a way that Cary found both fascinating and a little terrifying. Especially since their eyes were closed so they couldn't follow each other's movements visually. And they weren't touching, so it wasn't something they could coordinate through feel. Obviously, it had to do with magic, and their bond as a triad, but even knowing that didn't make the process seem any less creepy to Cary.

"This doesn't look good," Lucy said quietly, leaning a little around Marianne to whisper near Cary's ear.

"Nope," Cary said. "Where's Jaxer?"

"He vanished into the trees when the vampires appeared," Marianne said, also in a whisper.

"He didn't tell you where he was going?"

"No," Lucy said. "I didn't even notice him leave."

"I saw him slip away," Marianne said. "But only just. Might have missed his disappearing act if I hadn't looked away from the gathering hive at just that moment."

"Where the hell did he go?" Cary muttered. "And where are the other Protectors?"

"And why are there all these vampires here?" Lucy said quietly. "Don't they hate you?"

"Yes. Yes, they do."

"Do they know you're here to help?" Marianne asked.

"James would know. He was in on all this from the beginning." Although, she'd never really found out *why* since vampires didn't normally deal with demons. James hadn't seen fit to elaborate on the reasoning behind his part in all this. "But also, now he knows…things have changed with me."

Despite knowing he knew, knowing that Holland knew, she couldn't quite bring herself to say the words aloud for just any of her collected enemies to hear.

Not that the witches would be able to hear anything just then.

They dropped their heads back, moving into a sort of circle so that the very tops of their heads almost touched. Their hands came out to their sides. Their shoulders stiffened.

They'd looked like this when they'd swapped bodies with the Angel.

Did that mean they were going to do that now? Bringing her here *now*?

Cary's heartbeat hammered. She'd expected them to be able to talk with the Angel without having to swap bodies. And she'd expected the Angel to be busy doing…whatever it was she had to do to manifest here in this realm.

The idea that she was going to have to face the Angel right away without mentally preparing for it—even though she *knew* it would happen at some point because it had to or Lud couldn't be killed—was panic-inducing. She took an involuntary step away from the witches. And wasn't even entirely sure why. She'd seen the Angel kill from inside a containment circle, while occupying the witches' bodies. They hadn't built that circle this time. There wasn't even the illusion this time that the Angel would be somehow contained.

Wait…

Why hadn't they built a containment circle?

She didn't have time to ask aloud as their bodies started to shiver, a low-level vibration running visibly through them.

The hairs on Cary's arms stood up. The back of her neck prickled. A feeling like ants crawling over her skin made her want to itch and fidget. She leaned back, intent on asking Angie if she felt all this, only to hear Angie murmuring quietly under her breath.

Cary recognized the spell. Angie was building a protective circle. Whether it would work against the Angel of Death…

A clap of thunder sounded in the distance. The bang loud enough Cary jumped. Then she scowled at herself. What the fuck had made her think she could be a superhero of her own making? What a ridiculous idea. She jumped at fucking thunder.

Justina straightened her head and the other witches followed her in a wave of motion, too coordinated to be natural. When Justina opened her eyes, they were solid white.

"We have come," a voice emerged from all three women at once. The sound coming from the triad was like an echo coming from far off, growing more substantial and louder as it neared, but crawling over the top of itself as it moved. "We are here. Cary Redmond."

The Angel of Death herself.

Talking to Cary. Instead of her own son.

Oh boy.

37

"**M**other," Holland said, ignoring the fact that his mother had greeted Cary first instead of him.

His tone was more deferential than anything Cary had ever heard from him before. Even the lilt of the English accent he'd adopted seemed to drop away a little. She'd have never considered someone to sound *more* formal with *less* English accent in their voice, but here they were. Somehow that's exactly what happened when Holland greeted the entity that was his mother.

This was all so very weird.

A cold burst of wind moved through the circling trees, ruffling the leaves, and making Cary shiver. Even the heat from the sword the Lud-lookalike had left buried in the ground couldn't offset the chill in Cary's bones. The fall night was scented with pine and her own stress sweat, and filled with the sounds of night insects and a collective group of people—and monsters—all holding their breaths.

Okay, she couldn't technically hear everyone holding their breaths. But she was sure they all were. She certainly was.

From the corner of her eyes, she saw Angie's hands subtly drop, a gesture too deliberate to be just an idle movement. Cary narrowed her eyes and softened her gaze a little. And there, at the edge of her peripheral vision, she could see the faint blue light of Angie's protective circle. She couldn't see the edge in front of her, but she was aware of it if she didn't try too hard to see it.

Being able to see magic was a new and pretty cool trick. Without her Protector shields interfering, she seemed more able to pick these things up.

Or maybe that was just because she'd been absorbing a lot of different magic already that night and was likely to get hit with more before the hour was up.

Where the hell were Jaxer and the other Protectors? She could really use an indestructible shield or two just then. She trusted Angie's magic and Angie's circle would be a good strong one. But this was the Angel of Death, and normal rules just didn't apply.

Cary wasn't even sure her Protector shield had ever been anything more than a security blanket when it came to the Angel. But, boy, had it made her feel more secure.

Right now, even within Angie's circle, she felt vulnerable and terrified.

"Cary Redmond," the Angel said, in her echoing, distant voice, "you have come to protect my son from his father."

Cary noticed how the Angel hadn't bothered to return her son's greeting. Or how Holland stiffened slightly at the snub.

She swallowed hard, to wet a very dry throat, and made a conscious effort *not* to lean into Deacon for strength. Given the last time they'd been touching she'd somehow picked up some of his leopard feelings, she didn't think them touching right now would be a good idea.

"Hi," Cary said to the Angel. "Yeah, I suppose that's what I'm here to do. Uhm, how long do we have? To plan and…stuff?" She winced. Wow, she was bad at this part. The Angel *had* to know Cary was no longer a Protector if Holland knew.

There was an echoing of sound, then a reverberation, like the first sounds arrived then bounced back into the sounds behind them and mixed everything up a little. The words spoken eventually untangled themselves enough that Cary could understand.

"He has found a way through," the Angel said. "He anticipates victory here. We cannot exist in this plane to kill him. He thinks. He will attempt to kill our son here."

"Yeah, yeah. But, uhm, how long do we have?"

It occurred to Cary that the Angel's sense of time had to be vastly different from her own. Even if the Angel said "soon," that could mean, like, another year or two. She'd said "soon" before and now they were three weeks later. And a lot of stuff had happened in those three weeks. Or at least in the last week.

The witches, in unison, turned their heads toward Holland. "The sacrifice is ready?" she asked him.

"Wait, no." Cary stepped forward, despite herself. "No sacrificing. I've already said that. No sacrificing. You're an angel. You can figure out how to incarnate, or whatever, here without it. No sacrificing."

Three heads turned back so that Justina's white eyes once again focused on Cary. "It is the only way. We must be there in a corporeal form to kill him. We cannot do that without a sacrifice."

Cary closed her eyes and let out a slow breath. "Then we move this fight somewhere else. I don't care. Whatever has to happen to eliminate the sacrificing part needs to happen."

"You cannot travel to the demon god's realm."

No. Cary was well aware. Human body and all that. Still. She didn't say anything immediately.

Which earned her a hissed, "You are not going into a demon realm to die," from Deacon.

"I know, I know," she hissed back.

"Unless…" Angie said.

And for a heartbeat, it felt like everything in the clearing went silent. Everything stilled. Even the insects in the trees. The breeze. Everything just stopped.

Cary turned slowly to look at Angie. "Unless, what?"

"I'll be the sacrifice," Sheldon said, stepping away from a scowling Eriana.

"You will not," Eriana said. "I didn't just spend the last few weeks making you better only to have you die now."

"I'm useless otherwise," Sheldon said. "What the hell use am I to anyone?"

"That's for you to figure out," Cary snapped. "And you can't figure it out while you're dead. So no. No sacrificing." She glanced at Eriana. "Tie that boy down if he tries."

Eriana gave a sharp chin lift in assent.

"You can't," Sheldon said. "It's my choice."

"I don't care," Cary said. "This isn't a choice anyone is going to make."

"I told you there was a volunteer," Holland said. "Didn't I?"

"You can shut up. This is all your fault."

"My fault?" He put a hand to his chest. "I didn't ask to get born only so that my father could escape his destiny."

"Yeah, and that sucks too, but you're a demon, and I care a lot less. Especially since you're an asshole."

Holland's brows lifted, but he smirked at her, and that only made her want to smash her fist into his face. The violence of the thought startled her enough, she glanced down to make sure Deacon wasn't touching her. He wasn't. Violent thought about enemy demon was all her own.

That was good or bad?

She cut a hand through the air. "No one is sacrificing. No one is dying. Am I clear?"

"Someone has to die," the Angel said.

"Lud. Lud can die. That's it."

"Everyone dies. Everyone comes to dance with us."

"Yes, yes, creepy scary reality. I know. Stop already." She faced Angie. "What was your 'unless' about? If it's someone else doing some sort of sacrificing of their lives, though, the answer is no."

Angie's lips twitched but her smile never formed. She exchanged a look with Sebastian.

"You haven't done it in years," he said quietly, his own English accent a balm where Holland's felt like nails on a chalkboard in Cary's skull. "You still sure you want to try?"

"Of course I am," Angie said.

Sebastian ran a thumb over Angie's cheek. "This isn't the usual demon realm. Even demons can't access it. It might not work."

"Unfortunately," Angie said, leaning into his touch a moment before straightening away, "I already know it will."

Sebastian frowned at her as he dropped his hand back to his side.

"I'm missing something," Cary said, her gaze jumping between Angie and the demon hunter. "Something that feels pretty important."

"And dangerous," Lucy said.

"Seems very very dangerous," Marianne added.

Angie raised her hands, palms up. "I…have a particular talent that I have been running away from for most of my life. Except for a very short period of time, when I…worked with the demon hunters."

Cary narrowed her gaze on Angie. "A witch working with demon hunters?"

"It's a long story we don't have time for," Angie said. "But what you need to know is that…" She scowled and looked around the clearing. "Too damned many people here," she muttered.

Cary put a hand on her shoulder. "Don't. If this is something you've been running from, I'm not going to ask you to confront it now, here. We'll find another way."

"You have a choice, Cary Redmond." The Angel's voice echoed in the clearing. "We will kill the demon god. It is his destiny. Where we do that is of no consequence to us."

Well Cary sure as hell wasn't sacrificing anyone to get the Angel here. But if the Angel didn't incarnate here before Lud, there was no way to get rid of Lud. But she also wasn't going to ask her best friend to do something she didn't want to do. Just because Cary had been thrown into the middle of all this, didn't mean anyone else needed to sacrifice anything.

"You have three hours," Holland said into the silence. "Three hours before my father rips into this realm."

"How do you know that?"

"My mother just told me," he said, as if talking to a child.

Cary snarled at him for the tone. But realizing his mother had been able to talk to him without anyone else hearing, that the Angel could select who heard her, even speaking through the witches, was terrifying.

"I can teach you a lot in three hours," Holland said. "But that won't change the choice before you, Ms. Redmond. A sacrifice. Or the demon witch's alternative. Those are the only ways."

"Why does Holland seemed to know what you can do?" Cary murmured to Angie while keeping her focus on the demon.

"More of that long story," Angie said. "There's a reason I avoid demons."

"Demon witch?" That wasn't the first time Cary had heard someone refer to Angie that way. But it *was* the first time in years. And Angie had never told her what the term meant.

"You'll see," Angie said. "If we get to that."

Sebastian and Angie exchanged another long look. Cary got the feeling a lot went into that look.

"We could kill them all," one of the vampires behind James hissed. The rest of the vampires laughed.

Cary sighed and rolled her eyes. She would have preferred not having so many vampires hanging around during all this. It was like they were just waiting, like vultures, to clean up after the blood had been spilled.

And Cary couldn't shake the feeling that, before the night was out, they'd get their wish.

Blood would be spilled.

38

"Teach me what you can," Cary said to Holland. "We only have three hours. Teach me how to fight your father. The rest..."

Well, she didn't know. But she wasn't letting Sheldon sacrifice himself. And she didn't want Angie to do something she didn't want to do—had in fact actively avoided for years—if she didn't have to.

"How long can they remain body swapped with the Angel?" Cary asked, nodding at the triad. The high wind moved through the clearing, cold and sharp as the night got darker, but none of the wind seemed to touch the witches. The eerie way their clothing and hair didn't move even when a sharp wind blew past them was...a little too freaky to think about.

"As long as the Angel needs them to," Holland answered.

Cary sighed. That didn't sound good, not for the triad anyway, but who was she to intervene. The witches had made this deal. She gestured at Holland. "Okay, let's get on with this. We don't have much time."

"Or we could just eat you now," one of the vampires murmured, moving forward.

James raised a hand without looking at any of his people and the hive fell silent. The vampire who'd moved forward snarled but fell back behind James again.

"We'll just wait out of the way," he said to Cary.

"I really wish you weren't here right now," Cary said to him.

He smiled his big, teeth-flashing smile that she found so very disconcerting. "I know. But I wouldn't miss this for the world."

"It may be the end of the world, you know?" Cary snapped.

"I'm very tempted to quote a song lyric here," James said. "But actually, I'd rather our realm didn't end just yet, so…"

He flicked his fingers at the hive, and the vampires all flowed backward toward the trees, like the shadows of fast-moving clouds, flowing over the ground, silent but for some quiet hissing and the flash of yellow eyes and white white teeth.

"We'll stay out of the way until you need us," James said.

"Or until there's a glut of blood to feast on?"

He smiled again, but this time kept his mouth closed so he didn't flash his teeth. She blinked, and he was gone.

Presumably, he'd joined his hive at the edge of the trees, but she couldn't see him there, or really any of the vampires clearly. Just shadows, and those occasional flashes of their yellow eyes. But the hair prickling on the back of her neck assured her they were still there, watching.

"Do you want us to keep an eye on them?" Lucas murmured quietly to Deacon, nodding at the vampires.

Deacon gave a sharp nod. "But stay close. Don't engage unless necessary."

"Yes, my prince," Lucas said in that formal way he used whenever they were going into a fight.

Which should probably have made Cary suspicious. The last thing she needed was a leopard and vampire fight while she was trying to fend off a demon god.

As Cary watched the leopards stalk closer to the trees and those glowing yellow eyes, Marianne pulled something out of the purse she had hanging across her shoulder. It was a small enough purse, the size that would hold a wallet and cellphone and a few other necessities but nothing even so big as a tablet or hardback book. From the depths of that ordinary looking accessory, she pulled a small fold of cloth, a dark blue square of cotton. Maybe cotton. Cary wasn't an expert in fabric.

"What's that?" Cary whispered.

"Little extra," Marianne said. "When we need it."

Cary narrowed her eyes, but Marianne didn't answer. Okay. She trusted Marianne. She'd stop asking questions. But she was insanely curious. What Marianne could do with any single strip of fabric was always amazing, and Cary really really wanted to know what that particular bit of ordinary-looking material could do.

"If we're going to let Holland give you demon magic," Angie said, loud enough for Holland to hear.

He raised his brows at the "if" part of her sentence.

She emphasized it again. "If we let him give you demon magic to work with, I want it done inside a containment circle."

"Oh yeah." Cary faced Holland. "Yeah. We're doing this inside a circle. Last thing I need is to loose demon magic on accident." She looked at the others. "And you'll all stay outside the circle."

"No," Deacon, Angie, Marianne, and Lucy all said at the exact same moment and with the exact same tone.

The synchronicity was so perfect it kind of reminded Cary of the way the witches moved together while the Angel occupied their three bodies at once. Which was almost enough to distract her from the argument she was about to get into.

"I'll stay inside the circle too," Sebastian said. "Better to have a hunter here with the demon. Just in case." He turned his attention to Holland and the two men stared at each other.

Cary wondered if there was some sort of contest of wills going on in that stare. "What about the other demon?" she asked Sebastian. "The one in the woods that Holland brought with him?"

Holland raised his brows and smiled a little, but he didn't stop staring at the hunter.

"That one's been contained. It will stay where it is unless I release it," Sebastian said.

"Okay, well don't do that." She didn't need any more demons

running around than were already here. Holland was one demon too many actually.

The staring contest continued between hunter and demon. Cary looked between them. Then at the rest of her friends, who were *not* moving away from her impending demon magic lesson. And what little patience she had left grew perilously thin.

"Listen," she said, "I do not know what I'm doing here. I'm supposed to be learning—from someone I don't trust—how to use magic that might *slow down* his demon father. And that's gonna be dangerous."

"You managed it with other demon power," Angie pointed out.

"Inside a circle. With all of you outside of it." She winced. "Except Deacon. And I'd prefer if he hadn't been there too." Except that he'd been distracting the demon for her while she practiced Angie's spell, which took time.

Time she really didn't have.

Fuck. Holland was right. She didn't know how to do the stuff she needed to do with any of the magic she pulled in yet. She hadn't had time to practice any of this. To learn any of it. And she only had three hours to practice now before having to face an actual demon god while the Angel of Death still didn't have a way to incarnate here and kill that demon without sacrificing someone. Which Cary wasn't going to allow.

Every time she thought about their situation, the reality of just how fucked they were smacked her in the face.

"A containment circle is best," Holland said, blinking very slowly before looking away from Sebastian to stare at Cary. "I won't be taking it easy on you. Your friends will be safer outside the circle." His gaze flicked to Deacon. "And your leopard. It would be better if he didn't try to rip my throat out."

Deacon's eyes were full shifter yellow glow in the darkness. But he didn't rise to Holland's prodding.

In fact, he had his iceman expression on. The one that was all control and distance. She couldn't read him when he got that way, but she recognized his need to go there when he felt his control slipping.

There were other leopards around, and if his control slipped here and now, he was as likely to hurt them as anyone else. Or do other thing he'd regret later, like controlling them without their consent. She hated his iceman, but she understood why he was wrapping himself in that absolute control at the moment.

He didn't even blink at Holland's comment. He didn't say anything back. He just stared at the demon.

"Deacon is staying here," Cary said, against her own impulse to protect him. He'd lose his mind if he wasn't beside her right now. The fact that he had to assert as much control as he was only emphasized that fact.

And frankly, she wanted him at her back. She'd rather he was safe, but if they were both going to be in danger anyway, she wanted him close so they could protect each other. Even if she could no longer do that in her ordinary way.

She'd never thought she'd miss that damned job this much.

She faced her friends. "I'd rather you were all just outside the circle, though. I won't be able to focus if I think you're in danger."

"I'm staying," Angie said and raised a hand when Cary opened her mouth to object. "We've been working together on this. At least on how you deal with magic you absorbed." Her gaze flicked to Holland. "And I know how demon magic works. How demons work. I'm staying here with you, as much as anything to make sure what he tells you about how to use the magic is correct."

"And how would you know what's correct?" Holland asked Angie.

"Long story." She didn't take her attention from Cary. "But I've had more than enough experience with demons."

"More than she ever should have," Sebastian muttered so quietly, Cary wasn't sure she was supposed to have heard him.

Boy, she was curious about their story.

She shook off the need to ask questions and said, "Okay, Angie and Deacon and no one else. Sebastian can help from outside the circle." The less people she had to worry about, the better.

"We will return in two hours," the Angel said before anyone could object to Cary's orders.

Cary startled at the sound of her voice. The Angel of Death had just been standing there inside the triad's bodies, watching all this. And Cary had forgotten she was there. That felt really…stupid. Like, the height of stupidity to forget literal *Death* was standing a few yards away.

"Wait," Cary called. "We haven't figured out how you'll… incarnate without a sacrifice."

"There is always sacrifice," the Angel said. "Just as there is always death."

Cary wanted to say more, but the witches' bodies started to vibrate and tremble. They dropped their heads back simultaneously, their mouths opened wide, a flash of blinding light encompassed the clearing.

And when Cary had blinked back the spots filling her vision, there was only the triad, now passed out on the ground.

She knew from the last time this had happened that they'd be okay. They were here after all. But she wondered what body swapping with the Angel twice in one night, so close together, would do to them.

Something for the triad to worry about. Cary had to focus on her own task. Learning how to use demon magic.

Marianne handed Cary the square of blue fabric. "If you need it, drop it on the ground and step on top of it," she murmured close to Cary's ear.

Cary nodded, once again overwhelmed with questions, but recognizing if Marianne wasn't being specific there was a good reason and she needed to keep her own mouth shut.

Then Marianne pulled something else out of her purse. A long set of knitting needles. Cary raised her brows.

"I'll get bored waiting for you," Marianne said with a shrug that Cary realized wasn't as casual as Marianne was trying to make it. "Just want to keep my hands occupied."

Cary had great hope that whatever Marianne kept her hands occupied doing would be good for their side and bad for the demons' side.

Lucy's gaze jumped between Holland and Cary a few times. "I

can't help with the magic," she said quietly. "But remember what I've been teaching you about thinking less and letting your muscle memory take over."

Cary nodded, though she didn't trust her muscle memory completely. Especially when it came to using magic. She didn't have muscle memory for magic. She'd learned so much about so many different things over the years, including studying various kinds of magic and the theory behind the way things got used. But she'd never *used* magic on purpose until so very recently.

And now it was all she had.

"You've got this," Lucy said.

Cary really really hoped she was right.

39

As the people not staying inside the protective circle moved a few yards away, and Angie quietly built the spell that would encompass a small area of the clearing to keep those outside safe from what went on inside, Cary turned for a quiet word with Deacon.

She hesitated to take his hands, given how much control he seemed to be exerting. She didn't want to risk his control. But not touching him felt icky and wrong on so many levels, she gave in to the impulse, gently gripping one of his wrists. He was stiff, his muscles bunched and hard as a rock under her hand. He looked down at her, but there was no expression on his face.

"I get this iceman," she murmured. "I won't give you shit about it."

His expression remained the same, but there was a very faint twitch at the side of his eyes that let her know he appreciated her bad attempt at lightening the situation.

"Just don't do any violence unless necessary," she said. "This is going to be... Well, I don't know. I've never *purposefully* absorbed demon magic. I'm worried I'll hurt someone."

"You'll be fine," Deacon said, his tone so neutral, she knew that wasn't what he wanted to say.

"Of course. I'm too stubborn to do otherwise." She tightened her hold on his wrist briefly and murmured. "I love you."

"I love you."

His voice still didn't reveal any emotion, so the words sounded weirdly hollow, but since she knew he meant them, and that he was saying them now when he couldn't allow in any emotion, made her smile.

She patted his hand as she released him. "All right, big guy. Here we go."

She faced Holland just as Angie lowered her arm and a flare of bright blue flashed in the periphery of Cary's vision.

"I can see magic at the moment," she said to Angie. "If I don't look at it directly, I can see the circle."

"Good. You won't step into it on accident, then," Angie said.

"Any idea why I'm suddenly seeing magic?"

"Probably because you've been taking more in than usual tonight."

"Cool." Sort of. She'd have preferred more definitive answers. She wasn't going to get them, but they would have been nice. "You ready?" she said to Holland. "And are you sure you want to give me some of your power?" She wagged her eyebrows, just to irritate him. She couldn't help it. But also the bravado helped—a little—to settle her nerves.

Holland glanced at Angie and Deacon, both bracketing her. "You'll need to move away from her," he told them. "Just in case she can't handle this."

"If you make me explode, I will come back as a ghost and haunt you for all eternity," she told Holland. She hated ghosts so much the very idea of being one gave her the shivers. But she'd do it if this asshole she was trying to save killed her too soon.

She'd rather he didn't kill her at all, actually, but that was another story.

"I *can* control my powers," Holland said, raising his brow in a way that conveyed all the sarcasm.

Cary snorted.

Angie and Deacon had stepped back several feet, and Cary had tucked the fold of material Marianne had given her into the front pocket of her jeans. She frowned at the Lud-lookalike's sword. It was encompassed inside the circle with them because it was still buried in the ground between her and Holland.

"We should do something with that," she said. "It might react, I don't know, badly to demon magic getting thrown around." Actually, she had no idea if that would even be a thing. Still, seemed a bad idea to leave it just…sitting there.

Holland gave the sword a considering look. He stretched out a hand and the sword flew to him, slapping against his palm.

Cary gasped, despite herself, and Holland smirked. She snarled to hide her embarrassment.

Holland bounced the sword in his hand a little, as if rearranging his grip. Cary felt Deacon take a step closer. Then Holland thrust the sword into the air next to him. And the sword vanished.

"Where did it go?" she asked, staring at the area near Holland, looking for another rip in spacetime.

"I can't tell you all of my tricks, Ms. Redmond."

She considered flashing him a rude hand gesture. She settled for grumping, "Show off," and ignoring his smug expression. Waving at him, she said, "Okay, let's get this going. Time's wasting and your daddy will be here soon."

She was still a little overwhelmed with what to do about that.

Later. First, learn how to use any magic she absorbed in the coming fight—which was going to involve a lot of demon magic.

She kept herself facing Holland, so that the protective seams in her jeans that would deflect magic wouldn't dissipate anything he threw at her.

His lips lifted slightly as he stared at her. "I've wanted this for a very long time," he murmured. "It's…harder than I anticipated. Not just killing you."

She smiled. "I'm flattered? Does this mean you've changed your mind? Not willing to share, even to save your own life?"

"I haven't changed my mind. But it's amazing what one will do when there are no other options."

"Ha! Tell me about it." She waved at him again. "Get on with it. How do I use demon magic?"

"Feel it first." He raised his hand.

She winced. "Do not burn me up." Yet, she added silently.

She couldn't believe she was going to stand here and let him throw power at her. Every part of her screamed to run, duck, avoid. All those muscle memories Lucy had ingrained in her told her to move. Now. Not stand perfectly still and wait to get hit with whatever Holland threw.

He flicked his hand over, palm up, and a small ball of rolling lava-like flame appeared on his hand. The red and yellows of it melted and swirled together, folding on top of itself and reforming. A strangely real lava lamp without the lamp part enclosing it. When he met her gaze, there was red in his eyes.

She had just enough time to regret all her life choices, then he, almost casually, flung the ball of lava at her. She half-closed her eyes, wincing as she held still, a close-lipped squeal escaping because she didn't want to give Holland the satisfaction of screaming but she really really wanted to scream.

The lava ball hit her mid-chest, in a flash of heat and power, and for a split second she was certain he'd just gone ahead and killed her. That she was about to immolate. And that sucked a lot. The lava seemed to melt into her, covering her chest, seeping into her bones. She felt a tingling along the seams of her jeans. But Marianne's spell couldn't do anything against what Cary had just purposefully taken in. She absorbed the full force of Holland's magic.

And it hurt like a mother fucker.

When the burn lessened enough for her to catch her breath, she groaned. "Your magic sucks," she said through clenched teeth, and looked down at her chest, half expecting to see a big gaping hole, despite the fact that she'd just spoken. She might be a ghost now. She didn't know.

There was no hole in her chest, which was nice, even though her body felt like it was still burning. Was this what Sheldon had felt, coming back into his body after swapping with Holland? She imagined being in Holland's body was way worse. Which gave her a lot more sympathy for Sheldon than she wanted to have.

On top of the burning, there was the pervasive tingles, but ratcheted up to the extreme. Not just bugs crawling over her skin. Whole armies of different kinds of bugs, streaming over her endlessly.

Damn. This was just a little bit of his power. She really hated to think what this would feel like if he'd really tried to kill her.

And worse, what would Lud's magic feel like if she took the full force of it?

Well, she probably wouldn't know for long because she'd be dead instantly.

The weight of what she was trying to do sucked at her again, pulling her closer to a hopeless, black hole of despair. Of pointlessness.

She pushed it aside. She had some magic to use before she burned up holding on to it. She could get depressed about her impossible mission later.

"All right," she muttered, trying to loosen her tight jaw a little. "What now? How do I get rid of this?" Because she really wanted to be rid of it, and a part of her just wanted to push it out in one big explosive release.

Which would probably not be good.

She resisted that impulse while she waited on Holland's explanation.

"Demon magic is all power and brute force, Ms. Redmond," Holland said, his voice deep, his accent weirdly more pronounced. "You'll have to control it, and use it that way."

Angie stepped closer and murmured, "Use that stubbornness of yours and will all the power he's sent at you into a ball of lava, like what he threw. Picture the lava rolling in your hand. Not overwhelming you, but all of it, every last drop of it, right there in your palm to control."

Cary focused on Angie's—significantly better and more thorough —explanation of what to do, and forced the magic coursing through her to her palm. It took a few tries. She kept losing bits and pieces of all that heat and they'd creep back into her bones. The frustration and anger she felt in those moments seemed to help, though, and she recaptured all that liquid-feeling magic, bundling it back together into her palm.

She wasn't sure the anger she was using to control the magic was a good thing for her in the long term. But somehow, it also seemed very appropriate to the kind of magic she was using. Of course she needed anger to control it.

Good thing for them all, she had a pretty decent well of anger in her gut at the moment. Fear, terror, inadequacy. But also a *lot* of anger to pull on.

When she felt like she'd gotten all the demon magic contained onto her palm, she considered the rolling lava ball. It looked similar to what Holland had created, but not exactly the same. She had trouble figuring out what was different. Maybe a quality of the light, the colors not quite the same. There seemed to be some blue rolling through the oranges and reds. Or maybe green? She wasn't sure. It just didn't look like the ball Holland had thrown at her. It looked…

More familiar.

Which was a weird thought she couldn't have explained if she tried.

Afraid to bounce the magic or accidently drop it and catch the entire clearing on fire, she said, "Now what?" mostly to Angie because she didn't trust Holland.

Holland waved his fingers in an easy arch, and a little rip in space appeared, revealing a hot, burning wasteland beyond. The hellscape pumped dry heat into the clearing like a furnace, and beyond the rip, the ground crinkled and crackled like cooling lava.

Lot of lava going on in this lesson.

Also a very very strong smell of sulfur. She gagged a little and put her non-magic-holding hand over her mouth and nose.

"Nice place there," she muttered. She half expected to see the Lud-lookalike's sword but nope. Just a volcanic hellscape.

Holland smiled. "How's your aim?"

"Sucks. Why?"

"Toss the…magic into the demon realm. It will burn this one if you try to use it here."

"Gee, that seems like something you should have mentioned before tossing this shit at me," she said, snarling at him.

He showed no signs of repentance.

Cary's gut tightened in fear. If she dropped this ball of lava on her hand, or missed that very narrow opening into the demon realm…

She pushed the worry away. What was done was done. She had to get rid of the magic. The longer she held it, the harder it was to keep it contained in that one spot. It kept trying to creep back into her, sink back into her bones. And she could actually *feel* it doing…something to her. She wasn't sure. Probably burning her insides. Whatever it was, it felt strong. Too powerful and overwhelming. And once again, she was struck by the need to just explode all this outward and get it away from her.

Not a helpful impulse just then.

She focused on the magic in her hand, then glanced at the narrow rip between realms, then stared at the lava a moment more. With a deep breath, and a silent prayer to the universe that she didn't miss, she turned sharply and threw the ball of magical demon power through the opening between realms.

The power left her in a rush. Not just like throwing a ball. A stream of power, a comet's tail of power, followed the ball. Surprised and a little terrified some of that lava would drip, she focused on streaming it into the demon realm, letting a realm that could take it, have it all back. The stream seemed to go on forever, the power driving from her in a rush that left her too breathless to even hiss with her fear.

The last of the power arrowed from her hand, and when all of it disappeared into the demon realm, she sagged and let her head drop.

"Cary?" Angie asked. "You okay?"

"Well that was new," she muttered.

"Too tired to continue, Ms. Redmond?"

She glared at Holland. But paused when she caught his expression. He was frowning, his head tilted to one side as he stared at the opening between realms. The look he gave her when he faced her again was unreadable, but…interesting.

She'd swear he was surprised. But no. That didn't make sense. He knew how demon power worked. He'd even seen what she could do with magic when she absorbed it. He wouldn't be teaching her how to use his power if he didn't know she could use it, so what was there to be surprised by?

When she narrowed her eyes at him, almost a question, he raised his brows and asked, again, "Too tired now?"

"No." She straightened to face him. She was tired. But even as she unslumped, she felt better. "I can do more."

"Cary?" Deacon's voice was quiet, and there was a little too much growl in it.

"I'm good," she reassured, turning to touch his arm briefly before thinking better of it. He was so desperately trying to hold his control, and she was desperately trying not to screw that up for him. "I'm good," she said again. "I can do more." She waited until he met her gaze as he didn't seem able to look away from Holland. When he did, though, she said, "You?"

He nodded. "Fine."

He didn't sound fine, but she'd have to let that go for now. Any argument she made would just unbalance him further.

She faced Holland. "Alright. Next up. Same thing to practice, or do you want to try something new?"

Though Holland's expression didn't change much, he said, "This again. Then we'll try something different."

4O

They worked for the next hour, Holland feeding her some magic, her feeling the heat stealing her breath, throwing the magic back into the demon realm, feeling better afterward.

He fed her the lava-type stuff for a few more rounds, and then he started throwing actual streams of fire at her. The sight of that fire hitting the middle of her chest and soaking in without actually killer her was a little disorienting at first, and Angie had to remind her to concentrate on what she was doing. Frequently. One shot of fire had nearly encompassed her entire chest before she got it all back under control and turned into a concentrated ball of power on her hand. The burning then had not been pleasant—she might have screeched a little between her teeth, half fear, half pain—but the minute she got the whole thing collected into a single spot on her palm, the fear part of that screech eased.

And once she had his magic back out of her, the burning went away. Every single time. Which was nice. Even the exhaustion that dragged at her briefly after expending all that magic seemed to ease quickly enough that she could continue.

The whole process was both different to what she'd done with Rory, with Angie, but also, similar. A lot of visualizing and concentration. Unlike using witch magic through spells, though, this was almost all about brute force will and effort. Forcing the power to do as she wanted. No specific hand gestures or appropriate words to direct things. Just her and her will and her stubborn refusal to light her world on fire with demon lava.

Her parents would be amazed at how important all her stubbornness would be one day.

The fact that all this wasn't sending her to sleep was amazing, and a little terrifying. What the hell was happening to her? Usually, this kind of expended energy—the level of concentration and focus it took to keep the demon magic from overwhelming her; the focus it took not to just release it all in a big whoosh, and instead use it properly— normally, this would have laid her out for hours or days afterward. Even earlier, after using the shield and the other demon's magic, she'd felt pretty exhausted right after.

But the longer she practiced with Holland, the quicker she recovered, the better she felt.

That…was probably bad.

She paused after throwing yet another stream of fire into the still open, and surprisingly empty, demon realm—why weren't there demons in there trying to get out? She'd better ask—and faced Deacon.

His jaw was less rock solid than it had been when they started this, and some of the iceman neutrality had melted from his expression. He looked ready to pounce now, not entirely…civilized. But he also didn't look like he had to expend quite as much control over his leopard as he had earlier. That, at least, was a good thing.

She almost hated to upset that balance. But she had to know.

"Hey, are my eyes going red at all?" It took years for that to happen to demon hunters. And even then, it was usual subtle, just a red light in the depths of their ordinary eye color. If the hunter had brown eyes, the color was almost unnoticeable, could be written off as an illusion. Light-eyed hunters had a harder time disguising that flash of red, which worked against them.

But given the way she was adapting to Holland's powers, even rebounding from using them so quickly, she was a little worried what absorbing all that demon magic was doing to her. At a cellular level.

She probably should have thought of this more before this moment.

Deacon met her gaze, holding it for a long moment. His jaw tightened again. "A little. Just a small red dot in the depths of your pupil. Not sure anyone without shifter sight would be able to see it."

Cary let out a huff of breath that ruffled the hair on her forehead that had escaped her ponytail. "That's going to be a thing after this."

"If you limit demon interaction for a while after this, it'll reverse," Angie said. "It did for me."

And wasn't that an interesting statement that would have to wait for later before Cary indulged her near-overwhelming curiosity.

Boy, she hoped the world didn't end tonight. She had *so many questions*. She'd hate to die without at least some of them being answered.

To Holland, she said, "Have I learned enough? I should practice some other things before your dad shows up."

"No," he said with a shrug. "There's a lot more to learn. But I'd rather not teach you too much."

She grinned. "Afraid I'll use it against you?"

"Yes," he said without any hesitation whatsoever.

He'd been considering her with narrowed eyes and a slight frown throughout their practice. Every time he threw power at her, there was a look in his eyes, something she couldn't quite explain, but it felt like he was waiting for her breaking point, waiting for her to fail.

If she didn't know better—and she absolutely didn't—she'd think he'd been testing how much she could take, throwing more at her with each effort.

The fact that she kept bouncing back seemed to worry him as much as it worried her. But probably for different reasons.

His admitting to that was…interesting.

"In that case, I should practice some more spells with Angie," Cary said. "We still have time before daddy demon shows up. Where'd your mom go, by the way? Also, why haven't any demons tried to get out of that rip in spacetime you opened up?"

"So many questions," Holland said.

"I'm a curious girl," Cary said with a grin that maybe showed too many teeth.

Holland made a sound she couldn't interpret, a sort of humming noise that could have been exasperation, or a contained growl of irritation, or just a neutral noise to respond without responding.

"Are you going to answer any of my many questions?" Although since there were only really two, she wasn't sure that counted as many. "Or are you just going to ignore them and keep staring at me like you've seen a particularly interesting bug?"

"The 'particularly interesting bug' remark is quite…apt."

She grinned. "Ants can carry weight far exceeding their own, mosquitos kill, and cockroaches will live forever. Don't underestimate the bugs."

"Indeed," Holland said with raised brows.

Another moment of silence before she snapped, "Well? Answers or not? I have other things to do right now if you're just going to keep standing there being all creepy weird staring demon."

His lips twitched at one corner, but she was pretty sure he wasn't going to smile. That was probably an angry twitch.

"My mother is preparing to enter this realm," Holland said. "No demons are exiting that realm because I'm not allowing it." He shrugged. "And because you've been throwing a lot of deadly power into the realm since it's been open. At sporadic moments and of varying levels of deadliness. There are many stupid demon species who have very little sense of self-preservation. But most are self-interested enough to avoid getting killed by random power bursts."

"Fair enough." She paused when the last thing he said sunk in. "Wait. Are you saying I could *kill* a demon with your magic?"

Because that was a big deal. Humans couldn't kill demons. Demon hunters sent them back to demon realms. They didn't kill them. They might injure them. They could hurt them. And they could definitely defy them. But they couldn't *kill* them.

"I think you should work more on your witchcraft," Holland said. "My triad will wake soon. Would you like their help?"

"No. Thank you."

But she didn't miss how this question-avoidance was deliberately obvious. He wasn't going to answer her question. And that was answer enough. He'd slipped—which in and of itself was pretty amazing—telling her that part about killing demons. Using his power, which was demon power that could kill demons, *she*, a lowly human, could kill demons.

Very very interesting.

She was still a little worried about how good she felt, though. Maybe absorbing more demon magic just to kill demons wasn't such a hot idea—pun intended. She wasn't sure absorbing demon magic was good for her long-term status as a good guy.

The fact that she hadn't accidentally killed any demons without realizing she was doing it was kind of nice to know. She hadn't considered that when throwing Holland's magic back into that realm.

"Before I move on to witchcraft," she said, "One last question."

His sigh was actually audible. He adjusted his stance, and straightened his suit jacket, each gesture filled with irritation. That was interesting, too.

"Did you lose anything throwing all that magic at me? I— accidentally!—drained Sheldon of all his power. It drains others when I take theirs. Did it drain you?"

She was almost certain he wouldn't answer that question. Or at least not answer it truthfully. But she wanted *him* to know she was aware of the possibility.

His eyes narrowed just a little when he said, "I have plenty more. And it replenishes faster than the average human. I lost nothing."

Huh. There was something in his tone when he said, "I lost," that caught her ear. She wasn't sure why. She'd expected exactly that answer. Whether it was true or not. She'd expected him to say exactly what he'd just said. But something about the "I lost" part…

Since he was not going to answer her question with anything more than that, she shrugged and faced Angie. A little surprised she could turn her back on Holland. That seemed silly stupid. There was no longer a Protector shield keeping him from killing her. But she'd let him throw his magic at her for an hour and he hadn't killed her yet. He'd managed to contain the impulse even though he really really wanted her dead. She figured he'd continue to wait until *after* Lud. After all, killing her now meant giving up the chance to torture her before killing her later. Wouldn't want to give up the torture part.

It helped her piece of mind, though, that Deacon hadn't really looked away from Holland this entire time. She was pretty sure if Holland sent out a sneak attack, Deacon would see and react before she could get dead.

"So, we practice witchy spells?" Cary asked Angie.

Angie gave her a narrow-eyed look that wasn't very different from the one Holland had been giving her. "You're okay to continue? Not exhausted? This stuff usually wears you out. And usually wears most people out, even if they're used to wielding magic."

She shrugged. "I feel great. I'm a little worried that I feel great, but since we have to face a demon god in just a few more hours, I'll take it. I'd be pretty useless to everyone if I passed out from exhaustion now."

"True. Still. I'm not sure taking in more magic is good for you."

"Too late to worry about it now," she said, even if she was also not sure she should take more in. "It's all I've got to help the fight. And I need to know what to do with what gets thrown at me."

"Lud will be throwing demon magic."

"But there are witches here, too."

"And shapeshifters and vampires," Angie said, her mouth flattening. "I'd love to know whose side the vampires are on."

"They're on the vampires' side," she said without hesitation. "James has said he doesn't want the world to end. I think he'll be on our side until after we make sure the world stays spinning. Afterward..." She shrugged. She didn't trust James as far as she could throw him. And since he was a vampire, and she didn't have super strength, she couldn't throw him at all.

Angie sighed. "Okay. A little more spell work. But without much magic. I'll teach you the words, the gestures. You don't need the magic to practice those."

Cary lowered her voice to a whisper. "Are we draining you, when you give me some of your magic to use?"

"Not much. Some. But you don't have to worry about draining me the way you drained Sheldon. I know how to handle my magic. And… The reason I'm here, what I can do to help… It's not witch magic."

"You ever going to explain that?"

She didn't want Angie to do something she didn't want to do. If they could avoid that, all the better. But without knowing what Angie was talking about, it was impossible to make plans so she could avoid having to do whatever it was Angie didn't want to do. Without knowing what Angie kept alluding too, Cary couldn't help her.

And given how much Angie was helping Cary just then, she really wanted to return the favor.

"It'll be fine," Angie said, not answering the question. "We'll see what happens once Lud gets here. We may end up with other options."

"Uh huh."

"Hands at the ready." Angie waved to her, straightening her shoulders as she turned all business. "We'll start with some defensive spells, things you can use for deflecting and protection. Then a couple of offensive spells."

Cary prepared to force her memory to work.

And hoped everything she'd been taught stuck when the time came.

41

The scuffing and grunts of annoyance, followed by a shout of denial pulled Cary from her efforts to get a particularly difficult series of hand gestures correct. She and Angie and Deacon—who hadn't stopped staring at Holland during Cary's work with Angie—all faced the noise.

Brandon was holding a vampire by the neck, out at arms-length, while Marianne scowled at the vampire and tugged Lucy closer to her side.

"Fuck," Cary muttered and jogged to the edge of the protective circle Angie had set.

She glanced at Holland long enough to make sure he wasn't interfering. He'd closed the demon realm they'd been using during her practice earlier. But he'd watched her work with Angie with a hawk-like keenness that made her itchy and nervous. He didn't follow her and Angie to the edge of the circle.

And neither did Deacon. He continued to stare at Holland.

She wasn't sure if that was a good thing or not, but at least someone was keeping and eye on the demon.

"What's happening?" she demanded when she got close enough to the gathered group.

Most of the vampires were still inside the tree line, their yellow eyes glowing in the darkness, but otherwise, impossible to see. There were two hive vampires in the clearing, though, and James stood to one side of the situation, seemingly watching without getting involved. The leopards were all standing in a half circle behind Brandon, their attention on the trees and the majority of the vampires.

Marianne waved to the vampire in Brandon's grip. "That asshole thought Lucy might make a nice snack."

"He was very wrong," Lucy said in a hiss to rival the vampires.

"She surprised him by tossing him over her head," Marianne said. "But the bastards are fast and he charged back at her with his teeth out."

"Brandon stepped in," Lucy said. "And I have to say, I'm very irritated that he had to."

Cary heard the irritation. But she also heard the slight tremor in her voice. Her friend being even a little scared triggered Cary's rage.

"Drop the circle," she said to Angie, her voice low, but her gaze on James. Or on his shoulder. Without her protector shield, her freewheeling eye-contact-with-vampires days were over. "I don't know why you're here," she said to the Master as Angie cut the circle, "but it's not to eat my friends. Or to let my friends get eaten. Not when we're here trying to stop *your* world from ending. Is this the kind of control you have over the hive? Or did you let them endanger my friend on purpose? Cause all of that is going to come back and bite you in the ass. Pun intended."

James narrowed his eyes at her, which she only saw from the corner of her eyes and with flitting looks because of the no-eye-contact-anymore part of this. She could tell his eyes were glowing faintly yellow, though. And his mouth flattened as he considered her.

"Your eyes are red," James said, a non sequitur that nevertheless felt like a threat.

"They are not," she snapped. "And even if they are, we both know it's temporary. And what the hell does that have to do with anything?"

"Kill the vampire who attacked your friend," James said.

"What? No. What?"

"It's your right. He broke a truce—even if an unspoken one. Kill him."

The vampire in Brandon's grip started to struggle against the huge bear shifter's hold, attempting to speak. The woods filled with a hissing sound that made the hairs on Cary's neck rise.

Brandon eased the vampire back onto the ground, but didn't release his neck entirely. And the fact that he did all this one handed was so impressive, Cary would have to mention that later. She couldn't believe she'd been sparring with someone that strong. He had most definitely been pulling his punches.

She looked between the vampire and James as the vampire babbled about mercy or something. Was he…scared Cary would actually kill him? Because, while she might be angry enough to since he'd attacked Lucy, and while she wouldn't mourn him if he ended up dead—because he'd attacked her friend *and* broken the Portland rules about trying to feed off the unwilling *and* he likely wanted *her* dead because most of the hive did—she had no intention of actually being the hand to kill him.

That wasn't her job. And also, she didn't go around killing people.

At least, not on purpose.

"What the fuck game are you playing at?" she asked James, because these were vampires and this had to be a game.

"Satisfying my curiosity," James murmured so quietly it was barely a whisper on the fir-scented breeze. "If you won't kill him, I'll punish him later."

The vampire started struggling harder against Brandon's hold at that, and there was panic in his pleading now.

Wow. He was more worried about James punishing him than Cary killing him? That didn't seem like a good thing.

"Just don't let any of them attack my people again," Cary said, her instinct to protect kicking in and irritating the hell out of her. "We're not here to fight each other."

"Although it would be interesting," Holland said.

Cary let out a loud, irritated sigh and looked behind her. Holland had joined them. Deacon stood between him and her and Angie. She hadn't even heard them move.

Some superhero she was. She really should have known she couldn't pull that off. She was a Protector. And the rest of this stuff was just… She wasn't ready for it. She wasn't able for it.

She shoved down the doubts because time was running out. Lud would be here soon. And she *still* didn't know how to get the Angel here without a sacrifice.

"You—" she pointed at Holland, "—stay out of this. No stirring more trouble just because. And you—" she pointed at James, "—stop running experiments tonight. I've had more than enough of those already." She glared at Holland. "We have some serious shit about to happen. And we're all supposedly on the same side. At least for now. So act like it." She snarled out this last.

The statement earned her some murmured agreement from the leopard shifters.

"Thank you for stopping him," Cary said to Brandon, waving vaguely at the vampire he still held by the neck.

"No one attacks sensei without consequences," Brandon said.

From the corner of her eye, she saw Marianne shiver a little.

"Thank you for your help, Brandon," Lucy said.

"Of course," he said in a friendly tone. He flashed her a gentle smile that was at complete odds with the threat he'd just issued the vampire.

Good to know he was on their side. And in control of his animal nature. Given Deacon's tentative control just then, it was nice some of their allies were not being overwhelmed by their preternatural instincts.

She glanced back at Deacon. He was facing Holland, not her, but his shoulders were still stiff and his body looked bunched and ready to pounce. None of the leopards seemed in distress, though, so Deacon was maintaining.

James brought her attention back to him. "You could issue your own consequences, Cary. I wouldn't stop you."

"You can stop trying to get me to kill one of your people," she said. "I have bigger fish to fry right now. But there will be no more infighting." She glared around the clearing. Mostly at the yellow-eyed vampires still inside the tree line. "You okay now?" she murmured to Lucy without taking her glare off the vampires.

"I'm fine," she said with a huff. "Just annoyed."

"You?" she asked Marianne.

"Fine. Good. Fine."

Cary glanced more closely at Marianne. She was, very obviously, not looking at Brandon and the vampire. Huh.

"Okay, then," she said. "I need to practice more witchcraft. Anyone have anything else they want to say or get off their chest? No? Good. Behave for a few more minutes. There will be plenty of demons to deal with soon enough." This last she directed to the vampires.

A low level of hissing in the trees whispered through the clearing, the noise coming and going in waves. Cary couldn't hear what they were saying. They were speaking at that subsonic level vampires could manage, and she no longer had Protector-enhanced senses to help. Even when she had, she couldn't always hear vampires when they hit these levels just outside human hearing range. But she was pretty sure she was glad she couldn't hear them now.

She really didn't want to know why the vampires sounded so excited.

42

*W*ith the vampires no longer causing mayhem, Cary was able to work on two whole spells with Angie before things went sideways.

The shifters kept a close eye on the vampires, who continued to hiss quietly in the trees. Eriana hovered over Sheldon, who sat to one side on a log, looking despondent. Marianne, Lucy, and Brandon stayed close together, next to the leopards, their attention divided between the vampires and Cary's lesson. Sebastian disappeared into the woods, only to reappear a few minutes later. He exchanged a look with Angie, then stood to the side with Marianne, Lucy, and Brandon.

Deacon continued staring at the side of Holland's face, and Holland continued to pretend Deacon's presence was inconsequential. Though, when Cary took the time to look a little closer, Holland's jaw was tight, his shoulders stiff, and he rocked onto his toes a few times. He looked ready to move at a blink.

So not as unaware of and unconcerned with the angry leopard king standing next to him as he'd like them all to believe. Good. He deserved a little discomfort.

The breeze got chillier as the night deepened, but the cool air was refreshing. Cary felt like she was expending so much mental and physical energy learning how to deal with magic, she was running hotter than normal. She occasionally envied shifters their fast metabolisms, but at the moment, she could do without running so hot.

"You okay?" Angie asked.

"Just warm. But I don't want to take off my jacket." She fingered the bespelled leather. "Kind of a security blanket at this stage, anyway," she murmured for Angie's ears only.

Although, with the vampires and shifters all around them, she was pretty sure that was wasted effort.

"It's not warm out," Angie said, frowning a little.

"Is it bad that I'm hot?" She was worried about what all this was doing to her. The consequences that might come and bite her later. But she didn't feel like she had a choice. Lud was due soon. The Angel would be back…somehow. And she needed to know how to not die in the next few hours.

But she was still worried.

From her expression, Angie was worried too.

Lucy and Marianne left Brandon and Sebastian to join them. "There's a problem?" Marianne asked quietly.

"Cary's running hot," Angie said.

"Your eyes are still a little demon-hunter red, too," Lucy said.

They all kept their voices quiet despite the fact that every creature in the clearing would still hear them. Cary was glad she wasn't the only one doing that.

"I've got something that might help," Marianne said. "At least with the over-heating."

She reached into her bag again, pulling out a sheet of pale yellow cotton. The material, folded into a soft, small pillow, looked ordinary enough. Nothing particular special about it. Not even a shimmer or embellishments.

"What's that do?" Cary asked, reaching out to touch the cotton without thought.

"Wipe your face and neck with it," Marianne said.

Cary did as told and almost immediate a cooling sensation swept through her, taking off some of the heat, like stepping into a cool, but not icy, lake on a warm day. It felt glorious.

"That's amazing," she murmured as she moved the fabric to her neck. "You could make a fortune selling these."

"I've started weaving the spell into the clothes of my clients having menopausal hot flashes," Marianne said. "It seems to help."

"Yeah it does," Cary said with feeling. She almost hated to give the little pillow of material back, but after she felt sufficiently normal again, she did. Very reluctantly.

"Better?" Angie asked.

"Perfect." Cary put her hands on her hips and looked around. "Except we have a clearing full of people who don't like each other. An edgy leopard king holding on to his control by a thread. A tricky evil demon with ulterior motives. Another demon contained in the woods. Some witches who still haven't regained consciousness. A former-wizard who thinks he's gonna be allowed to sacrifice himself to the Angel of Death. No sign of Jaxer or the Protectors. And a demon god due any minute." She sighed. "So, yeah, I'm peachy."

Lucy snorted a laugh that didn't have a lot of humor in it.

"If it helps," Angie said, "Sebastian banished Holland's demon minion in the woods."

"He did?" Cary's eyes widened. "When?"

"When he went into the trees a bit ago? Then. Holland having a minion whose purpose we couldn't predict seemed like a bad idea. He was probably just there to keep Sebastian distracted anyway. Holland hardly needs the help of a lower-level demon minion against his father."

"True. Except maybe for fodder." Cary winced. "How did you know all this?" Angie and Sebastian hadn't spoken before Sebastian went into the woods, or after he'd returned.

"We used to work together. We know how the other one thinks."

Which was a fascinating tidbit Cary wanted to know more about. Later. After they saved the world.

"And we'd discussed what to do about the random minion before things got hairy with you and Holland," Angie finished with a shrug.

"This all is starting to feel very…protracted," Marianne said. "Don't you think?"

"Like waiting for the other shoe to drop," Lucy said.

"What's taking so long?" Marianne said.

"What's the god waiting for?" Lucy said.

"The longer we stand around waiting," Marianne added, "the more likely our 'allies' are to get into a fight."

"Maybe that's the point," Cary said. "How the hell do I know? Demons are assholes."

"I heard that," Holland said.

"I meant for you to," Cary called back.

"All this waiting gives you time to practice, too," Angie said, ignoring Holland. "That feels strange. If I were a demon god, I'd want you to be as unprepared as possible so I could walk over the top of you."

"Maybe my preparation means nothing to him because he's going to walk over me anyway," Cary said.

"Maybe," Angie said, with a matter-of-factness that made Cary scowl.

"Still, the delay, the waiting, all of this…" She let out a breath. "Now that Marianne and Lucy have brought it up, it does feel, I don't know, maybe deliberate."

"But why?" Lucy asked.

"And what do we do to subvert any nefarious plans?" Marianne asked.

"And where the hell are Jaxer and the Protectors?" Cary said, but mostly to herself.

"You could ask me," Holland said.

"You're the demon asshole," Cary pointed out. "Why should we trust you?"

"You just let me throw my power at you and trusted I wouldn't kill you."

"Ha! No, I didn't. I was half convinced you would give in and try to kill me."

She glanced back to look at him with raised brows. He had the grace to not deny the facts.

"My father can't come through until midnight. This delay has nothing to do with you."

Cary scowled. "Why midnight?"

"Yeah, I mean it's midnight somewhere on this planet already," Lucy said. "What does the time have to do with anything?"

"He requires specific time and space coordinates to arrive," Holland said with a shrug. "When everything is aligned right for him to break through and lose the minimum amount of power stepping into this realm."

"Wait, by coming through at midnight, he won't lose as much power?" Cary said. "Since when has that been a thing?"

"Always," Holland said. "I entered this realm…unconventionally."

"Meaning not through tricking some poor bastard who summoned you."

"Meaning I came into this realm differently to most demons. And because I picked the right spacetime coordinate, I was able to drain as little of my power as was possible."

Well that explained a lot, she thought. But didn't say aloud. The fact that he'd been even more powerful before doing that still left her a little breathless.

"My father is finally going that route. But the spacetime coordinate is very precise."

"So not stalling and waiting for us to rip ourselves apart on our own, then. Good to know."

"Not that that wouldn't benefit him," Holland said. "But he'd hardly give you time to test your…skills, if this wait wasn't necessary."

"You know you could have told me all this earlier," she said.

"Where would be the fun in that." Holland smiled.

She rolled her eyes and faced her friends again. "So, delay explained." She looked at her cellphone after handing the cooling cloth back to Marianne. "And we have about twenty minutes before we hit midnight." Her gut tightened and churned. The protracted wait had left her impatient and restless to get on with things, but now that she knew exactly what time things would happen and that a demon god wasn't just going to descend on their realm at some point soon, but in exactly twenty minutes, her fears all ratcheted up into something that stole her breath.

Deacon was at her side in a blink, the suddenness making her startle.

"You okay?" he asked quietly, though his gaze was still on Holland.

"Great. Why do you ask?"

"Your scent."

Ah. "Fear spikes are kind of smelly, aren't they?" she murmured.

"You're not alone," Deacon said.

"But there are as many bad guys at my back as there are good guys." She nodded to the whispering mass of vampires in the tree. She didn't bother to acknowledge Holland among those enemies. Everyone knew where he stood. "And some of the good guys are still M.I.A."

He gently squeezed her arm, his gesture at odds with the tight line of his jaw and the hard yellow glow in his eyes.

She appreciated that he didn't try to say something soothing. There wasn't anything to say. Nothing that made any of this better.

But it was nice to know he was here with her. And that he had her back.

She stretched up to kiss his cheek, hoping to convey wordlessly what she didn't have the words for.

A nudge from Angie brought her attention around. Angie nodded toward the triad, who were finally pulling themselves upright after the body swap with the Angel.

Justina rose to her feet before the other two and looked at Cary. "Are you ready, sister?"

"Ha. Not even a little bit. Are you recovered fully?"

Justina smiled. "Enough for what's to come."

"Got a better idea of what that is than we do? Holland's information is…" She glared at him. "Patchy."

"We can't fathom the Angel's thoughts when we're in her body," Justina said. "But I can say, the time is upon us."

Cary glanced at the glowing white letters on the face of her cellphone.

Two minutes to midnight?

Damn.

That went fast.

43

After all the stalling and waiting, the moment of truth came so suddenly, Cary almost felt like she'd been taken off guard. Except they'd known all night this was coming.

Didn't stop her from being shook to her toes when the clock on her phone hit midnight.

The whole thing felt like something out of a movie. Lights and sparks and showy special effects. Instead of a simple tear in spacetime, like Holland had used, a circle of sparkling red lights whirled open, the round break in reality revealing a deep blackness beyond that Cary couldn't see into. Unlike the golden glow of the realm Holland had tapped, this one was just stygian. No stars. No fire. No sparks of light. No lava.

Wait, no. As she watched, across the back of the blackness, she saw a faint glowing line of red. Lava moving over a black field of rock at midnight on a moonless night. And the line of lava appeared and disappeared. It took her several precious moments to realize the line kept disappearing from sight because there were *things* moving in front of it, things that were thick enough to block her view of the tiny glowing line.

Things made of darkness and shadow.

Her heart pounded hard. She took an involuntary step away from the red encircled hole into Lud's realm. Then turned to face it, putting herself between that opening and the people behind her. Even the stupid vampires.

Deacon moved to her side, not standing behind her as he usual did. There was no reason anymore.

The reminder she didn't have shields didn't help the shrieking fear in her brain. But it was comforting to have him by her side.

Holland stepped back from the opening, moving to stand just behind her. She'd have been more amused if sounds hadn't started coming from the other realm. Hissing. Whispering. Screaming at an octave almost—but not quite—outside her hearing range. The almost-heard screams were the worst.

Or maybe that prize went to the chittering sounds.

Chittering sounds like nails on a chalkboard, setting Cary's teeth on edge.

"I hate that sound," Angie murmured quietly behind her.

"Which one?" Cary asked.

"All of them," she said.

"This is really awful, isn't it?" Lucy said. "Not just me about to piss my pants?"

"Nope," Cary said. "Really awful. About to piss my pants."

"You might want to wait on that, Ms. Redmond," Holland said. "Some of the…creatures in there are attracted to that scent."

"Oh good. That's good to know." Her gut tightened so hard with the fear, she thought she might throw up. Probably also something she didn't want to do.

And speaking of smells, the ones coming from Lud's realm were not the usual demon sulfur, rotten egg smell. That was there faintly. The distant lava carried a tangy hint of it. But there was a metallic sort of taste to the smell. Which seemed weird, tasting the smell. It coated her tongue in a way that should have set her on edge as much as the sounds. It didn't. She sort of liked that metallic flavor.

Which just freaked her out even more.

Boy, she could use a Protector shield about now.

"What are they waiting on?" Marianne said.

The shadows seemed to be massing just behind the circle opening, shadow upon shadow, all blocking the view of the distant line of lava now. The darkness didn't spill through, though. Didn't enter their realm.

"Is it a timing thing or an inflicting-terror thing, all this waiting?" Cary asked Holland without looking away from the shadows.

"Both," Holland said. "Inflicting terror is always a goal. Even when its simply a side effect of other goals."

"Good. Good to know." Because she was definitely feeling the terror now. And every moment that passed with the shadows pilling up against the entrance to her realm without spilling through into it was a moment of that terror growing. She'd hate for the effort at inducing terror to have been wasted.

Wait. No, she wouldn't.

The chittering sounds coming from the demon realm rose to a pitch that made the hairs on Cary's arms stand up. A noise piercing enough she wanted to cover her ears.

"This a demon god's realm?" she asked, just to keep from running screaming into the woods.

"A transition realm," Holland said. "The real realm would break your human mind in moments."

"Isn't that the point?" Not like Lud cared about her sanity, or anyone else's for that matter. Why bother with a transition realm?

"He could never get here directly. His realm can't connect to this one. He must pass through others to get here."

"That might be the only good news I've heard all night."

"It's not for the realms he passes through," Holland said.

"Ah." And now she had some sympathy for demons that got in Lud's path? That just seemed wrong.

"This was the realm he used when his human minion was summoning him here," Holland said.

"How do you know? You weren't there." He'd been hiding in a Naga cage, content to take whatever torture they inflicted on him to avoid just this. Fat lot of good that did any of them.

"It's the same transition point I used," Holland said.

"Did you answer a summons?" She new Holland hadn't gotten here by the traditional route, but still, she was curious. And the talking kept her mind from going completely blank with the horror currently consuming other parts of her body. She was trembling hard. She couldn't seem to stop it. So she talked to distract herself.

"No," Holland said—humoring her, she was sure. "I didn't need the summons to open the portal between this realm and that. I chose a time, a moment, like my father has, when passing into this realm would only strip so much of my power. And came through on my own." He paused as the shadows just inside the demon realm seemed to thicken, and a foggy sort of blackness finally started to ooze out, covering the grass. "Just like my father's about to do," Holland finished.

A huge shadow separated itself from the mass behind it, looming so far over Cary's head she had to tilt back to take it all in. At the top of the mass, red glowing eyes with cat's slit pupils stared down at her.

And an eerily quiet chuckle filled the clearing.

"Cary Redmond," Lud said in a voice Cary could never forget, even if she stopped having nightmares about their first encounter. "We meet again."

Cary's trembling made it hard to stand upright as the giant Lud-shaped shadow stepped into her realm with a shrieking sound that pierced the night.

Followed by a laugh that made her insides turn to jelly.

44

"*F*uck." That was the closest thing to speech she could manage in the circumstances.

Behind her, a lot of quiet, fearful noises and shuffling. She'd swear even the vampires were nervous about all this. But she didn't have enough brain power, or frankly enough sanity, to worry about the vampires.

Because the demon god Ho'Lud, in all his stygian glory, stood only a hundred yards away. Inside her realm. And even with some of his powers stripped because he'd just stepped in without the usual process to retain power, he was still the most overwhelmingly powerful thing she'd ever had to face.

Without her shields.

And with a body that soaked up the magic thrown at her.

Which might well kill her if that magic came from a god.

Since the Angel of Death was around here somewhere, she supposed the timing was good.

Also, she recognized that all these thoughts were not a good sign for her retaining sense and sanity.

Angie began murmuring something behind her, which Cary now recognized as the spell for setting a protective circle.

"Stop," Holland said, his tone low and warning. "If you give him a containment circle to work in, with all of us inside, he'll be able to reclaim some of the power he just lost."

"That's not how that works," Angie said, though she stopped her spell, and she didn't sound as positive as Cary might have liked.

"It is with gods," Holland said.

"Happened the last time," Cary murmured, her voice so dry she had to swallow hard to finish. "We contained him and it stopped him from going farther, but also returned all his powers."

"'Kay. Then. No containment circles," Angie said. "Good to know."

"Good to know," Cary repeated. She wasn't sure why. Her brain wasn't working properly.

"It is time to fulfill your destiny, son," Lud said, his attention on Holland.

Cary realized that was the same thing the "fake" Lud had said earlier. Which meant either the demons had a very limited vocabulary in human languages, or Holland knew exactly what his father would say the minute they were face-to-face again.

For some reason that thought struck her as interesting. Interesting enough, some of her slide into terror-induced insanity stalled. Curiosity had always been the thing to get her into trouble. But it was also the thing that, more than once, helped save her life and the life of the people she was protecting.

Now, it was the thing that let her cling to some semblance of sanity.

"What, exactly, *is* his destiny?" she asked. "I mean, we've discussed all this, and I kind of know, or have an idea. You need his immortality, the real stuff, not just the ordinary demon god stuff, but… How do you get it? Sacrifice? Body swap? Holland's been vague with the details, though he suggested it would be the body swap. But he's a demon, so I can't trust his information." There always seemed to be a lot of body swapping going on around these two, though, so it sort of made sense. "Some other option I don't know about? What needs to happen here for you to avoid your fate at the hands of the Angel of Death?"

Lud's head swung around so his cat's eyes were focused on her. "You need to die," Lud said.

"Well, yeah, I figured you'd say that. I mean, not the best history between us, right? Where did Buck drop you off, by the way? Not all the way home, I'm assuming?"

She was used to a shield, used to annoying bad guys until they went away. This wasn't an option here, not even a little. And yet, she Just. Kept. Talking. She hadn't meant to bring Buck to Lud's attention again. She just…

She didn't know what else to do. When you spent all your time being a shield, learning how to be a sword was tough.

Probably she should have practiced that part more before this moment.

"Your demon dog companion will die here, too," Lud said. "Your world will burn. But first, I will reclaim what is rightfully mine."

"There's a story in there," she said. "You and the Angel having a son. I don't want to know how, cause…ew."

Holland cleared his throat. She couldn't tell if it was a laugh or an actual choke and didn't really care. She was too scared and seemed incapable of keeping quiet so she just kept rambling.

"But why would she give you the thing you needed to avoid your own destiny of dying eventually. She says everything dies eventually."

"Like you, Ms. Redmond."

"Yeah, yeah, I mean…eventually. I'm still hoping to survive all this. But you know, been there, done that, so we'll see."

Lud's cat's eyes narrowed slightly.

She continued to ramble. "So I mean, she's destined to kill you, and you want to avoid that, so you have an indestructible son with the person…or wait, she's not really a person. The… I don't know. The Angel who's going to kill you. And if you do whatever it is you intend to do to Holland, you get his indestructibleness, and she can't kill you. I know all this. It's been repeated a lot. But I don't understand… Why and how? I mean."

She sucked in a breath and kept going. Unable to stop. "Why did she agree to have a son with you. Did she agree? If she didn't, that raises even more how questions I'm not sure I *want* answered. But she's the Angel of Death, why allow it? Why give you an optional out? It all seems pretty hinky, logic-wise. Doesn't it?"

Still not stopping… "And now everyone's here in this delicate little realm to end this prophecy stuff, but why here and not in your realm? I know, I know, she can't incarnate here very easily and it's hard for you to get here without stripping away powers. Which is why Holland came here. I understand that. That's logical."

Still talking. "And that fact that you have to come here to retrieve him is logical. He's here. There's nowhere else for you to go. But now, we've got this fight going on here, and it seems like it would be better fought…somewhere else, right?"

She just couldn't stop rambling. She knew they weren't going to even try to answer these questions. She was stalling for the Angel, she supposed, but the Angel needed some sort of sacrifice that Cary wasn't prepared to give, so there was no telling if she'd even be able to show up in person. Meanwhile, they had this big old demon god just waiting to kill them. And she kept talking.

Was she even breathing? She paused to pull in a deep breath. Better. Oxygen was good.

She was panicking. Big time. And the fear and terror were overwhelming her. So much for the last seven years of training. She almost felt like she was standing outside herself, watching as she slowly dissolved into a jabbering mess of humanity with no real coherence left. Lud would squash her like a bug, and she'd go down yammering.

As if to confirm the assessment of her detached self, Holland leaned closer and murmured, "You know you don't have your usual abilities here, right?"

"Yup," she said. "Well aware. Just can't stop. Not sure why."

"Have you gone insane?" He asked so matter-of-factly she almost laughed.

"Might have," she said. Then back to Lud. "Anyway, so why can't you guys take all this back to your realm. I know you have to do some realm hoping. But honestly, that sounds better than body swapping, which frankly sounds really bad. I would not want to do that." She raised a hand when Holland pulled in a breath and looked away from Lud long enough to glare at him. "No. Body. Swapping." Then back to Lud, "So maybe back to your own realm would be the thing to do. You'd have all your powers for fending off the Angel, right. And Holland would be restored to full power? Or no, wait, coming here is a permanent sacrifice. Unless you're a god. So wait, how does creating a containment circle give you your powers back again? I thought it was permanent. I'm really confused."

"Obviously," Holland muttered.

Deacon took hold of her hand, the gesture shocking her into silence. He hadn't been touching her much since the earlier incident where she may or may not have soaked up some of his shifter magic for the first time ever, so the contact was enough to stop her talking cold. She glanced at him. He wasn't looking at her. He was staring at Lud. His eyes glowed in the darkness, golden yellow and feral. His jaw was tight. The muscles in his shoulders and neck stood out with his tension.

But his touch on her hand was gentle. His fingers intertwining with hers held her in a firm, supportive grasp that wasn't confining. And the unspoken support and backing helped calm some of the overwhelming fear that made it feel impossible to shut up.

She let out a long, slow sigh. "Guess I don't need all the answers, huh?"

"You're not going to get them anyway," Holland said.

She ignored him, focused on Deacon instead. "Better now," she said to him.

He nodded and gave her fingers a gentle squeeze.

"You?" she asked.

He shook his head.

Well. That was something different to worry about. He was not good, or better, and yet he was calming her down.

Actually, that was pretty impressive.

The movement of vampires hissing and shifters growling behind her finally penetrated her blind fear. She realized more demons were spilling out of the hole Lud had stepped through. Most were shadowy creatures. The last time he'd attacked, he'd brought a few large demons, most of whom struck her as pretty typical. A bat-like being, a giant red one, lots of flames and lava involved.

These were different. All shadowed darkness like Lud himself. Blending with the night, their presence showing up when they blocked the view behind them, eclipsing the forest. But hard to see otherwise.

How the hell were they going to fight something they couldn't see?

She leaned into Deacon. "Can you see the demons coming through? Cause I can't very well."

Shifter eyesight was better, and Deacon's night vision was excellent. She'd never asked if he saw things in different ranges of light, but she knew some shifter species did. Could the shifters, or even the vampires for that matter, see the heat signatures of the shadow demons? If so, that'd make the fight a little more level.

For the shifters and vampires anyway.

"There's a faint heat signature," Deacon murmured. "But they're still hard to see."

His voice was very growly and deep, a lot more so than even an hour ago. The sound reminded her of the one and only time she'd seen him so out of control he'd nearly killed another leopard. To be fair, the leopard was a bad guy and she'd kidnapped Cary, but still. The fact that he was close to that place again was probably not good.

She squeezed his hand. He'd stopped her from rambling with that touch. She hoped she could help him keep control in return.

The shadows spilling out of the demon realm formed a wall behind Lud, dense enough to cut off her view of the forest behind them. She could only see Lud and shadow now. And her human brain did not want to process those shadows as anything. It scurried away from the occasional glimpse of red eyes in the darkness like a mouse trying to escape an owl. Actually, it was more like the mouse was trying to pretend the owl wasn't there and that owls didn't even exist. Her brain did not want to believe the danger in front of her was real.

Boy, did she miss her Protector shields.

Lud leveled an arm in her direction and she wasn't even a little surprised a sword that glowed a strange red-purple color materialized in front of her face, the tip of the sword only a few feet from her nose. Because of course he had a sword this time. Of course he did.

For some reason, she was reminded of Jaxer's father, when he'd let loose the curse that had overtaken him and nearly destroyed Faery. It was a strange memory in that moment. The comparisons were there, she supposed. But more, that was the time she'd died. And remembering her own death, facing another being of shadow and darkness, who'd also had a sword, seemed a little too deja vu.

"Could use Jaxer and the others about now," she muttered aloud.

"Yup," Deacon said.

"Yup," Angie answered.

"Hope he's okay," Marianne said quietly.

Cary did too.

Because they most certainly were not.

Lud swung his sword in a large arc.

Cary froze, too scared and too panicked. What did she do? What was she supposed to do now?

Angie leaned in close and touched Cary. Cary felt the flow of magic coursing into her. "Shield," Angie said in her ear.

And Cary started muttering the spell, moving her hands in the pattern to make the shield form, using the magic Angie gave her. Even as she heard Angie also murmuring a spell. Not the same one. But a spell nonetheless.

Somewhere to her left, she heard a trio of female voices also murmuring. The triad. Another spell. Hopefully against Lud since they were supposed to be on Holland's side in all this. Or at the very least, the Angel's side.

She turned a little to the side, so that her hip was facing Lud, so that any magic that got through would come up against Marianne's magical clothes and not swamp her instantly.

She finished the spell, raised her hands high, and watched the blue shield form…

Just as Lud's sword swung down.

45

  *C*ary watched Lud's sword drop onto the magical shield she held, a kind of detachment taking over because she'd moved well beyond terror. She was holding a shield made of someone else's magic against the sword of an actual god.

This couldn't end well.

Except all the fear and terror that had been shaking her to her bones had somehow vanished in those slow-motion moments as she watched the sword descend. She didn't feel brave or strong. It wasn't that. She didn't really feel anything at all. A kind of curious detachment, watching the sword drop, wondering if the shield would stop it or if it would cut through her shield like butter.

The stillness of those moments struck her, too. The collective breath holding—which might have been her imagination. The silence —which also might have just been her. She was hyper aware of the circling fir and oak forest, the rocky grass under her feet, the people behind her. But everything felt like it had stopped moving, or slowed to a crawl.

So that when the sword finally hit her magical shield, created from Angie's magic and her own stubborn need to keep Lud from killing everyone, the clanging sound nearly deafened her. Loud. And long. A giant clock bell ringing right next to her ear.

There was a moment for her to wonder how the hell a demon's magic sword and her magic shield made a noise like metal striking metal…

And then the world of motion and sound flowed in again, swamping her senses. Around her there were screams, and shouts and movement. Above her, Lud pressed his sword down on her shield. It took her a few seconds to realize he wasn't able to just slice through it, and she nearly whooped with relief.

Until she realized how much stronger he was than she was, and how she was sinking under the weight of trying to physically hold up that sword.

A hand at her back, she wasn't sure whose. But she felt the rush of some kind of magic. Wild magic. Full of heat and anger.

And strength.

She shoved upward, pushing the shield. And to her surprise, she managed to push Lud's sword up and away.

Where the hell did that strength come from?

She didn't dare look back, because Lud growled and swung his sword around again. But she had a brief moment to *feel* the strength now flowing through her. It felt…familiar.

The hiss of leopards not far away, the sounds of Angie chanting a spell behind her, Holland shouted something she couldn't hear. All of it blending in a kind of battlefield chaos she couldn't begin to decipher. She might have had a better chance if she had her normal shield and could take her attention away from Lud.

But Lud's full attention was on her—useful, if not necessarily a good thing—and she was wielding magic—magic!—that she wasn't used to wielding. It took a lot of concentration and focus not to drop the shield she'd built. Even more to keep Lud from slicing her in half.

She heard a growl just behind her, but it was a familiar growl. Her mate's growl. She found that sound really reassuring.

Then Lud brought his sword down hard again. The ear-shattering clang that shouldn't be happening. The pressure that nearly brought her to her knees.

And another surge of strength pouring into her from a single touch.

She shoved upward again, regaining her balance. And in a move Lucy had taught her—using hands and not a shield, but still—she swiveled sideways, sliding the sword off her shield to the ground.

The fact that she was using a magical witch shield like an actual, physical metal shield was not lost on her.

Lud's sword punched into the earth, searing the grass and turning the dirt to darkened glass.

Cary swallowed hard. So letting the sword get near her would…not be good.

She spun and lifted the shield in front of her again. She wasn't sure how she was using it like a physical thing. She'd never done that before. But it seemed to be working so she went with it.

Even the shape of the oval blue light in front of her, large, round, curving out from her, struck her as very physical-shield like. It was a lot larger than any shield she'd seen. Taking up the full length of her body and spreading out to the sides enough to protect anyone directly behind her. But she held it up with her two hands like it was made of metal and wood, and moved it around in swinging arcs like it was real.

And that strangeness might have distracted her if Lud hadn't pulled his sword from the ground and swung it back around to slam into the magic shield again.

She winced and prepared for the strength of his swing to slam against her shoulders and push her farther down.

It didn't. She was braced. She was ready, her knees bent a little to take the strain and be better balanced—like Lucy had been teaching her. She *knew* that sword slamming down on top of her magical shield would reverberate through her, maybe even hurt a little.

But…nothing. She heard the clang. Lud was so close, she could smell his very faint sulfur scent. She could see his head lowering to her as he pushed harder on the sword.

She frowned up at him. This was almost like having her Protector shield. Except, not. Because she had to hold this one up. She could feel her muscles working. She could feel the magic flowing through her into the shield. She felt this in a way she didn't feel Protector magic.

She just wasn't feeling any strain against Lud's strength anymore.

That was weird. She liked it. But it was weird.

And, she was certain, was a result of whoever had touched her and given her that strength. She'd laid odds that was Deacon. But Lud swung his sword up again and down again, hard, so she didn't have time to ask.

More noise around her. From the corner of her eyes, she saw more flares of blue light from witch magic. A fire ball streaked past from somewhere behind her and slammed into Lud. Shadows flew overhead, cutting off sight of the sky. Something boomed and Cary's hair stood up as electricity danced in the air. A moment later, a sizzling line of lightning slashed through the shadows overhead and barreled into the ground strong enough to make the earth shake.

Cary really wanted to see what that lightning had hit and who was throwing it, but Lud tried to push closer to her, tried to stab forward with his sword and pierce through her shield, and she really had to focus on him.

She had no idea why *he* was so focused on *her*. There were a lot more powerful beings around her. Beings stronger and faster and with a hell of a lot more magic to fight him. But for reasons surpassing logic, Lud seemed totally focused on destroying her first before moving on to the others.

That was good?

When she was a Protector, she was delighted with that sort of thing. She *wanted* the bad guys to focus on her. She wasn't a Protector now, though, and she wasn't sure this focus was optimal for her survival.

It did mean, however, that he wasn't getting to Holland yet, and that had to be good. At least, she hoped it was.

"You must die," Lud said to her.

"One day," she muttered. In her head, because she kept poking the cut, she also thought, Been there done that, asshole. But she kept that part to herself.

Hey, that had to count as personal growth, right?

"Today," Lud growled. "Your blood will feed the ceremony."

"Uh." That didn't sound like something she wanted to happen. Not even a little bit. "No ceremonies today," she said. "Planet's all closed to ceremonies. Of any kind." Especially the kind that required blood sacrifice.

Which also included the blood sacrifice that the Angel required to get here.

Fuck, they still had that to worry about.

A scream behind her nearly had her dropping her shield. Panic surged through her blood. That didn't sound like a demon scream. It sounded too much like one of her people.

Deacon at her ear, breathing hard, "It's okay. Focus on Lud. It was a vampire, and they're fine."

"You sure?"

"No one you love," he confirmed. "And the vampire wasn't even killed. They'll be good. They'll miss that arm, but they'll be fine."

Cary winced.

Lud tried to stab her again, so she missed her chance to ask Deacon how he was, and what was happening. She wanted to check on the others, to see with her own eyes that no one had been killed.

She didn't dare.

Something slammed into her back, a burst of power that rolled into her cells and through her body with a heat and speed that nearly took her breath. The pressure of the magic pouring into her made her stumble forward a step. She recognized that power, after spending hours tonight working with it.

Without thinking, she poured Holland's demon magic into her shield. She hadn't planned to and didn't do it consciously. If she'd thought about it, she might have realized he was giving her something to fight Lud with, some offensive magic to throw at the god as the witch magic in her system got used up.

She only recognized that the witch magic had been thinning, that her shield was contracting, when she poured that new surge of power into the shield on accident.

And it ballooned into a glowing, transparent, purple wall in front of her.

The shield knocked Lud backward—to her utter shock—and spread out in front of her, moving high overhead and off to her right and left past her peripheral vision.

A demon shriek cut off abruptly. Lud roared and charged her new shield. She blinked, too stunned by what had happened to try to move or respond to Lud's attack. The new thing she'd created felt too big to move anyway. But she did manage to keep her hands up and keep pouring power into the shield.

Lud slammed against it. And bounced backward again.

Okay, that was kind of cool.

Even her protector shield hadn't done that to him.

The sounds of more than one demon roaring and shrieking in protest made her ears hurt. She couldn't lower her hands to cover her ears but she really really wanted to. The poor shifters.

Deacon's presence behind her felt like a wash of cool air as heat pumped through her veins. He set his hands to her shoulders and more of that strength from earlier poured into her.

"What are you doing?" she asked. But the demon noise was too loud. She couldn't even hear her own voice over all that screeching. "Shut. Up." She shouted up at Lud because it made her feel better even if he couldn't hear her.

And since Deacon had somehow managed to give her more strength, she took that and also poured it into her shield. A part of her mind considered it would be nice if the shield dampened the sound.

The sudden silence hit her almost as hard as a blow.

"Uh," she muttered. When she heard her own voice, she let out a little sigh of relief. The demons' shrieking hadn't burst her eardrums. That was nice. "What's happening?"

Beyond her now bright purple shield, Lud's mouth was still wide open and he was motioning to the shadow demons around him. From the still open rip between the demon realm and her realm, more shadows poured out.

And now new creatures emerged. Things she hadn't noticed before.

Huge glowing white rock and lava beings, their brightness so sharp against the shadow demons it made Cary's eyes hurt. She couldn't even see them properly they were so bright and hard to look at.

They were big, though. There weren't as many of them as the shadow creatures. But they were big.

"This is all very bad, isn't it?" she said aloud, not to anyone in particular.

"Yes," Deacon said. "That's very bad. How did your shield stop all the noise?"

"Got me," she said.

"You're using all of our magic at once," Angie said from her other side.

Cary risked a glance at her. Her face was pale, her hair piled on her head in a messy bun, and her fingers shook a little when she raised them to wipe sweat from her temple.

"You okay?" Cary asked.

"Fine. I'll be fine in a few minutes. Calling multiple lightning strikes in a row from a clear sky is hard work."

"That was you?"

Angie nodded. "I tried for rain at first, but the bastards are too hot. The rain just turns to mist and that fog was making the fight harder."

"There's a lot going on behind me I missed," Cary muttered.

"You've got Lud's attention on you. That's helping more than you can know." She lowered her voice to say this last.

"He'll keep his attention on you, too, Ms. Redmond," Holland said from somewhere behind her.

The fact that he was behind her made her nerves prickles with unease. She kept her attention on the demon hoards beyond her shield, on the giant white light creature stalking closer to her, but it was hard not to turn and face Holland.

"Why's he so interested in me?" she asked. She had been very good at pissing him off the last time they met, so she wasn't exactly surprised he wanted to kill her. She was just sort of surprised he wanted to do it himself so much he was ignoring the rest of the fight to focus on her.

A giant light creature slammed what Cary assumed was a shoulder against her new shield. She felt the shock of that hit through her shoulders and braced her legs against the sensation, anticipating the shove would throw her off balance. To her surprise, though, it didn't.

Huh. Strong shield.

"Lud intends to use your blood to feed the process of stealing my immunity to death," Holland said. "He'll need more than your blood."

This said with a matter-of-factness that made Cary flatten her mouth.

"But he wants yours first."

"How do you know?" she asked. Beyond the fact that Lud had said something about using her blood for a ceremony out loud.

"Remember, when we're in the same realm, we're able to…read each other."

Right. Right. He'd mentioned that during the Lud-lookalike confrontation earlier.

Holland sighed. "That ability grows more intense when we're this close. I can't keep anything from him when we're in the same space. It's always been a problem."

"Ya think?" She had to work not to roll her eyes. "Does he know what you know about me now?"

"By now," Holland said, not sounding bothered even a little bit, "he knows everything."

Oh boy.

46

"So," Cary said to Holland through gritted teeth as yet another of the bright white demons joined the first bright glowing demon to slam against her shield. "So you're telling me he now not only knows *what* a Protector is—" he hadn't known that the last time they faced each other; only that she was one "—but he knows that I'm not one anymore. And that I absorb magic? Is that what you're telling me?"

She wanted to glare at Holland for not mentioning this issue *sooner* in the fight. It wasn't like he hadn't had enough time. They'd been working for hours before this. But *no*. He had to go and leave out a little thing like he and Lud know *everything* that was in each other's minds when they got close to each other, and *none* of it would be secret.

What an asshole.

As if he'd been reading *her* mind at that very moment, Lud started to laugh. She couldn't actually hear it, which was weird. But she watched him lean his head back and his mouth open wide and his chest pump and his shoulder bounce in a way that didn't look like a scream.

When a demon god laughed, that usually meant bad things for the surrounding humans and other assorted non-demons.

"This doesn't look good," Angie said.

"Nope," Cary agreed.

"You might want to brace yourself, Ms. Redmond," Holland said. And for once he didn't sound matter-of-fact.

The edge of stark warning and the sense that he was about to take a step back from her was not encouraging.

She had just enough time to brace, and then power slammed into the shield.

Not Lud's sword. Not Lud's hands. Not any of his demons. But pure power shot from the palm of Lud's hand. A stream of power like raw white light. Nothing like she'd seen him use before. The glare made her wince and she had to look away.

She held her hands up, her arms trembling with the effort, hoping the shield held. She poured more of the magic Holland had given her into it. More of the strength Deacon had somehow managed to give her into it.

From behind, she felt more power pour into her from Holland. And she sent all of it into the shield.

Then another shot from Angie. Everything went into the shield.

Another surge of strength from Deacon hit her just in time for her to steady her tiring arms. How the hell long had she been holding her hands out in front of her? It felt like forever.

She could hear Lud laughing now. Sound from beyond the shield had returned, as mysteriously as it had been dampened. She was pretty sure Lud said something aloud, too, but she couldn't hear him over the rush of blood in her ears.

And then more power slammed into her from behind. And more. Two new sources of magic. Neither familiar.

Whatever that new magic had originally been, she took it and poured it into the shield. Shielding was what she did, what she knew. Her every instinct was to block and defend.

She had no idea who had given her those new sources of power, but the magic flowed through her and into her shield in a wash of heat and cool that left her trembling. The contrasts and conflicts of the different magic in her cells blending into something she couldn't even describe.

More than heat. More than frost. An exquisite edge of sensation that was overwhelming.

But it wasn't pain.

Lud redoubled his efforts, slamming more power against her growing shield.

She gasped and took a step back, coming up against Deacon. More of his strength poured into her. She wanted to tell him to stop, he'd get too weak if he kept this up, but she couldn't form the words around her gritted teeth.

Shoving into the shield she pushed it forward a little. And other wash of different magic poured into her from behind.

She couldn't have remembered one of Angie's spells in that moment if she tried. She realized too late she might have used some of the power flowing into her to attack Lud. That hadn't occurred to her either. She just knew she had to keep all that magic Lud was firing at her away from her and from the people behind her.

A part of her realized she was protecting everyone in that moment, without the Protector power or magic, she was using what Holland and Angie and Deacon had given her, what two other people back there had given her, to protect everyone.

Whatever magic she was given, no matter its origin or original use, she was using it the way she'd been using her bosses' magic for the last seven years.

Letting it flow through her into a shield.

Her arms shook and she had to brace her legs against Lud's onslaught.

The Protector shields had been easier to hold up.

From her peripheral vision she got hints of shadow and light now slamming into the multi-magic shield she'd created. The other demons attacking. She felt the hits like small vibrations through the makeup of the shield. But none of it felt strong enough to break through.

Only Lud's white hot power pouring from his palm felt like it could get past her defense.

Some shouting behind her, she couldn't decipher. Movement in her peripheral vision. And then she felt the ground shiver under her.

"What's happening?" she said. Or thought she did. She couldn't hear her own voice even though she heard noise around her clearly. She might not have spoken aloud.

She shoved at the shield she held again, pushing it forward. A wave pulsed through it, flowing from her down the lengths of the wall she could sense but not see the ends of.

To her surprise, the power that Lud had been steadily pouring at her hit that wave of movement and zinged back at him and the demons surrounding him.

His own magic hit him a glancing blow in the shoulder and arrowed into one of the shadow demons.

The shadow demon screamed. And exploded.

Woah.

That was unexpected.

"You've used the shield as a weapon before," a voice said near her ear. "Do it again."

Jaxer! She wanted to turn and say something to him, but didn't have time. More of Deacon's strength poured into her. Then more magic she hadn't felt before from the other side. Was that Jaxer's magic?

She'd sort it out later. She took what she was given and the minute Lud shot some of that white hot power from his palm at her, she sent another wave through the shield. The wave caught Lud's attack and sent it ricocheting back into his own hoard.

Another couple of shadow demons exploded. And one of the glaring bright white demons turned to a solid mound of rock when hit.

That was weird.

And only what she could see happening directly in front of her. She didn't dare risk looking around, in case she missed another Lud attack, but she was aware of other things happening beyond her line of sight. Noise. Screams. Flares of magic and flashes of light.

She needed to keep those behind her safer. How did she do that with this new weird shield? Lud couldn't get through it. It was exploding demons, or turning them to rock. But there was still enough chaos she knew things were getting through.

"Use the shield more," Jaxer said, his voice near her ear, coaching her. "It's your weapon. Attack with it."

She sent another wave of movement through the shield. There was no Lud magic to deflect this time, but the movement still smack down a shadow demon flying right at the shield.

That would work.

Moving her hands to a wider position, her shoulders straining with the effort to keep her arms up, she swiveled and sent a stronger wave through the shield. This time it smacked a couple of shadow demons who had been attempting to charge it.

Useful.

She did it again, and this time knocked one of the large white demons back onto its ass.

Huh.

"Shame I can't shoot stuff from the shield," she joked aloud, because the fact that she could use a *shield* as a weapon was kind of blowing her mind. She flexed and pushed again. The shadow demon hit this time spun into Lud.

Lud smacked the demon aside, and it screeched in protest.

"What are you doing?" Lud demanded as he pointed his sword at her again.

Got me, she thought. This was all new. She really didn't have any idea what she was doing.

She just wasn't going to tell him that.

"Get out of my realm," she said. "We've done this before and it didn't end well for you. Leave. Now." She tried to pour a little of that supposed stubborn will she had into the words.

It had absolutely no effect on the god. Which...to be fair, was not unexpected. The one time she'd been able to make will work against Lud, she'd had a legendary demon hunter beside her adding her own strength of will—a considerable boost to Cary's not-so-legendary willpower.

"Your little tricks don't work on me, human," Lud said.

"You still need to leave."

Lud laughed and it wasn't a good sound. "Ah, but I can do this forever. And I have forever. You will die. Soon. You can't win."

"I'm not here to win, just stall. And I can stall until the end of days." She was good at stalling. And irritating bad guys. And holding a shield stubbornly.

What she wasn't good at was getting rid of bad guys when she wanted them to go away. And that's the thing she really needed to be able to do just then.

Because Lud was right.

He could keep doing this until either the Angel killed him or he got Holland. Even if he went away now, he could just come back. She had no doubt this spacetime window he needed to get here would happen again. All of their defenses and fighting were well and good, but if they couldn't permanently get rid of Lud, none of this mattered.

Shame she couldn't absorb some of his magic to throw back at him. That might send him packing for a while. She might be able to turn things he shot at her back on his army, but she wondered what would happen if she turned his own magic back on him, filtering it through herself.

The fact that she'd probably die before getting the chance to release anything because taking a hit from a demon god wasn't something her human body would likely survive was not lost on her.

Still, the idea was there, in the back of her mind. If she could take in some of Lud's magic, could she fight him better? Could she get him to go away?

Could she avoid the sacrifice that the Angel of Death required to incarnate here and kill Lud?

Lud laughed again. And again, Cary was not comforted by that sound.

"You will have to stall for eternity," Lud said. "I am unending."

"Until your ex gets here," she said.

She stumbled a little under the weight of holding up the shield for so long. Deacon sent another jolt of his strength into her. And some other magic from somewhere behind her hit her again, this the cooling magic from earlier, from someone she still had identified. The combination of the two powers felt like they were repairing her strength.

Eriana. Had to be.

But if she was throwing power at Cary, who was stopping Sheldon from allowing himself be sacrificed for the Angel to incarnate?

She needed to look around, to ask questions. She couldn't when she was the only thing between Lud and a full onslaught on her people.

"Where are the other Protectors?" she hissed at Jaxer. She could use the break now to regroup.

"Not coming," he said.

"What? Why?" Had Kupal Umsta stopped them? Was he preventing them from helping? That would really piss her off.

"Lud's loosed a lot of chaos around the country," Jaxer said. "The Protectors and the demon hunters are fighting his incursions all over the place. They can't come help."

Fuck. He'd done that the last time, too. Kept the demon hunters occupied while he tried to invade. The last time, from what she gathered, he'd gotten a bunch of humans who wouldn't normally summon demons to summon them, and things got out of hand fast. The distraction had worked. No demon hunters had come to help her with Lud that first time.

And it looked like they wouldn't be able to help now.

"That's why no one's showed up," Jaxer said. "They can't. There's too much going on everywhere else."

"Just in this country?" The Protectors were isolated to North America, at least at the moment. More were just starting to be trained in other places. But the demon hunters were international. Was this happening around the world?

"The word through Faery is it's happening everywhere," Jaxer said, his tone grim.

Lud's laugh shook the ground. "You see? There's nothing you weak creatures can do. I will have my son returned. And I will not be stopped."

So whoever was with her now, that was all the help she'd have. All that stood between Lud and Holland. No one else was coming to help.

No Protector shields to save the day—or at least keep things contained while they figured out how to get the Angel here.

Chaos and death, and her with no way to stop it.

The hopelessness, the helplessness swamped her. And she almost lowered her shield.

"That's what he wants," Holland said, moving into view just to her left. "Your hopelessness. For you to give up."

Holland turned to look at her, and while she didn't look back so she could watch Lud, she was aware of his direct and piercing gaze.

"Will you give up, Ms. Redmond? Will you let him win?"

Bastards. The lot of them.

But she couldn't let Lud win.

47

ud's laughter thundered through the clearing. The hiss and sizzle of the demons before her now the only other sound.

Even the vampires had fallen silent behind her. Whether they felt the same sense of overwhelming hopelessness or were currently calculating how to survive in a demon god dominated realm, she had no idea. She wouldn't put it past James to have a backup plan that involved making peace with the enemy.

But there were a lot of good people in this world. Cary just wanted to keep them all safe. How the hell did she, a single and pretty ineffectual little human, do that? Her only real skill was a stubborn refusal to move.

And now, it seemed, the ability to pour whatever magic sank into her cells into a shield.

"You cannot win," Lud said. "Time is on my side."

"There's so much cliché in those sentences I don't even know how to respond." Cary shook her head, pretending at more confidence that she felt. But she was worried about that part. The time part. How did they end this without the Angel of Death here?

"Shame we can't just shove him back into his realm," she muttered.

"You could try," Holland said. "The door, so to speak, is still open."

The off-handed comment made Cary frown. Could she just…shove them all back into the demon realm? She'd pushed things with her Protector shield before, and hemmed in people she wanted to stop. This wasn't a Protector shield. But she seemed to have more control over this one than she'd ever had over her Protector magic.

She rolled her aching shoulders. How long had she had her arms in the air?

Deacon's hands moved to her shoulders, another brief hit of his strength.

"Stop," she murmured, trying to talk quietly enough only he would hear. "You'll get too weak."

"I'm fine," he said. "I won't leave you to fight alone by draining myself. I have enough."

She wasn't sure why, but she teared up a little and had to force back the sentiment. Stupid feelings in the middle of chaos.

She sniffled and glared up at Lud. "I'd love you gone."

"Too bad," he said. He moved his attention to Holland. "You are fond of these creatures?"

"Fond might be…well, not precisely the right word," Holland said. "But I have enjoyed my time in this realm."

"You are done here. It is time to face your destiny."

"As Ms. Redmond would say, No."

Her lips twitched. She pressed them together so she wouldn't laugh. Why the hell did she find Holland amusing at the most inappropriate times?

"We need your mom," Cary muttered.

"She needs a sacrifice," Holland said. "I can arrange her incarnation. But it will take blood."

"What is with you people and blood all the time," she growled. "Everything is blood this and blood that."

"We're demons, Ms. Redmond. It's what we do."

She, quite childishly, gave him a raspberry.

Angie murmured something behind her and then she felt her closer.

"Even if you send Lud back to the realm he came through, it's not his own realm. But...but the Angel may be able to incarnate there."

"Then why hasn't she before this?"

"He never spends much time in any realm outside his own," Holland said.

"Why would I lower myself?" Lud said, proving that their quiet voices weren't quiet enough to escape demon god hearing. "The Angel can only attempt to take me when it is my time," Lud said, straightening and pointed his sword at Cary again. "And it is not yet my time."

"Just incredibly close," Holland said. Which made Lud growl. "He's right, though. There's a very precise time schedule for these sorts of things. No jumping the gun and taking him early. He will die when he dies. But she will need to be there when it happens to take him."

Something in that phrasing sort of belied everything they'd been telling her about this up to this point. "I thought the Angel was destined to *kill* him. Right? That's what you've been saying. She's the only one who can kill a demon god. That's why she has to incarnate wherever he is." He was a demon god. Except for this weird... whatever it was, prophesy or whatever, that said he'd die, he was essentially forever. So... "I'm confused."

"You are human," Lud said. "It is your natural state to be confused."

"Ha ha."

She rolled her shoulders and her shield rolled a little. No one was charging it anymore, which she supposed was good. But the magic she'd been given to build it was going to run out eventually. She didn't dare lower it yet. The shadow demons were restlessly flowing around behind Lud. And the remaining white light demons seemed to be scraping at the ground like bulls waiting to charge.

But no one was attacking at the moment, and it took physical effort to keep this shield up. Unlike her Protector shield. Which she still really missed.

"Is the Angel coming to kill him, or just to collect him after he's dead?" she asked bluntly. "I thought she was doing the killing."

"Well." She caught Holland's shrug from the corner of her eye. "The prophecy is a little fuzzy on that last point, actually. Now that you mention it, Ms. Redmond. It only says that she will claim him. That he will die."

Holland sounded thoughtful and he did that head tilt thing as he studied his father. Lud glowered back. Which was pretty impressive from a demon god. His red, cat-pupil eyes narrowed and seemed to glow brighter.

This whole time she'd been under the impression the Angel had to be here to kill Lud. That was what everyone had talked about. The Angel had to incarnate here because she was the only one who could *kill* a demon god. The assumption this whole time was that the Angel herself would be doing the killing.

Cary had even kind of been looking forward to seeing that. How did the Angel of Death dole out death to a god?

But…

But what if all their assumptions had been wrong? What if something or someone else killed Lud? What if his time was just up, and all this was happening because it was supposed to? Here. In this place and spot. Because this was just where he died.

But who could kill him? And how?

"You can't kill him, right?" she asked Holland.

"No. I can't. Any more than he can kill me."

"Right right, your more immortal than even a god. I get it. What I don't get is…?" How was Lud supposed to die in all this?

"I will not die," Lud said, almost as if reading her mind. "I will overcome this prophesy. And my son will enable that."

Yeah, she'd heard all that before, but…

This other thing had caught her.

What if… What if all of this was how the prophesy was supposed to play out? That was the tricky thing about prophesies, right? You got this hint of something that was supposed to happen, then you went out of your way to ensure it didn't happen, only to bring it about by those actions. If the prophesy had never been mentioned, no one would have done the things required to make it happen. That was the whole trick. Right?

In every classical myth, the revelation of the prophesy is what drove the prophesy to come true. That was the reason Jaxer's father hadn't wanted to tell him about the vision of death and destruction his mother had had of the end of Faery. He worried Jaxer would run into the prophesy through his own actions. That he'd bring it on by trying to avoid it.

So…

So what if they were always all supposed to be here in this moment?

What if this was how things were supposed to end?

Because this was where Lud was always *supposed* to die.

But…

How?

48

As Cary's epiphany washed through her, making the minutes feel like they'd slowed to a crawl, her shaking arms and waning concentration snapped her back to the present. Her shoulders shuddered and she nearly dropped her arms again.

Deacon physically held her up this time, supporting her arms with a gentle hold on her elbows.

Lud laughed again. The sound like metal scrapping against metal, high and piercing and very unpleasant as it echoed through the clearing. A sound that made her ears hurt and her brain recoil.

"You are too weak, human." He gestured at the shield. "And when this falls, we will swarm. I will have what I am here for."

"But…" She was still having trouble dislodging the idea. "You're here for death," she said. A little surprised she'd said that out loud, surprised by how right it sounded. "That's what all of this is about. You dying."

"I will *not die!*" Lud lowered his sword and a blast of fire shot from the tip, crashing against her shield so hard the shock reverberated through her arms.

She twisted her hands, sending a save through the shield that sent the fire ricocheting back into the demon hoard. A white demon melted.

A shadow demon exploded. And Lud stopped shooting fire at her, growling as he snapped his sword down.

Her arms trembled hard, even with Deacon holding them up, and numbness was setting in. Lud was right, she wouldn't be able to keep the shield up much longer. Even with Deacon's support and all the extra magic others were feeding her. Physically, she wasn't strong enough. Eventually, this was all going to catch up to her human body, and she'd collapse, and Lud and his demons would overwhelm them.

But she knew, she just *knew* she was on to something here.

The Angel had killed Zorianthus. The Angel did kill, could kill. And she'd done that while she wasn't incarnate here in this realm. She'd just been using the triad's bodies at the time.

So the Angel could affect this realm when body swapped with the triad. Holland had said she couldn't kill Lud that way, though.

Not directly.

Not herself.

But what if…

To Angie, she said, "The witches, they're back there somewhere?"

"What are you thinking?"

"They need to get the Angel here. Usual way. No sacrificing anyone."

"Holland said the Angel can't kill Lud that way."

"No. But she can still affect things in this realm when she's in their bodies. She can affect ordinary humans."

Deacon's hands tightened on her arms. "No," he said.

Jaxer leaned in. "What do you think you're going to try?"

"She's not," Deacon said.

"Yup. I am. Because I think this is what is supposed to happen. I think this is what we're all here for."

She kept her gaze on Lud as he stared at her through the purple haze of her shield, but she leaned closer to Jaxer and Angie, relying on Deacon's support a lot now. "Death comes for everyone. When they die. As they die. That doesn't mean Death does the killing. Everything dies. She just collects them when they do. She *can* kill. She has the *power* to kill. But she doesn't have to be the *hand* that does the killing for things to die." She turned enough to look at Jaxer, leaning back more into Deacon. "She can send her power into this world, though. To humans." She lowered her voice. "*Through* humans."

Jaxer blinked and looked away, but she could see his mind working, see the wheels turning.

Marianne and Lucy closed in, forming up a tight circle with them. "I'm not sure I like the look on yours or Jaxer's faces," Marianne said.

"What are you going to do?" Lucy asked.

"Get the triad to bring the Angel here." She met her friends' gazes even as her arms trembled and Deacon had to tighten his support under her elbows. She didn't say what she was going to do out loud. But she watched as the realization dawned on them. She watched them figure out her plan.

And she watched every single one of them rebel at the idea.

Marianne shook her head. Lucy mouthed, No. Angie's expression tightened and she let out a long breath.

Jaxer blinked and looked at her again. "This isn't Faery," he said. "But it feels like the same moment."

She shrugged. "We weren't ever going to avoid this," she murmured. "Maybe this is why the Protector magic never came back. Maybe I *can't* have it right now. It would interfere."

"This is a crappy plan," Jaxer said.

She smiled, though it wasn't a smile full of much humor. "I always have been bad at plans."

"Which was my fault," he said, not rising to her attempt at levity. "But we'll talk about that later."

"If this works."

"If this works." His tone was grim.

Deacon set his mouth to her ear even as he boosted her arms when they flagged. She could feel the magic that had been flowing through her starting to fad. She was going to use up everything she'd been given soon. Not yet. But soon. Her body had converted all that magic into usable shield, but there was only so much others could give her. She was a little surprised she'd had enough to hold the shield this long, to be honest. Maybe she was getting some magic through Lud when he tried to break her shield?

That would be ironic.

Deacon's breath on her cheek was warm, and his scent filled her head, like surrounding her in a feeling of being home. She breathed in that feeling, that scent, knowing he was about to object to what she wanted to do, and that she was going to have to argue with him.

"If you die doing this," Deacon said, "I'm coming with you."

"No. No, don't do that." A tear slid down her cheek. Where had that come from? She didn't think she had the energy for tears right now.

"I'm coming with you," he said. "No matter where you go."

She blinked hard, her vision swimming. "I don't want you to die."

He nuzzled her cheek. "I can't be without you."

"Guess I better not die then," she said. "Because I don't want you to."

"Whatever works."

His comment was so strangely normal and out of place for his declaration, she let loose a surprised laugh.

He kissed her cheek. "I've got your back. Do what you have to do. I'm here."

"I love you," she murmured. Then louder, "Angie, go get the witches."

She kept her gaze on Lud as Holland sidled closer. "This won't work, Ms. Redmond."

"Oh, you can fuck all the way off with that negative attitude," Cary said pleasantly.

"It's impossible," Holland said.

"The witches body swap with her. I can do this."

"There are three of them. It takes three of them. Very powerful humans. You are one single human with no real powers."

She couldn't argue with that part. Her "powers" were stubbornness and this weird ability to soak up other people's magic. She kind of thought her stubbornness might be her real super power, though. Or maybe it was her kryptonite? She'd know the answer to that when this was done, she supposed.

"It's impossible," Holland said, "for you to do this."

"I have done some absolutely impossible things in the last year, Holland. I keep getting told 'Impossible!' And yet, here I am."

"You're going to die, you know,"

"Won't be the first time," she said, her tone downright cheerful now. Because irritating Holland made her feel better. And the more he tried to talk her out of this, the more she wanted to do it, just to shove it in his face.

She wasn't rebellious even a little bit.

She rolled her eyes at herself and stiffened her trembling arms.

"Don't say I didn't warn you," Holland said. "Although, I was sort of hoping you'd survive long enough for me to kill you."

"Yeah, yeah, yeah. No need to get all sentimental and mushy on me now."

Angie moved up behind her again. "They're starting the process," she murmured. "They think this will fail, too."

"Nice to have all the support and positive energy."

Angie's hand touched her back and another surge of magic rolled through her. Without thought, Cary poured it into the shield.

"You shouldn't do that anymore," Cary said. "You guys are draining yourselves too much, and you're going to need everything you've got when this shield drops." She refused to elaborate on *why* her shield would drop soon.

"I'll be fine," Angie said.

Jaxer put a hand to her shoulder and another surge of strength hit her. Fae magic was weird magic, but thanks to their time in Faery, it was also familiar. It bubbled through her blood like carbonation, making her a little giddy and light headed. But in a nice way. More Fae magic, but not from Jaxer, slid into her. She glanced back to see Eriana's hand glowing a faint blue.

Cary raised her brows at the healer.

"It'll help if this doesn't kill you," Eriana said. "And maybe even if it does."

Cary snorted a laugh. Eriana had brought her back once before. But she wasn't sure she'd be able to override Death this time.

"I can't give you magic," Lucy said quietly. "But I'll keep the bad guys away until you finish killing the demon god. Deal?"

"Deal," Cary said. "Don't get dead."

"You either."

Marianne pulled something from her bag, a very small piece of cloth that she shook out into something larger. A triangle of purple, sheer enough to see through. She tucked the material over Cary's shoulders and inside her jacket collar to hold it in place. "I whipped this up for you while we were waiting."

"A cape?" Cary said with a smile. "Is this my superhero cape? I thought capes were bad."

"Under the usual superhero circumstances, they are," Marianne said. "But I think we can make an exception for this particular cape."

"What's it do?"

"You need to move from where you're standing to a new place, fall backward into it."

"I'm not leaving you guys and ending up somewhere else entirely," Cary said, frowning at Marianne.

"It won't take you far. You'll pop up a few hundred yards away from where you fell. And it'll only work once. A break-in-case-of-emergency porting."

"That's super cool sounding and we will talk more about this particular piece when all this is done."

"Fair enough. But I'm not giving away my secrets."

"Ha! I never thought you would."

Marianne grinned. "Give me back that piece of cloth in your pocket."

Deacon reached in Cary's jeans pocket to get the square of fabric out since Cary couldn't lower her arms. He handed the little square back to Marianne then returned to holding Cary's arms up. She was trembling so much now, she was almost entirely reliant on his strength. But the fresh washes of magic had helped a little.

Marianne handed the fabric from Cary's pocket to Lucy. "This is for you now. You get into trouble, drop it on the ground and step on it."

"It's not going to port me way far away, is it?" Lucy said, looking defiant.

"No. Same as the cape. Short hop. Nothing more. But enough to get you out of trouble."

Lucy nodded and tucked the fold of material into her hoodie pocket.

A cold wind washed over Cary's back at the same moment as Lud tested her shield again with another blast of fire from his sword. The contrast of cold and heat felt weirdly well balanced.

Then Cary felt a tingling along her spine, an instant of warning, before a voice that echoed from realms far away, building and growing as it reached them said…

"I am here for you, Ho'Lud. It is time for you to die."

49

$\mathcal{S}$ ilence settled over the clearing, throughout the woods. The breeze stilled. Nothing moved. Even the chittering, hissing demons quieted.

The echo of the Angel of Death's voice hung in the air like a gong.

A shiver raced down Cary's spine and her gut tightened. What the hell was she about to do? This was stupid. This was a bad idea. This was going to get her killed.

She was going to do it anyway.

Lud let out a low laugh that melded with a growl to make a sound like nothing Cary had heard before.

"You cannot kill me like that," Lud said. "We both know your powers will not affect me in this realm. No matter what the human thinks." He flicked Cary a look. "And once I have our son, you will be powerless against me always."

Cary stared up at the demon god as he gloated. He was only a hundred yards away, not far for a creature that huge. Not nearly far enough.

She wondered if the Angel could read her mind? Angie told the witches what Cary's plan was. Or at least hinted at it. That knowledge would be in their heads for the Angel. Which meant the Angel had to know.

Right?

What if she didn't? What if Cary lowered this shield that was almost too heavy for her to hold up anymore anyway, and the Angel didn't take advantage? What if they were swarmed by demons before Cary could do anything?

What if they all died but Lud and Holland and the Angel?

Wow, would that suck.

"You know what to do?" Cary called over her shoulder. She didn't take her gaze off Lud as he stalked closer. Damn it, stop getting closer, she thought at him, hoping she could keep him back by that demon hunter will thing.

Didn't work even a little bit.

"Stop," Sebastian said in his deep voice, the English accent barely noticeable on the single word.

And Lud stopped.

Oh that was cool. Demon hunter will was Just. So. Cool.

Lud glared at the hunter. "Your will is weak compared to mine," Lud said. "You cannot stop me. None of you humans can."

Cary pulled in a deep breath and let it out slowly. Despite what he said, Lud didn't move closer, but his demons shifted restlessly around him.

"We good?" Cary called to the Angel.

"We are," the Angel said, her voice rolling in that echo like distant thunder, growing closer and moving farther away all at once.

Oh boy.

"Here we go," she said aloud. Letting out a panicked breath like she was about to jump into freezing cold water, she swiped her arms downward.

Dropping the shield.

The demons swarmed. Shouts, yells, a lot of chaos behind her. The feel of Deacon's hands flexing on her shoulders before he moved away to help the fight.

And then…

Something poured into her. Something that left her so overwhelmed it washed her away. She wasn't even sure how to describe it. Not heat or bubbles. Not cold. There was no real physical sensation she could put to it. Smoke. It felt like smoke in her blood, but smoke that had weight. Smoke that had mass. So much mass it was like getting sucked into a black hole, stretching her out to impossible lengths, breaking her apart from the inside out with the strength of the pull.

Yet she was also light. Insubstantial. Floating above the ground.

How the hell could she feel insubstantial and as heavy as a mountain all at the same time?

A voice filtered through all that confused sensation. She wasn't sure whose. There weren't really words involved, or if there were, she didn't understand them. The one voice turned into many. A cacophony. A murder of crows in her brain that was like nothing she'd experienced.

And yet, no fear.

That was the part that really amazed her. She had no more fear. What was there left to fear now?

She looked up. Lud hovered over her, his sword raised as if he intended to slice down through the center of her with it. But he wasn't moving.

She blinked and scanned the clearing. No one was moving. Frozen in mid-fight.

Angie's hands up as a streak of lightning angled down toward a shadow demon. Sebastian at her side with a flaming sword piercing one of the light demons—where had he gotten a sword?

Lucy mid-motion, her hands up as she tossed a demon over her head into a piece of material that Marianne had flipped into the air like a flag. And Brandon just behind Marianne holding a shadow demon by the neck up over his head, his other hand bunched into a fist, mid-punch.

Jaxer and Eriana, back-to-back, as lights of multi-color magic filled the air around them and the demons circling them snarled silently, leaning away from the Fae power.

Sheldon standing near the triad, dropping a bottle of something in front of a demon that raised up above him. The demon rearing back and away from the potion spilling into the grass.

Vampires caught in mid-flight, their fangs out as they dragged at demons, or were dragged by demons. James, his arms up, holding one of the white-light beasts over his head like he was about to slam it to the ground.

The leopards, in human and animal form, caught mid-leap onto a demon, or crouched and facing off against one.

Holland with his hand out and a line of flames pouring from him into a shadow demon, racing out the other side of the demon as the demon's limbs sprawled wide.

And Deacon, a few feet away, his claws out even though he was still in human form, his eyes glowing yellow as he prepared to take out the shadow demon flying toward him.

A stop-action moment in the midst of the battle.

The witches stood with their backs to each other, the light of the Angel encircling them. Justina's gaze was on Cary, but her eyes were rolled back in her head, showing only the whites.

"It is time, Protector." The voice rose on echoing waves into her mind, moving in and out of her hearing, rising and falling through the other voices clambering wordlessly in her head.

Cary faced Lud again. His darkness so deep he was almost invisible, and yet she could see him better now. Could lightless black glow? Because he seemed to be glowing in his darkness.

His red cat's eyes were narrowed. His attention on her and not the rest of the chaos. His sword moved toward her, but very slowly. So slowly she could have danced around him and had a tea party before the sword got anywhere near her.

That was a strange image. For an instant, she got hooked on the idea of sitting on the grass and drinking tea as she watched Lud's sword fall infinitely slowly toward where she'd stood.

The flow of power through her limbs grew stronger, heavier and smokier and lighter all at once. That strange sense of being both infinitely heavy and completely without weight sweeping her up again.

Her gaze settled on Lud's chest. There, she thought. Right at the center of him. If he'd been human, that's where his heart would be. That's where she had to go.

She moved toward him, wondering why she wasn't doing something like shooting death out of her hand or something. She glanced at Holland as she walked toward Lud. She'd been expecting to do something like that, throwing flame from her palm, like Holland had been teaching her, that flame piercing the demon god…

But no. That wasn't what she needed to do.

She stopped at Lud's feet, her head craned back to take him in. He was still staring at the space where she'd been, but as she watched, his eyes did move, his gaze slowly slowly slowly moving to look down at her.

She waited until he was staring at her again. Until his mouth started to open. He had very sharp teeth in that mouth. After all this time, she hadn't really paid much attention to his teeth. Strange.

Another flow of that heavy-weightlessness swept her and she pushed against the ground, bending her knees and jumping upward, but in slow motion. She floated higher, higher, until she was level with Lud's chest.

Then she set her hand against the very center of his body, that rock covering the lava flow of him, watching his slowly moving gaze as he tried to look at her again.

"Goodbye," she said.

Though she wasn't sure she spoke aloud. And her voice didn't sound like hers anyway. It didn't sound like the Angel's voice either, though. She couldn't say what it sounded like exactly. Or if she'd even used a word. Her brain translated what she'd intended to say for her, but none of that seemed to make sense.

Or even matter.

She pressed her hand into Lud's chest, letting it sink into him up to her wrist. Inside, he was lava and heat. The area around her hand started to glow as the lava inside him dribbled out around her wrist. Dripped down is chest.

She watched the flow a moment before looking back into his eyes.

They were wide now. The cat's eye pupils narrowed to slits. The red around his pupils brightened and faded and brightened in an almost hypnotic way. His mouth opened wide, and she was pretty sure there was a sound coming from him but it was too slow to make sense.

The hypnotic dimming and brightening in his eyes held most of her attention. She watched his eyes as lava dripped around her hand, falling to the ground. Smoke encompassed them, and the forest around them faded into that smoke. As insubstantial as everything else in this realm.

And when Lud began his slow-motion explosion, the slow breaking apart of his outer, rock skin, the cracks in his body, the way he dissolved into the lava that made up his insides, she watched that too. Like a movie. A special effect. Like something not real, but fascinating nonetheless.

Drip drip drip the lava onto the ground, hardening as it neared her foot. She watched it all, and somehow felt like she was watching it without her eyes, which was a really trippy sensation. Like she could see things she wasn't looking at. The bugs in the grass that died when the lava hit them. The grass itself dying but the seeds deeper in the soil that would replace it.

For some reason, she couldn't smell much. That would wig Deacon out. The lava, the sulfur scent, the dying grass and bugs, the slow slow explosion of a demon god. All that should have been pretty whiffy. The fact that she couldn't really smell much of it was interesting.

Would she remember all this later? Was this what it was like to be death? Or just to be a conduit for death? Or a conduit for the Angel?

Her mind didn't move fast enough to sort out any of those concepts. Mostly, she just felt easy in all this. It was meant to happen. All this was right. And destiny was being fulfilled.

Everything died.

When there was nothing but a pile of black crackling rock at her feet, she knelt down and set a gentle hand to the rock. It dissolved into ash, a slow collapse into dust swirling faintly in the air with just the barest of redness like glitter illuminating it.

That was kind of pretty.

She swirled the dust with her hand, whipping it up into a small cyclone and gently pushed the cyclone into the still open rift between demon realm and this one. When the ash reentered the demon realm, the tear that had opened between that realm and this swirled into a smaller and smaller circle until it finally closed.

There were other demons still here, though. Trapped in her realm now. That wasn't good.

She grunted and stood to face the chaos. No. There couldn't be anymore demons here. That wasn't right. They didn't belong here.

This realm was their death.

She moved among the frozen fighters and gently touched each demon, careful not to come into contact with those not supposed to die in this fight. There were a few that might have died, but…no. It wasn't their time yet. Not yet.

The part of her still "Cary" ducked from the knowledge swirling just beneath the surface, the knowledge that, if she wanted to, she could know when any of these living things around her were going to die. She didn't want that much knowledge, not consciously.

It wasn't her place.

Each demon she touched crumbled into dust. No dramatic explosions. Just a soft, gentle folding into dust that shimmered faintly in the wind.

From this perspective, the shadow demons were more distinct. She could see their horns, their teeth. The wicked curve of their claws. The black eyes with red pupils. An image she'd been better off without when she was a mere human, she decided.

The white-light demons weren't as bright now, so she could see their thick muscled bodies glowing in the halo they created, the sparks of red that pierced the white light, the almost fur like scales covering their bodies, iridescent and shimmery.

All beings were beautiful in their own way, she thought as she turned one of the white-demons to dust and watched that dust filter away in a breeze. Everything died. But everything was beautiful in death.

When no more demons remained, she looked around again. Only

the ones supposed to be dead were dead. As it should be. She blinked and realized she could now see more than just the living entities surrounding her. There were…others. Shadows.

Ghosts.

Ghosts moved around her, through her. Their cold touch…familiar. Their attention on their own aims, their own eternal quests. Only one stopped to stare at her for a moment. Cary stared back. The ghost was a young man, his style of clothes nothing she could identify unless she wanted to dig into those thoughts that would allow her to see too much. He was tall, thin, as insubstantial as the others. He blinked eyes that were huge and dark. Nodded to her.

And then moved on.

Interesting.

Before she could ponder the encounter longer, though, a voice like rolling, distant thunder came to her. Was her. And yet wasn't.

"You are done, now, Cary Redmond."

"Do I die now?" she asked. She hadn't bothered to look at the knowledge she knew was there to answer that question. Though, as she asked, her gaze settled on Deacon.

"Are you ready to die?" the Angel asked.

"No."

"Good. Because it's not your time. Yet. At least…this time."

Cary smiled.

"But we will dance again, Cary Redmond. You and I. We will dance again."

Cary shrugged. "Everything dies. Eventually."

"Eventually."

The word echoed, rolling in the distance as it faded away.

And the world around Cary flowed back into motion.

50

$\mathcal{I}$n the past, whenever Cary managed to channel a great deal of power, she'd invariably ended up flat on her back, and more often than not, unconscious and sleeping off the effects of channeling too much magic for days, sometimes a week. After she'd died in Faery, she'd slept for ten full days.

So she was completely expecting the exhaustion of channeling the Angel of Death's literal killing powers to wipe her out and send her to sleep for a while. With Eriana on hand, she'd hoped she'd survive the process—and the Angel was kind enough to confirm it wasn't her time to die—but she had still expected to end up in a state of senseless exhaustion.

What she had not expected, even in a little bit, was to feel…

Normal.

Deacon's hands on her face, so suddenly she nearly stumbled away from him, brought the whole "normal" thing to her full attention.

"You're alive," he murmured.

"Told you I didn't want you to die," she said. "I had to survive."

He sort of smiled, but it looked strained and tight.

She gripped his wrists in an attempt to reassure him. "I'm fine. Really. Great, actually." She frowned. "Really good."

He frowned back. "You're not…tired?"

"Nope."

"Not ready to pass out?"

"Huh uh."

"Sore or…feeling a little beat up?"

"Not even a little bit."

His frown deepened. "That's…"

"Weird."

"What's happening?"

"Got me." She looked at the triad. They were unconscious on the ground, still inside a protection circle. The fact that she could *see* the faint blue outline of the circle while looking directly at it was a little strange. But with the witches unconscious, that meant the Angel was gone. And she'd get no answers from either the Angel or the witches.

She looked around the clearing. Everyone who was part of her side seemed to be picking themselves up off the ground or looking around in confusion. She realized they hadn't probably noticed her walking around them destroying demons. That they'd probably blinked and the demons were gone.

That had to be disorienting. But also a good thing, right? She'd be happy to have the demon she was fighting magically die without her getting killed.

Angie, Marianne, and Lucy were the first to pull themselves out of the disorientation and charge her. She got swept up into a group hug that made her smile with relief. "You're all okay?" she asked, her face buried in Marianne's shoulder.

"We're good," Lucy said. "I'm never giving Marianne this hoodie back, though."

"Girl could not stop disappearing," Marianne said with a shaky laugh. "She'd stand there, let some bad ass demon move right in front of her, then toss them around like a sack of rocks."

"That was fun," Lucy said. "Also Marianne's magic cloth is the best stuff ever."

"Yeah it is," Angie confirmed. She leaned back first and stared at Cary. "How're you feeling?"

"Like myself and not on the verge of passing out. It's pretty weird." Angie frowned.

But before she could comment, a slow—and to Cary's way of thinking, infinitely condescending—clap interrupted them.

She pulled away from her friends and faced Holland.

"Well done, Ms. Redmond," he said. "I'm…impressed."

"Don't be an ass. I just killed your father for you by taking in your mother's powers. At the very least, you could mean what you say."

"I'm a demon, Ms. Redmond. Twisting words is part of my nature. But…" He shrugged. "The fact that you survived that is…impressive."

"Ha." She turned more fully to face him as Deacon took her hand and her friends lined up behind her. She was vaguely aware of others joining her—Jaxer and Eriana, Brandon and Sebastian, the leopards, even James was back there somewhere. She wasn't so sure about having James at her back, but there seemed to be enough friends behind her, she figured she'd be okay.

And they all faced Holland.

Who couldn't be killed.

And who still wanted her dead.

"Now what?" she asked him.

His gaze flicked over the people at her back before settling on her again. "I suppose I owe you something."

"You think," she said with a snort.

"What would you like, Ms. Redmond?"

"Not to die. And also not to have anyone I love die." At least not yet, she thought. But she kept that part to herself. Holland would just misinterpret it.

"You think that's an option?" he asked.

"Well…yeah. I do. I think it's an excellent option. I think it would make for a splendid end to my day. To not die. And to not lose anyone I love."

Behind her, Angie started murmuring and she could feel Marianne and Lucy both shifting positions. She sensed rather than saw Jaxer move up closer. Deacon's hand tightened on hers.

She held Holland's gaze.

"I've waited a very long time for—" Holland gestured at the surroundings, then at her. "For all of this."

"Well, now you can go about your business without worrying about your death destiny. Although if you're business is hurting people, we're going to have words about that."

"That's the problem, isn't it? Even without being a Protector, you're still…you."

"Is that an insult, Holland? That felt like an insult."

"I'm not sure, either, to be honest," he said, his mouth ticking up in a little smile. "I did, at one stage, harbor visions of enslaving you rather than killing you. Right away."

"Nice," she said.

"But I've changed my mind."

"About killing me? Good. Cause I would hate that."

"If I enslaved you, all these…associates would just come try to rescue you." He shrugged. "Well, some of them."

She was thinking the same thing. She had very big doubts that James would bother his ass trying to save her from anything or anyone. Deacon, however, wouldn't stop. Neither would Jaxer. And neither would her friends.

And if they tried coming after her, Holland would kill them. Which is something she really really didn't want.

"Yeah, enslaving me seems like a really bad idea all around," she said, quite seriously. "Plus, I'd suck at being tortured anyway. You'd get tired of all my pathetic whining within a day."

His smile widened. "You underestimate yourself, Ms. Redmond."

"You'd be sick of my whining within an hour, then?"

He chuckled. With other bad guys, that particular type of chuckle usually bode well for her. She was absolutely certain that in Holland's case, it did not.

"The world is probably a better place with you in it, Ms. Redmond," Holland said.

"That almost sounds like a compliment."

"It might be." He shrugged. "If I wanted the world to be a better place."

And without any other warning, he sent a spike of fiery heat from his palm, right into Cary's chest.

ary was aware of the heat pouring into her in the same way she was aware of the screams and shouts around her. She was still gripping Deacon's hand. She could feel that quite clearly. And the sight of Holland's blast of power hitting her square in the chest was... pretty disorienting.

But what was even stranger was that it didn't really hurt. It just pissed her off.

After everything she'd done for him. The bastard.

She lifted her free hand and threw all that magic right back at him, just the way he'd been teaching her all night. Except this time, she purposefully drove it back into his chest.

"Stop that," she hissed.

His own power slammed into him and sent him lurching backward a few steps. He blinked. And frowned at her. Still standing there.

Without a hole in her chest.

She looked down just to double check. Nope, no smoking hole. She'd seen him kill a dragon shifter with that casual spike of power. She should probably be more disturbed about the fact that she wasn't dead.

Not that she was going to argue with it.

"That was rude," she said with a huff. "You could have hurt someone."

What the hell was she saying? A part of her recognized this was all very strange and she should be dead. She wasn't a Protector and she wasn't indestructible now. But the Angel had said it wasn't her time yet, so she was certain Holland wasn't supposed to kill her. Yet.

But then, the Angel didn't work in the same sort of timeline as humans. And as Cary had learned first-hand, didn't have the same sense of time passing. "Not yet" to the Angel could have meant not this moment, but in about forty-three more seconds, that *would* be the moment.

Still, Cary wasn't dead. And she was really annoyed with Holland for trying to kill her. She'd recognized that as a defense mechanism to keep from going off the deep end later, she supposed. In that moment, all she could feel was irritation. And an edge of anger.

"Are we done now?" she asked. "Can we stop with all the throwing of demon power?"

He slammed another bolt of fire into her. Without word or warning.

She snarled and threw it right back at him, channeling everything he poured into her down into her palm as she sent all that magic careening back into his chest. She was like a walking boomerang now. She'd kind of preferred being walking Kevlar, but walking Magic Boomerang was good, too.

Especially now, when Holland's own powers sent him flying backward into a tree.

The tree cracked and with an ominous sounding crunch tumbled over to the side. Not close enough to endanger anyone with her, but still. Watching Holland hit a tree so hard it fell over was...wild. Especially because that didn't kill him.

Of course it didn't. He couldn't die. He was the son of the Angel of Death. Even *she* couldn't kill him.

But it was interesting how strongly his own powers, thrown back at him, knocked him around.

When he looked up at her from his sprawl on the forest floor, his eyes had gone full demon red. What did it mean that he was letting his demon side out?

Probably bad things. Very very bad things.

He stood, slowly, and snapped the jacket of his suit back into place as he stalked toward her.

"Can we be done with this, please?" she said, trying to reason with him even though she knew it was impossible.

"Never," he snarled and hit her with another shot of power.

She took one step backward, coming up hard against Deacon. Realizing he was right behind her and that if Holland succeeded in blowing a hole in her chest it would kill Deacon too enraged her.

She added that anger to the mix as she rebounded Holland's magic on him again. And all the other things she'd been absorbing that night. Demon magic, Fae magic, shifter magic, witch magic, Death. All of it poured into that concentrated spot on her palm before she sent it whipping out to slam into Holland.

"Stop that," she snarled back at him, a part of her actually willing him to just *stop* already.

And he did.

The power he'd been pouring into her cut off and he stood there. Blinking at her.

Whether from her will—ha! Not likely—or the fact that she wasn't dying, she wasn't sure, but he stopped firing power at her and just stood there. Staring at her.

After a few moments, he said, "Well. It appears we're at an impasse."

Angie leaned in close to Cary's shoulder and whispered, "We don't have to be."

"What do you mean?" She held Holland's narrowed, still very red, gaze, sure he could hear Angie.

"That thing I never talk about," she murmured. "That thing I've been avoiding and somehow keep slipping and referring to?"

"Yeah?"

"Ang," Sebastian's voice, deep and full of worry.

"Just this one time," she said. "One last time. For this one last demon."

Cary frowned and half turned. She didn't want to take her eyes off Holland, but she wanted to see Angie's expression.

"I've already found the perfect tree," Angie said very quietly. "I just need you all to drive him through it when I say the word."

"What are you going to do?" Cary asked.

Angie let out a sad, resigned sigh. "I'm going to open a realm breach into a demon realm." She swallowed hard enough Cary actually heard it. "And then you're going to send him through."

"I'll just come back." Holland smirked, proving he'd heard everything they'd said just fine.

"Not from where I'll send you."

"There's nowhere you can send me that I can't return from."

"How about your father's realm?"

"Impossible," Holland said. "Even a demon witch can't open a portal directly into his realm. I would know if it were possible." He gave a smug little shrug. "And no other realm you could send me to will be far enough to keep me away."

"Is he right?" Cary asked. "Can he just turn around and come right back?"

Sebastian answered. "He lost power coming here. If he's forced back to his father's realm this way, he won't have enough power to return."

"His father got here by going through another demon realm, not directly from the god realm," Cary pointed out. "What stops him from doing that?" She stared at the smirking Holland as she spoke. She really hated that smirk. She kind of wanted to wipe it off his face.

"He doesn't have the power to leave his father's realm anymore," Sebastian said. "It was a…condition of his asylum here. If he ever went back, he'd be exiled from our realm."

Well, the demon hunters would probably know, wouldn't they, since they were apparently the ones who'd given him asylum.

"That was one of the things I was doing, while I was gone," Angie said, still quietly, her voice sounding hoarse and jumpy. "Checking on the terms of his asylum. The powers he had left."

"So…" Cary narrowed his gaze. "If we send him back, he's stuck? He's…out of this realm for good?" Or at least for long enough for her to grow old and die naturally.

"No," Holland said, staring at Angie. "Because humans can't open a portal to my father's realm. Most demons can't get there. And for those who can, there's no way to get there directly from here. Not even a legendary demon witch can manage it."

Angie let out a long, shaky sigh. "Wouldn't that be nice," she said. But Cary got the impression she was mostly talking to herself.

"You sure about this, Angie?" she murmured.

Before Angie could answer, Holland shot another bolt of fire at them. But this time, Cary realized, he was aiming for Angie.

And wow, did that piss her off.

She stepped in front of Angie, took the hit of Holland's power and tossed it back at him so fast she got a little dizzy. Or maybe that was the rage that he'd just tried to kill one of her best friends.

Cause she was definitely feeling the rage.

"All right," she snarled at him. "That's it. It's one thing you trying to kill me. But I will *not* have you trying to kill my friends. You're out of here." She slammed more power into his chest.

Where had that come from? Whatever. She was too angry to care.

How dare he? Trying to kill Angie. Without even a smartass comment beforehand. Oh, she was mad.

She slammed him with another bolt of his own power. He stumbled backward as she advanced.

She was advancing? That was unusual.

Another shot from her palm. The bolts of power she sent into him were a strange color. Not the red flames he kept firing at her. A sort of mixture of red and blue and some sort of purple but also a faint gray color that hadn't been in there before. It wasn't like anything she'd seen before. And she only barely noticed. Because every time he tired to fight back, to hit her with another shot of his shitty demon magic, she sucked up the hit and churned it all back into her anger, into the next shot of her weirdly colored bolt of energy and magic.

She wasn't even firing flames at him anymore. It was, if she took the time to study the thing, more like a wizard's energy bolt, except it went on for a long time, like Holland's shot of demon magic. A line of power from her palm that only stopped when she closed her fist.

He hit her again, twice in a row, using both hands now.

And that just made her angrier. She couldn't remember ever being this angry before. And she was a grumpy ass anger machine when bad guys were being assholes.

But now... Now, she just wanted this bastard who'd brought all this down on them, who'd just tried to kill her best friend, who'd killed an innocent woman in front of her, who'd tried to corrupt a kid and turn him into a killer, who'd endangered her entire realm because of a family fight. This...asshole.

Oh, he had to go.

She took all the magic he poured at her—and he was pouring it at her now in long streams of power without stop—and she turned it around on him, sending shot after shot right into his chest.

Driving him backward as she advanced.

There was a part of her, somewhere far off and pretty quiet at the moment, that recognized all this was weird and maybe she should evaluate what was happening and what she was doing. Maybe he was walking her into a trap of some kind. Maybe she should stop stalking toward the unkillable and super powerful demon and take a moment to, you know, actually think.

But that part of her was so so quiet compared to her rage. The rage swept her up in a kind of righteous fire, and she poured all of it into him. This one, irredeemable, absolutely no questions asked, Bad Guy.

He'd just tried to kill Angie. In front of her. Casually. And the only thing that might have angered Cary more—or at least this much—was if he'd tried to kill Deacon.

She didn't give Holland time to even consider that, though. She stalked toward him, hitting him, again and again. Everything he threw at her, she threw back. The type of energy he poured at her changed.

She took it and kept firing. His eyes grew redder. And now she could see the cat's eyes pupils so like his fathers.

And for some reason, that made her even madder. She'd never have had to *meet* a demon god if not for Holland. She wouldn't have had to defend the world from that god. She wouldn't have lost leopard shifters in the first fight with Lud. People killed by Lud's human slave wouldn't have died.

It was *all Holland's fault.*

"Cary," Angie shouted, a sound Cary only barely heard above the ringing in her ears. "This way. Drive him this way."

Cary snarled and fired another shot of Holland's own power back at him. *More,* she thought. *Keep giving me more. I will burn you with it.*

That voice in her head, she wasn't sure who that was, and she was a little terrified of that anger. But she also wasn't prepared to give it up yet. Because Holland stumbled under her next hit. Not just took it, or backed away under the pressure. He tripped and stumbled backward.

His eyes widened as he glared at her. She wanted to laugh.

"Keep trying to kill me," she shouted at him. "Come on! You know you want to. Try it. Keep going."

She hit him again with another round of his own power, as well as all that other power filling her. The multi-colored magic she'd been throwing at him had, at some point, turned white. She barely noticed.

He hit her in the shoulder, in the chest, in the stomach. She took each shot like a punch, absorbing it, and then punching right back.

Pushing him backward, deeper into the trees, following the sound of Angie's shouts. She was only dimly aware that other things were going on around her. All she could see was the source of all this pain and evil. The source of so much suffering.

And she wanted him gone. Gone. Gone. Gone.

She roared in all that anger, because she had to get it out. Had to release it or it would tear her apart.

From the corner of her eye, she finally saw Angie, standing in front of a large oak tree. The tree was a little odd-man-out in the mostly fir woods, but it had a beautiful branching trunk, the kind with multiple large trunks splitting off from a thick base, forming natural Vs.

Angie was staring at that tree trunk, Sebastian at her back, holding her by the shoulders.

"Drive him to the tree," Angie shouted.

Cary did. She had no idea what Angie was doing. But it didn't matter. She trusted Angie.

And she needed Holland gone.

She fired, so fast her shoulders started to ache with it. So much magic, she felt like one big nerve ending alight with the zing of electricity.

Holland's roar only fueled her anger. She shouted at him again. Taunting him. Egging him on. The more of his power he fed her, the more she took and turned on him.

He couldn't stop hitting her with his magic or she'd roll over the top of him. But every time he threw something at her, she absorbed it and hammered him with it.

And, wow, was it satisfying to watch his panic, his realization…

He'd fucked with the wrong Protector.

Something flickered in the dark behind him, at the base of the tree.

Cary thought she saw a flash of red, but then nothing. Angie motioned at her, and Sebastian shouted something Cary didn't hear. Cary just kept driving Holland backward.

And then from out of nowhere, a leopard leapt past her and threw Holland closer to the tree. The flash of black fur came and went so fast, she barely had time to register Deacon had joined the fight.

A pulse of something like shimmering light beside Holland, and Jaxer was there. With a sword. Where had he gotten a sword? He slashed the glowing purple metal along the back of Holland's thighs.

Holland roared and turned on him, but the shimmering light encompassed him and he was gone again. Holland swung back toward her, his arm raised, and the black leopard hit him again from the opposite side, making him stumble.

As soon as the leopard was clear, Cary hit him with another bolt of magic. Still his? She wasn't even sure anymore. She fired again and again. Driving him backward.

In between hits from her, Deacon slammed physically against him.

Jaxer popped into sight and sliced Holland with his sword again. A bear the size of a small barn rose up behind Holland and tossed him into the air. Closer, closer to the oak tree.

Sebastian produced his own sword from…somewhere and swept it across Holland's chest, opening a gapping hole that almost startled Cary into inaction. Inside, where she'd expected…she wasn't even sure. Innards and guts. But Holland wasn't human and he wasn't filled with human stuff. Inside the wound burned heat and flame like a furnace.

Holland howled and started firing shots of power all around him. The bear took a hit and flew back into a tree. Cary screamed. So did someone else.

Rage overcame her momentary pause, and she threw everything she had at him. Firing directly into the wound Sebastian had opened in Holland's chest. All of her fire into those flames. All her anger and fear and pain. All of her.

She surged forward. Shot after shot. She felt Deacon at her side. Felt Jaxer on the other. Was aware in her peripheral vision of Angie, still staring at the oak.

And then she became aware of a noise. Like a chittering sound. Nails on a chalkboard high and piercing, filling the area. The sound set Cary's teeth on edge.

Fueled her rage by irritating her.

She drove another shot into Holland. He stumbled. Only a foot from the tree now.

He glanced over his shoulder. "No! I will not go back!"

Cary couldn't see what he saw. But she could smell the sulfur. And the chittering got louder.

"You will," she snarled, barely recognizing her voice it was so deep and gravely and somehow echoey. "You will go back. And you will never return."

She hit him with power, just as Deacon slammed into him, low on his thighs, just as Jaxer drove his sword into Holland's open chest wound.

Holland, despite flailing to stay upright, hit something low behind him, near the base of the tree. Tripped. Fell backward...

And vanished into the V in the tree trunk.

Cary could see it all then. Between the sturdy oak trunk, a black and red hellscape of lava and heat and flames, belching fire, columns of rock and ash and bones. Corpses on spits and spikes. Moans and growls and sounds she couldn't comprehend. And the demons. So many demons. Chittering beasts on all fours, their spiked tails high, their forked tongues flicking the air as they swarmed over Holland.

The screams and howls and ear-piercing screeches.

She felt herself falling into that world, that hellish realm, toward the screeching demons and the screams of pain and anger. Strong hands gripped her shoulders, keeping her upright, holding her back.

She leaned into Deacon, knowing who steadied her without having to look. She felt him. Through her skin, in her bones. And that sense of her mate, that knowledge that he was there, that he had her, allowed her to shake off whatever drew her toward the hellscape.

Sebastian murmuring to Angie. Angie's full body shiver. And then she turned away from the tree. A retching move that looked like it physically hurt her.

And the hellscape was gone.

Cary blinked at the oak tree. Nothing but an ordinary oak now. Nothing hellish burning between the V in the tree trunk. No more shouts and screams. No more ear-piercing chittering sounds.

Only a faint whiff of sulfur and burnt ozone lingered.

For a long moment, everything was silent, frozen. Cary blinked at the tree, wondering if she'd hallucinated everything she'd just seen.

But Holland was now, unquestionably...

Gone.

52

*C*ary stared at the oak tree for a long moment, trying to wrap her head around the fact that Holland was no longer standing there, roaring at her or trying to kill her. From the base of the tree, Lucy suddenly appeared as she stood from her crouch and dropped her hood. She glanced through the now perfectly ordinary V in the tree trunk.

"Holy hell," she said, her little girl's voice sounding a little stunned. "That was wild."

"I can't believe you tripped a demon like an old school prank," Cary said, shaking her head.

"He never saw me coming." Lucy grinned and held up the little square of fabric that Marianne had given her to port her short distances.

Cary touched her Marianne-made cape where it was still tucked into her jacket. "Damn. I never got to use mine."

"Maybe next time," Lucy said. "Also, I'm never giving this hoodie back."

Cary started to chuckle, but then she heard Angie's sharp exhale, almost a sob, and the real world came rushing back.

She hurried to her friend's side. Angie was turned away from the tree, her hands were shaking, and her head was bent so that her hair fell around her face, hiding her expression. Sebastian had his arms around her and was quietly murmuring to her.

"Angie, you okay? Are you hurt?" She slid around in front of her but was a little afraid to touch her in case whatever she'd done had left her nerves sore or... "What the hell was that?" she whispered.

"Long story," Angie said, and then laughed. The laugh sounded choked and tired. "I really hate doing that. And it's been a long time."

"Uh, yeah. But it was super useful just then. Thank you."

"He's gone." She wasn't asking.

"Are you hurt?"

"No, no. Just... I'm out of practice. And that realm is difficult."

That sounded like an understatement. "You opened a...what? A gate between the demon god's realm and this one." Again Cary spoke in a whisper.

"Yup." Angie finally looked up and met Cary's gaze. Her eyes looked haunted, but as she let out another deep breath, she smiled and it didn't look forced or strained. Just very very tired. "Not something I'd recommend doing very often."

Cary snorted. "I'll leave that one to you." She glanced at Sebastian. "You okay?"

"Fine. Now." His arms tightened on Angie and she leaned into him.

"Brandon's hurt," Marianne called, her shout loud in the quiet woods.

"Shit." Cary stared forward, relieved when she saw Eriana kneeling over the fallen bear shifter.

Marianne sat cradling Brandon's head in her lap. The tree he'd been thrown into had actually fallen sideways, taking down bunch of other branches with it. Lucy crouched beside Marianne as Eriana's blue hands hovered over Brandon's chest.

Since there wasn't anything Cary could do to help Brandon, she took a moment to look around.

James stood to one side talking to a female vampire Cary didn't know. The rest of the vampires were gone. Which was worrying, if she were honest with herself. She gave the surrounding woods a cursory look.

The leopards all seemed to be fine. Nicky held Jillian close, they were both naked, which meant they'd obviously shifted a few times, but neither one seemed to notice or be bothered by the cold breeze. They stood talking with Diana, who was still dressed, and Lucas, who was pulling his jeans back up. Obviously, he'd shifted during the fight, too. Caitlin and Sherri walked out of the woods not far away, fully dressed and looking uninjured. Everyone had survived this time. She nearly wobbled with the relief.

Sheldon sat on a log a few feet away, watching the shifters, his gaze hooded. She'd seen him keeping the triad safe during the fight. Protecting them from a demon when he didn't have any magic or physical strength of his own to call on. Using bought spells to fight the demons instead of doing something stupid like trying to sacrifice himself. She should probably acknowledge that out loud to him, that he'd done good, especially by not getting dead. Maybe. She still wasn't sure how to feel about Sheldon.

Finally, she turned to face Deacon and Jaxer. They were both staring at her with identical frowns.

"Uh?" She frowned back. "What's wrong with you two?"

"You're okay?" Jaxer asked.

"Not falling over?" Deacon asked.

"Not passing out?" Jaxer.

"Not exhausted?" Deacon.

"No," she said. Then she paused and considered the state of her physical health. "Uh. Yeah, still good. Even after all that. Little tired, I suppose. Rage is a draining emotion. And I'm starving. I could eat an entire pizza restaurant right now. But..." She shrugged. "Otherwise, I'm good."

"That's..." Jaxer started.

"Unusual," Deacon finished.

"You two are starting to freak me out with this completing each other's sentences stuff," she said. "I'm supposed to be doing that with Deacon, right? Not you two."

They didn't rise to her teasing, which was a shame.

"You channeled a *lot* of magic just now," Deacon said. He settled his hands on her shoulders.

And she noticed, unlike the other leopards, he wasn't naked despite having shifted to fight Holland. "Speaking of magic use," she said, patting his chest and tugging gently at his t-shirt. Not the first time he'd done that trick tonight, materializing clothes after shifting. "And whatever you were giving me during the fight." She touched his cheek. "You okay?"

"Fine," he said. Then blinked a few times and looked away from her. "Yeah. I'm…fine."

"What's wrong with you two?" Jaxer asked. When Cary gave him a look, he said, "No, I'm being serious here. Deacon never uses magic. And you've never channeled so much before. And every time before this that you have channeled a lot of magic, or used whatever you were soaking up, you either passed out or—" He cut himself off before saying the word, but she heard it clearly.

"Or died? Yeah, I know. This is a little weird." She looked up at Deacon. "Could we share your…whatever you were giving me. Strength. Anger. Could we do that because we're mates or because I'm a strange magic absorbing sponge?"

He scowled a little at her way of describing herself, but then shook his head and said, "I have no idea. We'd better talk to my mother."

"Oh boy." But since sharing his shifter magic and strength with her hadn't hurt either one of them, at least that she could tell, she'd leave the situation for another day. Very quietly, she said, "Everyone… survived, right?" Mostly, she was referring to the vampires, because they were all gone.

"Everyone survived," James said, appearing beside them so suddenly, she jumped.

"Don't do that," she snarled. Then, "All of your people are okay?"

"There were injuries. But they've recovered. No deaths."

"Well, that's…" Was relief too strong a word here?

James's quick grin flashed his fangs. Boy, she hated when he did that. Which, she knew, was why he did it.

"At some point," he said, his voice low, "I would like to talk to you about what happened tonight. What you…are now?"

"No," she said. "I'd prefer you viewed me as mysterious and unknowable."

Another teeth-flashing smile. "I'm relieved you're alive, Cary. I wasn't sure tonight would end that way."

She snorted. "Yeah, me neither."

"Until next time." He nodded at Jaxer and Deacon. And then vanished in that too-fast flash of movement.

She rolled her eyes. "Show off," she muttered. When she looked up at Deacon, she said, "I sure hope there isn't a next time."

"This was more than enough," he agreed. With feeling.

"You going to pass out?" she asked. Just to be sure.

"No. I'm good."

"This is weird, right?"

"It's weird. But we're alive so I'm not going to argue."

Jaxer was still staring at her with narrowed eyes. "You channeled the power of the Angel of Death."

"Yeah, that was wild. Probably want to avoid doing that again." She thought back to those moments, moving between the stillness of everyone else, to the ghosts that walked these forests. "I saw ghosts."

Deacon pulled her into a strong hug, and she smiled against his chest. He knew her so well. But…

"I wasn't afraid of them. That was maybe the weirdest part. I looked at a ghost, a bunch of them, and I wasn't afraid." She looked at Jaxer. "You think that'll last or was it just a once off because I was channeling Death powers?"

"We'll see the next time you meet a ghost," he said.

She shivered. "I think I'd rather not test this. I'll count it as a win and be happy."

"Definitely a win," Jaxer said, looking back at the oak tree.

"Will he find a way back?" she murmured.

"Good question," Jaxer said. "But it doesn't seem likely. At least not for a while." He faced Angie. "Right?"

"Right. Plus, he was…occupied when the rift closed." Her voice was deep and heavy with exhaustion. "That will keep him busy for a while, too."

Cary shivered again, remembering the swarm of demons piling on top of him.

"We'll keep an eye out," Sebastian said. "He's relinquished his protections here. Even if he does find a way out of his father's realm, and back here, we'll be waiting."

Cary let out a shaky breath as she leaned into Deacon and held Angie's gaze. "That's something at least."

And it was. For now, she'd count that as a win.

Not having to worry about Holland showing up to kill her at any moment was definitely a relief. The rest... The fact that she'd used the Angel of Death's powers to kill a demon god, the fact that she'd managed to hit Holland hard enough with his own powers to actually fight back, the fact that whatever she'd been using in her attack, all the myriad magics that had blended inside her to produce the magic she'd used in the fight... She'd have to examine what all that had done to her. Probably soon.

But for now, with all the people she loved most in the world outside her own family standing with her, alive and healthy, she'd count all of this a win.

Thanks to Eriana's healing, Brandon recovered from his injuries without any lingering problems. Marianne spent a great deal of time bringing him soup and fussing over him as he recovered. Cary resisted the urge to tease and, heroically to her way of thinking, didn't ask a lot of questions.

Lucy, true to her word, kept the invisibility hoodie. But she promised everyone she'd only bring it out when she wasn't around her mundane students.

Angie disappeared back home with Sebastian. She sent them all a few texts to assure them she was fine, but she needed some down time now. Since she had Sebastian to look after her, Cary figured her own fussing and worry could wait. Also, she had a *lot* of questions about Sebastian. But those would have to wait too. They were going to need a girls' night in the not-too-distant future.

The dogs welcomed Cary home without showing any signs that the demon chaos had affected them. Buck nudged her a few times, and there was a lot of sniffing involved, but he didn't seem bothered by the fact that she'd spent the night absorbing demon magic. Which was a huge relief. She buried her face in his thick, blond fur in gratitude for a long moment. Pickles greeted her with a deep, "Woof," that seemed to hold multitudes of meaning Cary couldn't begin to decipher. And Fred sat up and begged for a treat.

OVER THE NEXT WEEK, EVERYTHING SETTLED BACK DOWN INTO something resembling normal. Or as normal as things ever got in Cary's life.

Despite the chaos that had apparently kept the demon hunters, the Protectors, and huge sections of Faery busy that night, none of it seemed to have leaked into the mundane human world. Or if it had, the memories and video evidence had been taken care of.

Cary had a feeling that had something to do with Jaxer, and maybe her computer guru Chris, since Jaxer vanished after that night and didn't show up again for a week. It wouldn't be the first time he and Chris had worked together to scrub evidence of the paranormal from the internet—Chris with their amazing tech skills, and Jaxer with his amazing glamour skills. Since no one was screaming about demon attacks on the evening news, Cary knew at least something had been done to ensure humans continued on blissfully unaware of the near end of their realm.

For which she was grateful.

The leopards scattered again, no longer needing to be her bodyguard. Deacon's mother visited once, to make sure everyone was fine, but she didn't stay in Portland long, which made it easier for Cary to relax. They did ask Maria about the way Deacon had been able to share some of his shifter magic with her, even though she wasn't a shifter. Unfortunately, Maria hadn't had any answers for them.

At the end of that week, Jaxer showed up with Eriana. He didn't have a lot to say beyond the fact that he was glad she was alive. He didn't admit to the tampering he'd done with the human world to hide the near apocalypse, but he had smiled when Cary brought it up. They were saved from any awkward conversations involving feelings, her no longer being a Protector, and such, by Deacon's insistence that Eriana make sure Cary wasn't harmed by all the magic she'd channeled. She hadn't had any lingering side effects, hadn't had to pass out or go into a healing sleep. In fact, she felt perfect after all they'd been through.

Which worried the hell out of Deacon.

So Eriana agreed to give her a magical healer checkup. And because Cary worried about Deacon as much as he worried about her, she insisted he be checked as well. Just in case.

Eriana did a full healer scan of them both and declared Deacon perfectly fine—which was a relief to Cary—and Cary one giant step farther away from being an ordinary human—which was less of a relief. She was healthy, just a lot less mundane than she'd been before the fight.

They still didn't know exactly what was happening with her cells, but according to Eriana, she was healing at near shifter speeds now. There didn't seem to be any damage, per se, after channeling Death and all that demon magic. But she'd changed more after the battle, at a fundamental level. And there was no going back.

"I'm not dead," she said, attempting to put a bright-side spin on the whole thing. "I'm not exploding from absorbing too much magic. That's good, right?"

"That's good," Deacon said, but it didn't wipe the worry lines from his brow.

She did that part manually with her fingers. "So long as it's not killing me…" She glanced at Eriana for confirmation.

Eriana shrugged. "You're fine," she said. "Healthy as a…what's the human saying? Healthy as a horse?"

Cary chuckled. "Okay, so I'm healthy. Just not…mundane anymore."

"Right," Eriana said pragmatically.

As if that wasn't a life altering statement.

But then again, Cary had to admit, she'd never really been mundane, even when she'd thought she was. This ability to absorb magic had always been a part of her. And thanks to the years as a Protector, she'd built up a sort of resistance to magic, changed enough she could absorb it now without exploding. Absorb and *use* the magic she took in. So she didn't explode.

It was all going to take some getting used to, though.

RORY DROPPED IN TO CHECK ON HER AND MAKE SURE SHE'D SURVIVED. He listened to her retelling of all the magic she'd channeled—and not been killed by—taking in the story without comment, just nodded at the information. He asked a few questions about what Eriana had told her. But otherwise, he didn't have a lot to say about what had happened, except...

"I'm very glad you survived, Cary."

She chuckled. "Me too."

"Will you want to continue your lessons with me?"

"Yes, please, if you have time. I have a feeling I'm going to need them since I'm not a Protector anymore and also...very definitely different now."

Rory didn't argue with her assessment, but he didn't act as if it was something she should worry about either. Since he was a millennia old dragon, she imagined there wasn't a lot he did worry about.

SHE VISITED SHELDON ONCE AFTER THAT NIGHT. HE'D RETURNED TO his old apartment, to the basic bed he'd used to recover, still using the sheets, blankets, and pillow she'd given him.

He seemed...less surly on this visit, though. "I'm moving," he announced suddenly, after the initial small talk of checking in. "I have some things to figure out. I can't do that here in Portland."

She narrowed her eyes at him. "Things as in how to do magic again or get your wizard powers back or..." She trailed off before she could say something meaner. But the triad were still out there somewhere, and she didn't trust Sheldon not to go to them in the hopes they could help him get his magic back.

But he surprised her.

"No," he said, quite seriously and without a hint of the resentment he'd been throwing at her every time they talked about this. "No. I've... I have work to do. To...to atone for the lives I took." He didn't meet her gaze as he spoke. "Maria Jones is going to help me with that."

"You didn't kill any leopards," Cary pointed out, frowning at the news.

Other shifters, yes. But not leopards—only because Cary had stopped him. Still. Why would Maria get involved? Especially with the person who'd very nearly killed her own son. Maria was super protective of her family. Cary couldn't think why she'd *want* to help Sheldon after he'd attempted to kill Deacon and steal his body. Hell, Cary could barely tolerate Sheldon because of that, even if the result had been her meeting her mate and the love of her life.

She'd have to talk to Maria, make sure she wasn't planning on something…permanent for Sheldon. Cary hadn't gone through all the trouble of ensuring Sheldon wasn't killed only to let him walk off with Deacon's mother and let her kill him.

"I didn't know what else to do," he said, with a shrug. "Where to start. She showed up here." He gestured at his mostly empty apartment. They stood in the kitchen to talk because there were no chairs in the place still. "She said she had a job for me, if I was willing to do the work. That she'd help me find a way to…make amends for the evil I did."

"The fact that you're acknowledging you did evil seems a good first step," Cary murmured. As far as she could remember, it was the first time he'd acknowledged that, without any justifications or rejoinders or defensiveness.

She left him still a little worried about what he'd do next, and what Maria intended to do to him, but a lot less worried he'd return to a malevolent killing spree.

That had to be good, right?

Two weeks after the fight with Lud and Holland, Liruk and Wisat finally showed up. Appearing in Cary's living room as usual. Like nothing had changed or was different.

Despite everything being so very different.

"Everyone alive and fine?" she asked, before they could speak.

She'd texted with Frank and knew he'd survived the chaos of that night. But there was still a lot she didn't know. She'd managed to piece together some of the stories over the last week, though. The demon hunters had been busy rescuing humans from demons attempting to escape. Frank had done a lot of teleporting around to rescue humans from demon influence. Jaxer confirmed the Fae had come out of Faery at different parts of the world to help, in places where there were no Protectors and the demon hunters were spread thin. Since saving humans from demons wasn't something the Fae were known for, this had been almost as shocking as any other news.

According to Jaxer, they'd done it for her.

Which was super weird and would take time for her to process.

"The other Protectors?" she asked. "No one was hurt or killed?"

"We lost no Protectors," Liruk said, sounding a little stiff, even for her. "They acquitted themselves admirably."

"Good," Cary said. "Thanks for…sending them all out to help. I know it meant I didn't have a Protector of my own to help me." She grinned. "But I'm glad they could be around to protect innocents so I could focus on Lud."

Wisat and Liruk exchanged a look.

She narrowed her eyes at them. "What?" she said, her voice dropping as her suspicions rose.

"This will be difficult to explain, Prot—" Liruk started and then made a face. "Cary. Please let us finish before you…comment."

"This sounds really ominous and not good."

"It…may be good in the end," Wisat said. "This is why we'd like you to listen fully first."

"You guys freak me out with stuff like this."

Deacon came off the couch, where he'd been lounging so he appeared harmless, to stand behind her, hands on her arms. She took the support without hesitation.

"Okay," she said with a deep breath. "Tell me what you're going to tell me." And she'd try to keep her mouth shut. Though she suspected, given their expressions, that was going to be difficult.

"We weren't aware of most of this," Wisat started, quietly. "It was kept from us so that you would be able to fulfill your destiny without interference or…confusion."

She opened her mouth to ask a question then snapped it shut. Oops. That hadn't taken long.

"We were under the impression," Liruk said, "that your powers would return at the first moment you jumped in to protect an innocent."

"It's always how this particular test has gone in the past," Wisat said.

"And we were led to believe this would be no different," Liruk said. "But this was different. And we were kept in the dark." She sounded really annoyed by that. "Because you had to be without your shield, without your *Protector* shield, for any of this to work."

"You could not have taken in the magic you needed to with the shield in place," Wisat said, "to be strong enough to channel the Angel's powers when the time came."

"You would have died if you'd still been a Protector and attempted that," Liruk said quietly.

"So Kupal Umsta made the decision not to tell us the real point of this," Wisat also quiet now, "in case we gave too much away."

"You see," Liruk said with a huff, "he didn't trust us to let you face this without…doing something to help." She flattered her lips and scowled at the wall.

Cary blinked hard a few times at that. She wasn't sure what surprised her more, that Kupal Umsta thought they'd defy him to help her, or that they might have actually defied him to help her. Deacon's hands flexed on her shoulders. She had no idea what he was thinking, but she was stunned.

And she opened her mouth again to ask questions before realizing they weren't done yet.

"Among other reasons," Wisat said, "this is why the Protectors were not allowed to come to your aid."

"And then they were occupied." Liruk sighed. "So they couldn't help even though they wanted to."

Cary started to say, "They wanted to?" and get all mushy about it, before remembering to keep quiet. Also she was still a little too stunned and didn't want to sidetrack the conversation.

"You needed to face Lud without Protectors or Protector magic," Wisat, again quietly, "because what you did wouldn't have been possible otherwise."

"Or so Kupal Umsta says." Liruk, her mouth twisted into a disapproving scowl, huffed a little as she said this.

Cary pressed her lips together so she wouldn't chuckle at this very very inappropriate time. But for some reason, seeing Liruk so annoyed by all this took the sting out of it.

None of the confusion, but some of the sting.

"Now, though," Wisat said, giving Liruk a sideways look before focusing on Cary again, "we have the distinct honor of letting you know… You've passed."

Cary blinked and tilted her head in question since she was pretty sure she still wasn't supposed to be asking questions aloud.

"Your seventh year test," Liruk clarified. "You've passed."

Yeah, this was going to require an out loud question. "What does that mean? It's not even December yet. How? What?" Or more than one out loud question.

"Given what was required of you," Wisat said, "the period of your test was deemed fulfilled by Kupal Umsta. And you passed. You proved yourself more than worthy."

"So this means…?" She was a little lightheaded from the confusion.

"Now," Liruk said, "you have a choice before you."

More blinking.

"All Protectors are given this choice after passing their test year," Wisat said.

"You may now choose, with actual words and intentions," Liruk said, with a little twist of her lips that might have been a smile but might also have been annoyance. With Liruk it could be hard to tell. "You may choose whether or not you want to remain a Protector."

Cary leaned back into Deacon, knowing he'd hold her up without effort. That was nice. Knowing he had her back when gravity decided to reverse itself and her up became down and she could no longer make sense of words she'd known just ten minutes ago.

She blinked some more because it seemed to be all she was currently capable of.

"Cary?" The note of concern in Wisat's voice forced her out of her daze.

"Yes," she said, "still here. Still here. Just…confused."

"You've passed your test and are now in a position to make the final choice to be a Protector or not," Liruk said. "What's to be confused about?"

"Just…everything," Cary said, not even able to gather enough annoyance to scowl at Liruk's tone. She waved a hand vaguely in the air. "So, I can choose to be a Protector again?"

"Yes," Wisat said.

"Or not?"

"Or not." Liruk's tone was a little too neutral on that statement.

"If I choose to stay, what happens?"

"You continued to work for us," Wisat said, "doing the job you've been doing for the last seven years."

"With pay," Liruk added, as if that point was very important.

"And the glamour on your house," Wisat said.

Both points were actually quite important.

"And you'll come into your full powers," Liruk added.

"You've said that before, but…what does it mean?" For some reason, this point right here seemed to be the most important. The answer would determine whether she could do this…wanted to continue doing this…for the rest of her life.

She'd already proven herself incapable of *not* jumping in to save people. She'd been prepared to turn herself into a makeshift Protector so she didn't die doing that in the future. But now, they were offering her the chance to return to the job she couldn't stop doing anyway. With her "full" powers.

But what did that mean?

She was still processing the rest of the story, too. They hadn't thrown her under the bus by stripping her powers. They hadn't fired her. And the fact that her powers hadn't come back wasn't a deliberate punishment of some kind. Not an accident either. Not an unsolvable problem. It had been deliberate. But it hadn't been an indictment of her ability to be a Protector.

It had, apparently, been a necessary step so that she could channel the Angel of Death's powers and kill a demon god.

That reality was going to take some time to set in. Two weeks later and she still had trouble reconciling that she'd actually done that.

She blinked back to Wisat and Liruk, waiting for their answer. She needed to know what "full powers" meant before she made any decisions.

Wisat said, with an attempt at a smile, "With your full powers, you'll be in control from now on."

"You can call up the Protector shield whenever you want," Liruk said.

"Even to protect yourself."

"Full control of when it's up and when it's not."

"There will still be moments of it rising automatically," Wisat said. "When its needed. But you can choose to drop it at any time. Choose to raise it too, when necessary."

"Full control," Liruk said again, emphasizing the word control.

Which was very smart of her, because that was the part that struck Cary the strongest. Full control. The ability to use the Protector magic when and how she wanted—even to protect herself—and to drop it if it was interfering with something.

That was tempting. Very tempting.

"The shield should work better now too," Wisat continued.

"No more getting hurt," Liruk said. "Unless of course you drop it and get hurt."

Cary snorted at that. She wouldn't put that possibility beyond her.

"Any of the magic that comes with being a Protector will be yours to control," Wisat said.

"You need speed, or strength, you will have it," Liruk said, "as usual, but you will control those boosts."

"You will continue to heal fast. Although…" Wisat exchanged a look with Liruk. "Although, we understand that's less of an issue now."

"You've talked to Eriana?" she asked, still a little dazed.

Wisat nodded.

"Does Jaxer know…all of this?" That seemed important now, too.

"He was kept in the dark as well," Wisat said.

"He learned the truth just as we did," Liruk said.

Okay. That was…something she guessed.

Against her ear, Deacon murmured, "There's only one question to ask yourself, love. Do you want to be a Protector?"

"Yes," she said. Without even hesitating.

And wasn't that just weird.

Deacon kissed her cheek. "Then the rest is logistics."

She smiled a little at that. Logistics. The rest of her life. Doing this job. On purpose. No being tricked into it. And controlling the magic that flowed through her from her bosses. All of it just…logistics.

Because, when it came right down to it, despite everything that had happened, all the worries, the fears and insecurities, all the irritations, the outright anger, in the end…

She was a Protector.

"Guess I can't claim I've been tricked into the job from now on, huh?" she said. "That's a little annoying. I liked that complaint."

Liruk's lips twitched, but Cary couldn't tell if she was suppressing a smile or a scowl.

"Do I get a raise?" she asked, wagging her eyebrows.

Liruk's expression went full scowl then, but Cary swore there was some hints of a smile at the edges.

"Actually," Wisat said, smiling fully, "you do. All the benefits of before as well."

From under the window, where her three dogs had slept through most of this conversation, Pickles lifted her head and let out a very deep, "Woof."

Then she settled her head back between her paws and closed her eyes.

"Well, you heard Pickles," Cary said. "I can't turn down the benefits." She chuckled and shook her head.

"Does this mean…you accept, Cary?" Liruk asked. "Does this mean you will take the job of Protector? Of your own free will?"

"Dotting all the 'I's, huh?"

"I do hate to rob you of your favorite complaint," Liruk said.

Was that humor in her voice? No. That couldn't be.

Cary grinned. "I accept the job as Protector. With a pay raise to be negotiated later."

Liruk's lips flattened, but now Cary was sure that was a smile she was holding back.

Wisat's smile grew. "It is good to have you with us. Protector."

And before she could say more, they vanished.

"Uh…" She blinked at the empty spot by her fireplace where they'd stood. "So… Do I have my powers back now or not?"

"Want me to throw a book at you to test them?" Deacon asked.

That comment brought her back to their early days, when she'd proven her abilities to a worried mother by having her throw a book at Deacon. The memory made her chuckle, but also realize just how far they'd come over this last year.

"Wow," she murmured. "This has been a hell of a year. Hasn't it?"

"In a lot of ways," he confirmed before pulling her around into an embrace.

She sank against him without hesitating. He was all tall, and yummy smelling, and looking at her with so much emotion she felt her heart trip a little in her chest. What a year, leading her to all this.

Funny. But she wouldn't change a thing.

"You're sure about this," he said, not asked.

"You were right. It was a simple question in the end. And I'm just going to keep getting into trouble trying to save people. I might as well have the skills I need to do it without getting killed."

"I approve of that logic."

She snorted. Then she kissed him. Because he was there. And he was whole and alive. She was whole and alive. And life felt…good. So very very good.

When they came up for air, Cary was breathless, and ready to be done with talking, but Deacon's expression went a little serious as he stared at her, so she had a feeling they weren't quite done talking yet.

"What's bothering you?" she murmured. "The job?"

"No." He shrugged. "I've made no secret of hating your job."

She laughed.

"But after the last few weeks, I've decided it's a lot safer for you to have this job than not."

She couldn't argue with that.

"It's not the job issue." He frowned, and his gaze turned inward.

She touched his cheek, pulling his attention back to her. "What's wrong?"

"I have to… Since that night, when I was using my magic more, when I accidentally shared it with you, and then on purpose shared it with you… I haven't felt quite the same."

"Good different or bad different?" She straightened and patted at him like she could find the exact location of his injury and fix it. Although, *patting* an injury wasn't a very good way to *help* an injury she realized, and rolled her eyes at herself.

"Not necessarily bad," he said, taking her hands in his and kissing her finger tips. "But not as…controlled."

"Uh oh. Like when we met?"

"Not quite. Different. It's hard to explain. I don't feel… The stuff I managed not to do for many many years, I'm doing now without thought. I shift back to my human form already wearing clothing without thinking about it. I've done that three times since that night. I never use that skill."

She was very, acutely, aware of that fact because every time he shifted back to human and was naked it was impossible not to be aware of the fact that he was naked.

"What else?" she asked. "You haven't hurt anyone?" He'd beat himself up for the rest of his life if he'd hurt one of his people.

"No. But when they were scattering again, I… I felt how easy it would be to slip into compelling them to do what I wanted them to do.

It was so close to the surface. More so than… Except for the very few times I've coordinated their efforts on purpose—"

"Like when we rescued the leopard kids."

He nodded. "And after you were kidnapped—"

She winced.

"I've suppressed that ability so thoroughly, it doesn't come naturally. It takes an effort to use it. But…it wouldn't take an effort now. In fact, I feel like I could fall into that so easy. And, to be honest, that scares me."

She wrapped him up in a tight hug, as if she could protect him from his own fears. "What can we do? What do you need?"

He kissed the top of her head. "I spoke to my mother yesterday about this. She has some advice. But I'm not sure how well this will go over."

"Uh oh," she said again.

"She thinks… She thinks I need to go to Scotland."

Cary pulled back to look up at him. "Scotland? As in… Scotland?"

He nodded. "And I'd like you to come with me." He glanced at the fireplace mantel. "If your bosses will give you the time." He half smiled, but the expression dropped away. "I'll…do better if you're with me."

She nodded, trying to ignore the little leap of excitement in her stomach. He was upset and worried. She wasn't supposed to be getting excited about going to Scotland when he was upset. But…

Scotland!

She hoped none of the Fae minded. She was still a little nervous about showing up in Ireland or England and pissing off Danu and Tatiana. But did Tatiana have any control in Scotland? That was a different court, right? She'd have to double check, just in case. Because she was going to…

Scotland!

"Of course I'll come with you. But why Scotland? What's there that can help you with…all this leopard magic business?"

"You know my mother's been urging me to train this rather than suppress it, to use the magic?"

Cary was more than aware because Maria had tried to recruit her into bugging Deacon about it. She had refused to get into the middle of that argument. Let mother and son duke it out over whether he'd train his unique magic or not.

"There's only one person who can properly train me, outside of my mother. And having my mother try to teach me at this stage…" He shook his head. "We're too much alike. It would be a battle of wills that wouldn't help anyone."

She chuckled. Those were lessons she'd love to watch.

Maybe.

"This other person is in Scotland?" she asked, hugging him close again mostly because she couldn't resist resting her head against his chest. He had such a nice chest. All warm and strong, and boy, did he smell good. She sort of wondered if he was doing that on purpose so she wouldn't get upset about their conversation. Could he do that? Make his scent so distracting to her, she forgot what they were talking about? That would be some super power.

"They are," he said, answering her question.

Which only proved his scent had distracted her, because she'd completely forgotten what question he was answering.

"Which is why I need to go there."

Oh right! Scotland. "Okay. Then we'll go. When?"

"As soon as we can sort things out here. I'm not sure how long it will take."

That would probably be a little tricky, what with her just starting back as a Protector again and all, but she'd convince Wisat and Liruk. They owed her some down time before starting work again anyway. After all, she'd done such a good job at her seventh year test, she'd graduated early. More than a month early. Surely, they could afford to let her take a month to help her mate.

And if they argued, she'd sic Jaxer on them because she had a feeling he'd enjoy that argument.

"Perfect," Cary said. "I'll dig out my passport."

The last two trips she'd taken to Ireland and England had been through unconventional means and meant she hadn't even had her passport with her on those trip. She'd have to remember where she'd put the thing since she hadn't used it in… Uhm? Wow. A while. She hadn't been outside the country, except for those trips to Ireland and England, since becoming a Protector. She'd better make sure her passport was up to date. She might have to do an emergency renewal.

She was working out logistics, when Deacon tilted her chin up to face him, and she forgot all about logistics. Wow, he was handsome. Sometimes she forgot because she got caught up in other things. But then, out of nowhere, just looking at him would take her breath away. In those moments, moments like this, it surprised her all over again that he was hers.

His smile melted her brain. "Thank you," he murmured.

"You're taking me to Scotland. I should be thanking you."

"I'm looking forward to it," he said, leaning in to kiss her. Against her mouth, he murmured, "And I'm looking forward to introducing you to my grandmother. She'll be the one training me."

Cary blinked.

His *grandmother*?

Oh boy.

THANK YOU

Thank you for reading The Trouble with Death and Demon Gods! I really hope you enjoyed this Cary Redmond adventure. Originally, I'd planned on ending the series with this book. It felt right, a seven book series for Cary's seventh year test. I even had some idea of where all this was going from book one and thought I could finish it all here. But as you might have noticed, I couldn't quite wrap up everything there was to wrap up. Some things happened that surprised me in the writing, too.

So the Seventh Year Test story arc got its seven books. But there's more to tell in Cary's world. There will be at least one more book, because I want to go to Scotland with Cary and Deacon as much as Cary wants to go to Scotland. After that...we'll see. I love writing Cary stories a lot, so there may be more.

Until then, if you're interested in learning more about Angie's mysterious past, don't miss the Demon Witch series! You can start with the first short story, Moonlit Strange, and the first novel, Bone Lantern Witch, both out now. And look for more in that series coming in the fall of 2022.

If you want more Cary Redmond and haven't read the various short stories and novellas, there are a whole bunch of those available as single eBooks, and some collections of those stories which are available in both eBook and paperback.

To keep up-to-date on all my new releases and news, you can join my newsletter (https://bit.ly/KatSimonsNewsletter). New subscribers get a free short story set in my Tiger Shifters paranormal romance series, which isn't currently available anywhere else. The story was written originally for an erotic paranormal romance anthology, though, so the story is hot. Just so you're aware.

If you'd rather, you can find release and news updates at my website, visit my Facebook Page, or follow my author page at your favorite book vendor.

Thanks again for reading!

~Kat

Demon Witch Series

Cary Redmond Short Story Collections

BOOKS BY KAT SIMONS

Cary Goes to Hawaii

Cary Holidays

Cary and Dragons and Goblins

Cary's Galentine's Day

When Cary Met the Good Guys (Collection 1)

Dates, Dinners, and Other Disasters (Collection 2)

Witches and Weavers and Ghosts, Oh Boy (Collection 3)

DEMON WITCH SERIES

Moonlit Strange

Bone Lantern Witch

JOAN OF KERRY SERIES

Joan of Kerry: Joan and the Abhartach

Joan and the Leprechaun

HAUNTS AND HOWLS COLLECTIONS

Haunts and Howls and Guardian Spells

Tombstone Wizard

MORE BOOKS FROM KAT

Romancing the Leopard: A Tiger Shifters-Cary Redmond Crossover Novel

TIGER SHIFTERS SERIES

1 – Once Upon a Tiger

2 – Along Came a Tiger

3 – Here There Be Tigers

4 – Her Tiger To Take

5 – To Tempt a Tiger

6 – Down Will Come Tiger

7 – To Catch a Tiger

8 – What a Tiger Wants

9 – Taming Her Tiger

Tiger Shifters Series Vol 1 (Books 1 - 3)

Tiger Shifters Series Vol 2 (Books 4 - 6)

ABOUT THE AUTHOR

Kat Simons earned her Ph.D. in animal behavior, working with animals as diverse as dolphins and deer. She brought her experience and knowledge of biology to her paranormal romance and urban fantasy fiction, where she delights in taking nature and turning it on its ear. Her Tiger Shifters series combines romance and the otherworldly with heart-pounding action adventure. Her latest urban fantasy romance series follows the adventures of Protector Cary Redmond as she tries to manage her personal life while saving the world. A lot.

For something a little different, Kat also publishes fantasy romance, science fiction romance, and the occasional hockey romance under the name Isabo Kelly (http://www.isabokelly.com).

After traveling the world, Kat now lives in New York City with her family. She is a stay-at-home mom and a full time writer.

For more on Kat and her future books:
Website: https://www.katsimons.com
Newsletter: https://bit.ly/KatSimonsNewsletter
Facebook Page: https://www.facebook.com/KatSimonsAuthor